VÄKTARE

The first book in the Väktare series

KAIA LEIGH

BOOKS BY KAIA LEIGH

Just Drink

ACKNOWLEDGEMENTS

To everyone who's supported this book to completion from its inception sixteen years ago in another city, with another dog at my feet—and to the two dogs who lie there now, offering patient company through every season

Chapter 1

Welcome, to Dome Valley, the kind of place you go to film documentaries about missing hitchhikers.

I pulled over at the side of the road and checked the scrap of paper Dan had given me. Actually, it was a Post-it and he'd stuck it to my forehead. Hijinks had ensued. As a result, he had a sprained wrist, and I was in trouble with our boss. I was not in a good mood.

"Note for Liss — vamps at the Dome Valley forest fire sign."

Right up ahead was the sign. In the moonlight, I could just make out a little cartoon guy holding an arrow that pointed to red on the colour wheel. Apparently, the danger of forest fire was high right now.

It was early February, which in Aotearoa (aka New Zealand) meant the hottest month of the year, and I was sweating under two layers of leather. It was uncomfortable, but going into the forest alone, I chose caution over comfort. I'd rather have had Dan and Gracie with me, but thanks to the full moon, they were otherwise occupied—being werewolves and all.

I got out of the car and kicked the door shut.

Moonlight silvered the damp grass that lined the verge, turning the world monochrome.

I pulled my silver hunting knife, nicknamed 'Excalibur My Nightmare', and stilled myself so that I could feel the vibrations in the blade. The knife wasn't much use against vamps, but it could tell me when they were near.

There was no sound in the still night. No nocturnal birds, nothing moving up in the pines, no insect song. The moonlight hit the tree line and was swallowed up by the darkness as if the spaces between the trees were portals to another world.

I breathed in the tang of pine needles and started to walk.

After three steps, the ground turned to marsh. This wasn't just bad drainage. When the ground got soggy like this, it was a good indication there was a vamp breeding ground nearby. Something about the concentration of evil turned soil to mush, sludge welling up through the forest floor that stank of decay.

A pukeko hunting along the swampy side of the highway let out a shriek, cutting into the stillness. Their cries always made me shiver, reminders of a time when flightless birds weighing quarter of a tonne and standing three and a half metres high roamed this land, preyed on by the giant eagles that ate them.

I hit the tree line and paused. Above the scent of

damp earth and stagnant water came the stench of rot on the breeze.

Maybe I should come back during the day.

I thought of the condescending expression Dan would be wearing tomorrow if I told him I hadn't checked it out. 'Was our great Väktare scared to go alone after all?'

Yeah, nah. Why put off till tomorrow what might kill you today?

I switched on my torch and trained it on the ground. Pale coils floated on top of the marshy soil. Dead worms.

Movement caught my eye and I swung the torch in time to see a rabbit dart out from the trees. Its eyes were milky and sightless. It ran to the edge of the road then seized and fell over, stiff as a board. In all likelihood it'd been dead for a while, reanimated by the dark power seeping out of the ground.

I started walking, trying not to think of the bloated worm corpses collecting on the underside of my boots. In the torchlight the tree trunks looked scabrous, the forest floor littered with chunks of bark like shed flesh.

Whatever lived here was poisoning the hell out of the forest. This was the worst I'd ever seen it. It probably wasn't a good idea for me to be here alone. I'd do a reccy and get out—come back after the full moon once I knew what we were up against.

I should just go… but I was damn curious to see how many vamps it took to make the forest so sick.

With each step I took, a feeling of threat grew

around me until I could taste it on my tongue. This place pulsed with deep power. It came up from the earth, thick and violent, and it recognised me.

The silver knife began to throb in my hand and I paused to shut my eyes, feeling the metal sing in tune with the vibration of power all around me.

So, it really was vamps—and going by what I'd seen already, more than I'd seen in one place before. I felt a tug on the knife as if someone had wrapped their hand around it, but I knew better. Silver loves evil. Sure, it kills it, but it loves it first.

And my knife wanted me to go find something to love.

Chapter 2

I stayed cautious as I moved deeper into the forest, promising myself this would be a short mission. I'd go in, check how many there were, then come back with backup if there were more than I could handle. My max was two. More than that and I was going to need Dan and Gracie's help. I might be a Väktare one day, but right now I was only human, with nothing but my wits, a few millimetres of leather, and a wooden LED torch to protect me.

The ground under my feet felt firmer now, the moisture having been pushed to the edges of the nest's territory, away from the sleeping dead. I was getting close. Pine needles crunched underfoot and a pack of black beetles scurried in aimless circles, oblivious to the threat of being crushed.

The silver knife started to sing higher, a note I felt, rather than heard, like the vibration of a tuning fork.

I took another cautious step forward.

All the air sucked out of my lungs as power slammed into me.

I rocked on my heels and put a hand to the pendant around my throat. The power alone couldn't hurt me, not while I was wearing silver, but I could feel it trying to get in, pressing against my skin like cold fingers, seeking out my living heat.

I shone the torch through a gap in the trees ahead and there it was. In the clearing in front of me were eight coffins set into the ground end to end, so that they formed a circle.

My pulse thudded in my ears as the night hushed around me.

Something moved up in the treetops. I swung the torch upwards to see that the trees had grown into the centre of the clearing, tangled together to block out the stars. That couldn't be good. There was no way that was natural.

I played the torch over the canopy as a pinecone bounced off a branch and fell to the pine needles near my feet. I couldn't see anything. It was probably nothing. I mean, it's usually nothing when you're in a spooky forest in the middle of nowhere in the dark. Probably just the wind.

Heart pounding, I shone the torch back over the coffins. All the lids were open except one. I wondered where the vamps were and what they were hunting all the way out here. Yeah, they could live off animal blood, but the pickings would be slim in the forest. Deer, possums, rats. Pukekos. Please let them not be eating pukekos.

And then there was the one sealed box. I approached it warily. It could be a trap. It felt like a trap. But if it wasn't, this could be a fresh vamp, not ready to rise yet. That would be good. I could stake it and be home before Jack and Andy got back from running with the others, and still feel I'd had a productive night. We could get the rest of them tomorrow.

In daylight, the dark energy of this place would be subdued to almost nothing, but I knew where the nest was now. I could easily find it again.

I slid the knife into its sheath, flicked my torch off, and spun it around. The back of it was sharpened to a rather convenient point.

I pushed the lid off the coffin and took a step back. There was silence from inside.

Curious. Wasn't expecting that.

I flipped the torch around and ran it over the box's occupant.

He wasn't much older than me—maybe early twenties—and had wounds as if he'd fought hard against whoever had turned him. For a moment I felt a pang for the life cut short, the dreams destroyed, the future he'd never have.

The torchlight glittered off something attached to his blazer. A Young Nats pin. Oh well.

I tossed the torch in the air and caught it point down, letting the light play against the tree canopy while I aimed to strike the fatal blow.

There was a shriek from above, and a shape dropped to the ground a foot away and then scampered into the darkness. At the noise, the vamp's eyes flew open. I scrambled back out of reach as he hauled himself out of the coffin. The emptiness in his eyes left me in no doubt he was a newborn. All he cared about right now was where his first meal was coming from.

He scented the air, his pupils pinpoints in the torchlight, the whites of his eyes a jaundiced yellow.

"Hi." I gave him a wave to get his attention.

His head swivelled slowly towards me. I saw his muscles tense as his blood-hungry vamp brain kicked into gear. He snarled and threw himself at me, but he wasn't paying attention to the ground. His foot caught on a log, sending him sprawling.

He came up into a crouch, snarling like a dog, and turned his head to follow me as I circled him, those sickly eyes devoid of any humanity.

I found that sometimes if I talked to newly dead vamps while I murdered them, it distracted them and slowed them down. I figured it had to do with their dead brains trying to process speech.

"So you're probably thinking, who is this girl? Why is she here?"

The feral look in the vamp's eyes dulled slightly. It was working.

"They call me a Väktare. What does that mean? I have no idea. There is this one text that refers to the Väktare as 'Interfiere con cadáveres en posición vertical'," I said, "which I think means something like 'bothers upright corpses'."

He pulled his teeth back from his fangs and hissed.

"Are you bothered? Actually, you do look

14

bothered."

He lowered his head, his nostrils flaring.

"Come on. You know you want to."

He threw himself at me.

But as I braced myself for impact, a shriek filled the night, followed by thuds like heavy rain as creatures fell from the trees. I caught a glimpse of long claws and sightless eyes and realised they were possums, reanimated by the presence of the nest.

The vamp hit me while I was distracted and knocked me to the ground, the stake squashed flat between us. There was a creak of tendons as his mouth opened wider than was natural and he turned his head to one side to sink his teeth into my neck.

Crushed under his weight, I waited. Here it comes.

His teeth grazed my skin, followed by a howl of pain. He clawed at his mouth and I pushed him off. Silver. Never take off your silver.

I rolled away and he came after me, his fingers digging into the dirt as he dragged himself across the ground.

The great thing about vamps is that whoever makes them doesn't go around preying on martial arts schools and inner-city gyms. When I find them, they're hungry, mindless, and overpowered. They have too much torque for their impulses, and none of them know how to fight.

Whereas, I do.

I buried the torch end of the stake in the leaves, leaving the point aiming upwards. Oblivious, he crawled right over it to get to me. I sprang to my feet and leapt on to his back, shoving him down on the stake. I landed behind him.

The stake cracked through his ribs with a satisfying crunch, but my aim was off. Clawing at the stake in his chest, he let out a howl that cut off, choked with fluid. If there was ever anything human in him before, there wasn't now. I glanced up at the tree canopy. All this noise was going to bring more vamps to the party. I needed to end this, and fast.

He staggered to his feet and pulled the stake from his chest, along with a pulse of black liquid. He looked at it with a snarl, then threw it at me.

As I dodged out of the way, a reanimated possum ran under my feet. I fell to my hands and knees and the possum turned on me, puffed up into a furry ball of hate. With a screech, it raked my face with its claws before I could pull away, stinging my cheek.

I screamed back at it and pulled my knife.

The possum's filmed eyeballs followed the silver blade and it scampered away before I could carve it back to its natural state.

I'd gotten distracted.

Silent as a wolf, the vamp had come up behind me. He wrapped his arms around my waist and pulled me to my feet, his teeth sinking into my shoulder.

I kicked back with the heel of my boot as hard as I could and he let out a roar of rage. Free of his grip, I dived for the discarded stake. I rolled onto my back and as he threw himself on top of me, I thrust the stake up into his heart.

This time, I didn't miss.

He let out a shuddering breath that stank like meat left in the sun, and a pulse of black fluid trickled from his mouth and slid down my neck. Ah, the joys of young vamps and fresh decay.

As the magic that animated it left its body, the body blackened and bloated into a stinking corpse. With a grunt of disgust, I rolled it off me and got to my feet.

Seeing me alive and angry, the watching possums took to the trees again. I was glad. Dead animals creeped me out.

I put a hand up to my shoulder and felt two small holes. That was going to hurt tomorrow.

I looked down at the corpse and blew out a breath as I thought about what I had to do next.

The body was fresh for a vamp. The body was also ripe. This guy had been dead a week, maybe two. Once deanimated, vamps reverted to their natural state of decomposition. Anything older than a few years would simply turn to dust and bone if you staked it, but the young ones like this one — they left more of a mess.

Singing 'Be a tidy Kiwi, put it in the bin' quietly to myself, I dragged the vamp's corpse back to the coffin. I pushed the lid back on and without thinking, dragged fingers through my hair, smearing vamp rot into my split ends. Great. Time to get out of this forest. I had an early start in the morning.

Chapter 3

Jack was waiting for me in the lounge when I came down for breakfast. He and Andy had been my guardians since my parents handed me to the pack, and they took the role of foster parents very seriously.

"Got a vamp last night, did we?" asked Jack. His shoulder-length dark hair and amber eyes made him look a lot younger than he really was. Well, that and the werewolf genes.

When I turned twenty in a few months' time, he'd turn forty, but as I got older, people were starting to mistake him for some guy I'd hooked up with to defy my parents, rather than one of said parents.

Jack eyed the scratches on my legs with an air of disapproval.

"It was just a baby." I dropped down on the couch opposite him and prepared myself for a lecture.

Andy appeared from the kitchen and handed Jack a mug of coffee. He leaned in and Jack gave him a perfunctory kiss on the lips, before Andy dropped down on the couch beside him.

Andy's blond hair was still mussed from sleep and he hadn't shaved yet. He yawned, showing an impressive set of wolf fangs.

"So." Jack turned back to me. "Thomas called."

This was what I'd been expecting.

Thomas Daley, owner of Thomas! Cars, was my employer, and he'd been less than impressed by the Post-it incident yesterday.

Dan and I had known each other for nine years. We hunted together, drank together, and sparred with each other… a lot. Sometimes it got out of hand. Like when he'd stuck a stupid note to my face and I'd accidentally put him in a lock that sprained his wrist. It was a joke, but Thomas hadn't seen it that way.

"I didn't mean to hurt him," I said, aware that my tone said 'He had it coming'. Jack raised an eyebrow.

"Liss, don't. You know that in the human world, what you did would be considered assault."

I thought back to my squabble with Dan the day before. I was pretty sure if he was claiming he was injured, it was purely to get me in trouble.

"He's a werewolf! I'm human. Do you really think I could damage him with my bare hands?" I looked down at my hands. "Maybe if I had bear hands." I thought about that for a moment, then looked back up. "And even if I did, he'd heal in a day."

Andy clicked his tongue, annoyed. "That's not the point."

"Then what is the point?" I asked. I picked at the ends of my hair, shedding flecks of dirt onto the leather couch.

Andy gave me a long-suffering smile. "This is a huge year for you. You and Dan can't keep fighting like this anymore. When you come into your inheritance, people are going to expect more from you than... this."

Jack nodded. "You need to show some restraint, Liss. Some self-control. When you come into your power, you don't want people to be afraid of you."

I wasn't sure I agreed with that.

Sensing an argument brewing, Andy retreated to the kitchen. I heard him fill the kettle and click it on to boil.

Jack leaned forward. "Andy and I have been talking, and we're concerned. Concerned about the risks you're taking. Concerned about what living with the pack is doing to you. You could come into your power any time, and when you do, you need to be ready."

"It might not even happen," I said. "The books say it should have happened by now, but I haven't felt anything."

"It makes sense to be cautious, given the way things are attracted to you."

Well, he had me there. Things being attracted to me was the reason I was living with the pack instead of my parents.

"Regardless, Andy and I think you should look at your options."

"What do you mean?" I was suddenly suspicious.

Andy appeared in the doorway to the kitchen. "Liss, this life you're leading isn't normal for a person your age. I'm pretty sure this isn't what your parents would want for you."

I guessed we could always ask them, but since they seemed to have disowned me, I had to trust him on that.

"What are you trying to say?"

"We're saying, we don't even know what being a Väktare means in this day and age." He took a sip of his coffee. "We can barely translate the word, never mind decipher what your mystery powers are likely to be. And we're worried that you're relying on it too much to give you purpose when there are other, more important things you could be doing with your life."

It was true, no one in the pack spoke Old Wolf, the fusion of Norse languages most of our historic texts were written in — expect maybe Dan's brother, Karlo. And he'd always told me he couldn't be sure he'd translated them right.

The translations he'd given me included the one about bothering upright corpses, which he'd got from a Spanish text Dan's family had in their library. This bizarre roundabout labelling was in keeping with the Spanish people's reluctance to name werewolves outright in their local mythology, even though the lob hombre was described in the book as a protective, female creature with a passion for shiny gems.

The other translations he'd found for Väktare — which literally meant 'Guardian' in Swedish — were 'El buscador de los muertos' or 'the finder of the dead', and '*El buscador de los cadáveres verticales*' — the finder of the vertical corpses.

"Bet you wish *you* were a finder of vertical corpses," I muttered.

Jack ignored me. "Our concern is that the transition, if it happens, might make you an even bigger target. Which is why we think it might be best" —he winced at what he was about to say next— "if you put some distance between you and the pack."

"Distance? Things come after me, and you want me to be further away?"

"This" —Andy gestured to the living room, with its big-screen TV, pot plants, and area rugs —"it's not a normal life."

I raised an eyebrow. "I don't think it could get more normal, all things considered."

"We're just saying," said Jack, "that coming into your full ability may attract the kind of attention you don't need. We want you to experience some of the things other people your age do, before this… this thing, takes over. Or doesn't."

The kettle finished boiling and Andy made the drinks, setting a black coffee in front of me and a cup of green tea on the table for himself.

"Sweetheart, you work at a car yard. That isn't going to take you far in life. Jack and I would like to pay your university tuition."

I hadn't been to school since I was sixteen. I hated school. Most of school hated me. Most of what I knew —languages, maths, history —they'd taught me themselves.

"Why now?" I asked. "You're freaking out because I got a bit banged up?"

Jack raised an eyebrow. "Liss, you're like a tomcat. Every weekend you get 'banged up'. You go out on your own too much. It's not safe."

"But moving away from the pack is?"

"If you're not doing"—Jack waved his hand—"what you're doing, you're going to be safer."

"Don't you think this is a massive overreaction?" I countered. "I know how to take care of myself."

Andy gave Jack a meaningful look over his mug of tea. I could tell from his expression that he wanted no part of what was coming next.

"You won't be far. We'll still be in the same city. But if you're studying, you won't be..." he took a deep breath in.

"Around?" I said.

"Getting into trouble," said Andy firmly.

I nodded, tears burning my eyes. "Okay. If that's what you want."

Jack put out his hand. "Liss—"

I got up and stalked to my room, slamming the door behind me. They didn't want me here. They didn't want me around. I'd grown up, I wasn't cute anymore, and they were releasing me back into the wild.

I knew I was difficult. It wasn't as though I didn't know what I put them through. I'd always been a difficult child. I didn't throw stones or spit off overbridges or graffiti, but I was drawn to things that

23

children should run from. In fact, from as young as I could remember, when other children froze in fear at the sound of claws scratching the inside of the wardrobe door, I'd grab a torch and be disappointed when it turned out to be just the wind.

I'd never been afraid of the dark. Not as a child. I'd known instinctively what lived in it, and I'd known that the only power those things had was to induce fear. Since I had none, they were powerless to hurt me. I was a little older when I realised I'd been wrong about that one.

But because of that—because I'd taunted the things in the dark and sought them out—my little sister had lost her life to them. It was probably for the best. If she'd lived, she would surely have hated me, as much as my parents must have to hand me to the wolves one frosty June night and never speak to me again.

I'd learned my lesson that night. The thing we should fear is harm to the ones we love, not to ourselves.

Living with Jack and Andy, exacting revenge as often as I could, I'd felt somehow made up for that crime of vanity. As if my talent as a Väktare, a botherer of upright corpses—whatever—was useful. Something the world needed. Now, it seemed, I was the only one who thought that.

I lay on my bed, holding back tears until I got a headache, then pulled a box of tissues from under the bed and blew my nose noisily.

There was a knock at the door. Jack. He walked in

holding a small box in his hand and sat beside me on the bed.

"I'm pretty sure you took everything we said the wrong way," he said. "We're not asking you to leave the pack, we're trying to give you the best life possible."

"You want me gone."

"We want you educated. And independent. Definitely not gone. We want what any parent wants for their daughter. To see you succeed."

A wave of guilt washed over me.

"I'm being a brat, aren't I?"

He squeezed my shoulder. "You're smart, Liss, smarter than you give yourself credit for. And you're strong. You can hold your own with Dan, which is frankly impressive. But you're not a wolf. You're a human with a rare, arcane talent—and if I can put it bluntly, more than once, that's nearly got you killed. The world holds so much more than just revenge."

I wiped away a rebellious tear and hugged him.

He hugged me back so hard it elicited an undignified squeak. He grinned, the points of his canines showing, and held out the box.

"Here. This is from both of us. We were going to wait until your birthday, but I think you should have it now."

I opened the little box and pulled out a gold ring. It was set with a stone that glowed like fire in the morning sunlight.

"What is it?" I asked in awe. I didn't own any jewellery like this. Everything I had looked as though

I'd bought it from a travelling gypsy.

"It's called a *venulv* ring. The stone is sphalerite."

I slipped it on, then winced and slipped it off again.

"My hands are dirty."

He took the ring from me and slipped it back into the box. "Put it on when you've had a shower, but don't wear it out of the house for now. Liss, we just want you to know, we'll always be here for you. We'll *always* be your family. We love you so much. We've never regretted a day of knowing you. But can you do me one favour?"

"Sure."

"If you decide to name it, like you did your knife, don't call it something stupid like 'Excalibur My Nightmare'."

Chapter 4

I wore the ring to work, mostly to show off. I knew Jack and Andy were worried about me losing it, but I planned to put it in my desk drawer once I was sure Dan was sufficiently intrigued.

Dan was waiting when I got to the office. I'd forgotten it was my turn to unlock, and he'd graciously waited outside for me to open up, even though he had his own key. The first thing he noticed was the ring, but to my surprise he said nothing, just sat at his desk and sipped his morning coffee.

"What?" I sat down opposite him. "You're not talking to me now?"

He cocked his head, that doggy thing that most of the wolves did when they were considering you.

He looked pointedly at my finger. "That's a pretty serious commitment you've made there. I'm impressed."

My face coloured as he watched me over his coffee. "What are you talking about?"

Dan gave me silence as Thomas Daley, the car yard's owner, arrived. He strode up to me and said,

"Liss? A word?"

"We'll talk about this later," I said to Dan.

I followed Thomas into his office.

Thomas sat me down and closed the glass door to his office, completing the illusion of privacy by dropping the blinds.

"Okay," I said. "I guess I need to apologise first up."

He leaned back on a filing cabinet, arms folded. "Jack rang me. I'm satisfied that you're going to make a clean start. Am I right?"

I nodded.

"No more 'playful' violence, yeah? I know you kids think it's fun to wrestle, but when an employee gets his wrist broken, that's not fun anymore. You get me?"

I nodded again. Broken. That seemed *very* unlikely. I was going to kill Dan.

I realised Thomas was watching me and swallowed.

"Have you apologised to Dan?" he asked.

I shook my head quickly. "I was about to."

"Right." He held out a clipboard. "Go do that first, then start in lot C."

I nodded obediently and let myself out of his office. He rolled up the blinds again and watched as I went to Dan and said a brief apology. Despite the hard time he'd given me before, Dan was in a gracious mood.

"No prob, although I'm not convinced you mean it."

I glanced over my shoulder. Thomas had gone back to his paperwork.

"Dan, at the risk of sounding incredibly stupid, what did you mean about this ring?"

He cocked his head again, dark hair falling around his face, his brown eyes serious.

"You really don't know? Jack just slipped that ring on your finger and let you leave the house without taking the vows?"

I gave him a look of annoyance. "Let's go wash some cars."

The air outside tasted of sunlight. It was a gorgeous day to be working in the yard, the odd cloud scudding overhead, the sharp tang of sea spray in the air from the nearby ocean.

Dan leaned against a car as I turned on the hose.

"I can't believe you don't know," he said, for the fourth time.

I let the hose drift dangerously close to his shoes.

"Don't bother, De Witt, Thomas doesn't have infinite patience. Anyway, you need to stop being so defensive."

He had a point. I remembered how much delight I'd taken in 'breaking' his wrist the day before. And all he'd done was stick a Post-it to my forehead, with information that had led me to doing the thing I loved best. I guessed that counted as defensive.

"Dan, I'm doing your work here. The least you can do is tell me what you're *talking* about."

"Oh, you'd be doing that anyway," he said with a

lazy smile. "Thomas thinks it's only fair, since you put me out of action."

"Left you with one hand," I grumbled. But really, I didn't mind. I could feel the muscles in my arms starting to burn, and it felt good.

"So, what do I have to do to get you to tell me?" I asked.

I turned off the hose and dipped a brush into a bucket of soapy water. Sometime last night, a marauding herd of pigeons had splat-bombed the whole row.

There was a long silence, and I glanced over at Dan to see his expression had grown suggestive. He glanced down at the bucket of soapy water.

"Sure is hot out here."

He glanced shamelessly at my breasts, then back at the water.

"Oh, piss off." I turned back to the car.

He chuckled quietly then clutched his wrist and howled. "Oh the pain, please, don't hurt me again!"

Potential customers stopped and stared at us. Dan burst into a toothy grin.

"Put the teeth away, idiot," I hissed, my face burning with embarrassment.

"Oh, lighten up," he said, licking his fangs. "They might think dental implants, but they'll never, ever think 'werewolf'."

He had a point. I scrubbed vigorously at the white streaks on a wagon's bumper until the heat left my face.

Dan crouched beside me as I worked the spider

webs out of the car's grill.

"All I want," he said, "is revenge." Somehow, he managed to make 'revenge' sound an awful lot like 'sex'. I turned to find his face inches from mine, his brown eyes swimming with the beast beneath, his dark hair glossy as a raven's wing.

I blew my fringe out of my eyes. "Ahuh."

He straightened up and went back to leaning on the car. "I'm sure Jack and Andy will tell you tonight anyway," he said in his normal voice.

"Whatever," I said. Dan's games got old quickly. I also happened to know he had a date tonight, and it wouldn't be with the girl he'd been seeing the week before—or any of the girls from the weeks before that. I was so not interested in joining the ever-growing list of women who'd shared his bed.

He glanced at his watch. "You're doing well. It's already nine a.m. Not long to go."

By noon I'd finished the cleaning without tipping the water over my white car yard issue t-shirt, much to Dan's disgust. Now, back in the office, I was relishing the air conditioning and fuming about what the ring might mean. Vows? What *vows*?

Dan drifted past with another of his fragrant black coffees and stopped by my desk.

"Lots of insurance processing going on there, I see," he said.

I closed the browser, hoping he hadn't seen the words 'werewolf', 'vows' and 'ring' in the search bar, and gave him the finger.

He returned the gesture with a wicked smile and I grinned—until I looked past him and saw Thomas gazing my way. Thomas could, naturally, only see my side of the exchange. I waved Dan over to my desk.

"Sit down, name your price. What's it going to take for you to let me off the hook?"

He sat opposite me and set his coffee on the desk. "I named my price. You didn't take the offer."

He raised his cup and took a sip.

"I'm so tempted to knock that coffee all over you."

A flicker of worry ran across Dan's face. "I sincerely suggest that you don't do that," he said. "And I'm saying that because for all that you're a temperamental creature, I like you enough to not want you dead."

"What are you talking about?"

He pushed his coffee to one side and leaned forward as though he was casually chatting with me, but his expression was serious.

"All teasing aside, Jack and Andy should never have given you that ring without telling you what it means. It's a ring of promise, a promise specifically never to harm *us*."

"Annoying guys with huge egos?"

"A-ha, ha. Wolves, Liss. It comes from a time when humans who knew about us had a tendency to turn up with other humans armed with torches and pitchforks. And you know the Alpha Circle. No leniency on anything."

"Oh." I looked down at the ring. How could Jack

and Andy be so damned careless? "What would happen?"

"What would happen if you shoved your finger up Thomas's butt?"

I gulped. "Okay, so it's a ring of promise, and I'm supposed to have taken some sacred vows not to hurt the wolves. What, ever? No matter what?"

He nodded, his eyes boring into me. "I was kidding around before, but in all honesty, if I were you I'd give it back. This is too much responsibility for you."

"Why?" I shot back. "You think I can't control myself?"

"Well, yeah." He grinned and the tension in my shoulders eased. "But also because you're a Väktare. Picture it. You're out stalking a vamp when a wolf jumps you. He's not from your pack and you're in his territory. So, like as not, he's going to try and kill you. You. Can't. Touch him."

"Hammer time?"

He shook his head at me despairingly. "You know the punishment right? Same as it always is. You break the law, you get executed."

"Executed?" I looked down at the ring. "Why would they do this?"

He shrugged. "Maybe they don't like you that much."

With a last flash of teeth, he got up and sauntered back to his own desk, leaving me to stew.

Chapter 5

$\mathcal{I}$ found Andy waiting for me at the door when I got home. He ushered me in with a cold drink and sat me on the couch.

"Have you thought about what we talked about?"

"Wow, what happened to 'how was your day'?" I said.

Andy forced a smile. "How was your day?"

"Yeah, we need to have a little chat about this ring," I said, holding up my ring finger.

We both glanced up as Jack walked into the lounge.

"Is there something you forgot to tell me?" I asked. "Apparently I could have been executed today."

Jack broke into throaty laughter. "No, not quite. Dan wound you up, I take it?"

I nodded, more than a little annoyed with Dan at that moment. Maybe I should break his other wrist.

Jack sank into a chair while I folded my arms, fuming that I'd believed Dan.

"So, there are no vows or anything?"

Andy made a small noise in the back of his throat. I shot him a glance.

Jack steepled his fingers. "There *are* vows. And the ring is very important to our kind. But it's not quite as bad as Dan would have made out."

"So, is this all some coming-of-age ritual?" I asked. "Kicking me out of the pack, giving me a ring that means I can't defend myself?"

Andy slapped Jack's arm. "Stop tormenting her."

Jack put his head on one side. "What did you learn today?"

'That Dan is a bastard?"

He gave me a look that said he didn't entirely disagree. "Aside from that."

I sighed. "I don't know. Don't do stuff you tell me not to?"

He looked amused. "Maybe Dan's teasing isn't such a bad thing."

I glared at him.

Andy said gently, "Liss, we thought long and hard about giving you that ring. We considered every angle of what it meant for you. Yes, there's some risk, in that there are severe penalties for killing a wolf. But that's not a situation you're ever going to face. This was more about protecting *you*."

"Protecting?" I said. "What's going to protect me from a feral wolf that's trying to kill me?"

Jack lifted his shoulders in a hint of a shrug. "The Alpha Circle for one thing. And what about your pack, Liss? The ones who should be doing the fighting in the first place if you're ever threatened?

The point is, you can defend yourself — but you can't *kill* to defend yourself. That means when you enter another pack's territory, they won't see you as a threat."

"Unlike before, when they quaked in their boots."

He smiled patiently. "When you come into it, your power may be intimidating to other packs. We want to make sure it's very clear you're aligned to us, and that you're protected by us."

"You're turning me into a snack if I can't kill to protect myself."

'Snacks' was the nickname the wolves gave to humans... when they thought I wasn't listening.

Jack shook his head. "We're marking you as belonging to us. Hundreds of years ago, the wolves would gift rings like this to humans who worked with them — like the Väktare — in return for their promise not to bring harm to their kind. Without that, the wolves really had no compunction against eating humans they didn't like."

I blinked. "Was I at risk of being eaten?"

"There was never any risk," said Andy with a hint of exasperation. "No wolf is ever going to attack you as long as the Alpha Circle acknowledges you as ours. But you have to understand that in a modern world, the danger of exposure is higher than it's ever been. It won't hurt pack relations to let the other wolves know you're one of us."

I got it. Peace between wolf packs in the form of the Alpha Circle — the collective name for the alphas of each of the New Zealand packs — had only been brokered in the last thirty years. As long as I'd been alive, things had been peaceful, but the older wolves remembered a time when blood was regularly spilled and no one dared roam into another pack's territory unless they were there to try and claim it.

It was Abigail, backed by Kendrick, who created the Alpha Circle, bringing an end to centuries of bloody territory disputes. Together, they'd managed to convince all the country's pack alphas to agree to rules that would help the wolves move into the twenty-first century.

Although all members of the collective, known as ACPRs (Alpha Circle Pack Representatives, shortened to 'ACs' most of the time) were considered equals, the respect the Stokes gained through forging the Alpha Circle led to them unofficially holding the highest authority the wolves had in Aotearoa. If a vote was cast, Abigail usually got the final say.

They were also Dan's parents.

"Jack and I just want to make sure you're safe if you're not here with us. As you move out into the world, you're going to end up passing through or living in other packs' territory."

"I know to ask for TP."

"It's not just about traverse permission," said Jack. "The venulv ring will show the alphas that you take your loyalty to the pack seriously. And remind them that you're protected. It's a good thing, Liss." He nodded towards Andy. "We didn't do this frivolously. We've thought this through. Your talent is going to make you very interesting to other packs when you finally come into your power, and to head off any confusion around where you belong, the design of this ring marks you as ours. As Westlands pack."

Tears welled in my eyes and Jack held his arms out for a hug.

I got up and hugged him, and Andy threw his arms around us both.

I sniffed into Jack's shoulder. "So, I hear there are vows?"

Chapter 6

$\mathcal{J}$t turned out to be a long night of family bonding and at midnight I fell into bed, exhausted. Lying looking up at the ceiling, I realised I'd forgotten to call the others to arrange taking out the vamp nest. Crap.

I realised I wasn't going to sleep and sat up and checked my phone. Nearly 1 a.m. Not too late to text Erin.

I sent her a message. *'Want to hear something crazy?'*

'Sure,' came back a second later.

'Can't be bothered typing.'

'K. See you in ten.'

I grinned. Good old Erin. Slept less than most vamps. I threw on some clothes and sneaked out of the house.

Erin met me outside her place. She was dressed in her gothic best, including a pair of New Rocks that brought her up to my shoulder.

"Hey." I gave her a big hug and showed her the

ring. "Look!"

"Oh my god, that is *gorgeous*. Who gave it to you?"

"Jack and Andy. It's a werewolf thing."

"What's it for then?"

"Stops me getting eaten, apparently."

She raised an eyebrow.

I explained about having to take vows to prove my fealty to the pack.

"I have to learn this whole script in Old Wolf. Not for another month though. Which is good, because I have no idea how I'm going to remember a bunch of Nordic choking sounds."

"Do you want any help memorising it?"

"Yeah, that'd be cool."

We fell into an easy silence, our boots hitting the pavement in time, loud in the empty streets. It was nice to just be myself, without the constant pressure I felt trying to keep up with the wolves.

"So, where are we going to live?" she said eventually.

I looked at her. "What do you mean?"

"I mean, God, it's time I moved out of home too. Let's flat together."

I stopped. "Can you afford to while you're studying?"

"To be honest, I think my parents would *pay* me to leave at this point."

Both of her parents were accountants, so they could probably afford it.

I grinned, thinking of late nights playing video games, the two of us burning meals together.

Actually, that was a good point. Neither of us could cook.

"I don't think we should venture into something like this by ourselves," I said.

"Yeah," she mused. "Well, what about Corey?"

Corey was Erin's vampire-wannabe boyfriend. He was too short and too skinny to be taken seriously, and when he threw on his black leather coat and dropped his hair over his eyes, he just looked... cute. That was all you could say about Corey. He was like a kitten with a Skrillex haircut. I wasn't sure how useful he'd be.

"In this plan of yours, do you and Corey do anything other than have buckets of sex next door to my room?"

She laughed and threw me a wicked look. "Probably not."

I sighed. "If he can cook, I guess I can invest in earplugs. Anyway, do you want to play driver tomorrow night if we take out a vamp nest?"

While there was no way the wolves would put her in danger, Erin often acted as a getaway driver for us, staying with the car in case we needed to get gone in a hurry.

She nodded. "Sure. I take it you're going with Dan and Gracie?"

I sighed. "As always. They're the only ones who have time. I *was* hoping you'd made some new friends I could take."

She laughed and threw an arm around my shoulders. "You could always take Corey."

41

"Yeah, I don't think so."

Dan sighed when I asked for his help to take out the nest.

"There isn't anyone else," I argued. "It's you and Gracie or we just wait for them to spread."

He was sitting at his desk, paperwork fanned around him. He rested his head on one hand and looked at me through half-lidded eyes.

"I'm tired, Liss. And in case you haven't noticed, I've got a damaged wrist."

I looked at the crepe bandage doubtfully. He was a wolf—he should be healed by now.

He caught my glance and sighed again. He reached over and pulled the bandage off. The flesh underneath was pale from its day under cover, but even as I watched, his skin melted back to its natural olive tone.

"Well, I'm still tired." He tossed the bandage into the bin.

"Please, Dan." I hated begging, but the idea of those vamps running loose out there, preying on anyone unfortunate enough to stop near the forest at night, made my skin crawl.

Dan rolled his eyes. "Fine. But I'm busy tonight."

"Doing what?"

"Stuff for Mum and Dad."

Like I believed that. I wondered what her name was.

"I'll organise with Gracie for tomorrow night. How far out are they?"

"You're the one who gave me the directions."

"I just passed on the message," he said. "Ellen called it in."

Ellen was the alpha of the Northland pack, whose territory backed onto ours. Technically, Dome Valley was part of her territory.

"Well, about an hour. Tops."

"We'll have to leave work early then. I want more than a couple of hours of sunlight left if there's a bunch of them."

After promising to never ask Thomas to babysit my first born, should there ever be one, I managed to negotiate for us to leave early the following afternoon. I could tell by the way he smiled after us that he was glad we were playing nice.

We picked up Erin and Gracie on the way out of town and the four of us drove up the state highway, Dan's stereo blasting industrial music at ear-splitting levels.

It was half past four by the time we reached the billboard with its happy little cartoon guy and his informative arrow. Dan parked up near the tree line and Erin got into the driver's seat. In case of emergency, it paid to have the car ready to go, and it was a role she'd played for us many times before. She left the stereo on and rummaged through the glove box for something to do, finding a novel with a wolf on the cover.

"You read urban fantasy, Dan? Really?" she called out the window. "Is this, like, your version of

Woman's Day?"

Dan snorted as he pulled weapons out of the boot.

Gracie was her usual silent self. She was tall for a girl at five foot eight, with hair that graduated from black to silver as it fell to her waist. She'd joined the pack from somewhere in Scandinavia where apparently people were way better looking.

Today her hair was pulled back into an immaculate French braid and she was dressed in a short top that showed her midriff. I didn't miss Dan's appreciative glance as she walked past him.

She stalked to the edge of the woods and sniffed the air.

"What've we got?" Dan called to her.

She glanced back at him and held up six fingers.

"Six?" Dan turned to me. "You said seven."

I shrugged. "Maybe one of 'em ran off."

He looked doubtful as he handed me a mini crossbow. I clipped it to my belt and pulled out EMN.

"Why do you carry that ridiculous knife around?" Dan asked as we walked over to Gracie.

"Why, does it make you feel inadequate?" I asked.

He gave me a cool look. "Just don't trip and impale yourself." He strode on ahead, disappearing into the trees.

We fell silent as we moved further into the forest. We needed to be alert. The forest seemed far less spooky in the late afternoon sun, but I knew better than to feel safe.

Gracie, walking ahead, stopped and held up a

hand. She glanced back at Dan and he gave a nod. You almost got the feeling they'd done this before.

I flanked Dan, giving him room to fight. My own fighting space was necessarily smaller. My legs were shorter, and while the wolves could teach me their moves, I'd never have the physical strength and speed of their kind.

Gracie stalked into the clearing and levelled her crossbow at a coffin. Dan took the right side of the clearing, his own crossbow covering the coffins on that side. That left me to walk right up the centre. I wasn't overly fond of crossbows, but they were a practical necessity when taking out a nest this size. Just a shame silver hurt vamps but didn't kill them.

I held my knife in a relaxed grip, trying to keep the tension out of my arms so I didn't get fatigued before the fight. And there would be one. As I neared the coffins, I could sense what Gracie had felt. Six of the half-buried coffins called to the silver. I slid the knife into its sheath and unclipped my crossbow.

I flinched as a pinecone cracked underfoot, breaking the silence. Although I didn't know why we were sneaking around like this. It wasn't as though the vamps would hear us in their daylight-drugged sleep.

I walked to the first full coffin and aimed the crossbow at the lid. The coffin looked like solid rimu. I looked closer. It was nailed shut. Weird. They must be new vamps, not ready to rise without their maker nearby. I hoped the crossbow's tension would be enough to go through the lid.

The vamp inside stirred, sensing me near. He couldn't hear me, but he could sense danger as I tried to gauge where his heart would be. Dan and Gracie held their positions. With any luck, we could take out three simultaneously before the others were awake enough to do anything. If they woke, the sunlight would destroy them... eventually. But in that state of blind panic, they could still do a lot of damage before the radiation decayed them, which was why I preferred to shoot through the lid, rather than get the wolves to pry it open.

We exchanged a glance. It was time.

I squeezed my trigger as they did the same. The bolt pierced the lid with a crack that echoed off the trees. I got lucky—it found its mark. There was a wet sound of cracking bone and torn meat, and then a hollow thump as the vamp deanimated back to a rotten corpse.

I moved to the next coffin. Around me, I could sense a shift as his death stirred the rest of the nest through whatever weird telepathy they shared.

I took aim, but the vamp inside snapped awake before I could squeeze the trigger. An arm shot up through the lid and grabbed my wrist.

I frantically moved the crossbow to my left hand, but I was a lousy shot with my left. Also, the vampire was trying to pull me inside the coffin with it— through ten millimetres of solid wood.

Dan and Gracie closed in, and I could *feel* the other vamps moving in their coffins, hear them bumping against the coffin lids as the vamp that had me wrenched my arm down into the hole he'd made and sank his fangs into my forearm.

I screamed and dropped the crossbow. I pulled EMN. The blade sang as I struggled to pull my arm back through the lid. The vamp refused to let go, savaging my arm in the unseen darkness. I screamed as my bones were crushed by powerful jaws and knew bad, bad things were happening inside the box.

Blood pounded in my ears, a warning flashing in my brain that if I didn't do something soon, the vamp would just reach up with his other arm and tear my heart out.

My knife was not going through this lid.

I turned my head to one side and felt pieces of my arm being torn away. Black spots collected in front of my eyes as I hovered on the edge of passing out. I was vaguely aware that Dan and Gracie were fighting other vampires, heard their shouts through cotton wool as I concentrated on getting my arm back.

I was only going to get one shot at this. I tried to relax. One shot. With a defiant shout, I yanked my arm as hard as I could. Teeth tore through the muscle of my arm and the edges of the shattered wood shredded my skin as I stumbled away from the coffin. The horizon tilted and I fell into the leaf litter, fighting back the black.

Distantly, I heard the vamp roar as it tore the coffin lid off its hinges. There was a scream of tortured wood and the lid flew through the air and bounced off a tree trunk.

I had to get up. Was gonna die if I didn't.

I staggered to my feet. I refused to look at the ruins of my right arm as blood pattered onto the pine needles.

That sound. I know that sound.

Shielded from the sun by the tree canopy, the vamp launched himself at me.

All I could do was wound him as much as possible and hope the others would get to him in time.

As he lunged for me, I held the knife flat against my leg and tried to look helpless. Then, as he charged at me, I shoved the silver blade up into his armpit. Black fluid fountained into the air and he fell back, snarling.

He came at me again, this time wary of the knife. I laughed giddily, wondering if I was going to faint or feint. Faint or feint, that was funny.

As it turned out, he feinted; I fainted.

I came around to find Dan tying a piece of cloth around my upper arm.

"Don't look," he said hoarsely.

I ignored him and glanced over at the mess, numbly detached from what I saw. The bone was bared near the wrist, and chunks had been torn from the muscle of my arm near the inside of the elbow. I could see at least two inches of pale bone inside the mangled flesh, some of which was hanging off by what looked like a severed tendon. One finger didn't seem as long as the others.

I turned away to study the bark of a nearby tree. That was not me. Not my body. I was not going to lose an arm to some stupid vamp. Not my arm. Not my—

Chapter 7

I woke on the floor at the reserve. I turned my head to see someone had thrown a tea towel decorated with brightly coloured sheep over the mess on my right side.

Andy's face loomed over me. "She's awake. Liss, honey, listen to me, you're going to have to be strong. We need you awake to heal you. Do you understand?"

I nodded, not sure how I could hear him over the screaming. Was that me? I tried to put a hand to my mouth to check, but that bought a fresh burst of pain.

Jack put his hands on Andy's shoulders and moved him to one side. They shared a look and then Jack knelt beside me and picked up my good hand. His face was pale. My vision was fading again.

He squeezed my hand. "Liss, stay with me!"

I realised I was surrounded by wolves. They were all in human form, but I could feel their energy, their fear, crashing against me in waves.

Gracie knelt at my side and Dan joined her.

Jack squeezed my hand again. "Liss, keep looking

at me."

Silently, the wolves clasped hands, forming a circle. Dan laid one hand on my shoulder, another on my hip. He lowered his head and closed his eyes. Gracie and Jack closed the loop by placing their hands on his shoulders.

As the circle closed, the power started to flow. Each wolf added their essence to the circuit until a mass of energy ran through them, thrumming like a giant engine, quickening into a maelstrom of energy. It roared inside Dan like a tsunami waiting to crash.

He opened his eyes and they were lit with golden fire. Then he let go, and all that vitality poured into me.

All thought was obliterated under a landslide that crushed me breathless. My pulse thudded in my ears, way too fast, as my heart sped up to match the rush of power being pushed into me.

Sparks of light floated in front of my eyes, impossible to keep in focus as they burnt into the air and faded, like the imprint of fireworks against a dark sky.

It was overwhelming. It was too much. Liquid gold invaded every part of my body, flooding my bloodstream, drowning me.

At some point I gave in and surrendered to it, falling under as the pain washed away and the power swamped me.

"Liss! Come back!" Jack's voice in my ear.

Why would I come back? Everything had stopped hurting.

"Liss, please!" Andy's voice, full of terror, from somewhere nearby.

Dan's voice was suddenly in my head. *Come back, Liss. Today is not the day.*

Reluctantly, I pulled away from the warmth and into my body. It hurt. It was cold. The world was hard and stark and there was a bright light in my eyes. I blinked and realised it was just an ordinary incandescent downlight. Dan's face hovered over mine. There was something there I couldn't read — intense concern and something else. Elation? I closed my eyes again.

"Keep the connection," he said softly. "This might feel weird, but stay with us."

I could feel something happening in my injured arm. It hurt, didn't feel natural. I wanted it to stop.

"Hold on, Liss."

The sensation grew worse, a tingling, itching as if I'd been stung by stinging nettles. I tried to pull away but Dan sent me a thought: *'Nearly there.'*

The stinging got worse, and I felt the muscles in my arm knitting and re-forming around the bone, the bone itself rebuilding where teeth had crushed it, hot and molten, then growing solid, cooling to become a part of me. Then came the revolting sensation of skin repairing, stretching over the new muscle like thin tissue paper, then hardening, growing rubbery as blood began to flow through it, then soft and pliable and alive.

Was this what it felt like when the wolves shifted? If so, they were welcome to it.

The pain dulled back to an ache that pulsed through my body like a heartbeat, then slowly trickled away. Dan kept the contact long after the pain had stopped and I started to drift. This time, he let me go.

The circle broke, the last traces of power drizzling away. I heard a wolf fall back out of the circle, writhing under the change. Giddy, I opened my eyes as two more dropped. Dan's restraint showed in the sweat that broke out on his forehead, but he gathered me up and carried me from the kitchen down the hall to one of the bedrooms. He laid me on the bed and managed to get to the door before the change hit him.

He tore at his clothes and moments later fell to the ground on four paws. I caught a glimpse of steel-grey fur as he headed out to join the others.

A howl went up. Here at the reserve, a rural property owned by Dan's parents, the wolves were able to run free. The howl filled me, as it always did, with a mixture of ecstasy and loneliness, and a tear trickled down my face.

I turned my head to look at my freshly healed arm and blinked hard through a blur of tears. The arm attached to my right shoulder looked different somehow. It took me a moment to realise there were no freckles, no scars. I held up my left arm. Oh. That was the same. Not a freckle in sight.

The world lurched and I knew being awake wasn't an option anymore. I surrendered to the darkness and sank into it.

I woke to an empty house, desperate to use the bathroom. As I washed my hands, I looked up to see my face in the mirror. I stared, shocked. My skin was flawless. I looked like a painting, every pimple gone, every blemish. Even my hair seemed glossier. I realised there were no longer any split ends. How was that even possible?

I put a hand up to my face, then looked down at my hand in wonder. I looked as if I'd never stood under the sun. My nails shone like glass.

Dan appeared in the doorway. There was something even more smug and satisfied about him than usual.

"Have fun?" I asked as I dried my hands.

"Check you out," he said, eyeing me up. "Aren't you going to say thank you? Cosmetic surgeons can't do as good a job as this."

I stared at him. "What's that supposed to mean?"

He caught the first whiff of anger and stepped back, hands up. "I meant we did a good job, Liss. Nothing else."

I took a step towards him. "But you didn't stop there, did you? Was I not good enough before?"

"What? No! How can you be pissed at me over this? Look at your arm!"

I realised how ungrateful I sounded and was instantly ashamed. I splashed some water on my face and dried it.

"So, did we get them all?"

He blinked. "Oh. Yeah. I think so."

He wasn't telling me something.

"You think so?"

He looked away, fingers idly toying with the door frame.

"Just spill, Dan."

He dropped his eyes to floor. "We think there might have been another one—one who wasn't there when we turned up."

"During daylight? Is that even possible?"

He scratched the back of his neck as his gaze swept across the room, finally coming back to rest on me.

"I don't really know. Gracie said she caught a scent—something different. It was faint. If she hadn't pointed it out, I don't think I would have caught it."

"What was it?"

He shrugged. "Maybe nothing. Let's just stay out of the forest for a while."

Well, that was unsettling. Like Dan, I had a lot of faith in Gracie's instinct, and her sense of smell. But I was tired and I had a lot on my mind. It was easy to push down the nagging voice that whispered *something's not right*, and concentrate on my new, improved body—and the fact it was still alive.

Chapter 8

$\mathcal{I}$ woke the next morning in my own bed, convinced it had been a dream. I checked my arm and saw no freckles, no scars. Nope. Not a dream, then.

Battling nausea, I ran to the bathroom and knelt over the toilet. A vampire had actually done that to me. Torn my arm apart. I'd nearly died.

I threw up what little was in my stomach and shivered as I remembered the sensation of teeth tugging out pieces of my flesh, the wet, ripping sound. The pain.

I flushed away the mess and got to my feet to wash my face.

I avoided looking in the mirror, but as my hair fell forward, I saw what had always been a nondescript brown was now a glossy mahogany mass. I swung my head and the soft weight of it fell against my shoulders with a whisper.

If he got bored of the car yard, Dan would excel as a hairdresser.

Every inch of my body was healed of the nicks and cuts and scars that had accumulated during nine years of fighting the undead. It was creepy. I didn't look real.

The nagging thought came back to me from the night before, the fear that Dan had used the healing to make me more attractive. I shook it off. He'd saved my life—the wolves had saved my life. If the worst thing to come out of that was great hair, I would live with it and be grateful.

Jack and Andy had gone to work by the time I went down to breakfast. The house rang with sunny emptiness, a crystal sun catcher sending ripples of colour across the pale carpet.

I sat down at the dining table and checked my phone. There was a text from Andy.

'Make sure you eat, healing takes energy. Don't go out before we get back.'

I shrugged my eyebrows and opened the fridge, suddenly ravenous.

I was asleep on the couch when Andy got home early from work.

"Where's Jack?" I asked groggily. Jack usually got a lift home with him, as they both worked in the middle of the city.

"He's catching up with Abigail and Kendrick for a debrief on last night. How do you feel?"

I sat up. "Good. Tired. But good."

He sat beside me and touched my hair with wonder.

"I know," I said. "Shiny."

He lifted a lock of hair and checked the unsplit ends with amazement. "Did you let Erin know you're not moving tomorrow?"

I frowned. "No. Why am I not moving tomorrow?"

"Because you nearly died?"

"And now I'm fine. Nothing's changed, has it?"

He pushed my hair back over my shoulders and frowned. "Are you sure you want to move right now?"

I shrugged. "The first semester starts soon. For Erin's sake, I'd rather move now than later on." I wasn't ready to tell Andy yet, but I'd already decided I wouldn't be starting till the second semester—when I figured out what I wanted to study.

He made a face. "Well, it's up to you."

"It's not that far away. You can still make me dinner every night if you really want." I gave him a hopeful look.

He laughed. "Jack probably would, too."

My phone buzzed as he hugged me, and I checked it to find a text from Erin.

"Speaking of which, apparently we're starting tonight."

"I want to get healed if this is what happens," Erin said, as we slit open the many boxes that littered the lounge floor. "It's mostly your hair. You *know* your hair looks great now."

"And before?" I asked, holding up a craft knife as a weapon.

"The words 'rats' and 'nest' spring to mind." She grinned.

"Bah." I pushed an open box to one side with my foot. "Did you see it?"

She shook her head. "They were really weird about me watching, so I got a lift home from the reserve. They were pretty worried about you. I think they thought you were going to die."

I sat down on a box of bedding.

"Yeah, next time I go out hunting, I'm gonna wear long sleeves."

She gave a tight-lipped smile.

"What?"

She pulled another box towards her and stabbed into the packing tape. "Next time."

"This is kinda my life. So, yeah. Next time."

She concentrated on the boxes and wouldn't say anything else.

The next day was Saturday.

"Corey should be here soon. You know, he's been a vegan for about six months now." Erin threw a bag of flour into one corner of the pantry. "We can still cook meat, just not when he's home." She glanced at me apologetically.

I was already regretting this. Missing out on Jack's cooking was bad enough without the prospect of going meatless forever.

Erin stopped unpacking her shopping and looked at me anxiously. "Are you sure this is okay?"

I nodded. "Fine. He doesn't eat meat, but I'm gonna."

There was a knock at the door. "That'll be him."

Erin jogged to the door and pulled it open.

Corey walked in. He was wearing mascara. He held up a pineapple and flipped his hair back from his face. "Happy Housewarming."

As it turned out, Corey wasn't vegan anymore; he was trying 'just being a vegetarian'. I took that to mean he'd cope while I ate all the damn meat I wanted.

He threw his coat over the back of a chair, and loitered about while we tried to find places for all our things.

"Where's your stuff?" I asked, annoyed with tripping over his booted feet. He was stretched out across the hall, leaning against the wall.

"I'll bring my stuff when you guys are settled. Don't have much."

"Could you, maybe, be more useful?"

He shrugged. Erin stepped over him carrying a bedside table.

"Can I help with that?" he asked.

"I'm fine!" she said, eyes flashing annoyance. I saw his point. He gave me a 'what can you do?' look and I went into my bedroom and shut the door.

Now that everything was in place, it wasn't so bad. Cramped, as all student flats tended to be, but it'd do.

From the room next door, I heard low murmuring, then noises I didn't want to think about. We needed to look at sound proofing.

I pulled on my jacket and took myself for a walk.

Chapter 9

By Friday I'd gotten used to the weird noises coming from the room next door and had finally got a decent night's sleep.

I woke hungry and prowled out to the kitchen to find Corey finishing off the last of my cereal.

He looked at the box, then back at me.

"Do you want me to get some more?"

I shook my head and took to ransacking the cupboards. "Cereal won't do it this morning anyway."

"I can give you a lift to work if you want."

Oh yeah, work. The job that paid for my new home. At least, until I started studying and the accumulation of lifelong debt kicked in.

"When are you leaving?"

He checked an imaginary watch. "About ten minutes."

"Where's Erin?"

"Shower."

I went to the bathroom door and banged on it. "I need the bathroom!"

After the world's fastest shower, I threw on clothes and headed out the door.

I got to work five minutes late, my wet hair at least slightly less shiny. As soon as I walked in the door, Dan made a beeline for me.

"What are you doing here?"

I looked at him in surprise. "Er, coming to work?"

He glanced at my arm. "How does it feel?"

I flexed my muscles. "Well, I shifted house over the weekend. I feel great, actually."

He broke into a relieved smile. "Ready to work at the car wash, then?"

"What? Am I still doing penance?"

"Damn straight."

Corey and Erin were cooking together when I got home. There was a small cloud of smoke near the roof and I sighed, my predictions of blackened food becoming a reality.

"Jack texted me to ask if you were okay," Erin called, over the bubble of boiling water and the roar of the extraction fan. "He said you weren't answering your phone. He said to come over to theirs tonight. Dinner's at six."

I pulled my phone out of my pocket. Damn thing was on mute to keep Thomas off my back. Us millennials were apparently way too attached to our phones. As if *everyone* wasn't too attached to their phones.

I went down to my bedroom and shut the door. Muffled laughter floated into the hall as I texted Jack to let him know I was coming.

I left Corey and Erin flicking salad dressing at each other and started the walk to Jack and Andy's.

Walking felt great. I felt like a cat; fast, lean. A hunter. I leapt over a drift of fallen leaves and landed lightly.

Somewhere inside, I was aware I was romanticizing something too serious to trivialize. I'd nearly lost an arm. I'd nearly lost my *life*.

I stopped prancing about and put my hands in my pockets. This feeling of invincibility wouldn't last. I didn't train every day, didn't eat the right food. All too soon, I'd get careless and some vamp would slaughter me. What was I thinking? I wasn't a wolf — the only power I had was the ability to feel evil, to find it. And whatever supernatural inheritance I might receive, I'd still just be human.

Footsteps sounded behind me. I turned and scanned the darkness, my heart racing.

As if somehow rabid vampires would be wandering the suburban streets. I put my head down and kept walking. Whoever it was, they were going someplace, just like me.

The footfalls grew louder. I tensed as a man passed me, a messenger bag slung over his shoulder, white earbuds slung around his neck.

I let out my breath and laughed at myself. It wasn't the footsteps behind me that I had to fear. It was the ones I couldn't hear that I needed to worry about.

Andy pulled me into a hug when I arrived and ushered me to the kitchen where Jack was cooking something that smelled heavenly. I glanced around the kitchen and sighed at the spotless surfaces, the spices in alphabetical order in their rack. The visible bench.

To be fair, the spices weren't always in alphabetical order. Sometimes Jack put them in colour order, to make an earthy rainbow.

We sat down to eat, accompanied by some band called *Arcadia* that Andy loved and no one else had heard of.

Jack passed me the salt before I asked for it, then poured a Heineken into a glass. I grinned at him.

"So," Andy said, stealing the salt, "how do you feel after your near-death experience?"

I looked at him. So did Jack.

"You're ever tactful," said Jack.

Andy shrugged and took a sip of wine.

"No need for concern," I said, "I'm fine. I'll feel even better when people stop asking how I am."

Jack frowned. "As tactless as Andy is uncharacteristically being, you had your arm chewed down to the bone. It's natural for us to worry about you."

I sighed. "I feel amazing. I know it won't last, but for now, I feel great." I took a mouthful of food and sighed in pleasure. "You are a cooking god, Jack."

They exchanged a glance.

"What? What's going on?"

Andy ducked his head and concentrated on eating. Jack studied the plaster ceiling for a moment.

"Andy and I have been talking—"

"Oh, no, keep me out of this," muttered Andy.

Jack shot him a look, then said, "Have you decided what you're going to study yet?"

I sat back and let my fork drop to my plate. I'd been moved out for a week.

"I wasn't expecting the Spanish Inquisition."

"Nobody does," murmured Andy.

I took Jack's hand and couldn't help notice the way he looked down at mine. Even the tiny scar I'd got from learning how to spin EMN was gone.

"I'm happy with my life. I like working for Thomas. I like my friends, I love my family. I'm happy. I will study, but what's the rush?"

He squeezed my hand and pulled away, reaching to one side to grab a stack of course brochures from where they were sitting on a spare chair.

"I picked out some courses that I thought you'd like. Just take a look. If you want to go, we'll do everything we can to help you. If you don't, that's fine too."

Sure. Totally my choice.

I picked up the top brochure. "The University of Waikato?"

"They have some great degree options."

"You mean like Auckland University, Massey University, and Auckland University of Technology—all those universities that are, like, thirty minutes' drive away?"

Andy concentrated on his dinner.

"Why do you want me to leave town?"

Of course, I knew why. Because there hadn't been any reports of vampires south of the Bombay hills in nine years. There were also no wolves in that part of the country because it was what was known as 'free traverse' land—land no pack could claim, because it was the only thoroughfare from one place to another. Which meant they could visit me whenever they wanted to without having to notify a pack and ask for permission.

"They have a great film studies programme, and I know you've talked about that before. And they have psychology," said Jack.

Erin was studying psych. What a coincidence.

"You want me to ask Erin to move her degree to another university?"

"It was just an observation," he said placidly.

"I'll think about it," I muttered.

But I wouldn't. There was no way I was leaving Auckland. No way.

The next night, Erin and Corey announced they were going down to the waterfront.

"There's a new club opening," said Erin, handing her eyeliner to Corey. I sat on her bed and watched them touch up each other's hair.

"Oh yeah, Pulse. I heard about that."

I knew I didn't sound very enthusiastic. I'd spent the previous night going over stupid course brochures. Now I'd gone from being completely satisfied with my life to wondering what the hell I was supposed to do with it.

There were so many degrees, and they'd all make me sound so much smarter when I went for a job interview. Job interview? I *had* a job. I had two jobs.

Erin finished her eye shadow, then turned and leaned on the dresser. "Aren't you going to get changed?"

I looked down at my clothes. "Wasn't planning to."

She shook her head sadly. "Come on, let's get you spruced up. Unless you're saving yourself for Dan?"

I gave her a furious look and stalked back to my room to find something hot to wear.

I had nothing hot to wear.

As I dragged a comb through my hair, she dropped some of her own clothes on my bed.

"Try these."

I was afraid to look.

She held a top that barely qualified as clothing in front of me. "You know, he's too old for you anyway."

I stopped fighting my hair and looked at her. "He's twenty-three."

"That's... a hundred and sixty-one in dog years," she said helpfully.

I rolled my eyes and looked at myself critically in the mirror. At least my hair still looked great.

When I was finally dressed, she stepped back and gave me an appraising look. "This is good. You should stop saving yourself for Dan more often."

Chapter 10

From the outside, the club was straight out of one of my nightmares. Pounding bass thudded up through the pavement, and red light spilled out through the gaping maw of the door. And there were people. Lots and lots of people.

I cringed away from the crowd as we made our way to the bar. The music and the heat were thick, still early enough to be rich with the scent of deodorant and perfume, but I knew from grim experience that in a few hours the air would be heavy with sweat and the stink of booze and cigarettes.

Beside me, Erin's face was flushed with excitement. She grabbed my sleeve and pulled me with her and Corey to the dance floor.

As much as I loved the music, I couldn't get into it.

When Corey and Erin started dancing as if they were auditioning for an adult movie, I escaped to the bar and ordered a drink.

As I sat on a bar stool, thankful to take the weight off my feet, I felt a prickle of unease.

I looked around. There was no one behind me. But

when I turned back to my beer, there was a guy sitting on the stool next to me. He noticed me staring and glanced up. I looked away, embarrassed, my skin crawling. Something about him just wasn't right. But this was a public place and he was just a guy. Nothing to worry about.

He probably seemed creepy because he wasn't a were-anything, and because he was looking at me. Men never looked at me. Except with an expression of slight bafflement when I started speaking.

I decided to pretend he wasn't there, and concentrated on shredding the bar mat.

"Are you by yourself?" he asked, swivelling on his stool to face me.

His eyes grazed over Erin's choice of top and I blushed.

He smiled at my embarrassment. "Don't worry, it suits you." He held out a hand. "Sorry, should introduce myself. I'm Brandt Lamont."

The way he did it was weirdly formal for a nightclub, as if I was supposed to know who he was. Maybe he owned the club. I didn't really keep up with who was who on the Auckland scene; he could be a visitor from Hawke's Bay for all I knew.

I took his hand to shake it and froze. There was a subtle pressure in the way he laid his thumb against the back of my hand, as if he might pull me off the stool and drag me somewhere. The sweat suddenly cooled on my body and I could smell mountain air and the damp chill of glaciers. My skin itched as if things were crawling on me.

He cocked his head to one side and said, "What did I do?"

His voice was low enough to blend with the music but somehow I heard him.

I took my hand back and got off the stool. What to say now? Guys in bars just didn't approach me. I realised I liked it that way.

I gave him an apologetic smile and backed away, leaving the last of my beer behind. As I stepped back onto the dance floor, the mountain cool drained away, replaced by the sweaty throb of the nightclub.

What the hell just happened? What the hell was that?

I pushed my way into the crowd and made my way back to Erin. She and Corey were locked in what was possibly an illegal act. They fell apart when they saw me, laughing and hungry.

I waved a hand up by my face to say I was hot, and pointed to the door.

Erin nodded and made driving motions. I held up my hand to indicate I'd catch a taxi. Silent conversation over, Erin latched back to Corey's mouth, while I found the door and let the club vomit me out into the street.

Ah, blissful fresh air. I took a few deep breaths, ignoring odd looks from the bouncers, and walked down to the quay.

The water that lapped at the dock was inky black, ripe with salt and the stink of diesel from moored yachts. I sat down on one of the old railway sleepers that stopped drunk people from falling into the harbour, and watched the oily water lap against the dock as the sweat cooled on my arms.

My skin started to prickle again. I turned to see Brandt come out of the club. He stopped by the bouncers, head bent in conversation, then glanced up, straight at me. I looked away, hoping his interest was nothing more than a guy liking a girl in a club. My stomach tightened as I waited for him to stroll over.

When he didn't, I looked back to see him disappearing into a bar further up the waterfront. So, interested, but not *that* interested.

I sat in the salty breeze until curiosity got the better of me.

I headed back past the entrance to Pulse, weaving through the thin stream of clubbers towards where I'd seen him disappear.

The glowing sign above the entrance read 'Slice'. The logo was a wedge of lime on the rim of a glass. A spill of green light poured out onto the pavement where the pillars either side of the entrance were uplit by colour-changing lights.

It looked classier than the places we usually went. I glanced down at my nightclub-appropriate clothing and sighed. At least at this time of night, it was mostly empty.

I wandered up to the bar and picked up a cocktail menu.

Brandt watched me from a stool at the bar. His chin rested on one hand, his fingers covering most of his mouth to hide a smirk.

I ordered a mojito, since it was a drink I'd heard

of, and sat next to him, wondering what was supposed to happen next.

Eventually he stopped smirking and took a sip from an orange-red drink garnished with a spiral of orange peel. He held up two fingers and said, "Peace?"

I snorted, nearly sending my drink all over the bar. I managed to get myself under control and looked at him properly.

He sounded English. Not cockney English, but fancy waistcoat English, which made no sense, since he was wearing a leather jacket and jeans.

He looked like an off-duty rock star, with short, dark hair and grey eyes that glittered with amusement. He looked casual-trendy, annoyingly wealthy. Smug.

He let me look him over, then held up his right hand to show me he was wearing a ring. The orange stone caught the light like a trapped flame. Sphalerite. The stone was cut differently than mine was, but nothing else looked quite like that.

"Okay," I said, not able to keep the question in any longer. "What *are* you?"

I was sure he wasn't a wolf. I'd have felt that a mile off.

He grinned, showing the sharp points of his teeth.

The world blacked out except for the tiny part of it that showed his lips drawn back from bright, white canines. You know the ones. Some people call them 'fangs'.

"You're not a wolf," I said, keeping my voice low.

Slowly, he shook his head. "No."

What other supernatural creatures had teeth like that? For all I knew, there were all kinds of things out there in the dark that I didn't know about.

"Friend or foe?"

He smiled. "Your choice." He watched me over his glass as he sipped his drink.

"Just tell me."

He put his head on one side. "I believe you would call me *un cadáver vertical.*"

My throat was suddenly dry. "I have to go."

He rested his head back on his hand, watching with amusement as I slid off my stool. "Don't you want to know more about me?"

"That's a whole lotta nope." I backed towards the door.

He watched me go with an expression I'd seen in Dan's eyes when he went nature, a look that belonged in an animal's eyes. It was not a look I wanted to see on a human face. But then, he wasn't human, was he?

I *knew* guys didn't look at me in bars.

I stumbled outside on my stupid, impractical heels, fumbling for weapons I knew weren't there.

He was going to follow me; he was going to kill Erin and Corey. He'd kill Jack and Andy and everyone I loved.

My heel caught on the planks of the boardwalk and I wrenched it free, resisting the urge to run, Jack's voice sounding in my head: *Don't look like prey.*

I needed a weapon. I needed to kill him before he killed me or my friends, or anyone else for that matter.

I reached Pulse and checked behind me to see if he'd followed me. There was nothing to see — but that didn't mean anything. I turned back to the mouth of hell.

A wave of heat and noise rode over me as I struggled across the packed dance floor, looking for Corey and Erin. Where the hell were they? Tears stung my eyes and I blinked them back, eyeliner blurring my vision. Elbows and full drinks jolted against me as I cut a path through the throng.

I found them in the middle of the room, Corey's tongue in Erin's throat. His hands were nowhere to be seen. I pulled him off her unceremoniously, fear making me desperate. It was too close in here, the wild beat of the music making the blood thunder in my ears.

Erin saw my face and her annoyance fell away. She grabbed Corey by the hand and started to lead him off the dance floor. He cast me a dark glance as I followed but didn't protest.

Outside was a different matter.

"What the hell is wrong?" he snapped, while Erin tried to calm him.

"We need to get out of here," I said, "There's a…" I glanced at Corey. "There is a… stalker, out here, looking for us."

Erin didn't completely understand, but she picked up on my fear. Corey, however, puffed up like an angry cat.

"Some guy, out here? Wouldn't it be a bit hard for him to stalk us in there?" He jerked a thumb towards the club.

I shook my head, biting back panicked words.

"I think we'd be better off somewhere else."

"Home?" asked Erin.

I shook my head. "He might follow us there."

Corey rolled his eyes. "God, where is he? I'll deal with the creep."

Erin caught my eye and I knew I looked terrified. She put a hand on Corey's arm. "Babe, don't cause a scene. Let's just go somewhere else." She turned to me, some of my panic in her eyes. "Karlo's, downtown?"

The club was run by one of Dan's older brothers who was, unsurprisingly, named Karlo.

I nodded. "Yeah."

We hailed a taxi and got in, Corey still fuming at not being allowed to do his manly duty. I wondered how he would have handled facing an older, muscled, better-looking version of himself. A version with fangs. An idle thought flashed through my mind — *that's probably how he sees himself.* I grinned.

Erin nudged me with her elbow. "What's funny?"

I shook my head. "Nothing, really."

Karlo's was packed out with wolves, and Corey must have noticed that most of the people in there were taller than him and broader through the shoulders. There were a few civilians who'd been turned, rather than inheriting the gene, but even those had been chosen for the robustness of physique required to survive changing once a month.

Did anyone notice, I wondered, how quiet this place got on a full moon? Did anyone ever notice the pattern of entertainment, that big-screened sports and first-drink-free nights followed the lunar calendar instead of some more logical schedule? That most of the bar staff took those nights off?

I led the others up to the bar.

"Hey, Liss, nice to see you." Karlo grinned down at me from behind the bar. He had Dan's straight, dark hair, only his was pulled back in a ponytail while he worked the bar. His power flowed over and around me, as it did from all the others to varying degrees. It was hot in the air, a thick musk that smelled of home, of family, of comforting safety.

I ordered drinks and took a look around the club. This place was a casting agent's dream. Most of the Westlands pack was there, along with some of the Northland wolves. There were others I didn't recognise, probably visiting from the Midlands.

A girl caught Corey's eye, tall and beautiful with dark skin and blue eyes. He stared, transfixed, and she gave him a shy smile as she walked back to her friends with their drinks.

Erin dug an elbow into his ribs and he glanced back at her with a grin.

"What is this place?" he asked, leaning across her.

"Some friends own it," I said, speaking up to be heard over the noise. "We'll be safe here. I know half these guys."

As if to prove it was true, another of the wolves recognised me and drifted over. Glenn, Dan's oldest brother.

"Hey, Liss. Hey, Erin." Despite being in one of the more upmarket clubs in town, Glenn looked like a band roadie, dressed in a black metal t-shirt and jeans.

His long hair was streaked with silver, but he wasn't actually going grey—it was just his natural hair colour.

Corey watched him warily. He clearly didn't like that he knew Erin.

I took Glenn to one side and spoke low, knowing his wolf hearing would pick out the words above the din.

"There's a vamp stalking us. I don't want to take these two home until I'm sure he's sludge."

He frowned, his dark eyes full of concern. "You're sure it's a vamp?"

I nodded and tapped one of my front teeth.

He grinned and tapped one of his own.

I shook my head. "I swear to God, he's no wolf. I didn't even feel him until he was two inches away. And he's wearing a venulv ring."

He glanced around the club and caught Karlo's eye. He mouthed something, or possibly said something I couldn't hear, and Karlo nodded. He gestured us back behind the bar.

I grabbed Erin's shoulder and shouted in her ear. "Back soon."

Out the back, the music and chatter fell back to a muffled din. Karlo wiped his hands on a tea towel and gestured for me sit down at the staffroom table.

"What's going on?"

"There's a vamp roaming around the waterfront that I need to take out."

"A vampire? On the waterfront? Are you sure?"

I thought back to Brandt's shiny white teeth and condescending smile. Okay, so he could be something else. But why would he lie?

I realised Karlo was waiting for an answer.

"Do vampires ever work with wolves?" I asked.

He looked at Glenn. "Not that I'm aware of."

"So, if a vamp had one of those promise rings, he'd probably have taken it off someone else? Maybe someone he'd killed?"

Karlo frowned. "Maybe."

"Then we need to take him out."

Both Karlo and Glenn fixed their gazes on my freshly healed arm.

"What?"

Glenn looked down at his drink, but Karlo put a hand on my shoulder.

"Liss, if you didn't feel him coming, chances are he's an old one. Those vamps in the forests—the ones you've taken out until now—they've been babies. Two, three years... maybe five years old, tops."

I stared at him. "So, how old can they get?"

Stupid question, really, immortality and all that. I just hadn't given it much thought until now.

"They get *old*. And they get clever. Some of them

you can't tell from humans unless they want you to."

"If you don't want to come, that's fine," I said. "But if I let him go, who knows who he'll kill tonight if I let him go?"

"I didn't say I wouldn't come," Karlo said irritably. "I just don't think it's a good idea." He turned to Glenn. "Can you watch the bar?"

Glenn nodded. "Yeah. But Liss, Karlo's right. These old ones, they're better left alone."

I stared at him.

"Okay, fine." He pulled out his cellphone. "But at least wait until I call Dan and Gracie. You want decent backup for this."

Dan wouldn't be available tonight, I knew that much, and Gracie wouldn't come without him. If I waited around, he'd just disappear and come after me and mine later. I had to do this now.

I strode towards the door back to the main bar, but Karlo stopped me without any effort. He spun me around and forced me to look at him.

"Liss, he could be stronger than you can imagine, faster than you'll ever be able to comprehend, older than the land you're standing on. You can't do this by yourself."

I picked up a piece of kindling from the basket by the door.

"Are you coming or not?"

With a look of frustration, he untied his apron and threw it down on the staffroom table. "Just promise me, if things get out of hand, you'll run."

And leave him there to fight alone? Wasn't going

to happen. But I knew he'd feel better if I lied.

I nodded, and he followed me back into the bar.

Erin caught my sleeve as I strode past.

"Stay here until I get back," I said before she could speak. "If Corey tries to leave, get Glenn to convince him not to."

She nodded, her face paler than usual.

Outside, a cool breeze had sprung up off the harbour. I stood on the pavement and looked up. There was too much cloud to see it, but I knew it was only one day to go until full moon. No wonder we were all on edge. Even though I wasn't a wolf, my body still responded to the moon. Probably all those years of feeling the energy building in close quarters.

Karlo sniffed the air, then looked at me. "You're *sure* it was a vampire?"

"That's what he said." I felt doubtful myself, but there was only one way to find out.

I started walking back towards the waterfront. So far, Brandt had wanted to play with his prey, see what it would do. That was fine with me; I was learning things here that I clearly needed to know. For instance, that there were vamps other than the mindless, blood-crazed animals I'd killed.

It occurred to me that a smart vampire wouldn't come after me while I was keeping company with a werewolf.

I stopped walking. "What was that?"

Karlo looked around like a dog hearing a cat fight three blocks away. "What?"

I nodded towards an alley that led into the industrial precinct. "I saw something."

"Wait here," he said. He walked into the alley, his nose to the air.

I waited until he disappeared and started walking again, trusting Brandt would find me.

Logically, the best way to take him out was to look harmless, and pack a punch he wasn't expecting. Walking around with a werewolf wasn't going to do it. No. This needed cunning and finesse. And what better time to learn both of those things than now?

People were giving me strange looks and I realised it was the piece of wood in my hand. I pushed the makeshift stake into the waist of my tiny skirt and let my jacket swing over it. There was no way he would take me here in the middle of a crowded city street. No, he'd wait until I left the main drag.

I turned into a side street and started back towards the wharf. The street was mostly deserted, flanked by silent office buildings on either side. A group of goths turned a corner and clattered past in chains and boots, a travesty of the dead thing I'd set out to find.

As I passed the looming hulk of a parking building and moved into the narrow lane that led back to the waterfront, the clouds opened up to reveal a scatter of stars. It was pretty, despite the light pollution. The breeze off the water grew stronger, more pungent. I could feel the panic ebbing away, replaced by a strong, hard anger.

I would *not* cringe in fear, I would *not* let others fight my battles, and I would *not* let a vampire threaten me. I was the one who hunted them, not the other way around.

I turned a corner into the industrial precinct. A shadow flitted across my path and I stopped, scanning the darkness. I strained to see what was behind the construction fences that lined the sides of the road, seeing only the silhouettes of piles of rubble and dormant machinery. Far above, a light on a crane blinked off, on, off, on. I tore my gaze away, feeling lightheaded.

I realised a hand was touching my face and turned slowly to face its owner. It was like moving through golden syrup. Brandt's pale face was inches from mine. My hot breath touched his face; he was not breathing.

The night was silent, just the two of us there, alone in the street under the winking eye of the crane.

Brandt traced cold fingers across my cheek and then stepped back, breaking the contact between us. I stared at him, my brain fogged with confusion, trying to comprehend how he could be the same as the things I killed in the forest.

He smiled and moved his head, urging me to say something.

"You don't look dead." My voice was a whisper.

He tilted his head as if to say, '*Ah, you!*' and backed away to lean against the wire-loop fence.

We watched each other for a long moment. Then I remembered something. I pulled the stake from my belt and looked at it. I looked back at him.

He put a fingernail up to his mouth and flicked the bottom of one of his fangs. Cold drizzled down my spine. He'd been watching me at Karlo's. I'd known he'd be watching me, so why was I surprised? Why wasn't I killing him?

"So," I said, finding my voice. "Is there anything I should know?"

"About... killing me?" he asked, surprisingly able to follow my train of thought. He dropped his hand and drummed his fingers against his leg. "Let's see... yes, yes, there are a few things."

He looked back at me with a dazzling smile. I found the hand with the stake in it was hanging limply at my side and raised it again, holding the stake like a dagger.

"Well?" I said.

He looked incredulous. "You want me to tell you what they are?" He made a face. "Really?"

He stepped forward and my skin tried to crawl away from the slick presence that moved with him. He took the stake gently from my hand and tossed it over the fence. I watched it fall with a tiny clatter and felt nothing. No fear. No anger.

"What have you done to me?" I asked.

My eyes followed his glittering sphalerite ring as he reached out and tapped my nose. *Boop.*

"Nothing any decent vampire couldn't."

"Then I've only ever met indecent ones."

He laughed. "I have a proposition for you. How would you like to work for me?"

I looked at him, bemused. "See, this is what happens when we don't invest in mental health."

He gave a snort of laughter. "Well, it was worth a shot."

I shook my head trying to break whatever spell he had me under that was stopping me attacking him. It worked, a bit, and I started to feel the ache in my legs from standing still so long. I shifted cautiously, putting my feet into a balanced fighting stance.

Brandt watched this with apparent amusement. He leaned back against the fence, his hands behind him.

"If I wanted to, I could kill every last one of your pack. I could torture the little goth girl until she screamed out her wish that she'd never met you. I could come to you in the night and taste you at my leisure, then dump you into the ground for your pack brothers to hunt."

My body was mine again, bar some shaking. I advanced on him.

"You're a virus, vampire. You're that oily stuff that leaks out of cars when they get old."

"You mean oil?" he asked.

I ignored him. "You're lower than... than fish crap." I guess I was having a wharf-themed moment. "Stay away from my pack."

I was nose to nose with him, the scent of his power sounding violent warnings in my head.

"Or you'll what?" he said. "Insult me to death?"

I drew power into my arm and punched him. He was tall, but he didn't weigh that much. The punch pushed him back into the fence. For a moment his eyes widened in surprise and I backed away, readying myself to fight in my stupid skirt and my stupid, stupid heels. I knew one thing for sure. I was never letting Erin dress me again.

His eyes narrowed and he stalked towards me.

I aimed another punch at him and he simply moved out of the way. He was fast, every movement liquid grace. I aimed another blow at him, fuelled by anger at how easily he'd manipulated me, but there was no way I could hit him.

As I recovered my balance, he slipped behind me and hooked a foot behind my knee. I fell hard. Shards of broken glass stabbed my palms as I pushed myself to my feet and spun to face him.

He was gone.

I scoured the darkness, looking for movement, a hint of a shadow darker than the rest. There was nothing there.

Grimly, I brushed the glass from my hands and spoke, somehow knowing he could hear me.

"Leave them alone."

The lessons of tonight wouldn't be forgotten. Never again would I underestimate his kind. I needed to know more. I needed to talk to Jack.

Chapter 11

I checked my phone as I walked back towards Karlo's. Two hours had passed. Two hours! What the hell had I been doing for two hours?

The wolves gave me silent looks as I walked up to the bar.

"Where the hell were you?" said Erin.

"Let's go home."

She gave me a dark look and pulled on her jacket as Karlo came up to me.

"You disappeared. What happened?"

"I found Brandt. Or, rather, he found me. We talked and he took off."

"You talked? For two hours?"

I shrugged, unable to look him in the eye.

"Well, we'll have someone watch your flat until sunup."

"Thanks." Yeah, because after sunup we'd be safe. From the creepy old vampire who could make people lose hours at a time.

As much as I wanted to talk to Jack and Andy, I wasn't keen on waking them at 3 a.m. We caught a cab back to the flat and Erin and Corey went straight to their room, leaving me to wonder what the hell Brandt had meant when he asked if I wanted to work for him. Doing what?

I leaned against the porch railing and waited for the sun to rise so I could sleep. A shape stirred near the gate and I raised a hand in greeting. The wolf at the gate waved back. I rubbed my eyes and knew I couldn't stay awake much longer, and headed inside.

I slept through the day and woke late afternoon to find six unread texts on my phone. It seemed someone had told Jack and Andy about what'd happened. And I'd forgotten it was vows night.

The scent of spicy mince wafted through the air as I walked up the driveway to join them for an early dinner.

After hugs and Andy's once-over, we settled down to eat in the short time we had.

"So, tell us about last night," Jack said, forking lasagne into his mouth.

Andy looked up sharply.

Jack's tone was casual, but I could tell by the way he concentrated on his food that he was working on staying calm.

"I met a vamp in that new nightclub, Pulse— down by the waterfront. He said his name was Brandt. Sounded English."

Andy handed Jack the salad with a frown. Not quite the reaction I expected when telling them I'd met a walking, talking, thinking vamp in a nightclub.

Jack helped himself to the salad then handed it to me. "Karlo was upset that he wasn't able to find you."

"I had to go after him. I was afraid he'd come after Erin and Corey. They're not packed with supernatural goodness like you guys."

Andy was silent, sensing an impending lecture. He hated conflict, and went to any length to avoid it. I was guessing Karlo hadn't told Andy what'd happened, and Jack hadn't told him either, since he was still in the room.

Jack picked up his wine glass. "Karlo said you disappeared for two hours. He and Glenn couldn't track you."

There was still no sign of concern in his voice, but his wine was getting some pretty serious scrutiny.

"He's old, he's fast, and he's smart. Glenn and Karlo said you guys know all about vamps like this. So, fill me in."

Jack shifted one shoulder in a shrug. "We're aware of them. We don't tangle often."

He took a sip of wine and finally turned his amber gaze to me. "Did you deliberately lose Karlo last night?"

The look in his eyes made my skin prickle. I thought about lying, but I was never very good at lying to Jack.

"I didn't think he'd come after me if Karlo was there."

"So—I still don't understand your thinking."

I hated having to explain this to Jack. He already

knew the answer. We'd talked about it before—my attraction to danger. The thing inside me that made me want to find out what was in the dark.

"I went to find out what he wanted."

He nodded slowly, his face tight with disapproval.

"And did you find out what he wanted? Or did you just put yourself needlessly in danger?"

I looked down at my hands where nicks and cuts used to be. "He said he wanted me to work for him."

Andy frowned. "Work for him? Doing what?"

"I don't know," I said, "but probably not repairing consumer electronics."

Jack's eyes bored into me. "Don't be flippant. Every year you survive despite yourself. I've tried so hard to instil some kind of... survival instinct... in you—but every time you step out that door, you walk straight towards the deepest, darkest hole in the earth you can find and start digging for monsters."

My face burned. Being under his gaze at this point was almost physically painful.

He leaned forward. "Do you want to die? Is that it?"

"No! I just... I wanted to *know*."

He shook his head, his jaw clenched tight as he considered me. "This is why you need to leave. This is why you need to be forced to live a normal life, Liss. Because you can't be trusted to make that decision for yourself."

My hands, resting on the table, clenched and unclenched. "Maybe you should have told me what was out there."

He took in a deep breath and I felt the agitation of energy that surrounded him drop back a notch.

"Okay. Yes. That was clearly a mistake. But I didn't think you'd ever face one of his... kind. As long as you were with the wolves."

I shook my head in disbelief. "Why? Why did you think this would never happen?"

"Because the whole point of you being here for the last nine years was to keep you safe!"

I hadn't seen him this angry before. He never had to raise his voice. If Abigail and Kendrick hadn't been around, he'd have been the Westlands alpha. It was in his voice, in his presence. Even the Stoke brothers deferred to him. He spoke, we did as he said.

Well. Mostly.

I avoided his gaze as he took a deep breath in and let it out again.

Andy sat back in his seat, his eyes on his food. He'd stopped pretending to eat.

"So," I said, into the awkward silence. "These old ones ponce about drinking cocktails and putting out job offers, rather than chewing people's arms off. Is there anything else I need to know?"

Jack took a mouthful of food. He chewed for a while then swallowed. When he looked up, his anger had given way to something that looked more like guilt.

"When you came to us nine years ago, you were traumatised. Abigail suggested that hunting things you could successfully conquer on your own might help you find yourself again. It's not a small thing, to watch someone you care about be murdered in front of you. People have ended up in psych wards for less."

Abigail should know. She had a degree in psychology, among other things.

Unconsciously, I put a hand up to the silver necklace around my throat.

Jack nodded towards it. "I made a mistake when I gave that to you. And that damned knife."

I gave him an injured look but he reached across the table and took my hand.

"I made a mistake in giving them to you, and telling you they were *enough*," he said. "I wanted you to feel safe. I wanted you to stop screaming through the night. But I didn't count on how little it would take for you to become overconfident again."

"But you did make me feel safe," I said in a small voice. "You taught me how to fight. Do you want me to be afraid?"

He sighed through his nose. "Maybe. At least, more afraid than you are." He took his hand back and picked up the lasagne dish. "You're not to go after him."

I frowned at him. "He threatened us."

"He's probably just bored. You have the pack. You're safe." He emptied what was left in the dish on to his plate.

As the spoon scraped against the glass bottom of the dish, Andy tugged it out of his hands. "Before you lick it out."

He ruffled Jack's hair as if the past ten minutes

hadn't happened and took the dish into the kitchen.

Jack smiled after him, and dug into his lasagne.

"What about the ring?" I said. "Did Karlo tell you he had a *venulv* ring, like the one you gave me?"

Jack stopped with his fork in the air. "No. Are you sure?"

I nodded. "He made a point of showing it to me."

He looked down at his plate. "Not good. That could mean he's working with a pack."

"Yeah, about that," I said. "If he is, it seems really dangerous for me to be wearing a ring that promises I won't kill wolves, on pain of execution."

"I'll speak with Abigail tonight," he said. "But this just reinforces how important it is to keep out of trouble right now."

"I'll be sure to stop going to nightclubs, then," I said sarcastically.

Jack raised an eyebrow. "Just stick with the wolves and don't start any fights. That's all I'm asking."

"And if he comes after me? Or Erin?"

He gave me a grim look. "Then the *pack* will deal with it."

After dinner, we drove out to the reserve. We arrived just before eight, under a full moon.

As we got out of the car, I drank in the fresh scent of the bush.

Abigail and Kendrick greeted us at the door and walked us through into the sunken lounge.

It was Abigail's Maori heritage that gave three of the five Stoke brothers their dark hair and olive skin, while Kendrick, who'd immigrated to New Zealand from England in the 60s, had given his paler skin and grey-streaked hair to Glenn and Ben.

"Liss, I believe you've met Ellen before." Abigail gestured to a blonde woman with a formidable physique.

Ellen was the alpha for the Northland pack. Because Auckland was so close, we saw a lot of her pack. The Northland wolves were pretty much free to come and go as they wanted.

Ellen worked as a stunt driver for local film productions, which meant she spent a lot of time in and around Auckland. It was a dangerous way to make a living, but it helped that as a wolf, she was virtually death-proof.

It also made her a fortune and paid for her overpowered car, a dark grey Nissan R35 GT-R that always looked as if she'd just finished polishing it, then taken it for a drive with Barry Crump.

She shook my hand and gave me a friendly nod. I'd met her a couple of times, as she made a point of visiting all the pack alphas at least once a year, and acted as an enforcer on behalf of the ACs when one was needed.

"And of course, you know Tane." I'd first met Tane, whose name was pronounced 'ta-nay', on a trip around the South Island with Jack and Andy and he'd stayed with us a few times since when he had business in Auckland. I'd always liked him. An IT professional like Jack and Andy, Tane looked like one of those start-up owners from Silicon Valley. He ran the Upper South pack, another close ally of the Westlands. He and Jack usually found an excuse to play Call of Duty when they got together, but I didn't think that'd be happening tonight.

Abigail handed me a glass of wine and smiled encouragingly. I murmured hellos to Tane and Ellen and gulped my wine. Jack put a hand on my shoulder with an amused smile.

"You'll do fine. You've memorised the vows?"

I nodded. I was at least fifty percent sure I had.

Abigail stood me in the middle of the room and invited the others to sit down.

"Kia ora koutou katao, welcome everyone, and thank you, Ellen and Tane, for being here to witness Alessandra taking her vows. Today's ceremony is one that hasn't been performed in living memory, but it's one that was very important to our kind back in the cold North."

She put a hand on my shoulder.

"I've had the honour of knowing Alessandra for the last nine years, and I've seen her grow from a somewhat difficult child into the compassionate and slightly less wilful young woman she is today."

The bastards all laughed.

"Today's vows are not made lightly, and Alessandra knows the penalties for breaking them." Abigail turned to me. "However, in the spirit of the vows, we also wish to reassure you that the wolves are your allies, and as long as you respect these vows, the Westlands pack will protect you with their lives."

I swallowed hard, both moved and terrified of the

weight these vows carried. Jack gave me a slight nod, reassuring me everything was okay.

"Liss, do you have the ring?" said Abigail.

I held out my hand.

"All right, Liss, please recite the vows to us in Old Wolf, and then in English, so that we all witness that you understand the full implications of the oath you're making to the wolves today."

I nodded and took a shaky breath.

"Jag svär vid de gamla gudarna, trohet till vargarna i väst, og å aldri skade eller ta livet av en ulv i nord, sør, øst eller vest, ved dødsstraf. I swear by the old gods allegiance to the wolves of the West, and to never harm or take the life of a wolf of the North, the South, the East, or the West, upon penalty of death."

Abigail nodded, pleased. "Very good. And do you understand that this oath you're making today means that should a wolf attack you, you must incapacitate them without killing them, or risk the death penalty?"

I nodded. I didn't think it was fair, but then the wolves would also fight to defend me. In theory, being part of a pack was about never standing alone. I should never have to fight a wolf, never mind have to kill one to survive.

Abigail put her arm around me as the others stood to shake my hand.

"Tane, Ellen, do you have any questions?" she said.

"Liss, do you have any sense yet of what kind of power you might come into?". asked Ellen.

"Not really. Deep power's really strong to me now—I can feel it a mile off. And the animations seem to be more attracted to me too. I got attacked by dead possums last time I raided a nest."

Ellen looked surprised. "Has that ever happened before?"

"No, that was new. And super creepy."

Andy frowned. "You didn't mention that."

I winced with embarrassment. "I forgot."

Tane gave me a penetrating look. "Liss, have you made long-term plans for after you come into your abilities?"

I glanced at Jack and Andy. "I don't even know if I'm going to… come into my abilities, that is."

"We're encouraging Liss to go to university," said Jack.

Abigail looked delighted. "Oh, that's wonderful, Liss! Do you think you'll study locally?"

Not if Jack and Andy had any say in it.

"We were thinking Waikato University," said Jack. "Or even Massey, down in Palmerston North. Give Liss a chance to get away from here and concentrate on her studies."

Ellen looked confused. "That's a long way from home."

Jack smiled awkwardly. "Abigail, could I have word with you?"

She nodded and they moved out on to the porch. I was guessing he was going to talk to her about Brandt and the venulv ring.

Kendrick refilled our glasses. "Can I suggest a

toast?" His eyes twinkled as he raised his glass. "To Alessandra De Witt, first of her kind in Aotearoa, the Unblemished, Väktare to the Westlands pack, friend to the wolves, and terrible namer of inanimate objects."

"Cheers," I said, raising my glass to the general merriment at my expense, the clinking of glasses, and under the intense scrutiny of Ellen Kauri.

Chapter 12

I arrived home to find Erin sitting at the dining room table. I knew instantly that Corey wasn't around. Something to do with her not being attached to him at the mouth.

"Hey." I sat at the table opposite her.

She was working on a scrapbook. She held up a photo of the two of us, our arms slung around each other's shoulders.

"I like this one," she said. "Even if you are all pre-healed in it."

I grinned and reached for the photo, but she held it out of reach.

"Relax, you have to have a 'before' picture."

I snorted and watched as she stuck it into the book with adhesive skulls and roses.

"Did you guys have a fight?" I could tell from the faded black tracks down her face that she'd been crying. She kept her eyes on her work, but tears were forming.

"He's just so jealous. God, that sounds so soap opera. But seriously, he's determined that last night had something to do with an ex-boyfriend."

"Of yours?"

She nodded. "I keep telling him he's insane, that whoever the guy was, he's your stalker, not mine."

"Cheers."

But I could see how someone as insecure as Corey might see Erin as a tough girl to hold on to. In addition to being extremely pretty, her confidence was the most alluring thing about her. And she was smart without being pretentious, something no one else I knew was able to pull off. I guess I would have been jealous if I hadn't been so fixated on killing things. And if I hadn't loved her to death.

I gave her a friendly shove. "He's an ass, Erin. Dump him."

She grinned at me, wiping the tears away with the edge of her thumb.

"I've got that on a t-shirt somewhere."

"Hey, why don't we go out? Go see what the boys are up to."

She brightened up and shoved the rest of the loose photos into the front of the book.

"What will Corey think?"

I gave her a long look. "Seriously? He'll think he shouldn't have been such an ass."

Ben's house was where we normally went to hang out. Ben was another of Dan's brothers. There were five in total, with Glenn the oldest in his early forties, followed by Karlo and Ben, who were in their thirties, and then Dan and his baby brother, Tai, both in their early twenties.

I don't know how their mother did it. Five werewolf boys in one home. Still, I loved them all. Abigail and Kendrick made good kids.

It was a full moon, which meant the wolves would take a night off from their usual haunts to get together, drink, and then later on run together at the reserve.

They did the drinking at Ben's flat because Abigail and Kendrick valued peace and quiet. As alcohol didn't stay long in the wolves' systems, they could let off steam, then drive out to the reserve half an hour later and run, without worrying about drink driving.

I usually avoided these get-togethers, because nothing reminds you you're different so much as seeing everyone else taking pleasure in something you can't. But tonight, their revelry was exactly what Erin—and I—needed.

We walked up the driveway to the sound of music and laughter. Ben was standing on the porch drinking a bottle of beer. He waved to us.

"Hey, you." He gave me a kiss on the cheek, then patted Erin on the head. She slapped his hand away and he grinned.

"Just because you're a freak of nature," she said.

He shrugged. At six foot two, he towered above us both.

"Hey, Erin!" Luke, blond and blue-eyed, ran up and engulfed her in a hug. I left her on the porch and went inside.

The inside of the flat smelled of testosterone. The

brothers and their unsuspecting human friends were playing a drinking game in the middle of the lounge floor. Dan's shadow, Gracie, was nowhere to be seen, which didn't really surprise me. Gracie wasn't much of a people person, and I'd never seen her drink. She'd join the rest of the pack for the hunt at the reserve though—she never missed an opportunity to run with Dan. Not that I was jealous. Why would I be jealous?

Dan gave me a wave as he downed a shot. The rest of the circle cheered.

Ben took me into the kitchen and sat me down with a beer.

"So, I hear you've been stirring up the wrong crowd."

God, did everyone know? Of course they did. It was pack business now.

"Just some aged vampire who thinks he's hot stuff."

Ben cocked his head and stared at me without blinking until I met his gaze.

"What?"

"I don't like this silence, Liss. Normally we can't shut you up. What's the deal?"

A shout came from out front and we both jumped up. I pushed in front of Ben and raced outside.

Corey was standing by the gate, looking the tiniest bit terrified. Luke had his arms pulled up behind his back, and I hoped he was being careful. Even if he hadn't been a wolf, with his strength he could snap every bone in Corey's fragile body without trying.

"Let him go!" Erin shouted as she tried to pull Luke away from Corey. Ben and Tai came out of house and walked purposefully across the lawn.

I held up my hands. "Guys, I'll handle it."

They stopped and folded their arms, their expressions making it clear that if I was going to ask them to back off, I needed to deal with the problem myself, and quickly.

"Tell this idiot to get off my boyfriend!" Erin snapped at me. I turned back to her. Corey's face was a mixture of pain and fear, and I could see that Luke was struggling to be gentle.

"Who are these people?" Corey cried desperately.

I sighed. "Luke, you can let him go. He's a friend."

Luke's eyes had bled to wolf-gold, his pupils blown out wide. "He smells of vampire."

Okay, that was a problem. But not one breaking Corey was going to solve.

I could see Luke was losing it. If he snapped, Corey — and maybe even Erin — would be nothing but fresh meat to his moon-addled brain.

"You're drunk and you're an idiot," I said. "Let him go."

Erin crossed her arms and glared at him. Ben came to stand beside me. His body language as he faced Luke was very clear. His presence pushed out from him, warning Luke to back off.

Luke looked from me to Ben, his eyes that feral yellow, his canines pointed and gleaming in the moonlight.

I growled low in my throat. I might not have had

teeth to threaten him with, but since the vampire attack that'd nearly killed me, I hadn't left the house without my blade. I pushed my jacket back and Luke's gaze followed the gesture. Corey's eyes widened as he caught the glimmer of silver.

"Ow, let me go!" he cried as Luke's grip tightened.

I could see Luke was struggling to hold on to his humanity with so much threat around him.

Ben lifted his lips back from his teeth, just enough to show fang. In a pack, hierarchy won most fights, and Ben was above Luke. The warning was subtle, but it was familiar enough to reach Luke's wolf brain.

With a snarl, he let go of Corey's arm. But buoyed by the full moon, his beast wasn't done. His eyes fixed on me, nostrils flaring, his canines exposed.

Corey stumbled away rubbing an arm that apparently still worked, and Erin took him off to a safe distance and started damage control while I faced down Luke.

"Back off. We're pack, remember?"

Ben shifted his posture slightly, flexing, and Luke's eyes flickered to him, the wolf in him on the verge of clawing its way out of his body of its own accord.

"Liss?" Tai's voice, behind me. "You need to get Corey out of here, now."

I walked slowly around Luke, his eyes trained on me, his teeth almost locked into a snarl.

The others closed around him, ready to restrain him if he tried to attack. The laughter had died, replaced by a hush that let the full absurdity of the music's lyrics float out into the street.

"Come on, Erin, let's go."

Erin put her arm around Corey and we started back to our flat, Corey casting one last glance behind him at the silent mass of people standing like statues in the garden.

"Are all your family complete psychopaths?" Corey asked.

We were sitting around the kitchen table, Erin staring at the bruises on her boyfriend's pale skin.

"He didn't even do anything, Liss. He just turned up and Luke went psycho."

"That guy needs a muzzle," said Corey.

I looked at him sharply but there was no telling look in his eyes. The house smelled vaguely of incense and underneath it… pot.

I leaned forward and caught the scent of it on him.

"Were you smoking dope in this flat?" I asked.

He gave a half shrug. "So what?"

Erin punched his shoulder lightly and he winced. "You didn't tell me you had some!"

I wasn't impressed. I didn't have anything in particular against pot, except when it was in my home. Then it became a problem.

"Where'd you get it?" Erin asked.

Corey saw my expression and became defensive. "It's just weed."

I put my hands on the table and channelled Andy's disapproval.

"Who gave it to you?" Luke had said Corey

smelled of vampire. My senses were nothing like a were's, so I'd have to take his word for it.

"Some guy. Just a friend of a friend."

A chill ran through me. "Did you know this guy?"

He shrugged. "Not really."

"But he sold you drugs."

"Yeah, that's what normally happens when you go to a drug dealer."

Erin bit her lip, and I knew she was thinking the same thing I was.

"What did he look like?" I asked.

Corey looked from me to Erin. "What's the big deal?"

"You know that guy, that stalker the other night?" Erin asked. "We're just worried that it might have been him."

"Because—" I thought desperately. "He might have sold you bad drugs."

"Why are you asking me this?"

Time to be creative. "That guy, Luke, who grabbed you, he could smell the drugs on you. And—"

"And he thought it smelled bad," Erin finished. "Like, dangerous bad."

Corey looked at us as if we were nuts.

"Uh, he probably thought you were going to share some of the... bad drugs, with Erin," I added. "Our friends are very protective."

"Jesus Christ. Well..." He shrugged and waved a hand in the air. "He was tall, dark hair—just some guy, you know?"

"Was there anything different about him?" I

pushed.

Corey thought for a moment. "He was wearing a ring, I remember that—a fancy ring. He kept playing with it."

Not good.

Erin shot me a glance and I tried to not show how scared I was. Somehow Brandt had insinuated himself into Corey's circle—and now he was selling him dope? Although, I guessed, that was probably the best way to get into Corey's circle.

Corey looked at me with a thoughtful expression.

"Did I hear that guy say something about vampires?"

No, no, no, no, no. I put a hand to my mouth and yawned as I thought up a lie. Best stick as close to the truth as possible.

"Yeah, he thought you looked like a Twihard." That felt more natural than our recent discussion about 'bad drugs'. Marginally.

Corey scowled at me.

I made my excuses and went to my bedroom. More than anything I wanted to talk to the wolves, but not right now. Not with the full moon rising. As far as I knew, Corey was stupid, not dangerous, but full-moon wolves wouldn't see him that way.

The best thing to do would be to wait until tomorrow.

I sent Dan a text, knowing he'd see it when he got back to the reserve in human form, and then lay in bed staring at the ceiling until I finally fell asleep, dreaming of vampire drug-dealers.

Chapter 13

I woke to a noise at the window and rolled out of bed, pulling my knife from under my pillow.

The sound came again and I pulled back the curtain. It was Dan. He gestured to the front door and then disappeared. I checked my phone. 3 a.m.

I groaned and pulled on some clothes.

It had been raining and the world was damp and shiny. Dan was dressed in a sleeveless singlet that showed his muscular arms, a concession to the humidity. He looked as if he'd just had a shower, his hair hanging in damp spikes.

"I heard what happened," he said, his eyes roving over me.

"Where were you while it was happening?"

He looked embarrassed. "Some of those shots didn't want to stay down. Did Luke hurt you?"

I snorted. "He wouldn't. But he smelled vamp on Erin's boyfriend and took exception."

Dan ran a hand across his stubble and looked thoughtful.

"Why'd he think the guy was a vamp? Were there

bite marks? Has he been slaved?"

"Slaved? I don't know what that is."

"You know, the vamp bites you but doesn't turn you—takes your mind, but leaves you human, uses you to carry out his daytime tasks."

Slaved. Jesus. That had never occurred to me. Anyway, Corey was so covered in chains and layers, you'd never see bite marks.

"Well, Corey said he bought dope from this guy, and I recognised his supplier as Brandt from his description."

"Brandt?"

"The vamp I ran into the other night."

Dan stuck his hands in his pockets and gave a small sigh. "Do you trust him?"

"Who, Corey? About as far as I could ball and flick him."

He nodded. "We need to find out if this guy— what's his name again?"

"Corey."

"If... Corey? You're kidding."

"No, really," I said. "He's cute too, in a nauseating kind of way."

Dan shook his head. "Okay, we need to find out if Corey is involved with this guy. It's bad enough that he's buying drugs—do you realise you could get kicked out of your flat if Andy finds out?"

Yes, I knew. Plenty of wolves I knew smoked pot, but not down our branch of the family. They'd negotiated cheap rent on this place so that we could afford it, and they'd be massively upset if they found out I'd let them down. Andy would be 'disappointed' and Jack would be—well, more than just disappointed.

"Find out if he's got a bite and let me know as soon as you do. Meanwhile, can I have a look at his jacket?"

"Huh?"

"I want to get the scent of this vamp."

I went inside and found Corey's jacket draped on the back of a chair and took it out to him. Dan held the leather to his nose and sniffed. His lips raised back in a snarl.

"Luke was right?"

Dan looked up, his eyes glinting with anger.

"You don't want to know half the scents on this jacket. Let's just say, Erin isn't the only one getting intimate with this guy."

"Wait—Corey's sleeping around on Erin?"

"Yeah," he said grimly. "With multiple partners."

I'd deal with that later.

He combed the jacket with his nose, stopping at the cuffs, and murmured, "So, that's your scent." He inhaled deeply. "The vamp's old, Liss. This guy would have to be over a hundred to have a signature like this, maybe twice that. Older than anything I've ever come across."

"What does he smell like?" I took up a sleeve and tried sniffing. All I could smell was Lynx body spray and leather.

"It's like… the old ones smell kind of like lavender dust. It's far more subtle than a fresh vamp—they smell more like rotting meat. But this guy smells like... I dunno. Like paper. I can smell his aftershave over the top—I'm assuming the scent that isn't 'Horny, for Teenagers' is his."

"You're saying he smells like a cardboard perfume sample?"

He handed the jacket back to me. "Kinda. Maybe. That's a bad analogy. I could say to you he smells justified and ancient, but I'm trying to be more specific here. I don't think you humans have ever smelled some of the things we wolves can."

I sniffed the jacket again. Just leather.

"Anyway, I've got his signature now," said Dan.

"Could you track him from this?"

He shook his head. "It's faint, Liss. Distinctive against a human scent, but not a scent I could easily follow. And there's always a chance we'd ending up chasing the wrong one."

I stared at him. "What do you mean, 'the wrong one'? How many old vamps can there be around here?"

He put his hands back in his pockets. "I don't know of any, but I wouldn't be surprised if there were a few. It's not like they announce themselves."

I took a step closer and looked up into his face. "Dan, how many of these old vamps are there?"

He clicked his tongue. "In a city this size, I'd guess there could be three or four hunting regularly."

He put out a hand to steady me as his words sank in. "You okay?"

"I'm just great, Dan. God, you guys must have

been laughing at me all this time."

He shook his head. "Liss, no one was laughing at you. The others don't care about vamps unless they come too close to the pack. But I'm like you. I think they should go. I wouldn't have helped you find those nests if I didn't agree with what you were doing."

How could I trust a word he was saying? Sure, he'd never actually lied to me as far as I knew, but he'd never told me more than a tenth of the truth, either.

He seemed to read my thoughts and dropped his hand back to his side.

"How would you have slept knowing this, after what happened to your sister?"

I bunched the jacket into a ball and stared at it. The same way I'd sleep now. With difficulty.

Erin was not impressed.

"Of course he's not a servant thingy, he's just dumb!" She was chopping onions, which always made her cranky.

I leaned back against the bench and handed her a tissue. She mopped at her eyes, then went on chopping.

"Just check it out," I said. "It'll help make sure the pack doesn't come after him. If he's clear, we tell him to not buy any more pot from Brandt and we leave it at that."

She looked up, worry darkening her eyes.

"They'd really come after him?"

I shrugged. "I don't know. But Luke's so overprotective, especially of you, I wouldn't be surprised. It takes the wolves a couple of days to settle back to normal, and a hyped werewolf is not a fun werewolf. Just find out before sunset tonight, for me. Please?"

She tossed the knife into the sink and shook the onion off the chopping board into a frying pan.

"He's got no bites, Liss. I have seen him naked a few times now."

I thought of Dan's comments about Erin not being the only one Corey was getting jiggy with, and wondered why I was so keen to stop Luke mashing his face into pulp.

"Dan said the bites might be really small, that some old vamps can do it without causing bruising."

Erin stirred the onion, sending a cloud of steam up to the roof. I leaned across her and turned on the extractor fan.

"Um, how can I put this? He has bites on his neck, and they're not from a vampire."

For a moment I thought she knew about his other girlfriend...s. Then I noticed her impish grin.

"Oh, kinky." But it came out half-hearted. It was awful knowing this rat was cheating on her, but I couldn't risk telling her until we knew more about what Corey was. She'd give the game away—probably by murdering him.

"He also said sometimes vamps who're hiding what they are, use needles to take blood from one of the other main veins, like the one in your arm. You know, the vein they take blood from when they do blood tests."

"Oh."

I didn't like the look in her eyes.

"Oh, what?"

"Well, he recently had a blood test—he has them every couple of weeks since that cancer scare he had, back before I met him."

"When did he have it?"

"Two days ago."

Before I could ask her how legit it was likely to be, there was a scuffle at the door and Corey clomped in carrying a shopping bag.

"Hi all." He set the bag on the counter and put his arms around Erin, nuzzling her neck. I watched him with disgust until he caught the vibe and turned to me. "Something wrong?"

"Nothing alcohol can't fix." I grabbed a handful of cutlery from the drawer and started setting the table. Out of the corner of my eye I watched Erin, saw the stiffness in her body, the wariness in the way she looked at Corey. She was going to give the game away.

"Erin, which way around do you put the knives and forks?"

"Here," she said, handing the wooden stirring spoon to Corey. She came to the table and fussed around putting things right.

"We've got three hours of daylight," I said in a low voice.

"I know," she hissed.

She went back to the kitchen and Corey glanced at me over her head. For a moment, his eyes filled with a hatred so strong I nearly asked him what the hell was his problem was. Then it was gone and he was just cute, lovable Corey.

We finished dinner and I glanced at the clock on the microwave. Half past six. Sunset was at eight. I tried to catch Erin's attention, but she refused to make eye contact. I needed to know what Corey was, *now*.

As soon as I could, I pulled her into the hall. "Sorry Corey, period stuff."

He raised a hand and made a face of disgust.

Erin folded her arms as I shut the door behind us. "Look, he can't be a human servant. We've been together for over a year."

"Are you sure he needed that blood test?"

She gave me a sullen look. I guessed I understood. Finding out your long term partner was a rat was hard. But one way or another, I was going to pull this relationship down tonight. I didn't want her sleeping with him again—not knowing he was sleeping with other people.

"I told you about the cancer scare," she said. "He has blood tests every week or so to check his white blood count."

"As long as you've known him?"

"Yes."

"Doesn't that seem too often to you?"

"I don't know much about cancer," she snapped

back.

I debated whether or not to tell her about his cheating there and then, but this was hard enough for her.

"You must know something's not right."

Corey pulled the door open. "Sorry for interrupting." He put his arm around Erin. "Do you mind doing the washing up tonight, Liss? Season nineteen of Supernatural starts tonight. We'll go into our room so you can put on some music."

Before I could say anything, he led Erin down the hall to the bedroom.

I sat at the kitchen table as the sun sank down behind the hills, knowing I was going to have to tell Erin he was cheating. It was the only way she was going to believe Corey wasn't who he pretended to be.

As the moon rose, I felt its pull. Even though it was no longer full, I felt anxious from years of living with three days of full-moon weirdness a month. Like the time Jack and Andy stood in the yard watching a cat licking itself on the fence—for an hour. Or the time I came down to find dinner wasn't cooked. Or on a plate. Or dead yet.

Finally Erin finally emerged from her room, flushed and uneasy. It was obvious she'd found something.

She tugged me outside on to the lawn. "Two marks, but they're not small enough to be needle marks—just over an inch apart. He said they had to put the needle in twice because they missed the main vein."

"Where is he now?"

She glanced back at the house. "Watching TV naked."

I did not need that visual.

"What happens now?" she said. "If he's a servant-whatever, will the wolves come after him?"

"I don't know."

Brandt had wanted us to know about this, otherwise Corey wouldn't have told us about him. Or was this Corey's idea of a cry for help?

A howl went up somewhere close and we both jumped.

"Was that—?"

"Just a dog, I think."

Inside, the bathroom door slammed. Erin glanced back at the house, tears glistening in her eyes. "Is he evil?"

I thought back to the night down at the harbour, of the feeling of being in thrall. Of Dan's warning that Corey was cheating on her.

"I don't know. Probably." I sighed, trying to figure out how to break the bad news. "There's something else you should know—"

Corey came out onto the step, a towel around his waist. "What should she know?"

Erin advanced on him and shoved him hard.

"That you're a freaking vampire servant, that's what!"

A slow grin grew on his face. "I'm a what?" But he

was taunting her, not denying it.

She smacked a fist into his chest and he stumbled back a step, then caught her wrist. She twisted out of his grip and stood in front of him, fuming.

"Come on, Erin, that's what you love about me. The wicked mojo, the boosted stamina."

Yuck.

"Creep," shouted Erin. "Liar!"

She turned her back on him and came back down the steps. "Call Dan."

I folded my arms. "I don't think that's a good idea. You'll cooperate with us, won't you, Corey?"

He looked down at his half-naked body and then back up with an arrogant smile. "I'm in the *mood* to cooperate."

On second thought, it might be nice to have wolf backup. I pulled my phone out and dialled Dan, hoping he'd still have hands to answer with. Corey leaned on the doorframe and watched. There was no answer. It must be later than I thought.

I put the phone away and advanced on Corey, pushing him back into the house. As I reached the door, he put his hands on my hips, pulling me towards him.

"I like this side of you."

I backhanded him, hard. He collided with the wall, fury crawling across his face.

"Go get dressed," I said. "We're going for a drive. You're going to show me where you met with this pot dealer."

He sneered at me. "Make me."

I put my hand to my belt and pulled out my knife. "Okay."

He took one look at the knife and started backing down the hall to the bedroom.

"You have one minute. Then we—that is, me and EMN here—will be joining you."

I gave him a parody of his lascivious grin. With a last look at the knife, he retreated to Erin's room.

Chapter 14

The way I saw it, we had two choices. Tell the pack and run the risk of them hurting Corey—or Erin and I could take him for a drive at concealed weapon-point and find out where Brandt was camped. EMN would tell me if it was the right place—we didn't have to get too close. Then we could cut Corey loose.

What exactly I'd do after that, I wasn't sure. I only knew I wanted to face him again, prepared and composed. I wanted to show him he didn't scare me.

I figured if he'd wanted to kill me, he'd have done it by now. Whatever game he was playing, wasn't over yet. And it was my move.

Corey came back out of Erin's room in jeans and a short-sleeved t-shirt, flexing his stringy biceps to draw attention to the bite marks. As if we'd forget what he was.

He leaned against the table, smirking.

"Vampire right in your own home and you never even guessed," he said.

I snorted. "You're not a vampire, Corey. You're a wannabe. And why you'd want to be one of those things, I have no idea."

"You should taste this power, Liss," he said.

"No thanks, I like to keep my blood in my body."

"I was thinking you could taste my—"

"Sooo," I interrupted, changing tactic. "You're Brandt's pet now—"

"Renfield," interrupted Erin. I glanced at her and she held up her phone. "I just looked it up. Human servants are called 'Renfields' after Dracula's human servant in the Bram Stoker novel. It's totally canon."

I blinked. Yeah, I was not going to call him that.

"His *pet*. Without going into just how incredibly lame this sounds, tell us how to find your master."

He put a hand up to the blood at the corner of his mouth, and were... were his canines were just the teeniest bit sharper than they used to be? It had been a while since I'd seen his mouth open without Erin attached to it.

"I'm not going to take you to him. Firstly, I have no idea where he is. I met him at a friend's house. Secondly, if I took you to him, he'd tear me to pieces."

"Literally?" I asked hopefully.

He gave me a caustic look. "So, what happens now?"

Well, he was probably telling the truth about not knowing where Brandt was. And it was likely his master would be pretty upset at being given up if he *did* know. So, what would bring this vamp out of hiding? What could I do to Corey that would get his attention?

Lucky for the dweeb, Erin made the decision for me.

"Just throw him out, Liss. There's nothing else we can do."

I considered him and saw that he didn't like this plan at all. Were we not playing according to the script? Good.

"Get his things," I said to Erin. I kept my knife out and handy as I urged Corey towards the door.

"Here's the deal. You stay out of our way and we'll try not to hurt you."

Erin arrived and hurled his few possessions at him—his phone, a hip flask of bourbon, some unwashed clothing, and his leather jacket.

He pulled on the jacket, pocketed the flask and the phone, then stood at the bottom of the steps with his clothes in his hands, lip curled into a snarl.

"You don't deserve me, Erin. I should have known you wouldn't be able to cope—"

"Oh, shut up." I slammed the door.

Muffled words came through the door. "You were a crap lay, Erin! I know what *real* sex is now—"

I wrenched the door open and stalked down the steps towards him.

"You just had to keep talking."

Erin was at the top of the steps, arms wrapped around herself. "Please, don't hurt him!"

God, she was too good for this prick. I pointed my knife at him. "Leave!"

"I haven't finished talking to Erin."

"Oh, yes you have."

"What are you going to do?" The condescension in his voice reminded me that Corey really didn't know that much about me.

"Leave and you won't find out."

He started back towards the house and I swiped the knife at him.

He raised an arm to block the strike but he was way off. I wasn't aiming at his chest. Instead, I slit his t-shirt down the side, leaving a shallow scratch from armpit to waist that would hurt like buggery in the shower.

He stumbled back and looked down at the cut. "Bitch!"

He threw his unwashed clothes on the lawn and stalked down the drive.

"Don't call, Erin," he said, without looking over his shoulder. "You've already been replaced."

In a rage, I gave chase, and he broke into a run. My knife caught his retreating back, carving an 'X' in the back of his leather jacket.

"Where are you going?" I called after him. "The wolves'll find you, asshole. They love the smell of blood on a full moon."

He gave me a last terrified glance and hightailed it.

Erin was shaking when I came back inside. I pulled the duvet off her bed and wrapped it around her. She snuggled down on the couch and the floodgates opened.

I understood. She felt utterly betrayed. A day ago, Corey had been the warmth in her life, a reason to smile, someone she trusted and... bonked a lot. Now she was left cold, knowing there was no going back, fighting the impulse to go to the one person who normally made the hurt go away — the person who'd caused it.

She cried until she was spent, then closed her eyes, exhausted. I got a damp facecloth and laid it on her forehead. She murmured her thanks, and once I was sure she'd be okay, I grabbed a jacket and headed out.

As much as Corey had protested he wouldn't lead me to Brandt, I hoped I'd scared him enough that he'd want protection.

As I walked into the street, the cold of the night rising up around me, I cursed the stupid ability I was supposed to have that didn't even let me feel old vamps or their servants.

Someone fell into step with me. Without looking, I knew instantly who it was.

"Hey, Dan."

I could feel the power trembling around him as he reined in his inner wolf.

"You were right. Corey's Brandt's human servant."

His power swelled and I knew the wolf wasn't far away.

"Feel free to go nature, Dan. Don't stay all upright for me."

"Change, here, in the street?" There was contempt in his voice. "So, we're following Corey? Why?"

"Because I think he'll run to Brandt."

"Another good reason not to follow him."

"He's playing with me."

"So don't play."

He was right, I shouldn't be doing this. But there was no way I could leave someone like Brandt out in the night to come after me 'at his leisure'. No. I needed closure. His bones, in the ground.

We walked in silence for a while, Dan pausing at street corners to scent the air, making sure we didn't miss a turn.

"What are you going to do when you find him?" Dan asked.

"I don't know. I think I can talk to him. If he'd wanted me dead, I'd be dead by now." I glanced at him. "So, why are *you* here?"

"Because I have a feeling he has a hold on you, and I'm not letting you face him alone again."

"A hold." I snorted.

We kept walking. There was a warm push of energy at my back and I knew that others would soon be joining us. Their energy had a violence to it that made my pulse quicken.

"They can't rip Corey apart," I said softly to Dan, knowing that the others would hear, but hoping that their wolf brains would be too busy singing with the moon to understand I was implying they had no self-control.

"They won't," he said. "Not while I'm here."

"Who called you?"

"Erin," he said. "She realised you were gone and

was worried you might get yourself in trouble."

I guessed that was fair.

We reached an alleyway and Dan reached out and stopped me. It felt as though a tonne of iron had landed on my shoulder.

"Ow."

"He's in there."

Now that he mentioned it, I could hear distressed breathing and a soft scraping as Corey pressed himself into the corrugated iron fence.

A cold nose nudged the back of my leg and I answered by holding a hand out at my side, asking for restraint. There was a wistful whine, answered by snuffling and claws scratching concrete as wolves melted out of the shadows into the patchy yellow streetlight.

God help any late-night insomniacs witnessing this.

"You can come out now," I said to Corey, and started into the alley.

Dan dragged me back. "He smells wrong. But I can't explain how."

He cocked his head, scenting, listening. I waited, chafing with the urge to go shake Corey until his unusually long teeth rattled.

Dan squeezed my shoulder and pulled me back level with him as a shadow flowed out of the alley, followed by the figure of a man. For a moment I thought it was Brandt—but it was just Corey. Well, not *just* Corey. The frightened kid was gone, replaced by someone who stood tall, oozing confidence. As I watched, he pulled off his jacket and tugged his t-shirt over his head to stand bare-chested in front of us.

His wound was a glistening line against his pale skin.

Dan growled softly and the rest of the wolves answered. I had no idea who was who right now; I just hoped they respected Dan's leadership as the son of the Westlands pack alphas.

Corey strode towards us with a grace that wasn't his. It made him look far more threatening than he actually was. So, a vamp could pass some of his preternatural nastiness on to his pets. Good to know. Kinda *late* to be finding out now.

"You want to meet the master?" He held his hands out as if to show he was unarmed. "That will not be happening."

That wasn't his voice. Hearing Brandt's words coming from his mouth ramped my pulse up another notch. I was out of my depth here. I wanted to run, but that wasn't an option.

Corey/Brandt ran a fingernail in a line down his chest. A trickle of liquid welled from between the ragged edges of his skin. He did the same on the other side of his chest as I stood frozen in horror. With a grin, he pushed his nails into the wounds and began to peel the skin away. The tissue underneath was black, not red. What the hell had Brandt done to him?

The smell of carnage filled the air, and I heard Karlo's voice in my head, explaining that the word 'carnage' came from the Latin root 'carn' meaning flesh. In this case, rotting flesh.

I wanted to look away but couldn't. You can't look away from evil for even a moment. That's how it gets you.

He held out his hands, stained with black, stinking fluid.

"Chow's up."

That voice.

The wolf at my right tensed and sprang.

I heard Dan shout as the pack surged forwards.

"Stop them!" I begged him, but his eyes had grown wide. His pupils expanded until all I could see was black, surrounded by the rolling whites of his eyes. Then the dark circles snapped to pinpoints in an expanding circle of amber as the wolf inside pushed to get out. He fell to his knees, his eyes pleading with me to understand.

I closed my eyes as the wolf fought its way out of his skin and when I opened them again, he was indistinguishable from the rest of the pack.

The wolves boiled around Corey, driven mad by the stink of blood and undeath, urged on by the near-full moon and the fear they felt from me.

The thing that wasn't Corey anymore raised its arms gleefully to the sky as it was pulled down into a mass of fur and scrabbling paws.

I staggered back a step at the sounds their teeth made as they tore into his flesh. The growling grew guttural, heads shaking as pieces were pulled away from bone, the wet, thick sound of tearing meat.

A thin scream cut the night, Corey's own voice, strangled almost instantly by a wolf's jaws closing around his throat.

I turned and ran, stumbled and caught myself and ran on, lungs burning, as if I'd never stop running again.

When I reached the flat, I locked the door behind me and stood leaning against it, shaking. I couldn't believe what'd just happened. I partied with these guys, I worked with them, wrestled with them, baked cakes with them. They were my family. My murderous, monstrous family.

In a daze, I went into the lounge to check on Erin. Woken by the noise of my coming home, she stirred and peeled the facecloth away from her forehead.

"Liss! Are you all right?"

No. I would never, ever be 'all right' again. I wanted to bury myself under my bed covers, wanted to hide myself somewhere so deep, so far under the earth's surface that I would be blind to the images in my head. To the fear of what might be coming next.

She grabbed my sleeve and tried to stop me roving uselessly, unable to form coherent thought.

"What happened?"

I looked into her pale face and knew I could never tell her what I'd seen. But I had to tell her something. After all, Corey wasn't coming back.

"They're mad tonight, out of control."

"The wolves? Mad enough to kill?" Her voice trembled.

I stared at her, tortured. "I'm sorry," I whispered.

A sob hitched in her throat. "He's dead?"

I nodded.

She put a hand to her mouth, her breath coming in gasps. "How?

"They lost control."

Her eyes widened. "Are we safe?"

I shook my head. "I don't know." Something thumped in the wind outside and we both jumped.

"Let's go to Jack and Andy's," she said. She grabbed her car keys from the key holder and pulled on her jacket.

"No! We can't. The moon."

Jack was most likely a wolf now. God, I hoped he wasn't one of the wolves in the street.

"But, we should get in the car at least?" she said. I could see she was in shock, her fingers trembling.

She was right—the car meant distance between us and them. I opened the door cautiously. No sign of the wolves.

We jumped into her two-door hatchback and she backed out at full speed, taking off down the street as if we were in a Ferrari instead of a Honda.

It only took ten minutes to leave Hobsonville behind.

"Where are we going?" I asked in a voice dulled with shock.

"Town," she said. "Bright lights, plenty of people, no fur."

Her voice was flat. She'd gone into survival mode. Erin's reactions to the things she'd seen, hanging out with me and the wolves, never failed to surprise me. She'd go quiet when things got bad, knowing we'd deal with it later. Any other personality type wouldn't have survived our friendship.

She drove us to a café that served to the early hours of the morning. It was a Monday night, and there weren't as many people as I'd have liked, but the three other patrons of the café were better than nothing.

I stared into my black coffee while Erin sipped a latte.

"Are you going to be okay?" Erin asked.

I shook my head slowly, trying through the fog to decide what to tell her.

She took a sip of her coffee, tears shimmering in her eyes. "Was it quick at least?"

My face flushed with shame as I remembered attacking Corey. I'd started this. If anyone was responsible for his death, it was me. A cold weight settled on my shoulders, and I knew in that moment that if I ever told Erin the truth about this night, it would end our friendship.

"I've never seen them like that."

She sniffed and wiped her eyes. "They're werewolves. What do you expect?"

The couple sitting a few tables away from us gave us a strange look. But there was no need to laugh it off. No need to pretend we were playing role-playing games. No one would believe me if I ran around the café screaming 'run for your lives, the werewolves are attacking'.

If I told her I thought Corey had been dead for a while, she would know she'd been sleeping with a corpse. If I told her he was eaten alive, she would run and never look back.

"It was over so quickly, I don't think he felt anything."

She didn't believe me—I could see it in her eyes. But she was grateful for the lie.

"Thanks for standing up to him. I can't believe I didn't see what an asshole he really was."

"He still didn't deserve to die."

"I know," she said. "But still."

I swirled my coffee and wondered why I couldn't have just left it all alone.

The moon was still high in the sky when we left the café and the streets were empty, light rain glistening on the road. My pulse jumped as a leaf drifted down from an oak tree and stuck to the windscreen, flapping like a wounded bird. Otherwise, the world was still.

I pictured the pack running home, beads of rain caught in their fur, their muzzles dipped in blood.

We parked in the driveway, as close to the house as we could. As I got out of the car, the world smelled cold and wet and lonely.

I opened the front door, an itch of danger pressing against my back, and was glad to have that solid piece of wood between me and the outside world.

Inside, Erin threw her keys on the dining table. "We should get some sleep."

"I don't think I can."

"Well, I'm shattered." I could see she was worried about leaving me alone. Leaving *me* alone. She was the one who'd just lost her boyfriend.

"Go. It's okay."

After she left the lounge, I sank down on the couch. How the hell was I ever going to sleep again, after what I'd seen?

And what had I seen? Was that thing still Corey? Had he, in the last few moments of his life, felt the pain of tearing teeth, felt hot breath panting against his wounds? Was he locked inside, feeling everything but unable to save himself?

I turned off the lights in the lounge and twitched the curtains aside so I could see out.

I took in a sharp breath as a shadow appeared around the corner of the street and trotted down the damp footpath towards the house. The animal stopped, ears perked as though it had heard me. Its face turned towards me, its eyes dark hollows.

The moment passed and it carried on past the house with a purposeful gait.

I spent the last few hours of darkness huddled on the couch, staring at nothing until the moon sank behind the houses and the sky washed the lounge with the pale of approaching morning.

Chapter 15

I woke mid-morning on the couch and went down to my room where the heat of the day lulled me into a fitful sleep, broken by nightmares of the kind I hadn't had since I was a child.

It wasn't as though I'd never seen the wolves kill before. And whenever we did fight together, there was blood, gore, sometimes misplaced internal organs. But we'd never killed a living person. Never someone who had a name, someone I'd had a conversation with.

The vampires I'd slaughtered had been more animal than human, and not the cute, furry type. The kind of animal that you kill on sight, because if you don't, you know you'll be its dinner. There aren't many animals like that. In fact, that's mostly just vampires.

I woke, hot and sweaty, to the sound of my phone ringing from across the room. I fell out of bed and answered it.

"It's Dan. Where are you?"

"Where do you think I am?" I asked, anger in my

voice. "I'm at home."

"I need to see you."

"No! I don't want to be around you right now."

"Liss, we need to talk about this. Come over to Jack and Andy's tonight. We'll talk this through."

I let out a bitter laugh. "You do realize that if I hadn't known it was you, I'd have been fighting on Corey's side last night?"

He sighed. "Liss, you were raised by wolves. You need to be able to deal with this kind of thing if you want to keep doing what you do. You're a Väktare— look, I can't do this over the phone. Just come over."

He hung up, leaving me feeling sick and empty. There hadn't been one ounce of remorse in his voice.

I checked the time. 5 p.m. Dinner was usually at six—I had just enough time to make myself look human.

Walking into Jack and Andy's house after the night I'd had was like waking up to Christmas day. My flat was functional at best. Their house, though, that was a home, a home I missed.

Dan, Jack, and Andy were already seated at the table when I arrived, my customary half an hour late. A half-full bottle of wine sat in the middle of the table and their glasses were empty. They'd been there for a while, it seemed.

"Alessandra, honey, come and sit down." Andy jumped to his feet and took my jacket, draping it over the back of a chair for me while Jack poured me a glass of wine.

Andy gave me a smile and a wink as he swung back towards the kitchen to grab more wine.

I stared down at the table, unable to look at Dan.

Dan cleared his throat. "So, firstly, I just want to say that last night…wasn't… normal."

I gave a choked laugh and picked up my knife, turning it over in my hand. "No, stop, I hate small talk."

"No, really, Liss, look at me." I met his gaze. I wasn't sure what I would see—the flat gaze of an animal? The unflinching stare of someone who killed without mercy or regret? But while he was doing his best to control it, there was a shadow in his eyes that told me he was anything but okay with what had happened.

"Something was up. It wasn't just bloodlust last night; it was something far more powerful. We were pulled there, driven there. And Liss, Corey was more dead than alive before Brandt released his mind. He tore himself apart, that bastard… made him tear himself apart. I've never seen anything like it."

Sitting beside him, Jack's eyes bored into mine. "This is the first time we've crossed swords with a vamp this old, Liss. What he did to Corey was a warning. The way he controlled the pack was frightening. We don't want this guy as our enemy."

I stared at him, dismayed. "So—what—we just leave it at that? He kills Erin's boyfriend and we just walk away?"

"Yes," said Jack firmly. "I don't think he'll come after us if we don't antagonise him. But maybe it's time to dial back on the vampire hunting for now."

"We tried leaving him alone and look where that got us."

"You tried to find him," he said. "Despite my specific instruction to leave him alone."

A knot formed in my jaw. "And if he threatens me again? If he threatens my friends?"

"A threat is a threat," said Jack. "We'll take precautions, but we won't act unless we have to. Chances are he's just toying with you. Some of the old ones... they get bored. Ignore him and he'll go away."

Seriously? How afraid were they of Brandt that they were willing to overlook what'd happened with Corey?

I leaned back in my chair as Andy brought out dinner. If they weren't prepared to do something about Brandt, I would.

"Talk to us, Liss," said Dan.

"I just don't get it. How are you so casual about this? You just ate my flatmate."

Dan licked his lips. "There's no way I can make you understand. The pull was so strong, none of us could fight it."

I leaned forward. "Doesn't that bother you?"

He took a swallow of wine and his expression was unreadable.

I looked at the steaming heap of roast meat in the middle of the table and shuddered. I pushed my chair back. "I'm not hungry."

"Liss, please, have something," said Andy. His

eyes pleaded with me, but I had to get out of there.

"Sorry, I have to go."

I pulled my jacket back on as I headed out into the night. The sky was clear, and in the cool air I felt some of the tension drain away.

Maybe going to University outside of Auckland wasn't such a bad idea. If I wasn't allowed to do anything when evil showed its face, maybe it was time I went and learned to do something other than kill.

Chapter 16

Palmerston North in early August was grey and miserable. Damp wind swept my hair back and tangled it around my shoulders as I walked back to my car from the lecture theatre. The air was wet and heavy, and there were warnings that a cyclone was on its way.

At least lectures were finished for the day. I could go home, hole up, and try and figure out how I was going to complete this semester's papers when I'd slept through half my classes.

The wind picked up as I pulled out of the student car park, trees tossing their branches, power lines swaying overhead.

It had been five months since I'd moved there, joining Massey University's second semester intake.

While I told myself it was a good thing to put distance between myself and the wolves, moving so far away left me feeling dislocated. I missed Jack and Andy, missed the reserve, missed being within walking distance of my extended family.

I joined the flood of traffic leaving the city for the

suburbs and let myself drift into the stream as rain spattered against the windshield.

As I unlocked the door to my flat, the darkness and the silence of the place made me hesitate. I stood on the threshold, the silence in front of me, the storm at my back. It took effort to step into the house.

I flipped on the hall light and closed the door behind me, grabbing the remote for the TV to fill the house with some kind of background — anything but the brooding silence.

As I sank down onto the couch, my phone rang. I checked the number. Unlisted. I'd been getting a lot of those calls lately. I'd answered the first couple, but whoever was calling always hung up. They didn't come at strange times of the night, and I didn't sense any threat there, so eventually I'd just stopped answering.

But now, sitting in the silence, any kind of companionship was welcome. I swiped the screen and held the phone to my ear.

"Hey, Liss, how've you been?"

Dan.

"Hi." It came out as a whisper and I cleared my throat. "Hi. What's up?"

There was a pause and I could sense Dan choosing his words carefully. "I just wanted to see how you were doing. No one's heard from you in months. I spoke to Erin and she said she transferred down there but you decided not to flat with her — which doesn't make any sense to me... but anyway. I just wanted to know if everything was okay."

This was so not Dan. Dan rarely asked about anyone's emotional wellbeing. At times, I thought he was barely aware of his own. Someone had put him up to this, probably one of my foster parents.

"Tell them I'm fine," I said tersely. "It was time I went out on my own anyway."

Dan sighed. "I'm flying down tomorrow night and I'd like to catch up."

"Why?" I asked, surprised. I couldn't think of any reason he would have to come down this way.

"To be honest, to talk to you. Since you left town, we've done some investigating and we know a bit more about our mystery vamp. I think we need to be prepared for him to resurface. Jack and Andy are worried about you living on your own. Why aren't you living with Erin?"

Because I didn't want her to get *killed*.

I chewed the inside of my cheek and wondered if I wanted to see him or not. I decided I probably did.

"Okay," I said. "Text me a time and a place and I'll be there."

I hung up without waiting for his answer. The TV chattered aimlessly about cleaning products and life insurance while the rain slid down the windows and overflowed the clogged gutters. All of it meaningless noise. Nothing mattered to me right now. Nothing could convince me to keep my eyes open.

I curled up on the couch around the warmth of my phone, tears trickling down my face as the darkness swallowed the house into itself.

The next day was Saturday, a welcome change from the early starts and confusing lectures that marked my weekdays. I stayed in bed till midday, then spent the afternoon reading a book, reluctant to face the cold.

Only when I realised I had half an hour before I was supposed to meet Dan did I pull myself together and throw myself into the shower. I pulled on a long coat to keep off the misting rain, and painted on some eyeliner.

I arrived at the restaurant ten minutes late and stood at the door, a tremor in my hands. I'd fought to keep the image of Corey's death out of my head for months and had managed okay. But now, about to see Dan again, I was close to having a panic attack.

The memory of Corey tearing his own skin open, and of the wolves sinking their teeth into him, worrying off chunks…

This wasn't helping.

I pushed down my anxiety and opened the restaurant door. Warmth and noise rolled over me as I stepped inside. I found Dan's table and sat down opposite him.

"You came alone?" I asked, as I draped my coat over the back of my chair.

"And hello to you too," he said. He gave me a grin I knew well. Flirty, dirty Dan, in the flesh. "You look great."

He gave me an appreciative look that I didn't understand. I was tired. My shoulders sagged, my hair was a mess.

He realised he wasn't working his usual magic and dropped the act.

"Seriously, Liss, it's really good to see you. We were all worried about you. You need to call Jack and Andy—you don't just walk out and never say another word to the people who care for you. And who, I might add, are supporting you."

I sighed and slumped in my chair. "I know. I'm a shitty stepchild. But in my defence, I am adopted."

He gave me a wry grin and I felt a glowing kernel of warmth inside. I *had* missed talking to someone who got my references.

"So, what do you know?" I asked.

A waiter swung by to take our drinks order and Dan waited until he'd gone, then leaned forward.

"It's bad, Liss. After you left, the killings started. Nothing as dramatic as—" He stopped, realising his mistake, then started again. "Nothing obvious to the untrained eye, but we know it's vamps. A vamp. Given the pattern, Brandt seems the most likely culprit."

Our drinks arrived and I took a swallow of cider.

"What's the pattern?"

Dan picked up his fork and twirled it between his fingers. "The first death was a drug dealer up Ellen's way. The second was a recidivist drink driver in South Auckland. The next victim was a convicted rapist out on parole in Howick. The most recent one was a woman in Swanson. We don't know what her history is, but when we plotted it on a map, we got a—"

"A cross," I said.

"Pretty much."

"How do you know it's a vampire?"

"I figured you wouldn't be keeping up with the news or you'd have called. The media's speculating it's some kind of vigilante serial killer. He's been draining blood from the bodies and leaving it in a milk carton at the scene. He has our attention." He put the fork down. "We don't know if this is a game, or if he's trying to tip our hand and force us out into the open. But you were right. He's not going away."

"Jesus." I took another large swallow of cider. Dan still hadn't touched his beer.

"Jack and Andy didn't want me to tell you. But the fact is, without you, we can't find this guy. There's no scent trail—even Gracie can't track him. And, if he decides to head your way, we'll be too far away to help you."

"Ah." Now it became clearer. "Sooo, what you're saying is, after telling me my skills were largely useless, you want me to help you hunt him?"

Dan lifted his beer with a sullen glare. "If you want to put it that way."

"And here was me thinking you were here because you were genuinely concerned about me."

"Liss, it's only a matter of time before he heads down this way. What do you think he's going to do when he gets here?"

I gulped my cider, finally feeling the buzz I'd been hoping for. I finished it and put down the glass, my head spinning.

"I believe Jack's instructions were to 'ignore him and he'll go away'."

Dan's eyes darkened. "This isn't a joke."

I spread my hands. "What do you want me to do about it? I can't track him either."

"No sign of your power?" he said.

"No." I sighed. "Sorry to disappoint you. Again."

He raised an eyebrow. "Really?"

"Maybe it's me that's disappointed."

"That's more likely," he said. There was a flicker of anger in his voice.

I didn't care. For years he'd alternated between flirting with me and dating everyone *but* me. And 'dating' was a euphemism. Dan's relationships didn't tend to get to the meet-the-parents stage. I was tired of thinking he cared about me only to find out he wanted something. Tired of watching him and Gracie growing closer than we'd ever be, while he pretended he was attracted to me. Just generally tired of *him.*

"As far as Brandt goes, the only way I can deal with him is if he shows himself to me. I can't even sense him unless I'm holding EMN. If he comes—and let's face it, *when* he comes—I guess I'll give you a call as he's tearing my throat out. Until then, maybe you guys should leave him to it. Sounds like he's doing a good job."

I stood and pulled on my coat. "Tell the pack I'm doing what I was told to do. Minding my own business and getting an education."

Dan scraped back his chair, but I was already

heading for the door.

"Liss!"

I let myself out into the night and pulled in a lungful of damp, smoky air. Tears stung my eyes and rolled down my cheeks.

I broke into a jog and got into my car before Dan could come after me. I needed to be alone. No, not alone. Just away from him.

Chapter 17

Days rolled into weeks. I barely noticed them. I'd expected a phone call, a text—some kind of pursuit. But my phone stayed silent.

I threw myself into my studies, slept, flipped pages without taking anything in, and felt the loneliness seep into my bones like the damp that rose from the floorboards in my dingy flat.

Finally, I couldn't stand it any longer. I texted Erin and told her I needed to see her. She turned up at the flat half an hour later with two bottles of red wine and some Indian food.

"How are you, chick?" She pulled me into a hug and I burst into tears. We moved to the couch and Erin grabbed a box of tissues on the way.

"So, tell me what's going on. I've been really worried about you, but you didn't answer my calls."

"What calls?" I was genuinely confused. So was Erin.

"I called, I texted." She grabbed my phone and scrolled through it. "Here."

She held it up and sure enough, there were her

messages, her phone calls, all logged, along with dozens of calls from Jack, Andy, and Dan's blocked number. I blinked, confused.

"I have been pretty out of it."

She got up and dished out food, coming back with plates and a bottle of wine poured into two huge glasses.

While we ate, she asked about my studies, about the flat. I found I couldn't tell her much. I didn't really know what I was up to, couldn't remember the last paper I had written. All I could tell her was how I felt, that deep, grey feeling inside. When I finished, she was silent and thoughtful for a moment.

"Don't take this the wrong way—but it sounds like you're depressed."

That hadn't really occurred to me. I didn't really know what 'depressed' meant. I knew depressed people felt sad and lonely, but didn't everyone at some point?

"What would I be depressed about?" I asked her, and she gave me a withering look. "Erin, Corey was *your* boyfriend. If anyone's upset about what happened, it should be you."

Erin studied me for a long moment. "What happened wasn't my fault. I know that. I'm not so sure you can say the same."

"No, no, I'm quite sure it wasn't your fault," I said, taking a swallow of wine.

She narrowed her eyes. "Hah. She's funny."

"Someone's got to be," I muttered.

"I'm not trying to make you feel bad, but I know

147

how you operate. You feel responsible for everything, that you should be able to control everything. Maybe that's what your depression is doing—filling up your mind so you can't feel responsible for his death."

Maybe she was right. I should have protected Corey from the pack, even for Erin's sake, and I hadn't. I'd failed her.

Erin saw my face fall and slapped my knee with her hand.

"No! That's my *point*, Liss. It's not your fault! If you could have done something you would have. I talked to Dan—even the wolves didn't know how to deal with the situation. Remember all this happened because he chose to become that vampire's bitch. I didn't see what happened, so I don't know the details... and I don't want to know. But I know that if you could have, you'd have stopped it from happening. I bet there's a little voice inside you that keeps whispering horrible things in the back of your mind."

There *was* a voice, and had been for months, repeating over and over that it was my fault, that I was useless, that I was kidding myself thinking I had anything to give.

Erin took my hand and raised my wine glass to my lips. I took another sip.

"From now on, I'm going to be here with you. I see you have a spare room—I'll give notice and move in. We're going to get you well again."

My eyes shone with grateful tears, but the voice in the back of my head whispered that I didn't deserve

148

her kindness, and if she'd seen what the pack had done to Corey, she wouldn't have been so forgiving.

Sometime in the early hours of the morning, Erin crashed on the couch while I crept off to my hardly used bed.

As I lay in the dark, I could feel her presence in the house and realised I was no good at being alone. I belonged in a pack, and Erin was part of that. We were family. I fell asleep and slept the way I used to sleep, dreamless and free of the weight in my heart.

The next morning, Dan called, and this time I answered the phone.

"Hey, Liss." He sounded wary.

"Hey."

"You're not going to hang up on me?"

"No. No, you were right. It is my responsibility to deal with this."

Dan sighed with frustration. "Liss, it's not your *responsibility*. It's not your fault—"

"It *is* my fault. I started this by insulting him. I could have just left him alone."

He fell silent. We both knew it was true.

"If we hadn't encouraged you for years to use your ability, we wouldn't be here today. The fact is, it's no one's fault. But I'm glad you answered. I was scrolling through the newsfeeds this morning, and there's been another death."

Erin came out of the hallway, rubbing her wet hair with a towel. She saw my expression and mouthed 'Dan?'. I nodded.

"This one's a little closer to you, Liss. It was on the

university campus."

I dropped onto the couch, my heart racing.

"Liss, are you okay?"

"A kid?" I asked.

"Another douche," he said. "A small-time meth dealer. But the MO's the same. He's too close—you need to get back here."

I handed the phone to Erin and she put her arm around my shoulders while I fought for breath.

"What the hell is going on?" she demanded.

She listened for a long time, then when I'd regained composure, she handed the phone back to me.

I held it to my ear and took a shaky breath.

"Liss, are you there?"

I nodded, then realised Dan couldn't see that.

"Yeah, I'm fine. Just tell me what I need to do."

"Right now, the safest thing to do is get out of town."

"What?"

"Get to the airport and get on the next flight to Auckland. Just get out of there."

He wanted me to run. Yeah, not going to happen.

"We hunt him together."

"Are you kidding?" He sounded incredulous. "Look, we're heading down this afternoon, and we'll do everything we can to find him before anyone else gets hurt. But you've got to get out of there."

"No."

"Put Erin back on the phone."

"No."

Erin took the phone out of my hand and spoke into it.

"Yes. I understand. We will. Don't worry. Okay, bye."

I stared at her as she handed my phone back to me.

"You don't want to be responsible for anyone else's death? Then let's get out of here. Now."

She pulled on her jacket and slung her bag over her shoulder.

"I'm going to pack some clothes. I'll meet you back here in an hour. Be ready."

I nodded numbly and watched her go. I stayed sitting on the couch long after I heard her car pull away, a thought forming in the back of my mind.

The feeling. The feeling inside me that I'd felt for months now. The feeling Erin thought was depression, that I hadn't put a name to—was it that different to the feeling of dread that I'd learned to live with as a Väktare, that tug of evil I felt on the edge of a forest or at the entrance to an abandoned building in the middle of nowhere? That numbing sensation that had once powered me forwards?

Was Brandt somewhere near? Had he been here the whole time, poisoning my life with darkness, watching me shrink down into myself, confused and miserable?

Anger flared in the place where the dull ache in my chest had been the day before.

That bastard was messing with my mind. He was *playing* with me. He hadn't let me go—not by a long

151

shot. I was willing to bet my right arm he was somewhere nearby.

I got up and went to the bedroom. There, in the back of the wardrobe, were my leathers, my armour, my knife. My purpose.

I dressed and stood in front of the full-length mirror, seeing myself properly for the first time in too long. I'd lost some muscle tone, and I didn't have the same gloss I'd had after the wolves had healed me. But I was still me. A vampire's worst nightmare. Someone who'd taken out dozens of evil, undead monsters, who'd been covered in death and filth and walked out stronger.

I was Alessandra De Witt. And I was going to find Brandt and kill him, before he killed anyone else.

Chapter 18

First, though, I had to find him. For me to feel him this strongly, he had to be close by. I walked from room to room in the flat, seeing if I could get a fix on his location. If he was living next door, I should feel his presence more in one room than another.

But it was all the same. Wherever I went, the feeling was there. Now that I knew what was causing it, the feeling fuelled me on. I wanted to end this guy.

I grabbed my coat from the hook by the door and pulled it on to hide the leathers. Before I went out, I ran a hand through my hair to make it look... well, the way it usually did, and let my shoulders slump. If he was watching, I didn't want him to realise I was onto him.

I stepped out into the grey morning and looked up at the solid layer of cloud that hung over the city like a dirty blanket while I tuned into the world around me.

I set off down the road to see where the tugging sensation in my gut would take me.

Halfway towards the corner of my block, the

feeling faded. I turned the corner, tracing a circuit around the house.

As I approached the house that lay directly behind mine, the feeling grew strong enough that if this had been yesterday, I would have thought I had food poisoning. I was getting close. If Brandt was holed up nearby, he'd be vulnerable while it was daylight and I could find him and take him out before the others even hit town.

But... I did have a nagging feeling that taking him out would take more than a stake and some Kiwi ingenuity. How was I even feeling him when he was capable of concealing his signature? It was all just a game to him. How long had he been waiting for me to figure it out?

I slowed down, but couldn't get a fix on which of the dozen houses he might be in. The sensation just wasn't precise enough.

I loitered by a letterbox and looked around. The streets lay in grey silence. I pulled EMN and held it half concealed in my sleeve, that familiar quiver in my hand as the silver reacted to the presence of evil.

No car in the driveway. This could be the one. As I walked up the path to the house, I was aware of how bad this looked. If I broke into this house carrying a knife, and it was the wrong house, things were going to get messy.

I decided the risk of someone calling the cops was greater than the chance there was a vamp in the house and slipped the knife back into its sheath under my coat. I rang the doorbell.

There was a muffled thump of footsteps in the hallway, and a moment later, an elderly man answered the door. He leaned heavily on a cane, puffing from exertion.

"Yes?" he said. He looked me up and down. "Are you collecting for something?"

I was lost for words. "Um, wrong house. Really sorry. Sorry."

I backed away and headed back down the path as he shut the door with a grunt of effort.

Back on the footpath, I scanned the street. The villas on either side of my flat were rentals like mine, but owned by couples with kids who I'd seen in their yards often enough. They had cottage gardens and matching Labrador retrievers. I was pretty sure Brandt wasn't in either of those.

The house that lay behind mine was in a more prestigious street and was a modern addition; no fence and a stamped concrete driveway. It was on the market. Empty made sense. Empty but constantly full of estate agents and hosting open homes, not so much.

I walked back to the flat, frustrated. He was near, but without breaking and entering, there was no way I could find him by myself. Maybe Dan and Gracie could get a fix on him if they knew his general location. It was worth a shot.

I called Dan.

"Are you at the airport?" he said. "We're just about to board now to head down your way."

"I'm not going... and before you interrupt, he's

close. I'm not going to run, because we can end this today. He's close and it's daylight. This might be the only shot we get to catch him while he's vulnerable."

There was silence as he ran this over in his mind.

"I'd rather you weren't there."

"I know."

Silence, then a sigh. "Just don't do anything until I get there."

"As if."

He snorted. "See you in an hour or so."

Erin banged on the door a short while later.

"Are you even packed?" she said, pushing past me. She looked around the living room. "Liss, what the hell? Where's your suitcase?"

I shut the door. "He's here."

She looked around, panicked. "Where?"

"I don't know exactly, but he's close. I'm not depressed, Erin, I'm getting a Feeling. He's so close, his presence is toxic. He's been poisoning me for months, but because I didn't expect to find him all the way down here, I didn't even pick it up."

"So he's here—so we leave, right?"

I gestured to the walls. "Even if I ran, I could never come back as long as he's alive. And there's no point in getting on a plane when we can deal with him right here and now. The best thing we can do is wait for Dan and flush him out. As long as we have daylight on our side, it should be safe. Relatively, anyway."

Erin sighed. "Or we can get on a plane and let them deal with it."

I rubbed my eyes and then rested my face in the palms of my hands. The feeling of evil so close was making my stomach churn. But stronger than that was the growing excitement I always felt on a hunt.

"I want to be here. I want to do this."

Erin sighed again, exasperated. "You're freaking impossible."

We put on a movie and tried to relax, but I found it hard to sit still.

Finally, the doorbell rang. I checked my phone. He was on time. But I kept my knife in my hand as I answered the door—just in case.

As it was, Dan's bone-crushing hug nearly killed us both.

"Knife, Dan, knife!" He took it from my hand with a grin and held it out of reach.

"Say please!"

I kicked him in the shin and he winced and gave it back to me with a grin.

"Thought you wanted me out of town?" I said as he brushed past me. He'd brought Gracie. She gave me a faint smile and found a place to stand and linger, in her usual super tall and intimidating way.

"No, you're right, it makes sense to stick together under the circumstances. If he's as close as you say he is, we can get him done and dusted before sunset."

He scanned the lounge with an expression of distaste, taking in the faded couch, the black mould on the windowsills, and no doubt the scent of damp that permeated everything. "Nice place."

I slid my knife back into its sheath.

"*Anyway*," I said, "I figure he must be in one of the houses behind the flat or across the road. I can't tell for sure."

Gracie tested the air experimentally. "The vampire is near."

The way she said it in her thick Nordic accent raised the hair on the back of my neck.

"I thought it was just me," said Dan. He put a hand to his face. "It stinks in here."

She nodded. "It is very strong."

"Liss, could he have been in here?" Dan asked.

I glanced around the living room. "I don't think so." I remembered Brandt's ability to thrall. "Maybe. I'm not sure."

Dan gave Gracie a questioning look. "Change and see what we find?"

Gracie started to pull the curtains. I helped her, then went into the kitchen to make coffee while they changed. The wolves were never terribly concerned about changing in front of each other — or me — but I felt uncomfortable. It wasn't just the nudity, the intimidating beauty of Gracie's amazing figure, or Dan's firm abs and... other stuff. It was more that they were morphing from human to animal and the intermediary form was, frankly, terrifying.

Maybe if I changed myself, it would seem less alien. But every time they started to shift, the sheer *otherness* of it bent my brain. There was no better reminder that monsters roamed the earth than watching a human body break and reform into something else.

Before too long, two wolves stood panting in my lounge, heads down, tongues lolling. I grabbed a couple of bowls from the cupboard and filled them with water, and they drank greedily.

A few years back, I'd done some research to figure out what type of wolves they would be, if they were actually wolves.

As a wolf, Dan's fur was steel grey, his muzzle and ruff almost black. His build closest resembled a timber wolf.

Gracie looked like the same species, but she was smaller, silver and fawn, and so lightly built that if she were my dog, I'd have been upping her food intake.

Once they'd finished drinking, they prowled the house, Dan combing the floor with his nose, Gracie scenting the air.

They moved from room to room, sniffing the furniture, nudging open cupboards and circling my bed. Gracie moved under the trapdoor to the ceiling and reared up on her hind legs, one paw against the wall for balance. She scented the air and let out a yip. I went into the kitchen and grabbed a chair. I pushed the trapdoor open, then got out of the way. With incredible balance, she used the chair to vault her slim frame up through the trapdoor into the ceiling.

Dan came back down the hallway, ears pricked forward, his eyes on the trapdoor. A moment later, Gracie's muzzle appeared. She yipped again and I pulled the chair away so that she could jump to the floor.

Dan sniffed her ear and she shook her body in response.

"Anything?" I asked.

She waved her tail. Apparently not.

Dan trotted down the hallway to the bedroom and poked his nose between the curtains. He looked back over his shoulder at me.

"Want to wait till it gets dark, then check the rest of the neighbourhood?" I asked.

His mouth opened in a doggy grin.

"I assume you guys don't want to change back again. I'll go get some food." He sat and swished his tail against the floor in appreciation.

"Come on, Erin, let's go get Dan a Vindaloo." A growl from behind me made me chuckle. Like there was anything he could do about it.

As we drove down to the local takeaway, Erin sat in silence. I'd forgotten that she'd never seen the wolves shift before. She'd seen them in both forms, seen my family exhibit wolf behaviours, but she'd never seen the actual change itself.

"Shit, Liss," she said eventually. "Shit."

"Yeah, still gets me too."

"You could have warned me how weird it gets."

We lapsed into a more contemplative silence.

"Liss, what do you think it means that the wolves don't know where he is?"

I'd been pondering the possibilities myself.

"The whole time I've been in that house, I've felt it. Like a weight sitting inside me, like I swallowed

160

lead. He must have been living nearby the whole time."

"But... why would the wolves say your house smells like him?" she asked.

I didn't say it, but I was pretty sure we were both thinking the same thing. He had to be under the house. Had to be. It was the only explanation. I had a strong suspicion that the first thing Dan would do once it got dark, was head into the crawl space. Of course, by then, Brandt would be awake.

"Do you think he's there now?" she said.

The thought of him burying himself in the stale soil, sleeping *under* me, just to poison my life, was horrible. Beyond horrible.

We returned to the house with hot food—fresh meat from the butcher's for the wolves (their canine stomachs couldn't deal with greasy takeaways) and fish and chips for Erin and me.

It was already starting to get dark. The wolves chewed on the raw meat I'd brought them, pinning the flesh and ripping hunks of it away with a sound that made me feel nauseated. I had a flashback to that night with Corey, his eyes locked to mine as he tore at his own skin, the wolves sinking their teeth into his legs, crunching the bones in his arms, one's muzzle buried in his side, tugging out wet entrails.

I stepped outside and stood on the front steps, wishing I smoked.

Erin joined me. She didn't speak, but I think she guessed. It was a pretty grim realization for her, too, but being Erin, I knew she'd never talk about it

161

unless I brought it up.

Eventually the sun sank beyond the horizon and the last pale blues and greens faded to grey as night fell.

In the fresh darkness, a handful of stars scattered across the sky, barely visible against the light bleeding up from the city.

Dan trotted out onto the porch. I switched off the security light and we all stood bathed in the orange glow of the streetlights. He raised his muzzle to the night air and scented it. Gracie appeared behind him, her tail waving gently. With a huff, Dan started to search the foliage that ran along the side of the house. Gracie followed him, Erin and I close behind.

Dan found the wooden door first and pawed at it. I drew back the bolt and he slipped into the shadows. Gracie paused in the opening, scenting the wooden frame delicately, then cocked her ears forward and followed Dan.

Every part of me was glad that I wasn't going under that house. The feeling was stronger than ever, so bad I wasn't sure if I was going to be able to keep my dinner down. At the same time, I was drawn forward by the presence of raw evil.

I jumped as there was a crack of wood exploding from inside the house. I ran inside and found the lounge floor had been torn open by a vampire erupting through it. Gracie's snarling muzzle was attached to its pale arm and it was trying to get a grip on her so it could crush her. A growl came from the darkness beneath the floor as Dan savaged some lower part of it.

The vamp caught sight of me and reached for me. Its eyes rolled as it fought to get away from the wolves, black pupils pinpoints against the whites of its eyes. It looked as though it hadn't eaten in weeks, its skin tight against its skull, its fingers claws.

It raked the splintered boards with its free hand, tearing long scores into the wood as it tried to reach me, its mouth open and rimmed with blood where its fangs had torn open its lips. I fell back out of reach, tripping over furniture, as Dan clamped his jaws around its other arm and dragged it back.

Erin pulled me to my feet and clung to me, her breath coming in quick gasps.

I drew my knife as the floorboards shuddered with the impact of wolf bodies thrown against the underside of what was left of the floor.

In a daze, I held the knife in front of me, transfixed by the play of light along its length. The roar of the fight in front of me dimmed to the background and a voice near my ear said, *"Silver won't help you."*

The spell broke and sound ramped back up. What the hell was I doing? The knife was no use. I needed a stake.

I grabbed an overturned chair and smashed off a leg. Seeing I had a weapon, the wolves did their best to hold the vamp still, their eyes full of urgency.

I stepped forward and the vamp hissed at me, struggling to get to me. I lunged and shoved the stake into its chest.

It let out a shriek that made the wolves' ears pin

back, and collapsed in on itself, sagging into a sack of rotting meat. The wolves let go and the corpse rolled back into the hole.

I sank to the floor beside the wreckage of my lounge floor as the two wolves pulled themselves out of the hole. They shook decaying vampire and shards of wood from their fur, showering me with splinters.

Erin sank onto the couch. I caught her eye and she shook her head. "Unreal."

Dan huffed at me.

Both wolves were panting hard and I realised they needed more water. I pulled myself together and refilled their bowls. They drank deeply, sprinkling water all over the floor, then lay down to recover. I was glad to see neither of them was injured.

I couldn't stop staring at the gigantic hole in the floor.

I got as close to the edge as I dared and looked down. The space under the house was several feet deep and the light didn't penetrate far. But the smell of carrion and the stink of rot rose up out of the blackness.

"That wasn't Brandt," I said aloud, to whoever was listening. Dan snuffled the floor and then panted at me.

I realised the sick feeling was still there.

Dan gave me a long look and I closed my eyes as I realised he was about to change.

Once the sound of thumping limbs and cracking bones stopped, I opened my eyes. And shut them again quickly. Dan was still getting dressed. Dammit.

The image of his half-naked body was burnt into my brain.

"You can look now." He was laughing at me.

I opened my eyes in time to see Gracie pull her tee back on. Just standing next to her was usually enough to remind me I was human and she definitely wasn't. As I stood there in a daze, my phone rang. I checked it—no caller ID.

I held the phone gingerly to my ear.

"Did you get my gift?" Brandt.

"I thought you'd got bored and decided I wasn't worth the effort."

Everyone in the room fell silent, watching me.

"Oh, never, Alessandra, never. Since you brought yourself to my attention, I've found you to be terribly entertaining."

I growled. "Would you like to come and clean up after your surprise party?" I asked. "I've got a couple of friends who'd love to meet you."

"Cleaning is not my thing, I'm afraid, but we'll catch up soon."

"Coward." But he'd already disconnected. I fought back the urge to throw my phone at the wall.

Dan looked up, alert to something I couldn't hear. "We'd better clear out—the cops are on their way."

"My name's on the lease," I mumbled.

"Come on." Erin grabbed my arm and dragged me to the front door, Dan and Gracie close behind.

We got into Dan's rental.

"I'll give you and Erin a lift to the airport and wait until you're on a plane."

This time, I didn't argue.

Chapter 19

I sat with Dan and Gracie on plastic seats, sipping a bottle of water while Erin checked for flights that could take the two of us. I felt numb. Gracie sat with her fingers steepled, elbows resting on her knees, staring into space, while Dan laced his fingers together and stared at the pattern on the carpet.

I watched passengers pull their brightly coloured cases across the grey carpet and tried to imagine what their lives were like. If they'd ever had a vampire burst out of their lounge floor, or had friends who'd eaten one of their other friends.

Erin came back looking grim.

"The next flight's not for three hours."

I groaned.

"What time does it leave?" Dan asked.

"Eight thirty-five."

"Then I guess we wait here," he said.

I looked from Dan to Gracie, to Erin, to Brandt.

I choked on my water. Brandt was leaning against a column, his head bent over his cell phone. One by one, the others followed my gaze.

"Is that...?" Erin asked, trailing off.

Brandt looked up from his phone and smiled.

I got to my feet in a trance. The others stood with me, looking at each other for guidance. None of us knew what to do. We couldn't fight him. Not here. Not in an airport. We couldn't run.

"Don't—" said Dan, but I dodged his attempt to stop me.

I strode up to Brandt.

"Alessandra, how lovely to see you." Brandt dragged me towards him and turned me around. He held up his phone and took a picture. I pulled out of his grip and he turned the phone to show me the screen. "You could have smiled. That's not going on Instagram."

He looked past me and held up a hand. I glanced over my shoulder to see the others stopped in their tracks, unsure what he'd do if they disobeyed.

"Why are you doing this?" I asked. "Why torture me?"

He feigned confusion. "Aren't you the one who wants to hunt *my* kind into extinction? Isn't that your mission statement?"

I fumed, knowing there was nothing I could do to him.

Brandt folded his arms across his chest and chewed his thumbnail. His fangs were clearly visible to anyone who was watching. Only no one seemed to be.

"I don't think you should leave, Alessandra. No— no, hear me out." He put a finger to his lips.

"I know you don't like being useful, but before you get torn into bite sized chunks by another baby vampire, you could still make a contribution."

"Sorry, I gave at the office."

He gave me a condescending look. "You mean the car yard? The pinnacle of your career so far?"

I said nothing.

"And how are your studies going?"

Again I said nothing, determined not to react. As if sensing needling me wasn't going to get him anywhere, he folded his arms.

"All right, I'm bored now." He beckoned to me. "Come here."

I felt that compulsion, that tug at my stomach, and took a halting step towards him that put me close enough to smell his cologne. Something woody. Faint, but pleasant. Dan was right. He did smell like a cardboard perfume sample.

I had to look up to meet his gaze. He smiled down at me.

"For the past twenty years I've been quietly minding my own business. Then there you were, dressed in two inches of fabric, playing a siren in the grown-up world, when you clearly belonged in rompers in a sand pit. And then you decided you wanted to fight me, and that was just *adorable*."

Never. Letting. Erin. Dress me. Again.

"So fired up, as if you had any chance at all of resisting me."

"You're pretty resistible."

He was starting to look nettled. Good.

169

I felt the others move closer and Brandt cast his gaze past me. "Stay where you are," he said, in a low voice only the wolves and I could hear. "You know I can kill her and leave before she hits the ground."

They stayed.

"How about you get to the point?" I suggested.

He turned his gaze back to me. "Tasty morsel that you are, you've woken a certain… *lust*… for action, in me."

"Lucky me."

He went on as if I hadn't spoken. "So to liven things up, here's what we're going to do."

He continued talking, and when he was done, he winked at me. "Isn't this fun?"

He unlocked his phone and texted me the scowling selfie he'd taken earlier.

"Take care."

He strolled off through the airport and disappeared.

I turned back to the others in a daze.

"That was him," said Dan. "In the middle of a goddamn airport."

"Yep."

"I couldn't feel him," he said. "And then I could." His eyes were bright with anger. "What was all that crap about going to the Midlands?"

"I don't know," I said. "But we need to get out of here now."

As we walked back to the car, Dan's rage at Brandt's audacity boiled off him.

We got into the car and he gripped the steering

wheel so hard he made dents in the plastic. Gracie sat in the passenger seat, hands folded in her lap, inscrutable as always. Was she afraid? Angry? Who knew.

Brandt's instructions were that the four of us head to a town called Rotokawa in the central North Island. Midlands pack territory. The largest wolf pack in the country.

There, he wanted us to challenge the pack leader—a young werewolf whose father had just stepped down as alpha—kill him, and take up residence. *In Brandt's name.*

He had three rules that we were to obey on the pain of the death of our loved ones.

1) We were to drive straight to Rotokawa from the airport

2) We couldn't tell anyone what we were doing

3) We were to stay together at all times

We drove out of the car park in silence, all of us wary of Dan's scalding fury.

"We're not going to the Midlands, are we?" I said, as we turned on to the highway.

"No, we're not," said Dan through gritted teeth. "We're going home."

"He did say he'd kill—"

"He can try."

I leaned my head against the window as the emptiness of the highway sped by. Hypnotised by the white markers looming out of the darkness, I fell asleep.

My phone ringing jerked me awake as the first rays of dawn streaked the sky like smears of blood.

I fumbled it out of my pocket and held it to my ear.

"Liss, God, Liss, Jesus, you have to come home. You have to come home now. Shit, Liss, I'm so sorry, just... come home, please come home." It was Luke. He was crying.

The others were suddenly alert, listening. I choked, stopped breathing, my heart pounding.

"Please tell me," I managed to say. "What's happened?"

"Jack's dead," he said, a howl of grief in his voice. "Just come home."

The phone went dead. My head bursting with rage, I screamed wordlessly and smashed my fist against the door. The phone in my hand hit the window and shattered it. The car exploded with cold air and broken glass.

Dan pulled the car to the side of the road and got out of the car. He wrenched open my door and pulled me into his arms, crushing me against his chest while I raged and cried and screamed all the things I would do to Brandt.

Chapter 20

Gracie drove the last of the way home while Dan sat in the back seat with me. He pinned me against his chest with one arm and picked the glass out of my arm with his free hand while I screamed and fought him. And then, when I was burnt out, he cradled me in his arms and promised me Brandt would suffer in ways that hadn't been invented yet.

We pulled up outside Jack and Andy's to find two wolves I didn't know guarding the house. I was guessing they were on loan from Ellen. They watched us silently with red-rimmed eyes as we walked up to the gate. One put out an arm as Erin walked past him and shook his head.

"Trust me. Don't go in there."

She glanced at me and I nodded. Gracie handed her the car keys and she went back to the car while the rest of us went inside.

Andy was sitting on the couch, Jack's body in his arms. The couch was red, the cream carpet around it black. The ceiling was streaked with arcs of red.

If I hadn't known it was Jack, I wouldn't have known what was left was a person.

The others hovered at a respectful distance as Andy looked up at me, his face streaked with tears and smeared with blood.

"What happened?" I whispered.

"*Karlo,*" Andy snarled, his lips flecked with saliva.

I stared at him. "What do you mean, Karlo?"

"He walked into our house and tore Jack apart. Just tore him apart."

"No," said Dan, disbelieving. "Karlo wouldn't do this."

"Your brother just killed the only man I've ever loved," said Andy. "I saw him do it. Get out of my house."

Dan stared at him. "He wouldn't—"

"Get out!"

Dan put his head down and left the lounge.

I wanted to comfort Andy but I couldn't. Couldn't get any closer to the torn remains in his arms. Couldn't process this without seeing Jack's face, and Jack's face wasn't there anymore.

"Where's Karlo?"

"He ran to the reserve," said Andy. "It saved his life. He's being held for trial there."

Gracie approached Andy. She took his hand and looked him in the eye.

"Karlo did not do this."

Andy's face distorted with rage. "I saw him do it, Gracie—I watched him tear Jack's heart out! He didn't even get a chance to fight back."

Gracie looked as though she was translating the words she wanted to say in her head.

"Karlo will be proven innocent. Stay strong, Andy. Your pack needs you."

She squeezed his hand. She looked over Jack's ruined body with an expression of sadness, then went back outside.

"What can I do?" I asked Andy helplessly.

He shook his head. "Get out of here. Remember him as he was—not like this." He looked down at the mess in his arms. "Not like this."

I sank down on the front steps, my head against the stair rail, and tried to understand what had just happened.

It wasn't real. It couldn't be real, because Jack couldn't be dead. Jack was my dad. He would always be there. He was supposed to live long after I was gone.

I wrapped my arms around myself and rocked in place, the scent of roses floating around me, sweet against the metallic stink of death at my back.

Erin got out of the car, but I shook my head at her. I needed to be somewhere else.

I stood, still hugging myself, and walked down the path, past the roses waving gently in the morning breeze, past the gathered wolves, past Dan and Gracie. Dan gave me a worried look as I walked past, but didn't try to stop me.

I walked down the street and turned into the alley that led to the park near our home.

As I walked across the empty rugby field, the

sunlight cooled and I was thirteen again, smoking a cigarette that wasn't my first.

The light around me was tinged with blue, the sun low in the sky. Autumn leaves floated around my feet as I crouched to pick up the skeleton of a maple leaf. I straightened up, twisting it between my fingers as I dragged on my cigarette. Sometimes I took them home and Andy framed them and turned them into art. But this one wasn't complete. I dropped it and pushed my free hand back into my coat pocket to stay warm. As I started walking again, Jack fell into step with me.

I winced and stopped walking.

Jack took the cigarette from my hand. "Teenage rebellion?" He drew on it and breathed out slowly.

I shook my head. It wasn't even that. I just liked how it made me feel when I walked and smoked.

He put his hand out. I tugged the packet out of my coat pocket and handed it to him.

He held it up. "Tens. Not much of a rebellion."

He put the packet into his pocket and took another drag on the cigarette, then dropped it and scrubbed it out. He picked up the butt and handed it to me. "Put this in the bin. I don't catch you smoking again, I won't tell Andy."

He melted away and with a jerk I was running, the sun hot at my back. Still thirteen, I was jogging across the sports field with a Coke bottle half filled with water in my hand.

"Liss you dick, come back!"

I looked over my shoulder and saw sixteen-year-old Tai and eighteen-year-old Dan chasing me across the field.

Dan caught me and wrestled the Coke bottle out of my hand. He unscrewed it and took a swing. Tai snatched it out of his hand and took a mouthful, then handed it back to me.

I tasted the water. It wasn't water. It was vodka.

I took another mouthful, then another.

We sat on the grass, laughing, and Dan tickled me, forcing me to give up the bottle. My head swam from summer heat and vodka and laughter.

Dan sat up straight. "Oh shit."

Jack came striding across the field towards us. He pointed at Dan, then Tai. "You two, go."

Dan and Tai jumped to their feet.

"Leave the bottle," Jack growled.

Tai placed it on the ground, and the two boys sprinted to where their bikes were parked against the prefabs.

I stayed sitting on the grass and Jack stood over me, blocking out the sun.

"Give it here," he said.

I handed the bottle to him. He unscrewed the cap and sniffed the contents, then took a swig.

"Vodka," he said. "Suppose it could have been worse."

He sat beside me and took another mouthful.

"I just want to remind you that you're thirteen." He looked at me. "Do you understand?"

I nodded, and he took another swallow of vodka.

"I know I can't stop you drinking, but if you have

to drink, have a beer with Tai. Not with Dan. Okay?"

I nodded, confused, but I knew better than to argue.

"And tell Dan if he gives my thirteen year old daughter vodka again, I'll break his legs."

I came back to myself and realised I was kneeling on the grass. I put a hand to my face and wiped away the wetness there. When I brought my hand down, a tear trembled on the edge of my finger, glittering in the sunlight.

I got unsteadily to my feet. Before I could start walking again, night wrapped around me like, circling me until I was standing in the dark.

Fourteen now, Tai and I were walking arm in arm. Dan didn't smoke dope, so Tai had promised me he'd help me try it for the first time.

He handed a joint to me, his lips pressed together, his eyes watering.

I sucked on the crudely rolled spliff and coughed.

"Hold it in," he said, the words exhaled on a rush of smoke that clouded in front of his face.

I tried again. This time I held my breath and counted to ten. The tobacco mixed in with the weed gave me a head rush I wasn't expecting.

"Oh my God."

My knees buckled and Tai went down with me. We lay on our backs, staring up at the stars. Coughing and laughing, we passed the spliff between us, occasionally breaking into song as the dew soaked into our clothes, unnoticed.

Tai fell silent. He glanced at me and I sensed it too. We weren't alone. I sat up and looked around. Jack, half hidden in shadow, was leaning against the wall of the rugby club, his arms folded.

Tai started to get up and Jack held out his hand.

"It's okay. You're nearly done."

Tai looked guiltily at what was left of the joint, and was about to grind it out, when Jack strode forward and put out his hand. "Give it here."

Flustered, Tai handed it to him. Jack sniffed it and made a face. "You kids will destroy your lungs with this rubbish." He sucked on the end of it and coughed. "God, this is terrible."

He dropped it and ground it out. "Don't give this shit to my daughter again."

Tai stared at him, wide-eyed.

Jack handed him the butt. "In the rubbish, okay?"

"Yes," said Tai meekly.

Jack helped me to my feet.

"Am I in trouble?"

He shook his head. "Just keeping an eye on you." He turned to Tai. "First and last time, you understand?"

Tai nodded.

"I don't just mean Liss, I mean you too. You haven't passed your exams yet. Smoke what you want when you've finished university, but until then, stick to light beer." He turned to me. "And you, stick to killing things. That stuff dulls your reflexes. If you want to live, steer clear of it."

The night slid away the same way it'd come, like walking through a revolving door.

I was vaguely aware someone was following me, but I didn't care.

My head felt tight, my eyes clouded with tears.

There was a cluster of tan cinderblock buildings used by the local sports clubs that had a set of narrow concrete stairs running up the side of it—a fire escape. Up. That was where I wanted to go.

I walked towards the buildings, buffeted by the morning air. I reached the bottom of the steps and looked up the three flights of stairs that ended in a narrow landing at the top.

Jack's words from our last dinner together rang in my head.

You want me to be afraid?

Maybe. At least, more afraid than you are.

I squinted up at the blue sky then stepped onto the stairs, my boots scuffing the gritty concrete.

I made a mistake... telling you they were enough... I wanted you to stop screaming through the night.

Two gulls squabbled over a discarded potato chip packet, their shrieks tossed about on the breeze.

I reached the first landing and started up the second flight.

The warm wind gusted against me as I climbed.

I remembered our last strained hug goodbye, when I'd gotten on a plane and left Auckland. If I'd known that would be the last time I'd see him alive, I would never have let go.

You have the pack. You're safe.

I pulled myself up the final flight by the railing.

Do you want to die? Is that it?

I reached the top of the stairs and walked to the end of the narrow landing. At the end was a glass-panelled door, laced with mesh to stop vandals breaking the glass. I put my back to the door and slid down to sit on the concrete.

You have the pack. You're safe.

And if he comes after me? Or Erin?

Then the pack will deal with it.

But the pack hadn't dealt with it. And now Jack was gone.

Jack was gone.

Hot tears splashed my bare arms.

Whoever was following me reached the top of the stairs.

"Go away."

Dan shook his head. "You don't have to talk to me, but I'm not leaving."

I licked the salt from my lips. "I want to be alone."

"I know," he said. He sat on the top step and leaned against the railing, and after a while I forgot he was there.

That last conversation ran on loop, the words burning into my brain.

Do you want me to be afraid?

Maybe. At least, more afraid than you are.

The sun was hot and high above when Dan stood. He stretched and cleared his throat.

"Time to go."

I shook my head.

"Come on, Liss. I need to go to the reserve, and I'm not leaving you here."

I stayed where I was and he crouched beside me.

"Liss, I have to find out what happened." His eyes were glossed with grief, and I knew he was only holding it together so I could be weak. This was all the time we had. We were at war with an enemy who had the power to kill the strongest, smartest, and best of us. That I'd had any time to grieve at all had been a luxury.

"We've got to go now," he said. "Kendrick and Abigail are overseas and I want to make sure no one tries anything before they get back."

He straightened up and put out his hand and I let him pull me to my feet. He put his arms around me, surrounding me with his scent; a mix of faded cologne and wolf. "If Jack were here, he'd tell you to just deal with what's in front of you."

He'd have said more than that. If this had happened to Andy, Jack would have sat with me and helped me figure out how to keep Brandt alive while we dissected him. But Dan didn't know that Jack; the Jack who would have cheerfully and slowly murdered anyone who hurt me or Andy. Let him think Jack was all wise words and fatherly advice.

The four of us drove out to the reserve. I could tell that Erin didn't know what to say, could see the questions in her eyes, but I couldn't bring myself to tell her what Karlo had done. I would have preferred to keep her out of whatever came next, but she was in this too. It was too dangerous for her to back out now. Without the wolves, she'd have no protection at all if Brandt came after her.

The original house that stood on the land dated back to the 1600s and had been burned down and rebuilt several times, leaving brick foundations sunk into the ground in what the Stoke brothers had always jokingly referred to as 'the dungeon'.

At some point in its history, someone had built cells lined with iron sheeting down there—cells that no wolf could escape from. I guess when the cells had been built, the pack had had a use for them. Now, they were just a place to store gardening equipment.

We'd played down there a lot as kids. Dan's favourite game had been to lock me and Tai in the cells and pretend he'd lost the key. Thinking about it, I can't imagine why Dan and I had never got romantically involved.

The most recent house had been built in the 1970s, designed by an architect who'd modelled the roof to reflect the jutting hills that surrounded the reserve. As we drove up to the house, I was struck by how welcoming it was, how beautiful the landscape was— and how all that was changed forever by what was now housed in the basement.

Luke was standing at the top of the stairs to the basement playing bouncer when we arrived. He seemed calmer than he'd sounded when he'd made the call, but he was still a mess. He hugged me and

Erin, and gave Gracie a respectful nod. He eyed Dan with distrust.

"This is a death sentence for Karlo, you know that, right?"

Dan gave him a cool look. "If I have anything to say, it'll be to the ACs. Get out of our way." He stepped in close to Luke, seeming to grow two inches taller.

Both of them lifted their lips back to show their fangs.

Gracie stepped between them and put a hand out to Luke. "Let Dan speak with his brother before he is put to death. They are family."

Luke backed off and Dan pushed past him. He hesitated at the top of the stairs.

"I'll go with you," I said quietly.

He nodded.

We walked down the stairs into the dingy twilight of the makeshift dungeon.

The room below opened up into a row of iron doors along the far right wall, while a work bench, cupboards and shelving took up the left wall. Two of the cell doors on the right had small barred windows, while the door to the smaller cell at the end was just a solid piece of metal.

The walls were made of brick, and the air smelled of damp and moss.

In the middle of the room was a cage that looked like something from a Sherriff's office in a Western. Other than the back wall, it was made entirely from iron bars. I was guessing that was where you put someone when you wanted to keep an eye on them. Maybe someone who didn't have were-strength. The bars didn't look like they'd hold a wolf.

Luke unlocked the first cell on the right, where Karlo was being held, and stayed at the door while we went in.

Dan stood in front of Karlo and folded his arms. "What did you do, man?"

Karlo shook his head, tears in his eyes. "I don't know. I've been sitting here trying to figure out what happened. I don't remember how I got to the house. I don't remember going in or doing… what they say I've done."

He broke off and put a hand over his face.

Dan gave me a helpless look. We could both guess what had happened. Brandt had used his powers on Karlo and somehow thralled him into killing Jack—at the same time, taking out Abigail and Kendrick's second, my father, and Karlo, as a trusted advisor.

"I'm going to try and help you," Dan said. "This wasn't your fault."

Outside the cell, a growl sounded from Luke.

Karlo shook his head. "But I did it with my own hands! I killed him!"

"I can't explain right now, but everyone's going to have to trust me. This is not your fault," said Dan.

Karlo laid his head back against the iron wall and closed his eyes.

Luke walked back up the stairs with us. "What do you mean it's not his fault?"

"I can't tell you," said Dan. "Someone else could

get hurt. But we've got to convince the ACs not to execute Karlo."

We reached the top of the stairs and Luke folded his arms, filling the open doorway. "Good luck with that. I'd execute him myself if it was anyone else."

Dan bit his lip. "Luke, please. I loved Jack. He was a father to Liss. Do you think she'd be standing around if she thought Karlo did this off his own bat?"

Luke gave me a sullen look. "I guess not."

"Then just give us some time to figure this out."

"I'm still going to watch him."

Dan nodded. "You should. He might be a danger to himself."

We joined the others in the lounge where Glenn, Ben, Erin and Gracie were speaking quietly together.

"Hey Dan." Ben hugged his brother. "Abigail and Kendrick are on a plane back. They should get here early evening."

"Did they get you to call the rest of the ACs?" Dan asked.

Ben nodded. "The ones who can make it should all arrive tonight. A crime like this, they're not going to waste time. I'm going to pick a couple of them up from the airport later."

"So, what now?" I said. I kept forgetting why we were there. Then every so often I remembered Jack was dead, before my mind slid away again to think about anything—*anything* else. I found myself staring at a pot plant, wondering when it was last watered.

Glenn crouched in front of me. "Liss, how are you doing?"

I stared at him numbly. "My head hurts."

"I'll get you some painkillers." He took my hand and squeezed it. "We're all here for you, okay?"

I nodded, but my brain was already heading off somewhere else.

He came back a short time later. As I swallowed the pills he handed me, I remembered that while we were sitting around in the lounge, we were disobeying Brandt—which was what had got Jack killed in the first place.

I caught Dan's attention. "Can we afford to wait around? What if he does this again to punish us?"

"He?" said Glenn. "Who are you talking about?"

Dan gave me a look of exasperation then turned to Glenn. "I have no way of proving it right now, but I think you know who."

Glenn's eyebrows drew together. "The vampire did this? How?"

Dan shook his head. "I don't know."

My head was clearing to a dull ache, buoyed by fear of whatever was going to come next. There was no way Brandt was going to leave it at this.

"Come on, Dan, we have to go!"

He rounded on me. "No, Liss! We're not going anywhere. We stay with the pack!"

My phone rang. I gave Dan an angry look and went outside to take the call.

"Alessandra. You're not in Rotokawa."

The sound of his voice brought back the rage.

"What do you want, asshole?"

"Charming," said Brandt. "But much as I enjoy

this part of the process — the self-loathing, the recriminations, the general angst — time's ticking. You have somewhere to be. Go there. Now."

"You screwed up Brandt. When I catch you, I'm going to keep you alive while I cut pieces off you and put them in a blender, then feed the sludge to anything that wants to eat it."

There was a pause. "You sound awfully upset."

I choked back a torrent of obscenities. "You're surprised? After what you did?"

"You'll survive."

"You won't. When you killed Jack your countdown clock started ticking."

"Jack?"

"My foster father. That was his name."

"Liss, if someone's picking off the wolves, you might need to look closer to home."

I was so angry I felt lightheaded. "You'd like that wouldn't you? To see us turn on each other?"

"Turning on each other is the wolves' natural state. There's a reason they're the inferior species. You have your instructions."

He ended the call.

I turned to find Dan standing behind me. I could tell from his murderous expression that he'd heard the conversation.

"We have to tell everyone what he's done," I said. "He can't harm us if we don't let him get to us."

He nodded. "You're right. The only way he managed to kill Jack is by turning a friend into an enemy. Take away that power and he's got nothing."

We went back inside and called everyone together.

The wolves came into the lounge and sat on the couches that ringed the room, with folded arms and wary eyes. I think they expected Dan to try and convince them to let Karlo go. For that reason, I figured I should break the bad news.

I explained exactly what Brandt had done; what he'd said — what he'd probably done to Karlo — and then we sat in uneasy silence as the wolves argued among themselves. Everyone loved Jack. None of the wolves could comprehend how easily Karlo seemed to have been turned against him, how he could have been manipulated into tearing one of his own apart.

"You're saying he told you to go the Midlands or he'd start killing people?" said Glenn.

I pulled my knife and turned it over in my hands. "It was a threat. Just a stupid threat. I didn't honestly think he could hurt the wolves."

"And he didn't say how he'd do it?"

"No."

"If this is true, we need to get *all* the wolves here, right now — let them know the danger we're in," said Ben.

I shook my head. "Do you think that's wise? Any wolf that arrives here from now on could have been thralled by Brandt. What if that's his plan? Draw the alphas together and take out our leaders?"

I could see this hadn't occurred to Dan. He gave Glenn a worried look. "What do you think?"

Glenn shrugged. "It's possible."

"Look," said Luke, "we can second-guess this asshole's plan all day, but we have a duty to protect our own. There are enough of us here now that if a wolf goes rogue, we should be able to put him down. We just need to be vigilant."

"So—do we tell the Midlands pack?" I asked Glenn.

My phone rang. The number was blocked. It had to be Brandt. I pushed my knife back into its sheath and got up to take the call outside, but Dan pulled me back down.

"Here. So we can all hear," he said.

I swallowed and answered the call.

"I'm getting the feeling you don't understand your situation," said Brandt. "So I'll send you a reminder."

He ended the call. A moment later, a text came through to my phone. A link. The wolves crowded around me as I clicked on it. It was a link to an online video. The clip was only a few seconds long, but it showed Corey tearing—

I pressed the home button, screaming internally at the delay before the app responded and closed. Erin put a hand to her mouth and fled outside. I shoved my phone in my pocket and followed her.

She leaned over the porch railing and threw up.

"I am so, so sorry," I said.

She finished throwing up and one of the wolves politely handed her a damp paper towel to wipe her mouth. She tidied herself and turned to me.

"What the fuck, Liss?"

190

I shrank from the disgust in her eyes.

"I didn't want to tell you—"

"I can see why," she said. She closed her eyes. "Fuck."

I didn't know what to say. And she'd only seen the first few seconds, the part where Corey had started to rip himself apart. She hadn't seen what followed.

She opened her eyes. "I'm sorry, Liss, this is too much. I can't do this. I have to get out of here." Tears trembled against her long lashes.

Dan appeared in the doorway. "Please, you can't go." Erin started crying as he put his arms around her. "I know this is just about as bad as it gets, but I don't want you alone out there. It's not safe."

She looked up at him, one tear tracking down her cheek. "Dan, with respect, I've had about enough werewolf bullshit to last me a lifetime."

She pulled away from him and walked down the steps. Dan flashed a glance at me and I ran after her and headed her off.

"Erin, please stop! This is exactly what he wants!"

She shouldered her way past me. "Let me go."

"He was cheating on you! He chose to serve a vampire!"

She stopped. "So what? He deserved to die?"

Maybe, I thought, but I doubted she felt the same way. "No, of course not," I said out loud, "but he brought this on himself. He wanted to be part of the darkness and he got his wish."

She shook her head in disgust and continued

191

down the path towards her car.

I caught her arm and pulled her around to face me. "I'm not going to let him kill you too. You saw what he did to Corey. Please."

From the porch, the wolves watched us silently.

She glanced past me at the wolves. "They're not going to let me leave, are they?"

I shook my head. "We all love you."

Another tear spilled down her cheek. "Well, can I at least be by myself for a while?"

I looked back at the others. Dan nodded. "Luke will stay on the porch and keep watch."

She nodded and retreated to a wooden bench seat at the end of the garden.

I went back inside and sat on the couch. I had a bad taste in my mouth, as if I might be sick myself.

Dan sat beside me and picked up my phone. "How does he know?" he asked. "How does he know we're not where we're supposed to be?"

He had a point. "Maybe he's guessing," I said.

"—and you keep confirming it." It was a realisation, not an accusation.

"Or," said Tai, who was sitting on the other couch, "he's tracking the GPS on your phone."

He jumped up and took my phone from Dan. He checked the settings, then pulled out the memory card and the SIM card. He put the cover back on the phone and rebooted it while we all watched expectantly.

"Leave this with me. I'll make sure he's not tracking you or using the mic to snoop on you."

We all looked at the phone. Even though it wasn't possible without a SIM card, I still half-expected it to ring.

"I don't think he's ever laid hands on it, but I can't be sure," I said. "You know that mind thing he does."

"Let's just hope that disabling it doesn't piss him off." Tai headed upstairs with the phone.

Yes. Pissing Brandt off was not on my list of to-dos right now.

Tai kept my phone off the network while he 'fixed' it, which meant no more calls from Brandt. Not knowing what he might do next made me queasy, but I trusted that staying with the pack was safer than heading down to Rotokawa to start a war.

It was dark when Glenn returned from the airport with Abigail and Kendrick. As they headed up the path to the house, Dan greeted them and took their suitcases.

Abigail placed a hand on his shoulder and he bent his head so that their foreheads touched.

"Welcome home." Dan's voice was tinged with sadness.

She nodded and kissed his forehead, then put an arm out to me. I hugged her and she kissed the top of my head, then walked up the path to the house.

Kendrick put an arm around me and gave me a long look. I could see he was holding in his own grief. "Give us a few minutes then join us in the boardroom."

He carried on up the steps. As he crossed the

threshold I saw his shoulders fall, and suspected he would need some time to himself before he was ready to face me.

Dan followed Kendrick inside and took the suitcases upstairs to their room.

I followed him in and sat on the stairs until I thought it was safe to head up to the boardroom.

Dan was the first to join me. I threw a ballpoint pen at him and he caught it without looking.

He set it in front of me and quoted the bible; "When I became a man, I gave up my childish ways."

"Good thing I'll never be a man then, isn't it?"

He shook his head at me, as Abigail and Kendrick came into the boardroom. There was an awkward silence while Abigail checked her phone and switched it to mute. She set it to one side and folded her hands against the tabletop.

"Liss, before we start, I want you to know that we are here for you.

"Daniel, I'd like you to start at the beginning. We only have half an hour before the others will start arriving. I want to understand what we're up against."

Dan told her about the vampire we'd found under the house and finished with Karlo's protests that he had no memory of attacking Jack.

When he finished speaking, Kendrick and Abigail exchanged a glance.

"War?" he said.

Abigail shook her head. "I hope not."

Even though I'd grown up with the Stoke family, the air of gravity in that room made me very aware that Dan's parents were alphas—leaders that were to be obeyed. Generals, if it came to a fight.

Even Dan's body language was deferential as he spoke. "We've put the message out to all the wolves, including the Midlands pack. I think Glenn tried to call their new alpha too—not sure if he got through."

Abigail put a hand to her mouth, a gesture I recognised as Dan's 'thinking' pose.

"My suggestion would be that we get Ellen to head up a team and take this vampire out," said Kendrick.

"That makes sense," said Abigail. "But the risk is that he isn't working alone. It's a bold move—one vampire against *all* New Zealand's wolves. What makes him so confident?"

"Perhaps it's desperation?" said Kendrick. "He may be aware that Liss is close to coming into her full power. We know he's unhappy with her activities to date."

Abigail drummed her fingers on the table. "I think it's too soon to act. I want more information. Dan, can you please go and get Glenn? I want to know what Tristan had to say."

"Tristan?" asked Dan.

"The new 'alpha' of the Midlands pack, Nicholas Copeland's son. If the rumours are true, Tristan's deposed his father."

Her phone buzzed and she picked it up and read the text. "Ellen and Cole will be here shortly."

Kendrick gave me a nod. "How are you coping, Liss? This must be a very difficult time for you and Andy."

I swallowed. "I don't think it's sunk in yet."

He gave me a sympathetic smile. "Remember, Abigail and I will always be here for you."

I swallowed again, hard. "Thanks."

Truth was, I was doing everything I could to avoid thinking about Jack. And there was plenty to keep my mind occupied.

Soon other members of the Alpha Circle would be here and they were bound to have questions about how all this had started that I didn't particularly want to answer.

And then there was Cole. Cole Jenkins was the only second who was likely to attend the meeting. Just thinking he might turn up made me feel irritable in anticipation of how I was going to feel when he turned up. Cole and I had history—not the romantic kind, but the trading-insults-and-pissing-each-other-off kind.

Cole was one of those guys who refused to age. The wolves always looked younger than their years, but Cole seemed to have honed not-aging to a fine art.

He'd grown up in London as the son of wealthy parents, heir to a legacy he wouldn't inherit for another hundred years or more.

He wasn't an alpha now and never would be, but he was flying close to the sun as Ellen's second. He was stuck there because he couldn't be trusted—too temperamental, too ruthless—no people skills. But if things were going to get down and dirty, Ellen would call him in as her right-hand guy. I hated the guy, as did most of the pack. He had nicknames for all the wolves who ranked lower than him, and they were never complimentary. He called Dan 'Hair' or 'Zoolander', mocking him for over-grooming. If you knew Dan, you knew he hated people assuming he was vain, just because he was good looking. Inferring he was dumb, as well as vain, made him furious.

I wasn't a wolf, but that didn't mean I got a pass. Cole always made sure to call me 'love' or 'sweetheart', because he knew it pissed me off—although I noticed he never did it in front of Ellen.

Condescending, rude, arrogant—the guy was a bully. But Ellen kept him close for times like these, where a lot of blood was likely to be spilled.

I had to assume she knew Cole wanted her position in the pack—she wasn't stupid. But still, she trusted him at her side. I guessed she figured if things got out of hand, she'd deal with it. She'd certainly managed okay to date.

I realised Abigail was speaking to me.

"How's Andy doing?" she asked.

"Ben said he's not coming to the reserve because Karlo's here."

Kendrick's gaze dropped to the table.

"You know Karlo would never harm Jack of his own volition?" said Abigail.

I nodded. "I know. I know."

Erin knocked tentatively on the door. "Can I come

in?"

"Of course," said Abigail.

Erin pushed the door open. "The wolves won't let me leave," she said. "I was wondering—now that you're here—if I could go home?"

Kendrick glanced at Abigail. I knew they were both thinking the same thing.

"Sweetheart, I'm so sorry you're caught up in all this," said Abigail. "But this vampire knows your name. He's marked you as one of his targets. I don't think it would be wise for you to go home just yet."

There was a flicker of panic in Erin's eyes. "Are you... are you at war with him?"

Abigail picked up a pen from a holder on the table and turned it over in her hands.

"Possibly. I don't know what the word means for us in the twenty-first century. I don't know how many adversaries we'd face, or if any packs would back him. I don't know what he's trying to achieve."

"Would wolves really fight for him?" Erin asked. "How could they?"

Abigail shrugged. "Territorial disputes are not uncommon. In fact, what *is* unusual for our kind is how peacefully we've lived together in recent times." She put the pen down on the desk and sighed. "Regardless, winning a war isn't always about having superior numbers. Brandt's strategy seems to be pitting wolves against wolves, and we mustn't let him. We have to think carefully before taking any action that moves us towards a state of conflict with our own."

Erin nodded, and I could see in her eyes how over all of this she was. I understood her need to get away from the insanity, to process the horror she'd witnessed and find some peace again. But that just wasn't going to happen.

"This is my fault, isn't it?" I said to Abigail. "Hunting vamps, when there was peace between us? I started this."

Abigail shook her head. "We would have stopped you and Daniel a long time ago if we'd thought what you were doing would put us all at risk. We certainly never anticipated a vampire as old and powerful as this one would voluntarily call attention to itself."

Dan and Glenn appeared in the open doorway.

"Did you get hold of Tristan?" Abigail asked Glenn.

"He didn't answer. I left a message asking him to call me back, but I have no idea what's going on down there."

Kendrick looked at Abigail. "I suggest we discuss our next move when the others arrive."

She nodded. "Yes, I think that would be wise."

"What about Karlo?" said Dan. "Will he be put to death?"

"No one is going to hurt your brother," said Kendrick. "Don't worry about that."

Abigail got to her feet, signalling the end of our impromptu meeting.

"When the others arrive, send them up here. Liss, I want you to sit in on the meeting and talk the others through what's happened."

I looked at Dan, panicked.

He gave me an encouraging smile. "You'll be fine. Talking's your thing."

I narrowed my eyes and his smile changed to a smirk.

We went back to the lounge while Kendrick and Abigail went downstairs to speak to Karlo.

Tai came jogging into the lounge with my phone, out of breath. "Someone called. I didn't answer — they left a message."

I checked the call log. Blocked number. With trepidation, and a circle of curious wolves crowded around me, I called voicemail and put the phone on speaker.

At first, there was just noise — street noise, people talking, crockery and glassware clinking. Then Brandt's voice.

"I see there's a lot of activity around the petting zoo — what do the wolves call it, *the reserve*?" More sipping.

Coffee or tea? I wondered, mesmerised by the idea of a murderous vampire calling me from Starbucks.

"You can't possibly be stupid enough to think stalling me is a wise move, so I must assume you aren't answering your phone due to some wolf-imposed directive. Because I'm in a generous mood, I'm going to assist you with following my instructions. I've sent someone to pick you up so that you can get to Rotokawa where you have business to attend to. I do hope you get this message. Otherwise you'll be awfully upset by what happens next."

200

I ended the call and put my head in my hands. I was so angry, I was numb with it. I couldn't feel anything else if I tried.

A car horn beeped outside.

Ben went to the window. "Taxi," he said. "No passengers."

I got to my feet.

"Liss? Liss?" Dan put his hands on my shoulders. "We're not going anywhere. We're safe here. We just have to wait until the ACs arrive and decide what to do."

No. No, there was one thing Brandt wasn't going to let us do, and that was ignore him.

I took the steps down to the lawn two at a time and wrenched open the passenger door.

The cab driver looked at me in confusion, then past me at Dan's brothers with the same look of trepidation that most people had when they saw the Stoke brothers assembled in one place.

"Hello, ma'am, how are you today? Did you call for a taxi for four people, travelling to Taupo?"

He certainly didn't look like a criminal mastermind. He was just a taxi driver.

Dan pushed himself between me and the open car door. "Liss, please get back in the house. Thanks, but we don't need a cab, sorry for wasting your time." He pulled out his wallet and threw a fifty onto the passenger seat, then put his arm around me and led me away from the cab.

A gunshot shattered the night.

Dan pushed me to the ground. Ears ringing, I

shuffled around on my elbows to see blood painting the cab's passenger window.

"Oh, no, no."

I got to my feet, ignoring Dan's attempts to pull me back down, and wrenched open the car door. The driver's body slumped to one side, the gun trailing from his fingers. There were pieces everywhere — piece of... pieces...

I stumbled back from the cab and Dan walked up to the open door. He looked inside, then pushed the door shut. His face was pale.

I turned in a circle, fists clenched, no one to fight.

My phone rang. I held it to my ear.

"I understand your driver didn't work out. I can send another one."

"Don't you *dare*," I whispered. "I'm coming for you, Brandt. If you think I was hunting your kind before, you ain't seen *nothing* yet."

Brandt laughed. "That's the spirit. Now, do you want me to call you another cab, or do you want me to send the police out to clean up the previous one?"

Abigail strode out of the house towards me. She took the phone out of my hand as she reached me and ended the call. Her face was a mask of fury.

"Don't talk to him again, Liss. Look at me!" I did, but my eyes were unfocused and her face was a blur. "Don't let him manipulate you."

To the others, she said, "Get this cleaned up. Move the car to the back of the property, out of sight, in case we have more unexpected visitors. We'll deal with it later. The rest of you, get inside. I've had a call from Tane and Anton and they're on their way from the airport. Isabella Richmond's driving up from Hamilton tonight. We need to be coherent when they arrive."

Numb, I walked back inside, while Ben and Glenn set about the grim task of disposing of the cab driver's body.

At the top of the steps, I remembered something. I turned back and said to Glenn, "There's a photo in his visor. He had a family. He has a phone. Someone should tell them."

Trembling, I went into the house, the image of all those *bits* swimming in front of my eyes, the smell of death following me like a ghost.

Chapter 21

Not every member of the Alpha Circle cared about our problems and was willing to get involved, but Tane Kereti from the Upper South, and Isabella Richmond from the Waikato, along with Ellen and Cole from the Northland pack, represented our closest allies. Calling on Anton Gregory was a strategic decision of a different kind. Anton had skills other wolves didn't, which came from living at the far end of the earth without supervision.

I'd met him once before on a trip down South, and it wasn't something I was going to forget in a hurry. His home was a fortress, surrounded by ten feet of corrugated iron and barbed wire, and his pack called themselves the Southland Wolves. It was well known that the Deep South pack was basically a criminal gang, and where they lived, no other gangs operated. They wouldn't dare.

He'd supposedly built the pack from people who'd opposed him. They said he turned people he hated into wolves, and brutalised them into submission. Word was, he was responsible for taking out the old Deep South ruling family. But none of these were things people mentioned to his face.

Dan and I were outside on the porch when Ben got back from the airport with Tane and Anton. Anton gave me a polite nod and headed upstairs to the boardroom, but Tane pulled me into a hug, his brown eyes full of warmth. "Kia kaha, girl. We're here for you."

"Thanks Tane." It was hard to speak.

He took me to one side and handed me something. "Jack gave this to me, years ago now. I'd like you to have it."

He handed me a small velvet bag and I opened it. Inside was a silver pendant. The Gaelic design was the same as one Jack had give me, but like a separate piece of a larger puzzle.

Tane stood shoulder to shoulder with me as I examined it under the porch light.

"There are four of these that belonged to our wolf ancestors, here in Aotearoa. Jack inherited them. He gave one to you, and two to the Stokes when he joined their pack. This was his."

I glanced up at him. "Why did he give it to you?"

"It was a wedding gift. I introduced him to Andy. In return, when I got married to Jade, he gave me this."

I held it out to him. "He wanted you to have it. I shouldn't—"

He closed his hand around mine and pushed my hand back towards me.

"This pendant is an amulet of protection. Maybe

205

you'll keep it—maybe you'll give it to someone else who needs it. Either way, it belongs to you."

I put the pendant in my pocket and took a shaky breath in.

"I have to go—" he pointed to the stairs. "But I want to talk to you later. About Jack. Let's have a beer and a kōrero."

I nodded quickly. "I'd like that."

He put a hand on my shoulder and rubbed his thumb against my neck. "You were very special to him, Liss. Don't you forget how much he loved you."

He went inside and I leaned back on the porch railing. Dan put his arm around me and stood with me in silence.

Nothing felt real. I realised that part of me was waiting for Jack and Andy to arrive, to complete the pack gathering. Not having them there just felt… wrong. I wished I could text Andy to see how he was doing, but Abigail still had my phone.

Isabella turned up a short while later, a cigarette dangling between her lips. I'd met her before but didn't know her well. She was technically an independent rather than an alpha, as she had no pack of her own, but she was still a force to be reckoned with. She lived down near Hamilton, and much resembled what we Kiwis called a 'westie'.

Dressed in an animal print, figure-hugging dress and leggings, Isabella brimmed with Select brand energy and confidence. She finished her cigarette and flicked the remains onto the gravel and strode up to hug Dan. "How are ya, love?" she asked, her arms slung around his neck.

"Uh, good. As we can be," he said, his eyes slightly wider than normal.

"Good boy," she said, and kissed him on the cheek. She looked over at me.

"And how about you, love? You holding up?"

I nodded.

She gave me a wink and headed up to the boardroom in a clatter of silver bangles and swinging earrings.

Dan watched after her with an air of mild trauma.

The last to arrive was Ellen Kauri. We all heard her pull up in her Nissan GTR. People in the next *town* heard her pull up. The silence rang after the car's engine died.

Cole Jenkins was with her, as we'd anticipated. Glenn greeted them at the door and invited them in. Ellen gave us all a polite 'hello' while Cole simply gave the room a cool nod. "Where do we put our bags?"

"This way." Tai took him down to the bedrooms.

As Ben headed upstairs to tell the others Ellen had arrived, a collection of electronic noises sang across the lounge. I was the only one who didn't have a phone to check.

I watched Dan's face as he read the text and knew it was bad. He got up and I followed him outside. One by one, his brothers joined us. We stood on the porch, wondering what was coming next.

Dan held out his phone to me. The message read: *'Suffer the children.'*

Abigail and Kendrick joined us as we stood in the dark, waiting for Brandt to make his move. Ellen took a place beside me. "What are we expecting, Liss?"

"The last calling card he sent splattered his brains all over his cab," I said quietly.

"Would he really use children?" she asked.

I thought of Jack. I thought of the cab driver. Brandt would go as far as he needed to in order to get what he wanted. "Probably."

"Why's he doing this?" she asked.

"Because I insulted him."

Ellen looked at me sideways.

The security light snapped on. A small child, no more than four years old, stood on the lawn. He looked around in confusion. He caught sight of his silent audience and looked up at us, his chubby face streaked with tears.

"My mummy's hurt," he said. He stuck his thumb in his mouth.

Abigail walked down the porch steps and crouched beside him. "What's your name?"

He removed his thumb from his mouth. "Jack," he said. "Can you help Mummy?"

Jack.

Abigail straightened up and took the little boy's hand. "Where is she? Can you show me?"

The little boy began to tug her down the driveway towards the road. The rest of us followed, our footsteps loud in the still night, our breath misting in front of us. We reached the road and the child pointed to a patch of light a short distance down the road. Abigail hoisted the boy up and carried him as we walked towards the light.

As we got closer, I could see a car had crashed into the ditch, a single working headlight streaming into the brush. Judging by the smell of burning rubber, the car had skidded across the road and pitched nose first into the ditch. The woman behind the wheel was at best unconscious—probably dead.

"Is this your mummy?" Abigail said to the boy.

He nodded.

"Okay, sweetheart. We're going to help her, but I'm going to get my son Glenn to take you back to the house while you wait. Does that sound okay?"

The little boy looked at Glenn with wide eyes as Abigail beckoned him over. Glenn held out his arms and smiled. "Hi, I'm Glenn. Shall we go inside where it's warm?"

The little boy nodded, his thumb firmly lodged in his mouth. Glenn took him and carried him back up the road.

Kendrick stood beside his wife. "This is sick," he said. His voice was laced with anger. "Using humans because he's too cowardly to attack us directly!"

A siren rose in the distance.

"Okay, everyone get back to the house," said Abigail. "Kendrick, let's see what we can do for this poor woman, but I'm not hearing a pulse."

Kendrick stepped forward and crouched by the car. "Nothing," he said. "I can smell—"

"Yes," said Abigail. "I can too. She's gone."

I'd killed enough things to know what they were

referring to. When things died, they tended to lose control of all their muscles. There is no dignity in death.

Kendrick pulled the woman from the wreckage and laid her flat on the road. He started chest compressions as gently as he could with wolf strength. I heard a rib crack and turned away.

Abigail watched him for a moment, then turned to me. "I know this is upsetting, but please understand—this changes nothing. We stay together, no matter what happens."

"He'll just send more—"

"Liss! I will not let this vampire manipulate us."

I dropped my head, frustrated that she wouldn't listen. I knew she was wrong. We couldn't stop him manipulating us—unless we were prepared to let more people die. I didn't know how Brandt had caused this accident, but I knew if he could do this, he had a way to force me to do what he wanted. I was not going to let anyone else die for my mistakes.

I looked up as I caught a flash of something pale in the grass. Dan scented the air. He gave me a puzzled look.

"Did you see that?" he asked.

I nodded. "Can you smell something?"

"It's gone," he said. I strained to see in the darkness but eventually gave up. Dan's phone beeped.

With a snarl, he pulled it from his pocket and we read it together.

'How many more are you willing to sacrifice?'

I pulled his sleeve and he followed me down the road. When we were out of Abigail's earshot, I said, "He's right—how many more people are we going to let him kill? These people are completely innocent—they're not drug dealers and thieves. They're just people."

"That's why alphas make these decisions," he said, but he looked as upset as I was.

"Abigail's protecting the pack," I said. "That's her job. But who's going to protect the humans?"

He pulled away from me and started to walk back to the house.

I followed him, knowing full well the answer was *no one*. Humans weren't the wolves' concern. But they sure as hell were mine.

Inside, Glenn sat at the kitchen table with the toddler. The little boy held a mug of warm milk and looked far more cheerful now that he believed we were helping his mother.

I took a look at him and knew I had to act. My refusal to bend to Brandt's will had changed dozens of people's lives forever. Families had lost a mother, a father, a sister, a brother, a source of love—just as I had.

My plan was simple. Stop fighting. At least, until I could figure out how to win.

I leaned over the back of the chair where Ellen had left her jacket. "Is he okay?" I asked Glenn.

"He's fine," he said. "A few bruises, but he'll live." He frowned.

"What?"

"Some of the bruises aren't... fresh. And Liss..." He got up and walked over to me. He kept his voice low. "We found some pictures... in the cab from before. Of children."

Jesus H.

We shared a look, and I was pretty sure we were thinking the same thing. Every person Brandt had chosen to kill had done something most people would consider reprehensible. Not necessarily something you should die for, but not something you'd get an award for, either. A vampire with a conscience?

If so, how did my foster father fit into that?

"More please?" The little boy held out his empty cup to Glenn. Glenn took it from him and went to warm another mug.

While he was distracted, I snagged Ellen's car keys out of her jacket pocket, holding them tightly to stop them jangling. The little boy watched me with round, curious eyes.

"Where's Mummy?" the boy asked.

"I'm not sure," I said. "I'll go check."

I went outside to the car park.

Dan stood on the porch, scenting the air. "That smell's back again," he said.

I wandered between the cars, pretending to sniff the air. Actually, I *could* smell something... a faint chemical scent on the breeze. No time to worry about that, though.

I pressed the fob on Ellen's key ring and slipped

into the driver's seat.

I locked the car door and started the engine as Dan ran across the gravel. There was only one way to stop this. Brandt wanted me. I'd give him what he wanted.

Dan slammed his hands on top of the car's roof.

"What are you doing?" His voice was muffled under the engine's growl.

Ellen ran out onto the porch as she heard her car roar to life, but I ignored her and pulled out in an arc, forcing Dan to jump out of the way. He could have stopped the car by force but it would have meant damaging the car. You didn't damage Ellen Kauri's car.

I put the car in third and took off down the drive, sending gravel skidding out from under the tyres. Time to go find Brandt.

Chapter 22

The car ate into the night, the miles disappearing behind me. A light scatter of rain left the road glittering, stars against stars.

It occurred to me as I travelled at speed, that I'd only managed to grab a couple of naps in the last forty hours. The white lines ghosted in front of me, the reflective markers at the side of the road strobing past at the edges of my vision. I blinked hard and tried to make sure I didn't end up in a proverbial ditch, because if I did, it was going to be a while before anyone found me.

I had no phone, no way of contacting anyone. Rotokawa lay just outside the city of Taupo, and between me and Taupo were just under three hundred kilometres of open road.

At least with me on the road, it was pointless for Brandt to punish the others. Hopefully, he would leave them alone and concentrate on me. That is, assuming he knew I'd left. Which he would. I didn't know how, but he'd know.

I switched on the radio and opened the car

window. Cool air washed across me, along with the scent of damp forest and empty highway.

It only took two and a half hours to reach Taupo, thanks to Ellen's radar detector. I slowed back to the speed limit as the car's headlights picked out the first houses that signalled the city limits. The last thing I needed was more police attention.

I had no idea where I was going — no GPS, no maps, no address. I parked in the township outside a coffee shop and went inside. He'd find me. I knew he would. I ordered a coffee and sat down in a booth where I had some privacy. I reached for my phone automatically and felt oddly vulnerable without it.

Without my digital world to fall back on, I looked around. The place was long and narrow, with booths running down one wall, and a bar running the length of the other.

The walls were painted dark red and were decorated with huge beaten-copper shapes that gave the place a steampunk vibe. The smell of roasting coffee filled the air, the soundtrack 90s grunge. It was the kind of place Jack would have taken us and Andy would have hated.

With nothing else to do, I watched the other diners watch their phones with a tinge of jealousy. There was no real conversation to eavesdrop on, just the sound of milk being frothed over Anthony Kiedis singing about love and loneliness.

With nothing else to focus on, the grief hit me like a punch to the gut. Jack was dead. It was as if I kept forgetting. Or maybe I just hadn't accepted it was true yet. I leaned against the back of the booth and squeezed my eyes shut, smelling death instead of the aroma of ground coffee.

I opened my eyes as a waiter set a cup of coffee in front of me and drank in the steam. If I closed my eyes again, I could pretend it was still yesterday. The day before Brandt destroyed my world.

The table vibrated as someone sat down on the bench seat opposite me. I kept my eyes closed a moment longer and listened to my visitor take off his gloves and lay them on the table. I could sense him waiting.

I opened my eyes. "I came."

Brandt looked pissed. "How many people have to die before you do as you're told?"

I ground my teeth to keep from biting back. I needed to be smarter than I'd ever been before, if I was going to prevent more bloodshed. That meant controlling my temper. I pushed the anger and the grief into a tiny part of my brain for later.

"I'm here, aren't I?"

"Where's your phone?" he asked.

I shrugged and took a sip of coffee.

He pushed an iPhone across the table towards me. "Keep this on you at all times or the Stokes will receive more visitors. And answer it. Every call, every text I send you."

I picked up the phone and turned it over in my hand.

"What if I'm busy when you call, talking to a Nigerian prince who needs my help liberating his money? Or if someone finds a virus on my computer and wants to help me remove it?"

His look was chilling. "What's that on your hands?"

I was tired. I put down my coffee and looked at my palms, expecting, after the night I'd had, to see dirt, grease, mud. Nothing.

"Oh, it's *blood*," he said.

I laughed at my own stupidity. "I didn't have any spot remover."

He almost smiled.

"Why are you doing this?" I asked. "I haven't hurt you or yours. Seems as if I can't. You have nothing to fear from me and mine. Why? Why are you doing this? You don't seem unhinged. I don't buy that you're bored. This isn't boredom, this is cruelty."

A waitress stopped by our table and Brandt ordered a pot of tea. After she'd gone, he cocked his head and looked at me.

"You've never hurt me and mine," he said softly. "I suppose that all depends who 'me and mine' includes, doesn't it?"

I shook my head as I stared into my coffee. "I've never met anyone as powerful as you. You didn't come after me until that day on the pier. We exchange a few words and suddenly I'm your number one enemy."

He picked up the salt shaker and turned it in his hands. He held it out to me and shook it. "Exterminate, exterminate!"

My turn to give him a cold look.

"If you're implying I'm some kind of heartless killer, I think that's a little unfair. Vampires hunt humans. They take lives."

"They hunt to eat," he asked. "Like wild dogs or house cats. Or wolves."

"My—" I was about to say 'my people' but stopped. "The wolves don't kill people." Well, mine didn't.

"Just vampires," he said. "One graceful apex predator preying on another."

I finished my coffee as his tea arrived and ordered another one. He set down the salt shaker and poured hot water over a tea bag.

"Anyway, they didn't attack the vamps, I did," I said. "And now I'm yours, completely powerless. You have to be getting off on that."

He gave a soft laugh. "If only it were that simple." He added milk to the tea and stirred in a packet of sugar. "You never had any power of your own, Alessandra. Without the wolves beside you, you'd have been nommed by now."

I was about to protest, then remembered my arm being shredded by a single baby vamp in the woods. Brandt drank in my silence with his tea.

"But there's a rumour," he went on, drawing a circle in the air with his hand, "that you won't always be this helpless. Legend tells of a warrior who'll come into an arcane power on her twentieth birthday, a power that the vampires fear more than they fear... well, anything, since we don't really do fear."

"All a Väktare can do is find you. Hardly much of

a power."

"That really depends on who you lead to my door."

"And who says I'm going to inherit it on my twentieth birthday?"

My twentieth birthday was only two days away.

My second coffee arrived and I added a few more gulps of liquid anxiety to my already churning stomach.

"You're afraid of me," I said, my patience wearing thin. "So kill me."

"You're ready to give up?" he said. He sounded disappointed.

I laughed and shook my head. "You're not fighting me. If you were, I'd fight to the death. But it's not me you're hurting. It's innocent people. And I'm just not prepared to see anyone else tortured or killed in my name. Just end it, for Christ's sake."

On hearing me curse, a man reading a newspaper on his tablet cast a glance at me. Apparently talking about killing each other was fine, but cursing was unacceptable in a public place.

Brandt finished his tea and stood. He pushed his gloves into his coat pocket and offered me his hand.

"Come with me, Liss."

I ignored his hand and slid out of the booth.

"Where are we going?"

"To see the pack leader of the Midlands pack. I think you'll like him. He's about your age."

I hovered while he paid for our coffees and then followed him outside.

"We'll take your car," he said. "It'll make an appropriate entrance."

I got into the car, the iPhone heavy in my pocket.

Brandt got in beside me while I sat behind the steering wheel, staring into the darkness.

"Before you get ideas about driving into the wilderness and forcing me to kill you, remember, I can do this." He laid his hand on my arm. My focus pulled towards him until I met his gaze. Time slowed, sound distorting like a damaged cassette tape. His lips moved, but I couldn't hear his words. He lifted his hand and sound rushed back. My heart thudded in my chest and a convulsion of fear ran through me. The implication was clear. He could send me back. Send me back to my family as he had Karlo, an unwitting time bomb.

"Drive."

As I pulled away from the curb, I thought of my pack brothers and sisters, imagined what they'd be doing now. The ACs around the boardroom table, the Stoke brothers gathered in the lounge. Ellen may already be on the road, following me — and her car. Karlo sitting in his cell, waiting to be executed for a crime he didn't remember committing.

I did that, I thought. *I brought this down on us all.*

I thought of my sister, her eyes shut, her breathing ragged as her blood pattered onto the leaves around her.

As if reading my mind, Brandt patted my arm reassuringly. His touch was benign, carrying none of the weight of compulsion, but his touch still made my skin crawl.

He guided me through the streets and out into open country, where I opened up the GTR and drove as though I wouldn't see another sunrise.

We reached the Midlands pack alpha's country estate some time after midnight and drove through iron gates and up to the house, parking in one of those semi-circular driveways that I'd always associated with mansions full of annoyingly wealthy, condescending people.

I watched the car's display fade as I turned off the engine. It was after midnight. I knew I should be afraid, but I was in water so deep now, all I could do was float. Or maybe that was the sleep deprivation.

As we walked up to the door, Brandt positioned me in front of him. I noticed a camera set into the door as he rang the doorbell and guessed I did look slightly less intimidating than he did. His gloves and wool coat gave him a kind of Gestapo air that some people might correctly interpret.

The guy who answered the door had styled blond hair and pale eyes. He stood a head taller than me and was roughly my age. I was guessing he was the new pack alpha—so fresh he answered his own door. I didn't anticipate his would be a long and prosperous reign.

"You must be Alessandra," he said. That surprised me.

"Call me Liss," I said. "I'm sorry, I don't know your name."

"Tristan Copeland." We shook hands. "My sincere condolences about Jack."

I nodded, not trusting myself to speak.

He looked past me at Brandt. "You again."

Brandt inclined his head.

"It's the vampire," Tristan called over his shoulder.

Two wolves in human form came into the foyer and stood on either side of Tristan, radiating casual menace. One had tattoos running up his arms that crept across the patch of skin bared by the V-neck of his t-shirt, and the other was dressed in a hoodie and jeans.

The first guy stood with his arms folded, bulging his tattoos at us. The other guy had his hands thrust deep into the pockets of his hoodie. He blinked lazily at me and didn't seem overly concerned on his boss's behalf.

"May I come in?" Brandt asked.

Tristan blinked. "Why would I invite you in?"

Brandt pulled me back towards him and put a hand up under my chin, squeezing my throat. "Tell him why he should let me in, Liss."

My reaction, when someone grabs my throat, usually results in that person lying on the ground curled around a groin injury. But Brandt's magic touch left me stunned and gulping for air.

Tristan's bodyguards stepped forward.

"Uh-uh-ah," said Brandt. "If either of you moves again, I'll crush her windpipe."

I was losing consciousness, but with that skin-to-skin contact, there was no panic. Just a gradual darkening of the world as I went limp in his arms.

"All right! Come in!" said Tristan.

Brandt released the pressure. I staggered and found my feet, leaning against the wall for support. I put a hand to my throat as Brandt stalked around me.

The two bodyguards moved back to let him in, but they weren't happy.

Brandt strode into the foyer and looked around.

"Why are you here?" asked Tristan.

He stopped examining the chandeliers and said casually, "I came for a friendly chat. Shall we go into the lounge?"

"Joey," said Tristan. The guy with the tattoos stepped up to Brandt.

"You got any weapons on you?" he said. He was English. There seemed to be a lot of English wolves in New Zealand. His was not a fun accent. It was straight up murder-you-for-your-dentures gangster.

Brandt smiled, amused. "Weapons. No."

Joey's smile was easily as arrogant. "Yeah, didn't think so." The 'th' came out as an 'f'. He stepped back and gestured for Brandt to walk past him towards the lounge.

"Caleb?" Tristan said to the other bodyguard, whose vacant expression left me wondering how he'd got the job.

"We've got it," he said.

Tristan watched them escort Brandt to the lounge, and turned back to me.

"Are you hurt?"

I shook my head.

Tristan pushed the front door closed and held out his hand, inviting me to join him. I followed him to the lounge.

Brandt made himself comfortable in an armchair by the fire while Joey lounged against the wall behind him. Caleb took a seat, his hands still stuffed in his pockets, and watched me with cloudy grey eyes.

I stayed standing. I wasn't planning on staying longer than I had to.

Tristan took a seat opposite Brandt, and as he did, a woman walked into the lounge. She stopped and did a double-take.

"Tristan?"

"He was going to kill her," he said. "Liss, this is my sister, Riley."

Riley looked early twenties, but as a wolf, she could have been any age. Her skin was dark and flawless, her hair flowing in heavy ringlets past her shoulders. She could not have looked less like her pale, Nordic-looking brother.

She smiled at my confusion. "I'm adopted."

"Huh. Me too." I smiled back.

She went to a decanter of whiskey in a corner of the room and poured several glasses. She handed one to Tristan, one to Brandt, and kept one herself.

I guessed we weren't bonding after all.

Brand tilted his glass towards her. "Thank you." He put it to his nose and inhaled deeply.

"Why are you here?" asked Tristan.

"I assume, as the pack alpha, you're aware that I've asked the Westlands pack to assassinate you and seize control of your pack in my name?"

Joey let out a growl, and Caleb glanced at Brandt, surprised.

"Maybe you should have done your homework," said Tristan. He sipped his drink. "No pack in this country would breach the Alpha Circle agreement. Not for their own gain—and definitely not for yours."

"Things change," said Brandt. He glanced across at me. "For instance, this one. Very soon."

Tristan's gaze ran over me.

"You've not had a Väktare before," said Brandt. "And I suspect that very soon the rules, such as they were, will no longer apply."

Tristan leaned back in his armchair. "And why's that?"

"Because," said Brandt, "I now care about your affairs."

A muscle twitched in Tristan's jaw.

"I heard that your father stepped down after you instigated a vote of no confidence," said Brandt. "That must have been hard for him. Deposed by his own son."

Tristan glanced at his sister but didn't speak.

"Where is he now?" Brandt looked around. "In fact, where is *everybody*?"

Tristan's eyes narrowed, but Riley's indulgent smile didn't falter. In fact, she looked as if she was enjoying herself.

225

Tristan lifted his whiskey tumbler to his lips. "That's none of your business."

"Was your loss of faith in him," said Brandt, "and again, forgive me if I'm overstepping the social constraints of our relationship — anything to do with your father's discussion with the Alpha Circle about consolidating leadership under Abigail Stoke after young Alessandra here comes into her power?"

What?

Tristan's lip curled into a snarl. "As I said, none of your business."

Riley stood behind her brother's chair and put her hands on his shoulders.

"Our pack politics are private business, Brandt. And clearly the Westlands pack wasn't interested in following your orders. So why are we having this conversation?"

Brandt sat back in his armchair and laced his fingers together.

"It's true, they're rather reluctant and therefore ineffective," he said. "So I thought I'd come to you directly and see if we might discuss an alliance."

An alliance? Since *when*?

"Go on," said Tristan. Riley began to play with the hair that brushed her brother's collar. These two were not right.

"As you can imagine, it's in my best interests to *not* have the wolves united in one ravening horde, led by someone whose sole motivation is the extinction of my species."

"You're not a species," I interjected. "If anything,

226

you're the *remains* of a species. Like, literally the remains."

"Shut up," said Tristan.

I glared at him. "Or what? You'll hurt me? You really want my pack at your door? Because that's how you end up with my pack at your door."

He turned to me and snarled, baring teeth that were too long for a human mouth.

Riley patted him on the head. "Ignore her, Tristan. I imagine she's having a bad day."

I shook my head in disgust. "Brandt brought me here at great cost to a lot of people. You need to decide what you're going to do next, because if you're not going to kill me, I'm going home."

I headed for the door. In an instant, Caleb and Joey caught up with me. I had no weapons and they had were-strength, and they weren't overly concerned about hurting my feelings. They dragged me struggling and spitting insults back to the lounge and pushed me into a chair.

"If she moves, break her arm," said Tristan.

Joey's face twisted into a smile that made the skin crawl between my shoulder blades. These guys were not like the wolves I'd grown up with. These guys enjoyed being wolves entirely too much.

"Liss, really," Brandt chided me. "We talked about this. If killing your friends won't help you behave, we really will have no choice but to start breaking things."

His threat brought back my last vampire hunt with a sickening rush—looking down at my arm, the finger that was shorter than the others, the white place in the middle of my arm where the bone was showing...

I sat very still, waiting for spots to stop floating in front of my eyes.

"What kind of alliance?" Tristan asked, as if I hadn't spoken.

"Right now, the Alpha Circle is engaged with my distractions. But you're not part of the Alpha Circle, are you, Tristan? They didn't invite you to the reserve, even though you're the affected party."

Tristan sipped his drink and listened.

"They tried to get hold of you!" I said desperately. "I know they tried!"

"Caleb," said Tristan.

"Start with a finger," Brandt suggested. Caleb walked over to me and picked up my hand from the arm of the chair. I struggled to get away, but I wasn't strong enough. He put my little finger between two of his and snapped it like a dry twig.

I screamed as he dropped my hand, and cradled it while pain lanced through my finger.

"What the hell!" I shouted at Caleb.

"If she doesn't shut up, break another one," said Tristan.

I gritted my teeth as the pain became a hot throbbing. Riley went into the kitchen and came back with some ice wrapped in a tea towel.

"For the swelling," she said. "We'll splint it when we're done."

She went back to stand behind her brother, while

Caleb leaned against the wall by my chair.

Brandt cast me an amused glance. "If I'd known that's all that was required to shut you up, I'd have suggested it sooner."

Tristan was starting to get annoyed. "What kind of alliance?" he asked again.

"This girl is as much a threat to you as she is to me. As long as she lives, you will never have peace."

Riley frowned. "You brought her here so that we could kill her?"

Brandt smiled. "No. No, that would be unwise. I brought her here because her pack will follow her. But you don't need to be concerned with that... if I'm on your side."

"Why not just kill her if she frightens you?" asked Riley.

Brandt sipped his drink and said nothing.

"She's no threat to us," said Tristan. "She's your problem, not ours."

Brandt smiled down into his whiskey. "How very wrong you are. In two days' time, there will be no greater threat to you. Either believe me now, or have it confirmed at a later date. When it's too late."

Riley narrowed her eyes. "What do you think you know, vampire?"

He gave her an unsettling smile. "The Alpha Circle is not going to recognise your rule. For usurping your father's throne, you'll stand alone against all threats. Including me."

"I'm pretty confident that won't be a problem," said Tristan.

Brandt put his head on one side. "You are. And I'm curious about that. Why aren't you more concerned that a being as powerful as I am is sitting in your house while you're—well, if I can be so bold—largely undefended."

Joey leaned back in his chair, laughing quietly to himself.

Brandt cast him a glance. "No offence."

Tristan twisted his drink to the light. "All five Stoke brothers could turn up on my doorstop and I'd invite them in and offer them a drink, as I've done with you."

Brandt looked around the room, curious. "These two are nothing exceptional," he said, indicating the bodyguards. "So... which one of you is?"

Tristan leaned back in his chair. "Can't you feel it, vampire?"

Brandt glanced from Tristan to Riley and back to Tristan. Back to Riley.

"Oooh," he breathed, looking at her with wonder. "You've changed." He got up and walked over to her. He tilted her chin up. "I haven't seen one of you in the flesh before. I had no idea your kind were this powerful." He frowned. "You shouldn't be this powerful."

She smiled and guided his hand away from her face.

"Touch me again, Crimson Peak, and I'll show you what *real* power is. We cooperated before because we thought you might bring something to the table. Now, as you can see, we have other plans.

I'd advise you to stay out of our way."

"What have you done, Riley?" He sounded uneasy.

She smiled. "I went searching for knowledge."

Brandt's concern intensified. "Immortality from dark magic comes at a price, Riley. Usually madness."

That did not sound good.

"Best you stay clear of me then." She smiled sweetly at him.

Tristan stood. "Well, this has been fun, but as you can see, we don't need your alliance. And if you send anyone else to harm us, you'll find yourself clogging a Roomba."

Brandt took his gloves from his pocket. He glanced across at me. "Come on, we're leaving."

"No," said Tristan. "She stays."

I tried to stand, but Caleb pushed me back down and stood facing me, his hands clasped in front of him.

"Liss will stay with us until her pack arrives," said Tristan, "Which I have no doubt they will. After this conversation, I fancy a peaceful resolution, and handing her to them alive seems a good way to ensure that."

There was a flicker of displeasure in Brandt's eyes. Clearly he had his own plan, and this wasn't part of it. Tristan could see it too and smiled a shark's smile. You know the one, where there are teeth and dead eyes, and nothing approximating a smile.

"I could just kill your boyfriend," Brandt said to

Riley, keeping his eyes fixed on Tristan.

Riley shrugged. "Perhaps. But if you do, Caleb and Joey will kill Liss. And you still need her, don't you?" She tilted her head to one side. "What do you need her for?"

There was cold murder in Brandt's smile. "You're making a mistake. However strong you might be, you don't want to be on the wrong side of me."

"I think I'll survive."

He gave her a dark smile. "We'll see."

He turned crisply and walked back into the foyer. A moment later, the front door clunked shut behind him.

Tristan walked over to me. He looked down at my finger.

"That looks nasty. Does it hurt?"

"I've had worse."

He gave me an appraising look. "Well. Rest assured, you won't come to any more harm—but you really do need to learn when to shut up."

He walked back to the decanter and poured himself another drink.

I said nothing. That's self-control, right there. They say emotional intelligence is one of the biggest predictors of success in life. If so, I'd just moved one step closer to success.

Chapter 23

Tristan watched from his armchair as Riley bound my broken finger to the one next to it with medical tape.

"Is it really two days to your birthday?" he asked.

I winced as Riley added another layer of tape. I was not in the mood to be answering his questions.

I let the silence grow and looked around at Joey and Caleb, gauging the likelihood of more violence from them. They seemed happy chatting to each other as they waited for the others to arrive.

Tristan, however, was running out of patience.

"I asked you a question."

"Yeah, I heard you," I said. Riley finished up and took the first-aid supplies back to wherever she'd got them come from.

Joey stilled mid-conversation and fixed his gaze on me with quiet menace. "Are you going to answer the question?"

Caleb watched him with a slight smile as if Joey was about to do something amusing.

Joey got to his feet and walked over to where I sat.

He walked with the rolling gait of the bow-legged, every step full of muscle and threat. He leaned over me and put his hands on the arms of my chair.

"When someone asks you a question, it's polite to answer them."

If I kicked him in the balls and elbowed him in the face, what were my chances of not getting another finger broken?

"I'm told that most communication is nonverbal," I said. "For instance, I can tell from your body language that you quite fancy me."

His eyes glittered with amusement. "Trust me, you don't want that."

I believed him.

"Now answer the fucking question."

He straightened up and stepped to one side so I could see Tristan.

"Your birthday," prompted Tristan.

"Yes, Tristan, I will turn twenty in two days," I said.

"Lovely," said Joey, patting the arm of my chair. He went back to Caleb.

"Perhaps you should stay for a few days," said Tristan. "As my guest."

Riley came back into the lounge with a glass of water. She put it on the side table by my chair along with some painkillers, and took a seat on the couch.

"While that does sound lovely," I said to Tristan, "I prefer not to be the guest of people who break my fingers when I say something they don't like."

Tristan sipped his whiskey. "What if I promise it

won't happen again?"

"Yeah, right. You mind telling me how you know Brandt?

"We did some business," he said mildly. "But it's concluded now."

That did not comfort me at all.

"I could help you," said Riley. "With your power."

"What would *you* know about my power?" I asked.

She considered me with those husky-blue eyes. "More than you, I suspect. We have a lot in common." She left the couch and crouched beside my chair. "Close your eyes."

My pulse sped up. I was not keen to close my eyes in a room full of psychos.

"It's okay," she said. "I'm not going to hurt you."

I closed my eyes, against my better judgment.

"Now open yourself up to the energy. Can you feel wolf energy?" she asked.

I nodded.

"Mine's faint," she said. "I'm told it's different. You need to concentrate to feel it."

I breathed out and tried to relax. Sitting in the Copelands' lounge, I could feel the three wolves as distinct presences. When I paid attention, I could feel their energy, each one like an invisible bubble pressed against me. Tristan's energy was cold and unpleasant. Joey's was warmer and stronger—he was the real danger here. Caleb's energy was weak and pale, pushed back by the other two.

And then there was Riley. She didn't feel like a wolf. I tuned the others out as I'd learned to do after years of living with the pack, and concentrated on her. There was definitely something there. Her energy swirled like mist, constantly moving. It didn't have that familiar surface tension the wolves' had, but the longer I focused on it, the stronger I was able to sense it.

I caught a scent, like the smell of the bush after rain. Cicada song floated around me.

I opened my eyes. "What are you?"

"A shifter, like the wolves," she said.

"Any form?" I asked.

"Just the one," she said. "I can show you if you like."

"No," I said hurriedly. "That's okay. Canine?"

She nodded. "We have a few names—*skoghund, kuri ngahere*—forest dogs. We're rare. Almost as rare as the Väktare."

Before she could tell me her origin story, the doorbell rang. Tristan went to answer the door. That seemed to be his thing.

I jumped out of my chair. My people were here. Nothing was going to stop me walking out that door.

I got as far as the foyer before Caleb headed me off, and found Ellen standing in the doorway, flanked by Dan and Cole.

"Liss!" Dan tried to push his way into the house but Ellen put an arm out, blocking him. He looked at her in confusion.

"Tristan," said Ellen.

"Ellen," said Tristan.

I glanced back and saw Joey lounging in the doorway behind me, his hands in his pockets.

"Please, come in," said Tristan.

Ellen didn't move. "That's okay, thanks. We're just here to collect Liss."

Tristan folded his arms. "Yeeeeah, she's going to stay here for a few days." He gestured; "You can too, if you like. We have plenty of room."

Ellen pushed her leather jacket back. She was wearing a gun. And a knife. She probably had ninja stars in her pockets, for all I knew.

"Liss, come on, I want to get my car back tonight."

I didn't honestly think Tristan was going to let me leave, but I gave it my best shot. I shoved my way past Caleb and sprinted for the door. I got halfway across the foyer before Joey caught me. He swung me around and pushed me against the wall, then stood in front of me with an eyebrow raised, daring me to try and get through him.

Ellen's expression hardened. "Do you really want to do this?" she asked Tristan.

"Two days, Ellen. Riley can help her transition."

"Let us leave, Tristan. I don't want to have to use force."

I tried to get around Joey and he pulled me back. I cried out as he bumped my broken finger.

Ellen drew her gun and Cole followed suit, holding his gun pointed at the ground, waiting for Ellen's command.

Dan wisely backed away from the guns.

"Let Liss leave, Tristan," said Ellen. "I won't ask again."

Tristan glanced over his shoulder. "Joey, take Liss back to the lounge."

Ellen sighted her gun on Joey—and me. Very fragile, human me.

"Now, you don't want to shoot me," said Joey. "Not through her, anyway."

Holding me in front of him as a shield, he pulled me back towards the lounge.

It was now or never. I twisted out of his grip and dropped to the floor. In what seemed like the same moment, Ellen shot him in the chest.

Caleb fled into the lounge as Joey staggered away from Ellen. Ellen turned her gun on Tristan and pushed her way into the house. He put his hands up and watched her warily.

I joined Dan, while Cole manhandled Joey into the lounge. The gunshot wouldn't kill Joey, but if it'd hit his lung—which it looked as though it might have—that'd slow him down for a bit. I heard a second shot and guessed that Cole had shot Caleb for good measure.

I waited for a third shot and heard nothing. Where was Riley?

Ellen gestured with her head. "Okay you two, get to the car."

"There's one more," I said to Ellen. "She's not a wolf; she's a forest dog, whatever that is. Brandt was scared of her; we probably should be too—"

"Go!"

Dan caught my upper arm and pulled me away from the house.

A few feet from the car, Riley appeared out of the darkness. That enigmatic smile, those husky-blue eyes.

"The offer's still open," she said. Dan's eyes widened as he felt her presence. The shouting behind us dulled, replaced by the sound of cicadas and the scent of dry pine needles. I could smell rain on the wind.

Ellen and Cole were suddenly beside us.

"Word to the wise," said Ellen to Riley. "This is not how you gain power."

The corner of Riley's mouth twitched in the faintest smile. She stepped aside.

"Dan, Liss, get in the car. Cole, you can follow us in Dan's car."

Inside the car, Ellen holstered her gun and held out her hand for the keys. I handed them to her and the car purred to life.

As we took off in a hail of gravel, Ellen glanced over at me. "Never, ever take my car again."

"Tell me everything," said Ellen, once we were on the road. "Who hurt your hand?"

"His name's Caleb," I said. "Not a nice guy."

Ellen made a noise of disgust. "Did you see the rest of the pack while you were there?"

"No," I said. "Just Tristan, Riley, and those two thugs, Caleb and Joey."

"It's bad enough that he pushed his father out, but

pushing him out of his family home? That's low." She sounded angry.

I understood. Tristan had gone against everything the wolves believed in, disrespecting the rule of his elders, humiliating his father. It wasn't going to win him any friends.

"What happens now?" I asked. The throbbing in my finger was getting worse as the painkillers Riley had given me wore off.

"That's up to Tristan," she said. "Where's Brandt now?"

"He took off when he found out Riley Copeland's a forest dog. He must have been working with them, but it seems Riley's become more powerful than Brandt expected. They told him to get lost after he suggested they kill me."

Dan leaned between the seats and took my hand from my lap. "Is it broken?" he asked, examining my finger.

"I heard it snap," I said, and felt him wince. He gave my hand back.

"I guess Brandt got his war," he said, his voice loaded with anger.

"The Alpha Circle will decide if it's war," said Ellen. "War benefits no one. Especially a war engineered by a vampire. Let's get Liss home and decide what to do next."

Chapter 24

It was early morning when we reached the reserve. I got out of the car feeling lightheaded with exhaustion and could see Dan wasn't far behind in the 'God, let me sleep' stakes.

Ellen was surprisingly alert, but that was Ellen. She thrived on adrenaline, and unlike me, she'd probably slept at some point in the last forty-eight hours.

I went down to my borrowed guest room, not bothering to turn on the light. I pulled off my clothes and was getting into bed when Dan knocked on the door.

"Can I come in?"

"If you leave the light off."

He came in and shut the door behind him.

"Do you want company?"

So much of me wanted to say *yes*. I couldn't deny my attraction to him anymore and I couldn't tell myself he didn't feel the same way. But years of watching him shag his way through the female population had left me wary. I had no idea if his girlfriends overlapped—there definitely weren't any gaps between them. Did I really want to be just one more?

I was silent too long. He put his hand on the door knob. "Let me know when you're ready."

A slice of light moved across the room as he left, closing the door behind him.

I pulled the covers up around me, too exhausted to deal with complicated emotions. They could wait until morning, when I was sure I'd have plenty of time to think about them.

I woke to the sound of muffled screaming and tried to sit up, but something was pinning me down. I opened my eyes and stared into the twilight of the darkened room, realising simultaneously that a) the sound was coming from me and b) nothing was holding me down. It took a few moments for the paralysis to drop away and I sat up, breathing hard.

"Liss?" Dan's head appeared around the doorway. "Freshen up—they want you upstairs in thirty minutes."

He disappeared again and I looked wearily around the room. Someone, probably Dan, had dropped my suitcase in a corner while I slept. I bundled some clothes together and went to find a free bathroom.

I went upstairs to the boardroom with a clear head, ready to hear the ACs' verdict.

The mood in the boardroom was sombre. Sometime while I'd been sleeping, Andy had arrived.

He looked exhausted as he got up to hug me.

"What happened to your finger?" he asked.

"A guy called Caleb. Don't worry, Cole shot him."

"Is he dead?"

"Probably not."

"Shame." He gave me a small smile and squeezed my good hand, before going back to his place at the table.

The ACs sat me at the head of the table, with Abigail and Kendrick on my left, Ellen and Cole on my right, and Andy, Isabella, Tane, and Anton at the far end.

"How's the finger?" Kendrick asked.

"Trying not to think about it," I said.

"Ellen's filled us in on the situation with the Copelands," said Abigail. "We need to know what happened with Brandt and any additional information you can give us about this 'forest dog', Tristan's sister."

I told them everything that'd happened. When I was done, they exchanged meaningful glances.

"And you didn't provoke them?" Isabella asked. "Threaten them?"

As much as I had respect for the Alpha Circle, I didn't enjoy the reminder that I was considered incapable of self-control by pretty much everyone.

"I didn't lay a hand on any of them." I held up my broken finger. "They weren't as restrained."

"Thanks, Liss," said Abigail. "You can go now. I'll be down in a little while to have a chat with you all. Make sure you stay close to the house. We don't know what Brandt might send next."

As I reached the bottom of the stairs, my jacket pocket vibrated. I pulled out my phone, then realised it wasn't my phone, it was the iPhone Brandt had given me.

I opened the message with a sense of dread.

The whole thing read '...'. Brandt's way of telling me he wasn't done with me yet. I killed the screen and put it back in my pocket. I was tempted to hand it to Tai, since he seemed to know how to disable phones, but something told me that it was better to communicate with Brandt by phone than to have him send messengers. Or worse, have him turn up in person. I didn't know how that would go, but I knew I didn't want to find out.

Abigail, true to her word, came down a few minutes later. She gathered me, Dan, Gracie, and Erin into the kitchen and slid the dividing door closed.

"All right. You're all aware that this has become a very serious situation. From what Liss has told us, I think we can put Brandt aside for the moment and deal with the Midlands pack crisis. At this time, Nicholas Copeland, their deposed alpha, is missing. We're not certain, but we don't think Tristan ousted him through a vote. With no information coming out of the Midlands, we fear Nicholas—and possibly other members of Tristan's family—may be dead."

"Do you think Tristan killed them?" I asked.

"There's only one way to find out for sure," she said. "Normally, we'd stay out of other packs' business, but this is a particularly bad time to have instability in our ranks. I'm going to take some people to the Midlands to find out what happened."

"But according to Brandt, Liss is going to come into her power in two days," said Dan. "Don't you think he's going to come after her again?"

"He's had ample opportunity to kill her," said Abigail. "Even though he tried to hand her to Tristan and his crew, I doubt he expected them to murder her in cold blood. I don't think that's his intention. Keeping us in chaos seems a more likely motivation. To what end, I'm not sure. But to ensure the safety of the pack, Kendrick will stay here, with Ellen and Cole as backup."

Dan shook his head. "You can't go down there without enforcers. What if they're hostile?"

She gave him a cool look. "We have two priorities. To ensure Liss reaches her potential safe and unharmed, and to try and mitigate the risk of our social ecosystem being collapsed by this vampire."

She got to her feet. "We'll head out shortly."

Dan dropped his gaze and she put a hand on his shoulder. "Dan, a good leader capitalises on their strengths and recognises their weaknesses. I know mine. I won't take any chances. But if there's an opportunity to end this before it begins, I'll do what I need to do."

He watched her go with fear-filled eyes.

"Dan?" I said. "Abigail and Kendrick have led the Westlands pack for how long now?"

Dan refused to answer.

"Forty-two years," said Gracie.

"Forty-two years," I said.

He looked up, his eyes red-rimmed. "In my lifetime, there's never been violence between wolves. How are we prepared for it? I love my parents, but they're not fighters. Ellen is."

"I believe Abigail knows what she is doing," said Gracie. "Before you were born, she was a young, strong wolf. Now she is older, wiser, and even stronger. She has led this pack for over forty years and has survived raising you and your brothers. She has brought peace to the wolves of this country with the Alpha Circle, something no other wolf could do. Have faith."

Dan gave her a faltering smile.

The brick in my pocket vibrated again but I ignored it. We did not need any more complications.

Abigail left just before midday, taking Isabella and Anton with her. I knew the three of them would be okay, but Dan's nervousness was starting to rub off on me. I was sure Abigail knew what she was doing. We just had to trust her.

As for Riley, I had no idea what she was capable of. Anton claimed to have at least heard of the legend, but couldn't tell us if she posed a risk or not.

Abigail wouldn't be drawn on how long she'd be gone, but she was insistent that the wolves concentrate on the grand transformation that'd be taking place in a couple of days, and let her do her thing.

Despite everything else I had to worry about, I couldn't help feeling nervous about what might happen in two days' time. I had no idea what to expect. Would it hurt? Would I suddenly be all-powerful? Or would the change in me be so underwhelming I didn't even notice it? Maybe I'd already changed. That was a depressing thought.

My pocket buzzed as I sat in the lounge.

Dan leaned into me. "I can hear it."

"What?"

"Every fifteen minutes it goes off. We can all hear it."

Stupid werewolf hearing.

I pulled the phone out and turned it so he could see the screen.

'We need to talk.

'We need to talk.'

'We need to talk.'

I wondered if Brandt had created a shortcut, if he copy-pasted, or if he'd typed the same message every fifteen minutes for two hours.

"He's persistent," said Dan, but the tone in his voice said something far less polite. "Do you think he'll come after you again?"

"What would be the point?"

"That depends," he said. "On what he really wants."

"He told Tristan he was afraid that if the packs amalgamated, we'd come after him."

"That threat hasn't changed," said Dan. "He has no reason to stop now."

I turned the phone over in my hand.

"But—he has so much power. He turned Karlo—why would any of us want to go after him, if he's that powerful?"

Dan frowned. "I want to talk to Karlo."

I followed him to the top of the stairs where Luke was guarding the entrance to the basement.

"Out of the way, Luke," said Dan. "We need to speak to Karlo."

Luke folded his arms. "Orders from the ACs are that no one speaks to him until the trial."

"There's still going to be a trial?" I asked. "Isn't it obvious he's not responsible?"

Luke levelled his gaze at Dan. "You know our minds can't be turned. It's never happened before, and it hasn't happened now."

I looked at Dan. "What's he talking about?"

Dan looked at the ground.

"Dan?"

He glanced sideways at me. "No records of it to date. But that doesn't mean it didn't happen. Come on, Luke, nothing about this is right. I need to know how he did it. How Brandt made him do it."

Luke stared at him in silence. Dan let out a noise of frustration. "Fine, I'll talk to Dad."

"You do that," said Luke. "He's the one who gave the order."

Dan found Kendrick sitting alone in the upstairs boardroom. He looked tired.

"Can I talk to you?"

Kendrick motioned us in. "You can't see Karlo," he said, before Dan had a chance to say anything. Werewolf hearing caught more private communications than the NSA.

"Why?"

Kendrick sighed. "By order of the Alpha Circle. The only person who will speak to him before the trial will be Cole."

"Cole?" I said, alarmed.

Dan was just as upset. "You can't let that maniac near him."

"Dan, he's my son. I'm not going to let anything happen to him. But Cole's considered impartial. He's also skilled at questioning."

Dan put his hands on the table. "We all know what that's a euphemism for."

"He's my *son*," said Kendrick. "And he's a grown man. He's agreed to be questioned. That's all there is to it." He stood and Dan, who stood an inch shorter than his father's six foot one, visibly shrank another inch.

"Brandt's still trying to contact Liss. The more we know about what happened to Karlo, the better prepared we'll be for his next move."

Kendrick stared at Dan. To his credit, Dan held his gaze.

"What if Dan and I just watch?" I suggested. Kendrick's gaze slid to me. "After all, I'm the one Brandt's stalking. Shouldn't I have all the facts?"

Kendrick considered me. He put his hands in the pockets of his slacks and I could see him trying to decide if I'd keep my word.

"Please," said Dan. "Don't leave him alone with Cole."

Perhaps Kendrick had the same reservations we did. "I'll talk to Tane and Ellen," he said. "In the meantime, hang fire."

Dan gave a quick nod. I followed him out of the boardroom.

"What did he mean, Cole's skilled at questioning?" I asked Dan, as we walked down the stairs.

"It means he knows how to get answers," said Dan, "from wolves who don't want to talk."

We walked through the crowded lounge and out onto the porch, where Isabella was leaning on the railing, smoking a cigarette.

Dan leaned on the railing beside her.

She glanced at him. "Hello handsome."

He gave her a dazzling smile. "Hi Isabella. Hey, can I bum a smoke?"

I stared at him while she gave him a wry look. "I guess so."

She pulled out a pack, tapped one out, and gave it to him. He put it in his mouth and she lit it for him, shielding the flame with her hand.

"Thanks."

"Just don't tell your mother."

She finished up her own cigarette and flicked the butt into the garden. She went back inside, leaving us alone on the porch.

"What the hell?" I said, when she'd gone.

"Please don't."

In all the time I'd known Dan, he'd never smoked. And I'd known him since he was a teenager.

"But you don't smoke."

He gave a humourless laugh. "How would you know? You've been gone for months."

He took a deep drag and I had to admit, he certainly did look like a smoker.

"What?" he said. "You think I was happy with the way we left things?"

"I—what?" It dawned on me what he was saying. "I honestly didn't think you cared. Why would you care?"

His cigarette clamped between two fingers, he wiped his face with his hands, smoke curling into his hair.

"How long have we known each other, Liss?"

I shrugged. Maths was not my strong suit. "Nine… nearly ten years?"

"And in that time, how many girls have I dated?"

I started counting on my fingers. "Let's see, not counting under the age of sixteen, there was Dahlia—and I'm sure that wasn't her real name—she was year eleven. Then Brooke—although I think that was only two months in year twelve. Then that same year there was Charlotte and Emilia, then in year thirteen there was Evelyn, then during the one year you did at uni before you dropped out, Fleur, then Hannah—in fact, I wouldn't be surprised if you'd made your way through half the alphabet by now."

Dan exhaled smoke away from me. "And how

many boys have you dated in that time?"

My face burned. "Are you deliberately being an asshole?"

"No, come on, let's count them," he said. He held up his hand and extended a finger. "There was that nice kid who everyone thought was gay, and who turned out to be dating you because he was interested in Tai." He extended two fingers. "Then there was the douche bag who slept with you once and never spoke to you again."

"And Dominic," I said quietly.

"Oh, and *Dominic*. He was a class act. Nine months, and how many other girls was he fucking while he was going out with you?"

My eyes blurred with tears. This was why I'd never tried to date Dan. This cold, bastard part of him that slapped me in the face at the slightest hint we might get close.

"What's your point?"

He pulled angrily on his smoke. "It never once occurred to you that a decent guy might be a good alternative to that list of losers?"

I shook my head at him. "Yeah, of course, and where would I find one of those?"

He waved his cigarette hand at me, sending smoke in a lazy circle.

"I have no idea. No idea." He turned away from me and finished his smoke, flicking the butt into the garden. As he stalked back into the house, I sat down on the porch steps and leaned against the railing.

If I'd thought I could trust him, I would have tried

to make something happen. But the way he went through women, how could I? And then he got like this—cruel and dark and exactly the kind of guy my fathers warned me about. I respected myself too much to get involved with a guy like that.

But, a voice said inside my head, *not enough to keep out guys like Dominic.*

I'd loved Dominic. I was seventeen and he was sexy as hell, a couple of years older than me and smiley. He was fun—he had energy. Apparently, quite a lot of it. He wasn't sarcastic, and he didn't sulk when he didn't get his way.

I'd believed him when he said he was out with the guys, because that was who he was. Who I'd thought he was.

Tears ran down my face. *Screw* Dan. Screw him for making me feel small and alone and, more than anything, stupid.

I felt an arm snake around me as Erin sat down next to me.

"Is he being an ass again?" she asked.

I nodded. "Yep. We had our ten minutes of being civil, apparently."

She squeezed my shoulders. "The dude's got issues," she said. "Don't let him get to you. Not when you're surrounded by this lot."

It was true, Dan wasn't the only wolf around who'd indicated his interest, but a tiny part of my mind had always suggested that if I started something with another wolf, Dan and I would never be. Period. And I wasn't sure why that bothered me, when Dan could be such a gigantic tool. I was not going to be one of those women who was attracted to douchebags. I was going to find someone decent.

Preferably outside the Stoke gene pool.

Chapter 25

Fifteen minutes later, Dan appeared in the doorway, behaving as if nothing had happened. "Come on, Cole's going to question Karlo." I stared at him. "Now!" he said, and went back inside.

Erin and I exchanged a look. "I'm starting to see why you sprained his wrist," she said.

"I very rarely hurt Dan," I said, "but when I do, it's because he has a long history of being a dick."

She laughed as I got to my feet. "It's going to be okay," she said.

Yeah. With a friend like her, it probably was.

Before we went downstairs, Cole took us to one side.

"If you're going to sit in on this, there are rules," he said. "You don't speak. You don't interfere, and if I tell you to leave, you leave. Got it?"

We both nodded.

He scratched his neck, and I could see he wasn't at all comfortable about the situation.

"I need you to watch your expressions," he said.

"If I'm working with Karlo and you're standing behind me tearing that down, I can't do my job. D'you understand?" He looked at us both and shook his head in disgust. "Just, stay out the way."

There was tense silence between us as we descended the steps.

Luke unlocked Karlo's cell to let the three of us in, then locked the door behind us.

Karlo stood as Cole approached him and clasped his hand. "You all right, mate?"

Karlo nodded, not meeting anyone's eyes.

"Have a seat," said Cole. Karlo sat on the wooden bench that ran along one wall and Cole pulled up a stool. "Bit chilly in here, innit?" he said.

Karlo gave him a sad look that said he didn't care, hadn't noticed, had other things on his mind. His eyes were bloodshot from crying.

Cole pointed to me and Dan.

"These two are here to listen in, see if they can pick up some useful information. You okay with that?"

Karlo nodded. "Of course."

"Brilliant." Cole leaned forward with his elbows on his knees and his hands clasped in front of him. "What's key to me right now is that we save your life. You know, that lot up there, they're not sure what's happened, right? They're nervous. They don't understand how a wolf had his mind turned. So, my job is to help them understand. That's all. Just understand what happened."

Karlo nodded again. He pushed his long hair back

behind his ears.

"The one thing I'm most worried about is you beating yourself up. 'Cause I've seen a lot of people who've done a lot of bad things in my time, and I know that look. You feel guilty mate, don't you?"

"How could I not?" asked Karlo.

"Right, I know, I know. The thing is, in order to prove you're innocent, you need to believe you're innocent. So, no matter how bad you feel about what you did—what he made you do—you need to hold on to the fact that this wasn't your fault. And then I need you to help me to figure out *why* this wasn't your fault. Understand?"

Karlo nodded.

"Okay, now don't worry, I've done this for a lot of people and I know what I'm doing. I'm just going to jog your memory—that's all I'm going to do. Take you through what happened so we have all the facts. And in there, will be the truth."

"What if I don't remember?"

Cole nodded. "It's imperative, and I think you know this, that you do remember. So hold on to that and we'll start at the beginning."

Karlo looked past Cole at me and Dan.

Cole followed his gaze, then turned back to Karlo.

"Yeah, the other thing—ignore those two. They have to be here, and that's fine, but they're not going to help you out of this mess. So, concentrate on me, and let's get started."

Karlo fixed his eyes to Cole's face.

"Right. We're going to go back to the day of Jack's

death. What do you remember?"

Karlo thought hard. "I remember the night before," he said. "But nothing from that day."

"Right. So tell me about the night before. 6 p.m. Where were you?"

"At the bar. Just an ordinary night."

Cole nodded. "6 p.m. What were you *doing* at the bar?"

Karlo shrugged helplessly. "I don't remember."

Cole shuffled on his stool. "The devil's in the details, Karlo. I'm going to give you a minute, let you clear your head, then we're going to figure out what you were doing at 6 p.m. the night before Jack's death."

Jack's death. Jack's *murder*. Dan dug me sharply in the ribs with his elbow. I got it. My face. Always a dead giveaway, my face.

"You got on well with Jack, didn't you?" said Cole.

"Yeah, absolutely. Everyone did."

"And where would you say he came in the pecking order?"

Karlo eyed him warily. "He was Kendrick and Abigail's second."

"And you were all good with that, yeah?" asked Cole.

Karlo nodded. "Yeah, of course, he was a good guy. He earned it."

"A good guy. Yeah, I heard that too. A good guy. Okay, so, let's go back to the night before. Six o'clock. You're in the bar, the early drunks and the dinner patrons are starting to arrive. Where are you?"

Karlo swallowed. "I think I was out the back, supervising the orders."

"D'you do that a lot?" asked Cole.

"I keep an eye on everyone," said Karlo. "Just wherever I need to be."

"All right. You were in the kitchen at six. What about seven o'clock?"

"I... I spend a lot of my time out the back."

"Hanging out?" Cole asked with a grin.

"Yeah, you know, we play cards, I keep an eye on things."

"So who was with you that night?"

Karlo sniffed and wiped his nose. "Ah, Glenn was there. Ben, I think. Some of the others from Ellen's pack—they come and go, you know, they drop in for a drink or a chat."

"Good," said Cole. "That's great, you're doing great. So we've got Glenn, Ben—both your brothers—what about Tai?"

Karlo shook his head. "I don't... think so. Maybe?"

"Does he usually come to the pub?"

Karlo seemed unsure. "Sometimes."

"But not that night?"

Karlo took a shuddering breath. "Maybe later on. I don't remember."

"Okay, so seven o'clock, we've got you, your brothers Ben and Glenn, and maybe Tai joined you later on. Eight o'clock. Who've we got?"

Karlo licked his lips. "I don't know, I wasn't keeping track of time. We play poker, you know, just

259

out the back—"

"Who was winning?" asked Cole.

Karlo stared into space. He pressed his palms together and put his hands to his mouth. Cole let him think. "I think it was Ben."

"Okay, good, mate, that's good. Nine o'clock. What's happening?"

Karlo's composure broke. "I don't know! I don't know what time it was—I don't know who was there, I don't know what I was doing!"

Cole put a hand out. "Easy, easy, mate. He came in, didn't he? Brandt. Around nine?"

Karlo shook his head in frustration. "I can't remember!"

Cole leaned forward on his stool. "You can, mate. You can."

Karlo got to his feet, a finger pointed a finger back at his chest. "You don't get it—I can't remember! It's just a blur."

Cole stayed sitting. He pointed at the bench. "Sit down, mate."

Karlo stared at him wildly, his chest heaving.

"Sit down."

Karlo took a deep, shuddering breath. He wiped his sweaty palms against his jeans and sank back on to the bench.

"You need to concentrate. I can help you. I can give you a drug—"

Karlo shook his head. "No."

Cole carried on calmly, "I can give you a drug that'll help you relax. Help you calm down.

260

Whatever he's done to your brain, it'll help unlock it."

Karlo looked at him warily. "What drug?"

Cole pulled a small plastic bag from his pocket. It held a small yellowish-coloured pill.

"You'll like it," he said. "It's nothing you've not taken before."

Karlo gave a short laugh. "And that'll help me remember?"

"Help you relax, mate. Tell you what, I'm going to leave this here—you've got your water there, and I'll come back in twenty minutes and see how you're feeling. How does that sound?"

Karlo considered this and finally nodded.

"Okay. We'll see you soon."

Luke let us out of the cell and locked it behind us. Cole gestured to me and Dan. "You two, upstairs. I want to talk to you both."

Cole took us upstairs to the boardroom.

"I don't want you to come back down. I need to lead him through something he doesn't want to remember. That's hard when you've got an audience—it'll pull him out of the state I want him in."

I had to admit, things hadn't gone the way I'd thought they would. I'd thought he was going to threaten Karlo, even torture him. But instead, he was trying to be his friend. Trying to save him.

"We need to know," said Dan. "We're running out of time. Brandt wants to speak to Liss—we need to know how he managed to capture a wolf's mind."

"Don't you think," said Cole, "that's what I'm trying to find out?"

"We have permission to be there," said Dan. "I'm not leaving you alone with my brother."

Cole sat back in his chair. "So that's it, is it? You've got a problem with me, always have had. What'd I ever do to you, Dan? Tease you? Bit of ribbing every now and then?"

Dan's look was cold. "He's my brother. I don't want you taking his words out of context. His life's on the line."

"Oh, that is magnificent," said Cole. "You're actually accusing me of wanting your brother dead now, are you?"

Dan knew he'd gone too far.

"Cole, you obviously know what you're doing," I said. "Dan's just afraid for his brother. I'm sure you can understand that. Please let us stay. I promise we won't interfere."

Cole considered us both. "I meant what I said before. I need to get *your* brother"—he pointed at Dan—"to go back into a memory he isn't particularly fond of. If you interrupt me, if you do anything, if you so much as breathe too loudly, I will personally throw you out of this house. Do you understand?"

Dan nodded in sullen silence.

"All right, ten-minute break. Get a coffee, take a piss—I'll meet you back down there."

Dan pushed back his chair and yanked open the boardroom door. In his wake, Cole pyramided his hands and pointed them at me.

"Liss, I need you to promise me something."

"What?" I had a feeling whatever came out of his mouth next was going to annoy me.

"Don't let your emotions get the better of you. We're on the brink of war. Every one of us is trying to stop that from happening. No matter what you hear, promise you won't go off half-cocked again."

As if I was the emotional one.

"Let me worry about me."

I started for the door, but Cole shoved his seat back and got up, putting an arm out to block me from leaving.

"I'm not being an asshole," he said. "I'm trying to make sure we all get through this alive."

I stared at him, stony-faced.

"Liss, please. Promise me you won't leave the pack again."

Well, he had said 'please'. I nodded. He moved out of the doorway and I headed after Dan, suddenly feeling the need for a smoke myself.

Fifteen minutes of tense silence later, Dan and I joined Cole back in the basement. Karlo smiled at us when we came into his cell through half-closed eyelids.

"Feeling better?" Cole asked.

Karlo nodded.

"Great. Let's try again." Cole sat back on his stool. "Okay, I'm going to ask you to close your eyes and keep 'em closed. We're going to go back to that night."

Karlo closed his eyes and rested his head against the wall.

"Six o'clock. You're at the bar. You're in the kitchen. There's rushing about and food frying and orders coming in. Seven o'clock, you're out the back, playing poker with your brothers. Eight o'clock, playing poker and Ben's winning. Nine o'clock. What are you doing?"

Karlo's face twisted with anguish.

"Relax, mate, it's already happened."

Karlo's fists clenched and unclenched as he fought the memory.

"Someone's come into the bar," said Cole. "Who is it?"

Karlo, eyes still closed, shook his head. "Tai — and he's with a girl."

A girl? A friend, maybe?

"Who's the girl?" asked Cole. "Do you know her?"

"No," said Karlo, "she must be human — I can't feel her. She's got dark skin but incredibly pale blue eyes —"

Oh no.

Cole shifted on his stool. "What's happening?" he asked.

"They're dancing. Tai's heading to the bathroom. She's motioning me over." A pause. "We're talking. She says she wants me to *fucking God, no!*"

Karlo's eyes flew open and he jumped to his feet. Cole rose with him and put his hands on his shoulders.

"What did she want you to do, Karlo? Tell me."

"She wants me to kill someone and she's talking and I can... I can smell the forest and hear birds and smell blood—"

Cole tightened his grip on Karlo's shoulders.

"Why're you listening to her, Karlo?"

Karlo looked into Cole's face, his eyes wide and staring. "Because she can make me listen to her. Because she smells like rain after a thunderstorm. She talks and I want—I *have* to make her happy." Tears ran down his face.

Cole kept his hands on Karlo's shoulders and gently pushed him back down. He sat back on his stool.

"What happens next?"

Karlo shook his head.

"Close your eyes. Don't look at me. We need to know. What happens next."

Karlo closed his eyes and bent forward, his head in his hands. "She goes, Tai goes, and I go home. God. I went home, I went to sleep. I felt good."

"Okay, mate, we're getting somewhere. This is important. Did any of the others see this girl? Did Ben or Glenn see her? Talk to her?"

Karlo shook his head miserably. "I don't think so."

Cole pulled Karlo's hands gently away from his face. "Okay. Thank you," he said.

He stood and Karlo looked up at him. "They're going to execute me, aren't they?"

Cole sighed. "Not if I can help it."

Luke let him out of the cell.

Dan got to his feet. There was rage in his eyes.

Karlo put a hand on his brother's arm. "Don't go near her Dan."

He put his head back in his hands and I grabbed Dan's sleeve again and pulled him after me.

Cole left us at the top of the basement stairs.

"Don't tell a soul what you just heard," he said. "I need to talk to Kendrick, and then see if baby Stoke remembers anything from that night. Keep out of trouble till I come find you."

Chapter 26

Cole went up to the boardroom, while I stalked outside. "I'm gonna kill her. I'm gonna fucking kill her."

Dan followed me out and watched me pace.

"You really think she's got the power to turn his mind?"

I shrugged. "I don't know what she is, but you know Karlo's not weak."

He looked down in disgust. "Yeah, well, I didn't feel anything off her that scared me."

"So she didn't turn the bullshit ray on you. Doesn't mean she can't."

"I guess," he said. "So did Brandt tell her to come after us?"

I thought about it. "If he did, he wasn't specific. He seemed confused when I accused him of killing Jack, so maybe that wasn't his plan. And Riley set Karlo up before we'd even gone against Brandt's orders."

"Maybe he figured we would, and put some insurance in place. What were the chances we'd do what he wanted us to? The way I see it, they're both responsible."

And we knew where she was. I thought of my promise to Cole not to react to anything Karlo told us.

Dan read my mind.

"You can't go after her."

"Yeah, I know." But something else was bugging me. Why? Why would she work with Brandt at all?

"What if he's controlling her?" I said.

He folded his arms and leaned his back against the railing. "Is that likely?"

I shook my head. "I don't know. "I just don't understand why she'd come after us. Even if she and Tristan wanted to control the Midlands pack, what's that go to do with us?"

He shrugged.

Erin came out on to the deck. "How's it going down there?"

I told her what we'd learned.

She leaned back on the railing next to Dan. "Wow. So she can bend the wolves, just like that?"

Dan looked dubious. "Maybe."

"I don't see any other explanation," I said. "So yeah. Looks like she's our biggest threat right now."

I caught sight of Gracie sitting on a bench at the end of the garden, deep in thought. I walked down the steps to the garden and approached her.

"Hey Gracie."

She acknowledged me with a nod, her eyes fixed to a wildflower as she twirled it between her fingers.

"Have you heard of skoghunds? They're from your part of the world."

She squinted up at me, shading her eyes from the sun. "They are a legend. They do not exist anymore."

Dan and Erin joined us. "How long ago did they go extinct?" asked Dan.

She shrugged. "Four hundred, five hundred years ago. Assuming they ever existed."

Oh, they definitely existed.

"It was thought that they were a metaphor for the spirits of the dead," she said. "There is a prophecy—a warning not to wake them. Give me a moment to translate it to English."

She thought for a while, then said, "You may call the forest dogs to aid you in battle, but you will lose your lands to them. Awake again, they possess the land, and you will need their permission, or they must sleep again, so that you can walk freely on it once more."

That did not sound good.

The iPhone in my pocket buzzed. I pulled it out and we crowded around it.

The text read: *'Riley has your alpha.'*

"Dammit!" I said, "Does he know everything?"

"Yep," said Dan. "Seems like."

The phone buzzed again.

'I don't suppose your boyfriend needs two parents.'

Dan took the phone from me. *'Where?'* he texted back.

Three winking dots, then an address.

"If we tell the others they won't let us go," I said.

"What if he kills her?"

I shoved the phone back in my pocket as Dan's brother, Glenn, strode across the lawn towards us.

"You lot, get back inside. Kendrick wants to talk to you. We just got another text."

"Is it Abigail?" Dan asked.

Glenn looked grim. "No, from Brandt. Abigail's not answering her phone."

Dan looked up at the darkening sky, his breathing shallow with a mix of panic and anger.

"What did it say?" I asked.

"Queen takes queen."

Kendrick was waiting for us in the lounge. When the hubbub died down, he addressed the pack.

"I know that there's a great deal of angst about Abigail's mission to the Midlands, but right now it's more important than ever to not let this vampire manipulate us. If they want a war, let them bring it to us — to our territory. We will not be responsible for taking hostile action on their soil."

"What if he really does have Abigail?" asked Ben. "And we just let him kill her, the way he killed Jack?"

Kendrick's smile was strained. "He's taunting you. Surely you can see that."

Luke spoke up. "Shouldn't we go help her?"

"No," said Kendrick patiently, "To send more wolves would be considered an act of hostility, and it'll be viewed that way by other packs we need as allies. We wait until we know if this is just Tristan and Riley, or if more of the Midlands pack's

270

involved. If Nicholas needs our help, we'll support him. If he's dead, then we may need to act."

"But they hurt Liss... they were hostile first. Why can't we attack them back?" asked Luke.

"This is our decision," said Kendrick.

Luke dipped his head as Kendrick's power pushed out from him, an uncomfortable pressure that made my skin crawl, and the wolves look anywhere but directly at their alpha.

"What about just going after Riley?" I said into the uneasy silence. "As far as I can see, she's the real threat, not Brandt."

Kendrick stepped through the crowd and the wolves moved to let him through. He reached me and put a hand on my shoulder. It was a common gesture among the wolves and it could mean a number of things, from companionship to outright domination. Right now there was weight to his touch; a reminder that he was an alpha and his word was our law.

"Liss, you've got to be patient. In two days' time, everything could change. Brandt's counting on disrupting us here and now, leaving you vulnerable to exploitation. I won't let that happen."

I bit the inside of my lip while I found the courage to say what I thought needed to be said.

"I understand why you want us to wait—I do. And you're right. If the wolves go down there, it could spark a war. Which is why I'd like permission to go meet Brandt. Just find out what he wants. What he knows. He's not going to hurt me, we know that—

271

not if I do what he wants. I don't think he's working with Riley anymore. And I think she's far more dangerous to us than he is right now."

Kendrick gave me a level stare. "I'm not asking you to pretend nothing's happened. I'm not asking you to forgo avenging Jack's death. I'm asking you to trust that we know what we're doing and stay put for at least the next couple of days. There are larger forces at work."

We didn't have two days. Even as he was speaking, the phone was buzzing in my pocket.

"This is not about revenge!" I said. "Now that I know he won't kill me, I want to know what he wants. I want to stop anyone else getting hurt."

Kendrick's expression was one a man wears when he thinks if he stays silent, you'll talk yourself out of an idea. It wasn't going to work on me.

He sighed. "There won't be any more discussion on this."

"I'm going." I pulled away from him, but his hand landed on my shoulder again, an iron weight that stopped me mid-stride.

"You're not."

I would have taken him to one side to prevent embarrassment, but what would have been the point? Every wolf there would hear what we had to say, even through a closed door.

I turned back to him. "Kendrick, I'm not a wolf."

There was a warning in his eyes. He knew where this was going.

"Unless you plan on physically restraining me,

you can't keep me here."

"Let me ask you a question, Liss. Do you really want to walk out that door without the pack at your back?"

"Of course not. But I understand why it has to be this way."

"If you leave now, you'll be on your own."

Dan stepped forward to argue, but Kendrick put up a hand. His presence filled the air with a choking warning.

"No debate," said Kendrick. "This is too important. Liss, my primary concern is the safety of the pack. I can't let you put us all at risk."

"Meaning?" I knew being disrespectful was a bad move, but I was getting annoyed. I was trying to save human lives. It wasn't as though the wolves couldn't look after themselves, with their speed healing, their super strength and their heightened senses. Hiding when they were that powerful seemed to me to be... cowardly.

"Meaning to prevent further loss of life, if you insist on doing this, I will let you go. And so will the rest of the pack."

I looked around for Andy but couldn't see him among the silent wolves.

"Where's Andy?"

"He didn't want to stay here... with Karlo," said Ben quietly, keeping his eyes downcast so that he didn't meet Kendrick's gaze.

I was wasting time. "I need to go."

Kendrick lifted his hand and I headed for the

door.

Ellen spoke up. "Liss."

That one word held a volume of warnings, and I heard and understood every one.

Erin was leaning against the wall in the hall. "Just us then?"

I gave her an appreciative smile. "Yeah."

Dan followed us out on to the porch. "I wish you wouldn't."

I shrugged. "I don't see another option."

"Please be careful."

I nodded. "Always."

He rolled his eyes.

I cleared my throat. "Can we borrow your car? Erin's is still back at the flat in Palmy."

Without saying anything, he handed me the keys.

His gaze was flat, and I wondered if he was ashamed he hadn't backed me up. Too late now.

I checked the address Brandt had texted to the iPhone. It was only an hour's drive away. This would all be over one way or another soon enough.

The rest of the wolves filtered out on to the porch as we got into Dan's car.

Dan glanced from me to his father. He was clearly torn—but pack was pack. At the heart of Dan was a very obedient wolf.

Carrying the weight of the wolves' stares, I backed the car out and drove off down the drive.

No one tried to call me back.

We drove into the night, following Brandt's

instructions, and finally found the turnoff and drove down a dirt road into the forest.

I pulled up next to a picnic shelter and turned off the engine.

"Could he have picked a creepier place to meet?" Erin asked.

"I'm sure if he could have, he would have."

We got out of the car.

The night was cold, a breeze stirring through the trees like voices whispering on the edge of hearing. I hunched down into my jacket as I leaned against the car, unsure what to expect. He could bend both our minds, but I didn't think he would. I wasn't sure why... it was just a feeling. This was solely an act of faith—faith that my instinct was correct and this was the right thing to do.

With the car headlights off, all we had was weak moonlight. Somewhere in the darkness nearby, I could hear a stream flowing. The sound invoked a vision of slow-moving water filled with eels and choked with weed.

I shivered in the cold and put a hand up to the silver pendant around my neck. I wasn't getting much from it. If there was deep power in this place, the silver couldn't feel it.

Erin wrapped her cardigan around her and leaned against the car beside me.

"Can you feel anything?" she asked.

I shook my head. "I don't know how much warning we'll get with Brandt."

She was silent for a moment. "Do you think the

275

wolves would really kick you out of the pack?"

"I don't know. I'm so used to being around them, I forget they have these stupid arcane rules. I think Kendrick just needed to make an example. Those boys are hard to hold back when they're pissed at the best of times. If he didn't lay down the law, it'd be chaos."

The wind blew a scatter of leaves past our feet with a sound like hard-shelled things travelling on too many legs. I was glad we didn't have scorpions here.

The breeze picked up and I looked up into the trees, half expecting to see something there; a dark shape, or red eyes glowing in the dark.

"I've been thinking," said Erin. "About why Dan behaves like he does."

"Yeah?" I said, listening to her, but also listening to the forest. He couldn't be far away. I could feel something. I just wasn't sure what.

"I think he's in—"

Her words faded as what little light there was warped briefly, and then Brandt was two feet in front of me.

"Alessandra, thank you for coming. Erin." He nodded towards her.

"Fuck you," she spat.

Brandt looked taken aback. For a moment he looked confused, before his expression smoothed back to casual condescension.

"I'm surprised to see you out here all alone, without the dark-haired boy you both fancy."

I glanced at Erin in surprise.

"He's cute, okay? I'd never go there."

I shook my head and pulled my focus back to Brandt.

"Like she said, fuck you. What do you want?"

Brandt rolled his eyes. "You need my help, so let's be civil."

"Your help with what?"

He gestured to the forest. "Keeping you alive until you're ready to join me."

"Did you bring sweets?" I asked.

He looked confused.

"If you want to lure kids into your van, you need to bring sweets."

A look of annoyance flashed across his face. "You're quite safe from me in that regard."

I snorted.

"Alessandra, I'm helping you out. Don't be ungrateful."

Ungrateful? I slid EMN from its sheath.

"You need to know what you face," he said, ignoring the knife. "I've provided you with the opportunity to practice. I wouldn't squander it, if I were you."

"Why would you help me? I've already told you I'll never work for you. I'd rather die."

He considered me. "Don't be so dramatic. I'm trying to *help* you. And you'll change your mind at some point. It's only a matter of time." He glanced at Erin. "And finding the right incentive."

"You could force her... couldn't you?" said Erin.

"Isn't that what vampires do?"

He gazed at her, a slight smile turning up the corner of his mouth. "There's no point in taming a wild animal if you have to muzzle it."

Charming analogy.

I folded my arms, the knife still in my hand. "Why are we here, Brandt?"

He walked off a short distance, scanning the forest. Listening. He turned back to us. "You have enemies who could destroy us all if you don't destroy them first."

"Really? You think Riley's the threat now, not me, is that it? What's she got over you? Why can't you just kill her?"

He was silent.

"Seems to me if she meant you harm, she'd have come after you by now. Maybe it's not all about you."

The corner of Brandt's mouth quirked in a mirthless smile. One minute he was standing two feet away, the next he was a foot away, holding my knife. He held the knife out to me, handle first. I took it, spooked into silence.

"Don't worry about *why*, Alessandra. Worry about defending yourself."

He turned his back and walked back into the gloom.

"What am I looking for?" I called after him.

"Anything that seems as if it might want to kill you."

I glanced at Erin. "Screw this, I didn't come out here to play games. Let's get out of here." I patted my pockets, searching for Dan's car keys and found nothing. "You got the keys?"

She frowned and checked her pockets. "Nope."

From the darkness came a familiar jangle and the sound of keys flying through the air and landing in leaf litter. Where? Impossible to tell.

The breeze rose, rustling through the fallen leaves, bringing a scent of black water and the bitter tang of vegetation crushed underfoot. Moonlight silvered the ground around us, enough to navigate by if we stuck to the open. It was too dark to try and walk into the trees.

"Let's go back to the road," I said. "Maybe we can flag down a car."

Erin nodded quickly.

Neither of us liked the idea of something unknown watching us from the forest. I wanted to think Brandt was just doing this to torment me in his usual fashion, but there was a smell on the breeze that made me nervous. Something was out there.

We headed down the dirt trail, where the trees that hung over the track obliterated the light in dirty patches, leaving us to walk in the shadows for minutes at a time.

As much as I tried to be the big, bad thing in the night, I had to admit, the other things that could be out there made me feel like a kitten crawling around in a gin trap factory.

I fought the urge to run as the forest creaked around us in the wind, accompanied by that ever-present sound of water running and mystery thuds that reminded me of the dead possums I'd found in the forest on my last hunt.

The iPhone buzzed. I pulled it out and read as we walked through another patch of shadow.

'Wrong way! Behind you.'

I stopped. Erin glanced back at me. "Whatever it says, let's keep going. It can't be far to the road."

We kept going. Every now and then I caught a glimpse of what looked like a pale light in the woods that flanked the road. Then in a solid patch of darkness, I froze. I could just make out a canine shape, about the size of a Rottweiler. I was afraid to speak, to break the silence, in case it walked out of the trees and became real. Right now, I was hoping it'd resolve into something else—a tree stump, or a bunch of evil squirrels in a duffel coat.

I hadn't been afraid of the dark in years. Not since Jack had given me EMN and permission to stalk the things in my nightmares.

When I'd first come to live with Jack and Andy, my nightmares had followed me out of sleep and into my room in the middle of the night. They'd find me curled on the sofa in a ball, crying in terror.

They'd both taken turns comforting me in those first few weeks, but it was Jack who'd figured out what I needed.

One night as I lay on the couch, choking on tears, Jack came into the lounge. Instead of turning on the lights and trying to comfort me as he had in the past, he sat beside me in the dark and waited for me to calm down.

Confused, I eventually stopped crying and sat up. I remember his face in the dark, his eyes hidden in shadow. Suddenly afraid, I shrank away from him.

"What do you see?" he asked. "In your dreams?"

At the sound of his voice, the fear melted away. I crawled close to him, but he didn't put his arm around me. Not this time.

"He tears off her arm," I said. "And I kill him."

"You killed him," he said. "So why are you crying?"

I remember looking at him with wet eyes and snot coming out of my nose, thinking, *Why* am *I crying? Didn't I get the bad guy?* —and realising it wasn't enough. He hadn't suffered. He was already dead. He didn't feel pain or fear. Like a curious child pulling legs off a fly, he tore off my sister's arm. There was no answer to that. You can't deal with something like that by waiting for it to do wrong. You have to get there first.

"There are more," I said. "And I haven't killed them."

Jack's eyes were hollows turned towards me, the lights of the city glittering through the window at his back.

"Do you think they're going to hurt you?" he asked.

I laughed. I remember that. "No."

"But they might hurt someone else?"

I nodded. They were out there in the dark, curious and hungry, and there was no one to stand between them and kids like Zöe.

Jack held out a knife, the silver blade shining in the dim light. It was heavy and cold in my hand. Too heavy for me, back then. The handle was bound with leather I could smell was new.

"This belongs to the pack. But I think you should have it."

I ran my finger along the blade, feeling the outline of letters, but recognising none of the words.

"What does it say?"

"It's written in Old Wolf. It translates to something like, 'Fight bravely, die free'."

"Does it have a name?" I asked.

And that was where he made a fatal mistake.

So I'd fought the vamps and I'd stopped being afraid in the night because I knew I was doing everything I could.

But here, in this forest, my best friend at my side, my *best friend at my side*—oh God, what had I done bringing Erin into this?

"Liss?" whispered Erin. "What is it?"

Zöe was five, exactly five years younger than me, when she died, and she was a brat. She followed me everywhere, talked incessantly, and asked questions she already had the answers to.

Once she got past the age of tripping over things and hurting herself in her efforts to be my second shadow, I pretty much avoided her.

At ten years old, I was bulletproof. I could fight

the neighbourhood boys and win, could arm wrestle them all, swore just as much, ran just as fast, and I had one thing they didn't: complete confidence that I would always win.

So when I discovered the grave in the woods, I wasn't afraid—I was curious. Always attracted by the macabre and the sinister, I was the kind of child who buried a dead woodland creature with tears and sadness, then dug it up a month later to see what its skeleton looked like.

I knew the difference between dead and alive. Dead things didn't feel pain. They were empty shells, just the physical parts of us that decayed and went back to the earth.

The hills around our family home were densely forested, impassable in some places. But there were trails, some made by wild deer, some made by people. I'd go into the forest to find red-capped mushrooms and to look for cicada cases—the prehistoric and terrifying shells left behind when cicadas shed the skins of their larval forms and became harmless heralds of summer with gossamer wings.

I wandered those trails, enjoying the solitude, sometimes frightening myself by getting lost, and enjoying the thrill of trying to find my way back. To make sure I could find my way home, I broke the leaves of silver ferns, so that the pale underside of the leaf was showing.

One day, I wandered further than I'd been before. I'd been out all afternoon, even though rain was misting, mostly trying to avoid Zöe, who complained about *everything*, including dirt, uneven ground, and the smell of rotting leaves, and who was terrified of cicada cases, *even though* there was nothing in them.

My favourite game was to secretly attach one to her clothes, then wait for her to find it and scream.

That day, as afternoon gave way to evening, I found myself in a part of the woods I hadn't been before. Given I spent my life in the forest, that meant I had to be a long way from home. I was about to start back when I noticed something odd through a gap in the trees. I moved closer and saw that what looked like just a heap of earth, was in fact a heap of earth by a very large hole.

The soil smelled damp. I remember at the time, I just wanted to know what was in the hole. I walked up to the edge. It was very definitely a grave. I mean, you only dug a hole like that for one purpose. The other clue was that the hole was lined with a coffin. The lid was lying flat, chewed up and destroyed, half buried under the fresh soil.

It was just on dusk and the birds were roosting. I looked up and noticed there were none roosting in the trees above me. Odd. I looked around. There was no skeleton in the pit, so that meant whoever had dug it up had probably taken it somewhere.

I was excited. Someone else was just as curious as I was about what death looked like, and they'd done what I knew I was under no circumstances to ever do—they'd dug up someone's grave to have a look. And they'd taken the bones away.

That part was weird—I mostly wanted to look, maybe touch the bones, see what they felt like. See if I could face the dead with as much courage as I thought I could. But why take the body away?

I fancied myself a tracker and looked around the edge of the clearing. The sky had darkened to just the faintest hint of dark blue to the sky, but there was enough light to see a branch cracked open, exposing the pale wood inside. Something had come this way with the subtlety of a tornado.

I took off the small torch I wore around my neck and pulled out my penknife.

It wasn't hard to see where they'd gone—wherever trees had blocked the way, whoever had taken the body had crashed through, leaving a trail of broken branches, laced with the tang of fresh sap.

I picked up one of the broken-off branches and used it as a walking stick as I'd seen hikers do. I felt very clever, tracking this person by the trail they'd left behind.

As I walked, I sensed somehow that we were heading back towards the house. I don't know how—I relied on instinct a lot back then, and it rarely put me wrong.

It wasn't long before I found myself back on the main trail. No more smashed branches. I figured if they'd diverted off either side I'd see the carnage, so they'd probably taken the path. I kept going.

Twenty metres from where the trail opened up to our back lawn, I stopped. In front of me stood a man with his back to me. He was sniffing the air. I ran the torch over his back and saw his clothes were streaked with mud and sap.

Seeing the light play over the trees, he turned to face me, and I knew it wasn't a man.

The thing that stood in front of me had yellow eyes and dirt smeared across its face—had it chewed its way out of that coffin? The yellow eyes roved across me, and it scented the air again, its mouth working as if it was imagining what I would taste like.

As I stood frozen, Zöe came running across the lawn beyond, towards the trees where we stood, hidden from view.

"Aliss, Aliss, Mumma says come inside now!"

The vampire half turned towards her and fear poured through me. There was no time. As Zöe appeared, the vampire pounced. It grabbed her, one hand on her fragile shoulder, one around her throat. Its fingers dug into her flesh like claws and she screamed, a single constant note.

The vampire roared in her face and she burst into open-eyed tears, the kind that truly terrified children cry when they want to run away but can't.

The vamp lifted her into the air, holding her too hard, drawing blood where its fingers pierced her skin. It ran its nose down the side of her neck.

I only had one weapon and it was a stick. I knew what this thing was, had seen the movies. All I had to do was put the stick into the vampire.

Whatever spell of terror I was under suddenly broke. I dropped my torch, and holding the stick in front of me with two hands, I rushed at the vampire.

In the darkness, there was a ripping sound like a chicken leg torn from the carcass, a sound of tendons popping and wet meat tearing. Zöe went silent.

I speared the vamp with the stick as hard as I could, by some miracle piercing its heart. The thing collapsed in on itself, splashing me with putrid black muck.

I went back and fumbled for the torch and found Zöe lying on the pine needles, her left arm twisted off just above the elbow joint. A short distance away, the crushed remains of her arm nested in a pool of what looked like black stew.

I stared down at her, caught in the certainty this was a nightmare. I put a shaky hand to my face and wiped something away, then held up my fingers to the light. I had what looked like oil on my fingers.

This was real. This was real and Zöe needed me. Her eyes were closed, her skin deathly pale. Blood pulsed from the stump of her arm, between bones and trailing tendons, and pattered onto the leaves. I realised I was about to black out.

"Liss? I heard screaming." My mother. "Are you kids playing or is someone hurt? Liss?"

I gathered up Zöe in my arms and ran across the lawn towards the light.

I came back to *now* with those same black shapes swimming in front of my eyes. The memory I'd lived had only taken a moment to play out in my mind, and the shape was still there at the side of the dirt

287

track, watching us.

I swallowed. I wanted to move forward but my body wasn't in agreement. *Stand very still,* my brain said urgently. *Stay completely still forever and maybe it won't rip you both apart.*

Erin touched my arm. I took a shaky breath.

"Can you see it?" I said in a low voice.

"Are you looking at that tree stump?" she asked.

At her words, the shape resolved into what it was—just a tree stump. I collapsed into hysterical laughter.

"I thought it was a bunch of evil squirrels in a trench coat."

"We don't have squirrels," she said, confused.

"True. Vampires, werewolves, all kinds of other supernatural nasties, but no squirrels."

"Well, MAF's quite strict about the squirrels," she said.

"Ah, we really need to get out of here before I lose it," I said, wiping tears from my eyes.

We started walking again.

Although the dark had lost some of its menace, the moment we fell silent, I heard rustling from the long grass at the side of the road.

I glanced sideways and Erin gave me a slight nod. She could hear it too.

We reached a slice of open road lit by moonlight, and paused. We'd emerged from the shadows at the corner of a sharp bend. Beyond the bend, the road narrowed and was thickly wooded on either side, the trees huge and old, towering over the dusty track. I was pretty sure that beyond this bend was the main road. But the hills and thick woods all converged at this narrow bottleneck, and we'd need to pass through it to find what I was thinking of as freedom.

Behind us, a twig cracked. I knew there were plenty of creatures that'd be searching for food around this time of night, most of them small, furry, and harmless. But the other part of me, the part of me that at ten years old had heard that sound—that sound of roasted chicken tearing in the dark—knew that this time, we were in trouble.

Erin moved closer to me.

I nudged her. "Whatever you do, don't run."

She gave me an exasperated look. "I wasn't going to."

There was a crunch of loose gravel and a stone rolled out onto the road.

I caught my breath as I saw something pale in the long grass. Another twig crunched slowly, deliberately.

"Stay behind me," I said.

"There's something I've been meaning to tell you," said Erin. She reached behind her and pulled out a black-bladed hunting knife. I lifted the back of her jacket to see a sheath looped through the back of her jeans.

"How the hell did you pack that without me noticing?"

"That's really something you need to ask yourself."

Good point. Very good point.

"Carbon steel?"

"Silver—painted black. After the night where Corey was..." She trailed off. "I started carrying a silver knife. Learned how to do this, too!"

She spun the knife so that the sharp edge of the blade was now facing outwards. I was impressed.

"Ow." She transferred the knife to her left hand and sucked the cut she'd made on her palm. "Still working out the kinks."

There was another sound of twigs crushed underfoot, as if whatever was out there was annoyed we weren't paying it any attention. I could just make out a pale shape in the ferns. The shape growled.

"Let's keep moving," I said. "I'll watch our six."

"'Watch our six'. That sounds really badass."

"We are badass."

We started to walk, and the shape kept pace with us.

Shadow slid over us as we entered the covered part of the trail. I braced myself.

Sure enough, as soon as we stepped out of the light, the growling from the woods became an explosion of movement as something on four legs leapt at us, spraying gravel under its paws. I caught a flash of white fur and blue eyes as it came at me.

It knocked me down and I grunted as it dug its claws in to leap over me and tackle Erin. I rolled over to see what looked like a medium-sized pale dog standing over Erin.

It had a dense white coat and was the size of a

husky, but with smaller ears and a shorter tail. There, the similarity to a family pet ended.

Where dogs are cute and fluffy, this thing looked like a badly stuffed taxidermy, with distorted, lopsided features and dull eyes that didn't hold light the way eyes should. They were dry, I realised, missing that sheen of living moisture.

It was also glowing. Its lumpy, ill-fitting coat shed a radiance that put me in mind of Sherlock Holmes's famous Hound of the Baskervilles. Only this was no painted hound. This was just… wrong.

Erin was holding its jaws at bay with her knife, but the thing had her blade in its teeth. It rolled its eyes towards me as saliva and blood dripped down the blade.

Silver is poison to the wolves and to all shifters — it's not the only way to kill them, but it's one way, and it's effective at stopping their wounds healing in time for them to survive, if you know what you're doing. All I should have to do was sink my knife into this thing a few times. But then, it seemed to be quite enjoying its meal of silver.

It looked up at me with mad, blue eyes, then bit down on the blade and started to tug.

This was not right. Not right at all. Time to act.

I threw myself at it and got my arm around its neck, then slid EMN to the hilt into its side. The blade tip must have been only centimetres from coming out the other side.

The thing thrashed and growled and tore away from me. It moved a distance away, its head lowered, its mouth opened in a pant. Even as pale pink-tinged liquid ran from its fur and matted its coat, it just stood there.

Erin got to her feet. "Try again!" she yelled at it. "Come on!" She held her knife ready while the thing eyed her warily from a distance. It started to circle us, limping in a slow arc, its eyes fixed to my face, its tongue lolling.

"What *is* that thing?" asked Erin.

"I don't know, but Te Papa probably wants it back."

The ooze from the wound was now yellowish against the faint glow of its coat, and there was a chemical smell in the air. While I wasn't a hundred percent sure it was alive, it was at least as alive as a vampire. If I could wound it a few more times, I might be able to kill it.

The thing's jaws parted and it let out a growl. Strings of blood-tinged saliva hung from the corners of its mouth.

"You're failing," I said, moving to face it as it circled us. "Soon you won't have the strength to take me. Look at you, limping and wounded and all alone. Where's your master?"

Without warning, it sprang at me. I ate the stink of its fur as its paws hit my chest. It latched on to my knife arm and bit deep, shaking its head until I dropped the knife.

"Erin!"

She moved closer with her knife poised, while it thrashed like a shark.

"I'll hold it, you kill it!"

I rolled over, pinning it with my weight, and put my hands around its throat. Its rear legs beat upwards, raking my stomach, while its front paws clawed at my arms.

I looked up to find Erin frozen in place. "Erin!"

She looked at me in horror.

"I can't kill it while I'm holding it—you have to kill it!"

"In its face?" she asked.

"Yes, Erin, kill it in its face!"

The white dog's jaws snapped as it thrashed from side to side, trying to loosen my hold.

"Oh God, oh God, gross, gross!" said Erin. She poised her knife over the creature's head.

"Now, please!" I said, desperately trying to hold its head still.

She closed her eyes (never advisable when you're about to put a weapon into your enemy) and, holding the knife in both hands, drove it down.

There was a noise of pain that was part scream, part gurgle, and the white dog stopped struggling. Erin had driven her knife through its open mouth and out the back of its skull.

I rolled off it and lay on my back while I got my breath back. I put my other hand down to my ripped clothing and found blood where the creature's claws and teeth had torn through my leathers.

I flinched at a strange noise behind me—a sound of stitches tearing and the slight 'foof' of a pillow exploding. I was almost afraid to look.

"Liss." Erin's voice was a whisper in a night full of whispers.

I turned my head. Where the white dog had been, there now lay the body of a fair-haired man, his skull pinned to the ground by Erin's knife.

I turned away again. "Well, that's horrible."

I got to my feet with a groan and looked down at the corpse.

The man lay on his back, surrounded by shreds of white fur and hide.

"He exploded," said Erin in awe.

It certainly looked that way. As an animal, he'd looked like a grotesque mockery of a living thing. As a man, he wasn't much better. A Y-incision bisected his chest, sewn shut—I had to assume for burial. Whatever magic had animated him hadn't let him rot, and he wasn't rotting now. The fluid trickling from his side filled the air with an astringent stink that burnt the inside of my nose.

"Do you want to do the honours?" Erin asked.

"Not really," I said. But I already had my hand on the knife.

The chemical smell of the corpse made me gag as I pulled Erin's blade out of its skull, but at least there was no blood. I wiped the knife on my t-shirt, coating my clothes with pale liquid, and handed it back to Erin. She picked up my knife from where I'd dropped it and handed it to me. Now that the hard part was over, I wondered what to do with him.

Luckily, the problem solved itself. It took a moment to realise it was happening, there in the dapple cast by the trees. I frowned as dark shadows appeared under the man's eyes and spread, his skin darkening until his face turned black. His body inflated, ballooning until he was unrecognisable as a person, then deflated with the jerkiness of a grotesque time-lapse until nothing was left but skin stretched taut over bones. With a *foof*, the bones disintegrated into dust. Erin and I stared at the pile of dust, both of us in shock.

"That was convenient," I said.

She nodded. "Yep."

"What the hell was that?" Erin picked up a piece of fur. "Some kind of training dummy?"

I shrugged off my jacket to take a look at the wounds in my arm. Now that the adrenaline was draining away, the pain was setting in.

"Yeah, maybe. Brandt said he wanted us to know what we were facing. So... some kind of shifter, not immune to silver, but harder to kill than your average canine." I glanced up at her. "That was your first fight."

She held out her hand. "Hardly even shaking." She grinned.

I held out mine and winced. "Yeah, can't say the same."

I jerked around as the wind rattled the dead leaves at the edge of the trees.

"Let's keep going."

We kept going.

We reached the road a few minutes later, and I'd

never been happier to see a stretch of tarmac. The road curved through the open landscape with the woods behind us and grass-covered hills in front.

Something beeped. Rolling my eyes, I pulled out the iPhone.

'You did well. Expect more company.'

Great. I looked around. "Where are we again?" I said to Erin.

"I believe they call this 'the middle of nowhere'."

"We're gonna need a lift."

I thought for a moment. Did I know Dan's number by heart? No. Did I know anyone's number by heart? The only number I knew was Jack's cell because it spelled out 'werewolf'. He'd had it changed when I was younger, as I had a tendency to lose my phone and end up miles from home with no way of contacting them.

I swallowed and dialled the number. Chances were his phone was flat... but if I knew Andy, he'd have it with him.

No answer. "Dammit!" I hissed, then realised I'd got the answer phone.

"Andy, if you get this, Erin and I are in trouble. We're in Dome Valley —" I realised I needed to check the GPS for exactly where in Dome Valley we were. I ended the call and checked.

We'd only driven for an hour or so, so in theory... I did some maths. I wasn't good at maths.

"Hey, Erin, if we drove for an hour at a hundred ks an hour, that's like, a hundred ks to walk. How fast do people walk?"

She thought for a moment. "About five kilometres an hour, I think."

"Okay, so that means we should be able to walk back to the reserve in about…"

Twenty freakin' hours.

I dialled the number again. Andy answered on the first ring.

"Liss? Where the hell are you?"

"Uh, we're in Dome valley—"

"Where? I can't call your phone—the number's blocked. Are you okay? Kendrick said you walked out—"

"Whoa, Andy, calm down—we're okay, we're just stranded. We're apparently not far from Waiwhiu Road. Brandt lured us here, took our car keys, and set… something… on us."

"What?" he said. "Are you hurt?"

"We'll be okay, but ah, if you could come get us, I'd be really, really grateful."

Andy was silent for a moment. "But you're okay?"

"Yeah—we are, but we don't have Dan's car keys, so we're walking along State Highway 1—"

"You're not hurt at all?"

I fell silent. "What's going on?"

A pause. "Kendrick told me you excommunicated yourself."

"Not by choice."

"Did you really argue with Kendrick in front of the entire pack?"

"Well, I—"

"You can't do that!" he said. "You've put me in a

297

hell of a position."

"You're not going to help us?"

"Kendrick is my alpha," said Andy. "You know how this works!"

"You're kidding!" I exploded. "I left the pack so that I could help keep everyone safe!"

Erin took the phone from me. "Andy? How are you holding up?" She listened for a bit. "I understand. We'll be okay, we have each other. It would take days to walk back, so we'll hitchhike — it'll be fine." She listened a while longer. "We have weapons, we'll be fine. We'll be fine, Andy. Honestly, the last thing we need is for you to get—" More listening. "Okay, but you don't have—" More listening. "Okay. Dome Valley — we're walking along State Highway 1. Okay, if you're sure. See you soon."

She ended the call and handed the phone back to me.

"How?" I asked.

"He can deal with us being attacked by supernatural monsters, but the thought of us catching a lift with a stranger apparently gives him the heebie-jeebies."

"Good to see your psychology degree isn't going to waste."

We started walking, partly to keep warm, partly because we wanted to get the hell out of Dome Valley.

The night was quiet except for the shrieks of pukekos and the occasional morepork call. But I was sure we weren't alone.

I sniffed the air every few minutes but couldn't smell anything over the astringent stink of the fluid soaked into my t-shirt.

It was forty minutes before Andy's car rounded a bend, the lights curving over the hills, blinding after so much time in the dark.

He pulled over at the side of the road and jumped out, pulling me into a hug.

"I'm sorry I wasn't there to stand with you today."

"It's okay," I said, "I know why you don't want to be at the reserve. I'm trying to fix it, I really am."

"Oh, Liss. This is not your mess to fix."

"You know it is."

"Family, Liss. You didn't kill Jack—" He broke off and took a moment to compose himself. "We're family. We're all family and we'll get through this together."

He looked down at me, noticing my torn clothes. "I thought you weren't hurt?"

I shrugged. "I've had worse." I waved my hand. "Still got my arm!"

"Not funny," he said, shaking his head. "Now get in the car and let's get out of here."

As we drove, I explained what'd happened.

"You think he took it out there for you to practice on?"

"That's what it looked like."

"And you think it was a forest dog—like Riley?"

I nodded. "I haven't seen her shift, but I'd put money on it."

He glanced across at me. "I'm so glad you're both

299

okay. But for the sake of giving Kendrick some space to show his will's been enforced, we should go to the summer house, at least for the night. Then I'll make the case on your behalf for him to let you come back."

I loved the summer house. It had originally belonged to the architect who'd designed it, and featured a set of coloured slot windows along one wall. It was set on a private block of land out near the beach and was the perfect place to go when you wanted solitude. Although I understood why Andy didn't want to be at the reserve right now, the thought of him grieving alone made me feel sad.

We pulled onto the gravel road that ran along the beachfront. Wooded hills rose up from the shingle road on one side, scattered with a mix of wooden cottages and expensive glass-fronted beach homes, while dunes and tussock stretched down towards the waves on the other.

We turned into the gravel driveway that led to the house, which was screened by a bank covered in flax and scrubby coastal plants so that only the highest windows looked out to the ocean.

On the other side of the house, the land fell away so that the morning sun warmed the house before it fell beyond the horizon in the evenings.

Andy pulled the car onto the packed earth by the front door and unclipped his seatbelt. As I was undoing mine, he froze, head cocked like a wary dog. I knew better than to ask. Slowly, he let the seatbelt wind back into position, making sure the sound didn't obscure whatever he'd heard. Erin and I mirrored him. For what seemed like minutes, we sat there, Andy moving his head from time to time, scanning, listening to something I couldn't hear.

A moment before I heard a rustle in the flax, he tensed, his gaze fixed to the garden at the end of the car park.

Something melted out of the low bushes at the end of the drive. It was the twin of the thing Erin and I had killed, only this one looked slightly better put together. Not right—just less wrong.

Andy pressed the switch that locked the car's doors as the thing padded towards us and stood blinking into the streams of light from the car's high beams. It opened its mouth and panted.

"Is that Riley?" Andy asked.

"I'm willing to bet it's not," I said in a low voice. "It looks just like the one we killed earlier tonight.

"We're safe in here, aren't we?" Erin asked.

Neither Andy or I answered. It depended. If forest dogs had were-strength, then no, we were absolutely not safe. But the one Erin and I had just wrestled with had been no stronger than a normal dog its size— vicious and determined, but I didn't think there was anything preternaturally strong about it.

"Can it break the glass, Liss?" Andy asked.

"Should we really wait to find out?" I asked.

The dog chose that moment to leap onto the bonnet of the car. It lowered its head and stared at us. Its coat had that same faint luminosity.

"Uh, Andy, maybe we should get out of here?"

The dog reared up on its hind legs and brought them down on the windshield. It made us jump, but it was clear it wasn't going to get through the glass. It didn't have the weight. It tried again with the same results. Frustration lit its pale eyes. It leapt off the bonnet and started to circle the car. As it paced past my window, it kept eye contact with me until it passed around the back of the car.

A moment later, it jumped up against the rear window and let out a high-pitched bark.

I glanced back at it. "They don't have much of a survival instinct."

The dog paced around to the front of the car again. It lowered its head and growled.

Andy opened the car door. "You got the last one— I'll take this one." He stepped out of the car and pulled off his shirt. You didn't want to get tangled in your clothes while your enemy was staring you down.

The forest dog watched him its head tilted to one side. It shut its mouth and waited to see what he was going to do. Andy finished pulling off his clothes and threw them into the front seat. Then, with one fluid motion, he collapsed in on himself and became a wolf. I got out of the car, EMN in my hand, in case he needed backup.

The dog ignored me, its gaze fixed on Andy.

Erin got out of the back seat, her black knife blade nearly invisible.

I could smell the dog over the ripe ocean breeze that blew up off the dunes. It smelled dead.

Wolf-Andy advanced on the dog, mouth open, ears perked forward. His silver fur standing on end, he dwarfed the forest dog.

The dog licked its lips and stepped back a pace as Andy advanced. Andy paused as it pricked its ears. A moment later I heard it too—a howl riding the wind, rising from the nearby woods.

The white dog lifted its nose into the wind and howled. It wasn't a wolf howl, but a thin sound like a human parody of a howl. When the sound died away, it was answered by yipping and nervous skittering barks, like coyotes at nightfall.

Only there were no coyotes in this country.

Wary, Andy took a halting step forward.

I heard a sound behind us and glanced around. There was nothing I could see. When I looked back, Andy had the forest dog backed up against a low clay bank at the edge of the garden. It laid its ears flat and growled.

Andy pounced. The forest dog tried to flee, but in its panic, it couldn't find a gap in the bush. Andy latched his teeth to its ruff and dragged it back towards the car. Using his body weight, he rolled the dog under him and gripped its throat, pinning it.

I may have imagined it, but he seemed to have a look of distaste on his canine face at having the thing's fur in his mouth. As near as I stood to it, it smelled of chemicals and ammonia, dead and preserved.

The forest dog struggled under Andy and he bit down harder.

"Andy, kill it, it's already dead. More are coming."

There was a yelp, this time from the bush beyond the house. They were surrounding us.

"Andy!" I said urgently. "We're not alone."

Andy tightened his grip on the struggling dog, but he still wasn't killing it. The stink was overwhelming. If it smelled bad to me, it had to be awful for him.

More yips, closer now, only metres away, and from all sides.

Andy looked up. Instead of tearing out the dog's throat, he let go and backed away.

The yelps were getting louder.

"In the car!" I shouted.

Andy skidded around the car and leapt into the back seat while Erin jumped into the passenger seat. I slammed the back door and jumped into the front seat, slamming the door just as the white dog darted towards me.

I started the car and set it in reverse. As I backed into the turning bay, something thumped against the rear bumper. Something white and glowing faintly reeled away into the darkness.

I pointed the car back down the gravel drive and four more forest dogs stepped out of the tussock. They milled across the road like sheep, their ears pricked towards the car. I checked my mirrors and saw more behind us. One jumped up against the rear window and met my gaze in the rear-view mirror. There was human intelligence in those blue eyes.

I put my foot down and drove forward. Instead of scattering, the white dogs let themselves be buffeted

304

aside by the car.

One yelped as it was thrown forwards, then screamed as I drove forward over it. The scream stopped abruptly. The others began to run, keeping pace with the car, leaping and snarling at the windows. Teeth connected with the glass, leaving streaks of saliva across the panes.

I glanced in the rear-view mirror and found Andy's guilty golden eyes looking back. He shook himself in apology, but I was too busy driving to worry about his squeamishness.

I took the turn from the drive onto the metal road at full force, drifting Andy's car on the loose gravel. Stones pinged and bounced away from the tyres as I revved the engine and accelerated up the road.

"Liss, if we crash, they've got us," said Erin.

I slowed enough that I could correct safely if we slid out, while the white dogs renewed their efforts, bounding beside the car, leaping in the air like dolphins beside a fishing trawler, their blue eyes and pale fur like fireworks bursting at the edge of my vision.

At the end of the road, the gravel turned to tarseal. As the tyres gripped and we sped forward, I knew we needed to get clear of the bush. I didn't know why, but I was certain we'd be in danger until we reached civilisation.

We were well over an hour from Dome Valley, yet still, here they were. Maybe they knew the summer house's location and had waited there in hopes of ambushing us. Or, I had this horrible vision of them scampering at unnatural speed through the forest as we drove down the highway, their tongues lolling, their yellow fangs glistening.

The road away from the beach twisted up through the hills, and there were plenty of low-speed bends where, if I wasn't careful, I'd overshoot and send us plunging down a bank.

The dogs kept pace with us, occasionally body slamming the car and ricocheting off as if they'd been fired out of a cannon.

The road straightened out as we reached the crest of the hills and flowed down into a valley. I planted my foot and drove it up to one-eighty. The dogs were soon left behind, but they didn't stop. No, it was pretty clear that they were going to follow us no matter how far or fast we ran. I wondered if they were capable of tracking. I guessed we'd find out.

At the end of the main beach road was a set of traffic lights. As I slowed for the red, I checked behind us. I couldn't see them, but I knew I hadn't put enough distance between us to be sure we'd shaken them. The light went green and I drove out on the main highway. Here I'd have to be careful of speeding—if we were stopped by the cops and the dogs caught up, I wasn't sure what they'd do.

I drove at something approximating the speed limit, checking my mirrors with paranoid regularity for flashes of glowing fur behind us.

After twenty minutes, I'd seen nothing.

"Where are we going?" asked Erin, as we pulled onto the motorway.

"I don't know. Away from trees."

Andy whined.

"I'm sorry, you'll have to get dressed in the back of the car or stay as a wolf for now."

He stared at me in the rear-view mirror and huffed.

"You're going to try and tell me to go to the reserve, aren't you?"

He huffed again, twice.

"You know that's just leading our enemies there. Don't we have enough to worry about?"

He pricked his ears forward, then leaned between the seats and licked the side of my face.

"*Ngyah*, that was unnecessary!" I said, wiping away the spit. "I'm not going to the reserve. I'm not wanted, remember?"

He nudged my neck with a cold, damp nose.

"No!"

He put a paw up on my arm and curled his claws into my arm.

"No!"

He snorted, sending moist droplets across my face. I made the mistake of looking in the mirror again, just as his face started to morph.

As I've mentioned before, I don't like to watch. I'm very comfortable with wolves and people, but I am not at all comfortable with the form in between.

I dragged my gaze away, and a few moments later, Andy reached forward and got his clothes from the front seat.

"We have to," he said as he pulled on his shirt.

"We need to stick together."

"Don't you get it?" I argued. "They came out to the summer house to find you because you split off from the pack—and now they're herding us all into one place like sheep. What if that's what Riley wants? If they just wanted to kill us, why haven't they tried harder?"

"I want to know what they are," said Erin. "And why they look like stuffed museum exhibits."

"Me too," I said. "They're beyond spooky."

"Our greatest strength is the pack," said Andy. "We need to stick together."

"I don't like it." I kept my eyes on the road ahead.

"Whether you like it or not, the reserve is the safest place to be."

I slammed my hands on the wheel in frustration.

"Fine. I'll go back to the reserve. But don't come crying to me if we're all dead by tomorrow."

Chapter 27

While we drove down the network of rural roads that led to the reserve, I grew aware of pale flashes in the bush that lined the highway.

"Are you guys seeing this?" I asked.

Erin wiped the condensation from the inside of the car window.

"They're still out there," she said.

"The same ones?" I asked. "I mean, how could they have kept up with us?"

Andy wiped his own window, the squeak of the glass loud in the car.

"There's no way of telling," he said.

We fell silent, watching for those flashes of white between the trees. We reached a place where the bush receded from the road, giving way to open paddocks, and Andy let out a yell. "Jesus!"

I slammed on the brakes, my heart pounding, and he patted my shoulder.

"Sorry, Liss, keep going, didn't mean to scare you. Just... one of them just disappeared."

"Huh?"

"I saw that too," said Erin. "I thought I imagined it. It reached the edge of the tree line and you could see it jump into the air—and then it just vanished."

"Leapt into the air and vanished," agreed Andy.

"What is going *on*?" I said. The way they described it was giving me an uncomfortable itch between my shoulder blades.

As the car reached the trees on the other side of the open land, all three of us swore at the same time as a white shape appeared in mid-leap and bounded into the forest.

"You know where I think we'd be safest?" I said to Andy. "Somewhere where there are *no goddamn trees!*"

"Or over a dozen wolves that have ten times the strength of any of these animals. We'll be safe at the reserve, Liss. Just drive. I'll call ahead and let Kendrick know we're coming."

I sulked as he dialled, convinced it was the wrong thing to do, but unable to think of a better plan. If we drove into the city and they followed us, people could get hurt.

Thirty minutes later, I turned into the road that led down to the reserve. The area was heavily wooded, and I expected to see the forest dogs in full force as we drove up to the house—but there was no sign of them.

The wolves were waiting for us in the driveway when I pulled up. Andy leapt out of the car and greeted Kendrick. He took him to one side and explained the situation.

I exchanged a glance with Erin, reluctant to get out of the car. We were both thinking the same thing.

Awkward.

I couldn't put it off forever.

"They'll be fine," said Erin.

I nodded. 'Course they would.

Kendrick broke off speaking with Andy as we reached them.

"Get inside," he said to me. The look he gave me was icy.

"I know how to fight them," I said. "This is my mess, let me—"

"Get," he said, putting the emphasis on the 't', "inside."

I could feel the Stoke brothers' eyes on me as I walked between them and up the steps to the house. From somewhere near, a chorus of thin howls lifted into the night. Not wolf howls, but the forest dogs, with their weird, nearly human voices.

Inside, Ellen and Cole were deep in conversation. They broke off when they saw me.

"The prodigal daughter returns!" said Cole. Trust him to tease me at a time like this. "What can you tell us about what's coming?"

"You want the long or the short version?"

"Short, please," said Ellen.

"White dogs, reanimated, don't know how—when they die, they're people, but people who've clearly already died. Blue eyes, angry, but not as strong as wolves."

He gave me an appraising look. "This is very

311

important, Liss. Are these creatures related to Riley or the Midlands pack?"

"They have to be," I said. "They've got blue eyes like hers. And they glow. I haven't seen her animal form, but… what else would they be?"

He exchanged a look with Ellen.

"The question is," Ellen said to him, "do we treat them as Midlands or as an outsider threat?"

Cole shrugged. "Does it matter, if they attack us?"

"How delicate are they?" Ellen asked me.

"Oh, they're not delicate," I said. "I put EMN into one of them and it kept running until Erin shoved her knife through its face."

Both Cole and Ellen looked shocked. They glanced at Erin, who until this moment had been silent.

"You?" said Cole. "You killed it?"

"Oh," she said. "Yeah. Liss had it pinned down and I kinda… finished pinning it."

Cole raised an eyebrow, impressed.

The howls rose again, along with that skittery coyote yipping the forest dogs were so fond of. It sounded like a dozen people all shouting 'yeh-yeh-yeh-yeh-yeh' at the tops of their voices, one short cry after another in quick succession.

"What the hell is that?" said Cole, walking to the window. "Ellen, come and look at this."

She walked to the window, then reached back and flicked off the lounge light. Erin and I joined them. In the darkness, pale shapes were visible among the flax bushes, their eyes like reflective silver circles.

"Time to play," said Cole. We filed out onto the

porch.

A shout went up from one of the wolves, and I knew that they had their own silent line of intruders watching them from the wood-lined driveway.

The world hushed, as if every living thing inhaled at the same time.

I strained to see how many dogs were out there, my ears ringing in the silence.

One dog stepped forward, its eyes as flat as silver coins.

The silence broke. A sound started on the edge of hearing, a howl building like a fire siren that erupted into chaos as the forest dogs' voices rose in those thin wails and high-pitched 'yeh's to become screams— all-too-human screams.

I felt heat building inside me and put a hand to my chest.

"You okay?" Erin asked.

I nodded, then let out a gasp as a pain lanced through my chest. As if that breath had ignited it, the heat expanded and exploded inside me.

I fell to my knees, head spinning. My skin was slicked with sweat, trickling down my back. I couldn't feel the deck under my fingers, couldn't feel anything solid at all.

"Liss!" Erin crouched beside me, but if she was touching me, I couldn't feel anything. I could barely hear her over the pounding of blood in my ears.

The forest dogs' screams became shrieks that added to my panic. What the hell was happening to me?

I turned and crawled back towards the house on all fours, knowing somehow that I needed to get away from the light, that whatever was happening needed darkness. And cool. I needed to cool down.

Someone tried to help me up, but I pushed them away and kept moving, fleeing from the screeching chorus.

The world grew indistinct, nothing but dark shapes, carved apart by pale shadows.

I discovered cool tiles in the hall and placed my face flat against the floor. I considered staying there, but the shrieking was too loud. I had to keep going, had to get deeper into the house.

Was it my imagination, or was the noise getting closer, rather than further away?

People were shouting my name but the words were just noises, their shapes like aliens seen through gauze. They tried to touch me and I bared my teeth, warning them away.

I crawled into the dark hallway, feeling only the lightest sensation in my fingers as I pulled myself across the carpet, and pushed open a bedroom door. True darkness. I pulled myself into the room and collapsed on the floor, heat running through me in scalding waves.

Didn't know what else to do, didn't know how to cool down.

I ground my teeth together and tasted blood as the wailing carried through the walls of the house, too loud — *too loud!*

Someone was in the room with me.

"Get out!" I tried to say through a locked jaw. "Get out!"

The bedroom door closed and concerned voices rose, urgent but unintelligible in the hallway.

The forest dogs were closing in. Were they doing this to me? Was this their combined magic? Were they killing me?

I let out a scream that turned into a growl, and I wondered if I was turning into one of them.

Then, as one wave of heat burnt its way from my core to my fingers, a wave of cold followed like a flood of ice water.

I started to shiver uncontrollably, as that dark orchestra screamed around me.

I heard a voice—Ellen?—raised over the others shout, "What time was she born?"

I couldn't hear the reply, but I knew. And only I knew. 3:01 a.m. This was it. I was becoming.

The noise outside stopped. The waves of ice cold slowly bled away, and as they did, I felt something else building inside me. The music of the world, swelling up like heavy strings, the harmonies that lay under everything, building, throbbing through me.

If you stand alone on top of a mountain and stare down, the wind blowing up off the snowy slopes, the scree and rock dropping away from you, the cold stinging your eyes, while an eagle circles overhead—

If you stand on a beach, alone at dawn, watching the sun rise out of the ocean, painting cobalt blue with liquid gold, and feel the world inside you, knowing that you own it—are part of it—owned by it—

If you lay your palm against an ancient tree and feel that surging green life and solid strength reaching up to the sky—

If you've ever known for a moment that you are God, *that all the planet's songs are inside you, that you're connected with the Earth, made of the fabric of the universe and so attuned to it that your slightest action will ripple outwards and cause distant stars to explode—can send your mind out into the darkness of space and hold the entirety of it inside you—*

...then you know exactly how I felt at that moment.

I was aware of everything. Everything that lived, I could touch. I could taste colours, sense life as drops of dew weighing on a web that expanded out from me, so that my fingertips seemed to touch... everything.

The wolves were like glittering stars, heavy droplets of rain clustered together on the vast, giant earth ball that was our home.

The forest dogs weren't alive, but whatever animated them had its own colour, a muted dark blue against black. Knowing they were pale and phosphorescent, I painted that image over their shapes my mind and saw they were in their dozens— maybe as many as fifty ringing the reserve, all waiting, all connected back to something else— something brighter. Something that pulsed the bright blue of a husky's eyes, a shape shifting through the shadows, an unseen commander.

I lay flat against the bedroom floor and felt the

earth under me, felt it solid and deep and humming with power, the power that drove all of us, all things supernatural and all things connected to the supernatural.

I felt minerals in the ground and knew they had power that could be drawn on, felt the tiny creatures that lived beneath us as pinpoints of light in the darkness, like glow worms in clay. Felt not just the presence of all living things around me, but their emotions as shapes inside them.

The bedroom door opened and Andy knelt beside me. "Liss, sweetheart, are you okay?"

"Dan," I managed to say. "Please get Dan."

Andy got up, the shape of his love for me a pulse inside his light, and I felt the warmth of it dim as he moved away, like a cloud across the sun. A minute later, Dan came into the bedroom.

"Shut the door," I whispered. "Lie down beside me."

He did. I turned my face to his so that we were eye to eye. I could see him in both worlds, his physical shape in the dark, and his light, glittering through him.

I crept my fingers across the carpet towards him and he took my hand.

"See this."

I let the new world flood through me and into him.

He made a noise in his throat, and his fingers twitched in mine as he was swallowed into the vision.

I closed my eyes and soared with him, taking him up into the sky to look down on it all, all those glittering stars below, each one connected to all other living things.

It was hard to breathe as I struggled to contain that much presence. We were everything. We were *all* everything.

It seemed we flew into the cool night, breathing the damp mist of cloud, bathed in moonlight that washed us with power, but we didn't really fly—we contained it. Swallowed it all.

I had to let go, it was too much. I brought us back into our bodies with a physical jolt.

I opened my eyes and found him staring at me, his eyes glossy. He didn't speak—didn't have to. I could feel everything he felt, knew he was awed and humbled, excited and overwhelmed. Knew he'd never felt anything like that before, not even close, and that he'd never been more grateful to be alive than he was right now, lying on the floor, face to face with me.

We stared into each other and I knew he could see what was inside me too, connected to me in an impossible way.

Something was happening outside.

I sent out my new awareness and saw someone was approaching the house. It had to be Riley. I painted her image over the raw sensation and saw that it matched. I could tell she was in human form and that she was alone. Alone except for...

A new colour. This must be Brandt. Gold—molten

gold, with a force that was almost painful to push against. His shape, a shadow in that nightscape, sparked with golden electricity. Branches of it crackled up out of the ground, drawn up from so deep inside the earth that I couldn't see the source. Maybe from the molten heart of the planet itself.

He stayed back, and I knew he could sense me, my new power, and felt him grow wary. But he'd been expecting this, had known better than any of us what my inheritance might be.

Riley reached the ranks of wolves that blocked her path.

"We should help them," said Dan. His voice was coarse with emotion.

It was too much to hold, this power, this new awareness, what it might mean. What *did* it mean?

I let go of his hand and somehow got to my knees. I stayed there, head spinning, stars blooming in front of my eyes, until he helped me up. My damp clothes were cold. Dan went to the wardrobe, pulled out a t-shirt, and came back to me.

"Here."

I shed my jacket and pulled my damp t-shirt over my head. I stood in the darkness and realised I could see him clearly. His life glowed to my new eyes, as if he was painted with moonlight.

We stood, staring at each other. His heightened wolf senses would tell him all he needed to know about me. But now, for once, I could see what was inside him too.

He held out the clean t-shirt and I realised it was

one of his.

I took it and held it to my face, drawing in his scent and feeling in the texture of the fabric some part of his essence. I looked up at him. "She's waiting."

"There's time."

I dropped the t-shirt over my head.

As I opened the bedroom door, his arms snaked around me from behind. He bent his head and nuzzled my neck. "To standing on the edge of everything."

I turned my face to his and he kissed me. I shuddered, the feeling of being so close to him almost too much, as if we'd melted inside each other.

He let me go and I took a deep breath. "Let's do this."

Chapter 28

The wolves had known I would be a Väktare long before I did. I can't explain why my parents never told me that one day I might change—that this supernatural thing might be inside me. Maybe they just hoped it would never happen.

Andy had told me they knew about me years in advance, that the pack knew my parents and that I might inherit the talent due to some relative from some Nordic country having had it.

Jack and Andy had always insisted that no one blamed me for what had happened to Zöe, but when days turned into weeks, and weeks turned into years and they still didn't contact me, it became pretty obvious that they were doing more than just protecting themselves. They'd erased me from their lives and moved on.

Their faces were faded in my memory, shapes of light and shadow silhouetted against the porch light, where moths beat themselves to death against the naked bulb.

Jack and Andy had taken me away that night

wrapped in a duvet stained with blood. I hadn't even asked where we were going.

These two strangers had taken me to the house where I'd lived for the last ten years. I hadn't known who they were that night. I hadn't known where I was.

I thought back to Andy sitting on the bed that night, tucking me in while Jack watched from the doorway, and realised how shaken they must have been. The size of the bombshell that had landed on them. How they'd both taken it in their stride and managed to make me feel safe, while their own lives were turned upside down. I wasn't even sure how he and Jack were chosen to raise me—if they'd volunteered, or if the Stokes had asked them to take me in.

I'd felt so lost that first night, hiding under the duvet to get away from the unused smell of the spare room and how cold it was. To dampen the echo of voices from the hall, because there was so little furniture in the room to soak up the sound. To get away from the memory of that damp, metallic heat and the smell of my sister's death.

I remembered asking if Zöe was still alive and the silence that had followed.

There was silence outside.

Riley was waiting for me. She stood in human form just outside the line of light the security floodlights made across the driveway.

The wolves followed me with their eyes as I

walked between them. There was a wariness about them that told me they sensed the change.

Kendrick didn't argue as I approached Riley.

"Liss! You've found your power. How does it feel?"

"Like breathing in the universe," I said.

She laughed and it was musical. I closed my eyes for a moment, and in my mind's eye saw her colour shift as she experienced joy, changing from that pale blue to emerald green and back again.

"What's it like to be you?" I asked.

"Amazing," she said. "To be me, Liss, is to be—"

"A god?" I asked.

Her smile faded slightly. "What do you see?"

"Everything," I said. "I can see you're enjoying yourself."

"Then you know what I am," she said.

I shook my head. "I can see inside you, but I don't know what it means."

Her eyes caught the light as she watched me intently. "Where does my power come from?"

I thought of Brandt, the way he drew his power from deep in the earth. Where did she draw her power from?

She walked up to a nearby beech tree and placed her hand flat against the bark. I let go of what was real and solid around me and instead moved to the image inside my head.

Aaaaah. There it was. Dark green, so dark it was nearly black, veins of power that snaked through the air, connecting her with the bush around us.

"Anything that grows from the land gives me its power," she said.

She walked back to me and the strands of power followed her, still connected, threads of darkness against the night.

"Why are you here, Riley?" I asked. "What do you want?"

"Like you, I've been chosen. Do you know the story of the kuri ngahere?"

I shook my head. I guessed it was time for some exposition.

"More than six hundred years ago, a small group of skoghunds came to these islands as refugees. They were running from slavery and persecution in the cold north, where the Vikings used them as labour and soldiers — and emergency food on sea voyages if they made the mistake of shifting while they were at sea. They were considered less than human by their countrymen and were dying out.

"They found refuge here, and developed an alliance with the first people. But there was a... misunderstanding. The first people placed a curse on my kind. The curse that led to my blood lying dormant until Brandt gave me the means to unleash it."

"What do you want, Riley?"

She cast her gaze over the wolves, then looked back at me.

"Did you know that the wolves have placed a moratorium on breeding until a wolf dies?"

Kendrick stepped forward. "The Alpha Circle

makes these decisions as a whole. Our species walks a narrow line. The zero-sum policy prevents over-population, turf wars, exposure that would see us hunted and destroyed. We all have to live by the same rules."

Riley snorted. "With all due respect, Kendrick, it seems very convenient that this law was passed *after* having your *five* sons, consolidating your hereditary claim to the reserve for the next several hundred years at least. As it stands now, as the head of the Alpha Circle, Abigail Stoke is the highest authority among the wolves, and the rules you 'all live by' have in fact not affected you at all, while restricting where the Midlands pack can live, where we can hunt, and critically, how many children we can have."

This was all news to me.

"The Midlands pack is the largest in the country," said Kendrick. "Their numbers are far greater than ours. We have only our family and those we've adopted into the pack. Our footprint is a third of the Midlands'."

Riley turned back to me. "And did you know that our alphas were so afraid of upsetting the Stokes, they enforced a policy of mandatory abortion if an *accident* were to occur?"

Kendrick shook his head. "Riley, that's not something we would ever ask—"

"Be quiet!" she said to Kendrick, and to my surprise, he fell silent. "The death penalty, Kendrick. That's the punishment for breeding outside of the

Alpha Circle's restrictions. How else did you think that would be enforced?"

Kendrick's expression was tortured, but he said nothing.

"So, Liss." Riley put her head on one side. "How many forest dogs are there in the world that you're aware of?"

"Is this a trick question? Because I don't know if you count the cheap knock-offs or not."

"One," she said. "Just one. Just me. And I love Tristan Copeland, a wolf who is not allowed to have children."

I stood there, puzzled. "You want kids?"

She shook her head in amazement at how long it took me to get it. "Forest dogs—my species—have lived on the border of extinction for over six hundred years. We have no territory, no lands, no place here. We have been fugitives all our lives. If I die, there's no guarantee there will ever be another of my kind. Yet I'm forbidden to have children with Tristan, because he's a wolf."

"Let's organise a time to speak about this," said Kendrick. "We weren't aware of the unique nature of your biology. We would never have tried to enforce this rule on you if we'd known."

I could see that Kendrick just wanted to keep the peace, but Riley had the air of someone who was done talking. She might not have raised it with Kendrick and Abigail, but she'd raised it with *someone* and got an answer she hadn't liked.

Her silent army of glowing mutant dead watched

us, surrounding us on all sides. Even though I was sure the wolves would win if it came to a fight, it was going to get messy if they attacked us.

"You don't need to do this," I said to Riley. "Whatever you need, let's just talk about it."

She laughed, a sound layered with brittle anger. "I didn't come here to talk. I came here to end the Stokes' reign of oppression. Tell me, why is Abigail Stoke in charge of my reproductive rights?"

Kendrick put up a hand. "Riley, I understand. You've been heard. The moratorium is unfair on you and it needs to be discussed."

"That doesn't work for me. I'm here to tell you, Kendrick Stoke, that Tristan and I, as the new alphas of the Midlands territory, do not recognise the rule of the Alpha Circle anymore. We will live where we see fit. We will do as we see fit. We will breed as we see fit."

Kendrick's presence radiated from him as he reached the end of his patience. There was no way Riley couldn't feel it, but she didn't flinch.

"Riley, you don't want to stand against the Alpha Circle. If you do anything that risks exposing the wolves, we'll have no choice but to act against you."

Riley's eyes narrowed. "But there's no need. One out, one in, that's the rule, isn't it, Kendrick? Done. We've made space. Send no one else to our territory. You're not welcome."

She turned her back and stepped out of the light as a concrete weight settled inside my chest.

"What you do mean, you've 'made space'?" She

327

stopped, her back to me. "You killed Jack... so you could have a kid?"

She looked back at me. "If it helps, Liss, it wasn't supposed to be Jack. It was supposed to be him." She pointed at Dan. "A life for a life, a son for a son. But Karlo's mind wouldn't accept the suggestion, so I had to improvise. Sometimes that's what it takes to get people to take you seriously."

Something in me snapped. I launched myself at her, but Kendrick lunged for me and pulled me back.

"Liss, let me handle this."

He let me go and went after her while I stood in the dark with the light at my back, vibrating with rage. She'd killed Jack, not because Brandt had told her to, but out of spite. Out of *spite*.

"Riley!" Kendrick's voice rang with command. I felt the wolves flinch, felt their natural deference to the power in his voice.

But Riley wasn't a wolf.

Incensed, she turned back to face us, her face morphed into a snarl.

The high-pitched yipping started again, circling us as the nervous sound passed from dog to dog.

I could feel the anger in Kendrick as he spoke, each word falling like a physical blow, laced with power. "Riley, you need to answer for the murder of Jack Koestler. Come with me now and we'll hold you for judgement before the Alpha Circle. I promise you'll get a fair trial. But if you try to run, you *will* be killed."

The wind rose and lifted Riley's hair back from

her shoulders.

"You don't seem to understand, Kendrick. Your authority means nothing to me."

Kendrick advanced on her. All around us, the white dogs lifted their muzzles skyward and let out a high keening. *Aaaah, haaa, haaaa, haaa, haaaa,* part whine, part scream.

"Don't make me use force," said Kendrick.

Riley smiled, her eyes glittering with dark joy. "Change," she said softly.

A look of confusion came over Kendrick's face. His features started to contort. I could see him struggling to stay human, but whatever power she had was too much. He made a noise as though all the air had been sucked out of his lungs and fell to the ground, struggling free of his clothes as he became a wolf. He stood with saliva flecking his muzzle, his eyes golden and wild with anger.

He growled and Riley put a hand out and stroked his head.

"Good dog."

Kendrick's lips pulled back from inch-long gleaming fangs, but he didn't bite. For a moment, the Stoke brothers stood frozen, struggling to comprehend what was happening.

"You will learn to respect my kind," said Riley. "You've been warned."

She smiled down at Kendrick and spread her hand flat against his skull. I didn't know what she was about to do, but I knew it was going to be bad.

"Get out of my way!" Ellen strode out from the

pack and fired her gun twice into Riley, catching her in the chest. Riley crumpled to the ground. With a chorus of screams, the forest dogs charged out of the forest in a wave of white, glowing fur.

All around me, the wolves tore at their clothes and morphed into their animal forms, ready to meet their attackers. Ellen stood over Riley and fired another shot into her head moments before they both disappeared under a thrashing pile of white fur and yellow teeth.

The world filled with the sound of wolves and forest dogs tearing at each other, a storm of snarls and yelps of pain.

I stumbled back towards the house, blinded by colours bursting inside my head and smashed on all sides by the wolves' rage. Both worlds, the real world and the one I could see in my mind, were layered together, melting from one to the other like a bad acid trip.

I looked out into the yard, seething with twisting bodies and splashed with blood, and tried to find Dan.

Every now and then a reanimated forest dog would explode in a hail of shredded fur as the wolves dispatched dog after dog, leaving pale human corpses behind. The stench of death and chemicals stung my throat and made my eyes water.

I closed my eyes and let the world re-draw itself using the second sight of the Väktare and found Dan's dark red centre.

Knife in hand, I waded through the fight, kicking

away dogs that latched on to me.

I found Dan fighting three of them and sank my knife into one, stabbing it through the skull as it tore into Dan's hind leg. A second dog had its teeth sunk into his shoulder, even as he clashed, teeth to teeth, with the third.

I stabbed the dog latched to his shoulder through the skull and it fell away. The first corpse morphed back into a man's corpse, sending a flurry of shredded fur into the air like a ripped pillow.

Dan gave me a look of gratitude and threw himself at the third dog, barging it with his shoulder and rolling it onto its back. Without hesitation, he dug his muzzle into its throat and tugged. Instead of blood, yellow fluid sprayed from the wound. The stink of chemicals was like spilled bleach.

Dan stood panting beside me as we surveyed the battlefield. A wolf and dog rolled over and over, crashing into my legs. I planted my knife into the dog, killing it, and the wolf threw itself at another, even as the corpse at my feet exploded out of its fur casing and became another dead human.

I ran my gaze over Dan. One back leg was torn open and his shoulder was matted with blood. But the others needed our help. We exchanged a glance and launched back into the fight.

I couldn't keep count of how many dogs I slaughtered, but fifteen minutes later only wolves were left standing and we had a hell of a clean-up ahead of us.

I looked around but couldn't see Kendrick, Ellen,

or Cole. There was no sign of Riley, dead or alive. My legs were covered with superficial bites and scratches, but I'd live. I limped down the drive towards the road, sending my mind out searching for signs of the missing wolves.

Dan padded out of the shadows to walk beside me, his rear leg no longer dripping blood. It was good to know the supernatural beasts' bites would heal like any other on the wolves.

He came to stand beside me, his ears pricked, golden eyes scanning the darkness.

"I can't sense them," I said. "I don't know which way they went. But Kendrick's not on the property anymore—and neither are Ellen and Cole."

Dan shook himself and glanced back towards the house. I followed his gaze and saw Gracie, trotting beside Erin with slender grace. Erin had her knife in her hand. Behind them, other wolves appeared, their muzzles splashed with yellow chemicals and flecks of their own blood.

Dan glanced up at me. I placed my hand on his head and patted him for good measure. He gave me an amused look, but the contact worked.

'Find them,' he thought. *'Search further.'*

I found that, connected to him, I could do just that.

I closed my eyes and looked into the world with my new sight. The forest around us filled with the small, glowing stars of birds and insects. I pushed further out and found them, the wolves' stars glowing like tiny suns. Beyond them was a pulsing blue glow. Surely Riley couldn't still be alive?

Dan, sharing my vision, let out a growl. He pulled his head away from my hand and I snapped back to reality.

I didn't need to say anything. We would head for that blue life sign and make sure it went black.

Dan took a step forward and whined. He sniffed the air, then glanced back at the others. One of the larger wolves, possibly Glenn, raised his head and let out a howl that rose up into the night. An answering howl floated back from somewhere distant.

Ears pricked forwards, the wolves trotted past me one by one, picking up speed as they disappeared into the darkness.

Dan and Gracie stayed where they were. Dan nudged me with his nose.

"Go," I said. "We'll follow you in Kendrick's car."

As they faded into the shadows, Erin turned to me. "What will we do when we catch up with her?"

I shrugged. "That's up to her. But I hope I get to kill her."

Chapter 29

*E*rin drove—I needed to use my second sight. The wolves had taken off into the forest, which was great for them—but we needed roads. That meant matching available routes for cars with what I could see in the star-dotted mindscape.

Someone needed to invent an app for this. GPS overlaid with second-sight would be really, super helpful.

One question that was burning in my mind was where the hell Brandt was in all of this.

When I'd 'become', for want of a better word, I'd seen him at the edge of the property, lightning flowing up into him from the ground like crackling plasma—and now he was just... gone. Wasn't a Väktare supposed to be able to *find* vampires? Wasn't that our main claim to fame? And if so, why the hell couldn't I see him? I wished there was someone who understood this power that could give me some pro-tips on how it worked.

Not for the first time, I wondered where Abigail was. I hoped Brandt's message had just been to goad us and that she was okay.

I also wondered how the hell Riley had survived two gunshots to the chest *and* one to the head.

Erin broke into my thoughts. "There's a turn coming up—should I take it?"

I realised I'd stopped watching my internal map and pulled it back into focus.

"Yeah, if it goes right, go right," I said.

Erin had slowed down to a crawl; now she hauled the car to the right and started down a forest road.

"Where's she going?" I asked in confusion, as we turned on to a dirt track. I figured she probably wanted to stick to the trees, but this road led to the coast. What was she planning?

We reached a T-junction.

"Right again."

We turned onto a shingle road that ran along the top of a sheer drop that fell twenty metres down to the ocean. I was not comfortable with this.

I closed my eyes and checked for life signs. "She's not far ahead—watch out for—"

Erin slammed on the brakes.

I opened my eyes to see a wolf standing in the middle of the road, its head lowered. Its yellow eyes glimmered in the car's headlights.

"Is that Kendrick?" said Erin.

I was pretty sure it was.

The wolf bared its teeth. In my nocturnal landscape, his life force shone blue.

"I think Riley's controlling him," I said.

Riley stepped out from the trees. Yep. Definitely

controlling him.

We got out of the car.

"Kendrick!" I called to him as his snarls rose to a roar. "We're not going to hurt you. So please, you know—don't kill us."

He continued to snarl at us, his pupils blown out, his chest heaving with stress.

"All your friends are dead," I called past him to Riley. "This is not how you make new ones."

Riley laughed. "I can make more. Besides, who needs friends when you can control your enemies?" She stood beside Kendrick. "You've made a mistake, Liss. You're on the wrong side of history. It's not too late to change that."

I laughed. "Seriously? The 'join me' speech isn't supposed to happen until the climax, and no offence, this doesn't feel very climactic."

She narrowed her eyes. Kendrick's growl grew in volume.

I took a step towards her, the calm woman next to the snarling wolf. If I could touch him, I was sure I could break her grip on his mind.

"Give up, Riley. We'll give you a fair trial."

"A fair trial?" She was incredulous. "How can a trial be fair without anyone to defend me? How can a trial be fair when the penalty for breaking any rule is death?"

"You heard Kendrick. They didn't know you were a forest dog. I'm sure they would have made an exception."

"Are you honestly trying to convince me you'll

forgive me for killing Jack?"

I gave a shrug. "No, not really. You're fucked."

"Get in your car and drive away, or Kendrick dies," she said. "If you continue to pursue me, I will kill everyone you love."

My pulse beat faster. Maybe I didn't want her to give herself up after all. Maybe this was better.

The wind whipped up off the ocean and Kendrick whined, his eyes squinting in pain. I was guessing he was fighting her mind control and it wasn't much fun for him.

"Last chance," she warned.

"If you kill Kendrick, you have no collateral. And when the rest of the wolves get here, they'll tear you apart."

"No," she said. "They won't. But if you don't back off, they'll all take a leap into the sea."

Kendrick let out a high-pitched yelp and turned, every muscle tense with strain, to face the cliffs. He walked, one laboured step after the other, towards the drop.

"Stop!" I said, and lunged towards him. Riley raised a hand and Kendrick looked back at me, his teeth bared.

"He can kill you, or he can kill himself—or you can back off," she called over the rising wind.

The others couldn't be far away.

Kendrick took two more steps towards the edge of the cliff.

"Okay!" I said. I held up my hands, palms facing her. "Okay, we'll back off."

337

Kendrick's ears lay flat against his skull. He stepped to the very edge of the cliff, dislodging a pebble that bounced off the rocks on its journey towards the sea.

"Leave, now!" said Riley. If I'd been a forest dog, I was betting her voice would have held the alpha ring that Kendrick's had.

I shut my eyes and looked at her with my second sight. She was channelling bright green strands of energy from the trees and pushing blue energy into Kendrick in a steady stream. As strong as she seemed to be, the wounds in her chest and forehead were glowing masses of light. My guess was that trying to heal potentially fatal wounds, while controlling a mind like Kendrick's, was taking more energy than she could draw.

"*Leave!*" she screamed.

Kendrick scrabbled at the edge, fighting not to fall, as her impulse pushed at his mind.

The others would be here soon. We just had to stall her a little while longer.

"Okay, okay, we're gonna get in the car now." I gestured to Erin and we both backed towards the car. I opened the back door.

"Come on, Kendrick."

"Oh no," she said. "He's coming with me. I know you and your kind. You won't give up until I'm dead, unless you have an incentive."

"No offence, but I don't think Kendrick wants to be your pet."

She laughed. "The wolves are easier to control

than dogs. It's in their blood. They crave leadership."

"You know there's a difference between leadership and using a supernatural roofie, right?"

My heart was hammering in my chest. I wanted her to make a move. I didn't want Kendrick to die, but her hold on him was the only thing stopping me from murdering her.

Where the hell were the other wolves? I could see their stars among the trees, but they were faltering, moving in aimless circles.

"You have ten seconds to get in that car and leave."

Kendrick let out a yelp of pain as the wind whipped around us, scrabbling for footing as Riley urged his mind forward.

How much longer could she keep doing this, as injured as she was? I was betting not much longer.

As if to prove me wrong, the wind grew stronger, the creaking of the trees around us punctuated with the crack of snapped branches bouncing towards the ground.

"Okay! Okay, Riley, we're going!"

I glanced at Erin and we got back into the car. As we did, I closed my eyes and saw stars all around us as the wolves arrived. Finally.

Dan and Gracie streaked past the car and leapt at Riley. But as they launched into the air, Gracie's body twisted mid-leap. She caught Dan's ruff and pulled him sideways, sending the two wolves rolling over and over in a tangle of fur and teeth.

"Leave him!" Riley commanded.

Gracie broke away and trotted to her side. She stood facing down Dan, her teeth gleaming in the moonlight.

I closed my eyes and saw Riley had diverted her energy away from Kendrick into Gracie... which meant Kendrick was free.

He scrambled away from the edge of the cliff and disappeared into the forest. In my second sight, I could see him circling her, but Riley wasn't fooled. She raised a hand and Kendrick stalked out of the trees behind her, his ears laid back against his head, his eyes squinted in pain. He joined Gracie at her side.

Beads of sweat broke out on Riley's forehead as she struggled to suck the energy she needed from the trees. More branches cracked and the stem of a sapling at the side of the road ripped in two. Shreds of wood burst from the broken centre as if it'd been hit by invisible lightning.

Kendrick and Gracie snarled like hyenas, the fur raised in ridges along their backs. Dan growled back.

"Get back in the car and take him with you, or I'll have these two tear him apart!"

Dan took a step forward and Kendrick launched at him. He caught Dan's ruff and rolled him over, then placed a paw on his throat, and growled into his face with teeth that dripped saliva.

Dan pinned his ears back to his skull, his tail curled between his legs.

"I warned you!" thundered Riley. Her voice was so charged with power, it made lights bloom behind my eyes.

"Okay, okay. Dan, get in the goddamn car!"

Kendrick let him up and he scrabbled to his feet and trotted back to me. His slitted eyes were filled with murder.

"We're getting in the car, Riley. When we get back to the main road, we'll stop and wait for Kendrick and Gracie. If they don't turn up within ten minutes, I'm turning around and coming after you to end this."

Riley's voice lowered to a very dog-like growl. "Good luck with that."

I held the back door against the wind and Dan jumped into the back seat.

He reached out his muzzle towards me and I briefly rested my hand between his ears as I prepared to shut the door. The instant I did, a jolt of power ran through me. I could feel it—his energy, added to mine.

I closed my eyes as Erin got into the driver's seat. In my second sight, I could see the blue energy radiating from Riley was starting to tremble. Her wounds glowed white-hot. She couldn't keep this up.

'Now!' His thought in my head was filled with urgency.

"Go!" screamed Riley. Kendrick and Gracie stepped towards us, Kendrick still fighting against Riley's compulsion with every ounce of his being, while Gracie was immersed completely in her will.

'Distract Riley and she'll let go,' Dan thought through our shared link. His eyes fixed on my knife.

'If bullets didn't hurt her, I don't think I can do much damage with a knife.'

'All we need is a distraction.'

Screw it.

I stepped away from the car, drew back my arm, and threw my knife at Riley with as much force as I could, while Dan torpedoed out of the car towards Gracie, loose stones spraying out from under his paws.

The knife flew true and sank into her stomach. Riley staggered backwards and put a hand to her abdomen. She pulled out the blade and let it clatter to the ground. It wasn't going to kill her, but it'd done its job. She'd lost her hold on the wolves.

She sank to the ground, a hand pressed to the wound.

Free from her power, the wolves turned on her. But as they lunged at her, she put her palms up to face them, channelling what little power she could still manage. The wolves' teeth clicked together and they stood, muzzles frozen in snarls of fury, unable to move.

Blood pulsed from Riley's wound. She couldn't heal and hold all three wolves, but she wasn't ready to give up just yet.

Slowly, the wolves all turned to face me.

Dan growled. Saliva dripped from his jaws, slung back along his muzzle by the wind.

"Now I have three—what will you do?" said Riley, her voice hitching with pain.

"Wait for you to die?" I said.

She gasped and a pulse of blood ran from her wound.

I could feel her power shuddering like the handlebars of a bike on a dirt track. Dan turned towards her and I felt him push back against her — but while she was nearly tapped out, her answering surge of energy made him sink to the ground with his teeth locked together.

"How do you think... Dan's going to feel tomorrow as he's... picking pieces of your... flesh out of his teeth?" she ground out.

Before I could answer, shapes melted out of the trees. The rest of the pack had found us.

They swarmed around her, facing off against Kendrick, Dan, and Gracie.

"Stop, or I'll have them tear each other apart!" shouted Riley. She gritted her teeth with effort as she made one last desperate attempt to draw the power she needed.

The wolves stood with their forelegs spread, their teeth bared. Their energy rose around me, a whirlwind of anger and power.

A wolf leaned against me and I recognised it as Tai. I pushed my hand into his ruff and felt the maelstrom flow through me.

'Together', I thought to him. He tensed under my touch and I closed my eyes. It wasn't as hard as I'd thought it'd be. Maybe because the wolves shared some kind of connection anyway. But just thinking about channelling my power through him to the others made it come alive. Gold-orange lightning crackled over his fur and leapt to the other three, severing her hold on them.

"Now!" I shouted to the wolves. They surged forwards. Riley put her arms up, her fingers outstretched as she desperately tried to draw more power. I felt the juddering in her power increase to the point of breaking and pushed a last blast of power through the wolves, so that it leapt to her like grounded lightning.

She tried to scrabble away but the wolves surrounded her.

"Stay back!" I shouted to them.

I stalked towards her, Tai taking halting steps at my side, so we could keep the contact.

I reached Riley and pulled her to her feet. She swayed in place.

"Liss—"

I punched her in the face. She fell to her knees and I crouched in front of her, that golden power crackling between us. Dan brought my knife to me, holding the handle gingerly in his mouth, and I took it from him.

Riley's eyes fixed on the knife. I knew I should kill her now, while she was weak. While there was no one to tell me not to. I held the blade against her throat.

"Now would be a good time to apologise for killing my father."

A look of contempt entered her eyes, but she said nothing.

"I'll take that as a no. Either way, you're going to

die. I don't really care if you make peace with me or not."

I pressed the blade into her skin.

A growl sounded behind me.

I didn't turn around. "She's going to be executed anyway!"

Kendrick closed his teeth firmly around my wrist and a thought formed in my head.

'Not like this.'

"Then how?" I said aloud.

'We need to know if she really is the last of her kind before she's put to death.'

I shook my head in disbelief. Why? What would we do if she was? Put her in a cage and breed from her?

'I can't sanction making a species extinct.'

"She killed Jack!"

Riley, hearing only half this exchange, raised an eyebrow.

'Take her back to the reserve, Liss.'

Even his thoughts woke an impulse in me to obey him. But I wasn't his wolf.

I pressed the knife harder against Riley's throat and Kendrick dug his paws into the dirt and tugged at my arm. He was stronger than me.

I growled at him. He growled back.

"Are you all right?" Riley asked.

I gritted my teeth. "I'm going to take you back to the reserve. Unless you want to try to kill me again. Then I'd be quite happy to see who wins."

"He won't let you kill me, will he?" she said, with

a small smile. "Choosing the right side of history, Kendrick?"

Kendrick let go of my arm and I pulled Riley roughly to her feet.

"We're going to get into that car now and drive back to the reserve. At the first sign of you trying anything, I'll kill you and use you as a coat."

The wolves moved out of our way as I hauled her towards the car.

I pushed her into the back seat.

She sat back against the seat, a hand against the wound in her abdomen, an unsettling smile on her face. It wasn't the expression of someone who'd been defeated and was facing execution. It was the expression of someone who'd won.

"You drive," I said to Erin. "I'll ride in the back with her and make sure she doesn't cause any more trouble."

Erin glanced at the wolves. "Should we take one at least for support?"

I shook my head. "With her, they're more liability than help. You and I can take care of her until we get to the reserve."

I got in next to Riley.

As we pulled back on to the main highway, Riley gave me a look of pure contempt.

"So what will you do with your new power?" she asked. "Help support an oppressive regime? How very noble of you."

"This is not how you fight oppression," I said. "You killed Jack. You have no idea how much effort it's taking to not do the same to you."

"Yes, I do regret that." Yeah, she absolutely didn't. "It should have been Daniel Stoke."

"You think I'd be less upset if Karlo had torn Dan apart?"

She answered with a small smile that enraged me.

"You might think there's not enough space in the back seat of a car to punch someone to death, but you'd be wrong."

She snorted. "Alessandra De Witt, all class."

I sneered. "Just how alive are you right now?" I asked. "And how much of you is held together with cosmic duct tape?"

She blinked slowly. "Can't you tell, all-powerful Väktare?"

I closed my eyes and ran my second sight over her. The wounds I'd seen before, the places where the golden power had collected, were still there—but smaller. I was sure they were smaller. But that could be the power of suggestion. I knew one thing—Ellen hadn't missed. Any one of those three shots would have killed Riley if she were human. The wound in her stomach had stopped bleeding, but it was still open. That wasn't going to heal in a hurry.

"I'm not that easy to kill, Liss."

"I can see that," I said. "But if I take you on a ship, out into the middle of the ocean where there are no trees—I'm betting you'd fall apart like so much wet meat."

Her eyes glittered. "Are you planning on murdering me?" she asked.

I grinned. "Bitch, I might be."

We pulled up at the reserve a short time later and several of the wolves, now in human form, came out to the car to escort her inside.

She didn't fight as they led her down into the basement. In my second sight, her life energy was burning so low, I expected what little light she gave off to gutter and die at any moment.

There were four cells in the basement, and as we arrived at the bottom of the steps, I realised Karlo was still in one of them. This suddenly seemed like a really bad idea. But where else could we hold her?

Luke had a cell door open and waiting, the only cell that had bars, instead of solid iron walls. A cell we could easily see into.

Riley turned to face us as Luke locked the door.

"Don't mistake the wolves' penchant for justice for stupidity," I said to her. "If you try to use your power on any wolf here, you'll be slaughtered and your pieces scattered to the ends of the earth."

"There are no ends of the Earth," she said. "It's round."

I leaned in. "Then I guess the wolves will just have to eat you."

As Ben, Glenn, and I started back up the stairs, Karlo shouted through the small barred window in the door of his cell. "You can't leave her down here! Please! Don't leave her here with me!"

Glenn and Ben exchanged a glance.

Luke walked over and smacked the iron door with his hand. "Shut up, asshole!"

"Hey, Luke," I said, jerking my head towards Riley. "Aim it at her."

"If she does anything suspicious, call me," said Glenn. "Anything. Okay?"

Luke nodded and Glenn and Ben headed back upstairs.

I cast one last look at Riley. She wasn't drawing any energy. If she stopped drawing, did that mean she'd stopped healing? I guessed we'd find out.

I started up the stairs, and Karlo shouted out to me.

"Don't leave me with her! Please!"

I stopped on the steps and turned back to Luke. "Let me see him."

"You shouldn't—"

"Luke... he's not the enemy. Take pity on the guy."

He seemed about to argue, then thought better of it. He unlocked Karlo's cell.

Karlo was sitting on the floor, his back against the wall, his knees drawn up. I pulled the door shut behind me.

"It's her," he whispered. "I can feel her. In my mind." His eyes were red-rimmed, his olive skin pale.

"She knows if she tries it again, we'll kill her," I said.

He reached out a hand and grabbed my wrist, pulling me down to his level.

"Kill her. Kill her. You can't control her. I can feel her burning... burning in my brain."

I checked him with my second sight but couldn't see anything.

"Right now—you can feel her in your head, right now?" I asked.

He nodded. "Not controlling me, but it burns... Liss, it hurts so much."

He put his hands to his head and grabbed fistfuls of his hair, shaking his head in pain.

Gently, I pulled his hands down.

"Hey," I said. Tears ran down his face as he met my gaze. "I'm going to try and help you."

I had no idea what she'd done to him, but I got a sense it was something I might be able to fix. I closed my eyes and looked into his mind.

The light the wolves gave out was too bright—I needed to filter it down so that I could see what lay underneath.

I peeled away the light in layers until I could see Karlo's mind; the intricate patterns of electricity that were his thoughts, the energy that drove his brain. I looked for anything that seemed out of place—a colour, a shape, a broken connection. Finally, I found what I was looking for. I magnified it and dove in for a closer look.

It was a scar—at least, that's what it looked like. A place where multiple connections terminated into a shallow crater in his brain. I overlaid it with red so that I could see it clearly. As I touched him with my energy, I could feel how much it hurt for me to look at him this way. I was sure it wasn't supposed to hurt.

I sent energy into him, surrounding that tiny place in his brain that was damaged. I willed it to heal. I wasn't sure how to make it do that, but it was worth a shot.

As I ran golden energy over the scar, it glowed softly. He let out a cry and grabbed my wrist, but I knew it was working. The redness, the darkness that separated that part from the rest of his mind, shrank and dwindled away.

I felt his pain ease and opened my eyes.

Karlo looked at me in wonder. "I don't know what you just did, Liss, but thank you. Thank you."

He looked calmer now, more like the Karlo I knew; the guy with the immaculate shirts and the popped collars, who looked cool no matter how hot things got. But even as I was quietly celebrating being able to help him, grief flooded his eyes.

He covered his face with his hands. "Oh God, what have I done?"

"It's not your fault," I said to him.

He shook his head.

"I have to leave," I said, "But I'll come back and check on you later."

He nodded.

I left him with his head bowed, his shoulders shaking as he cried silent tears.

Luke let me out.

"What did you do?" he asked.

"I don't know how to explain," I said, "So I'll just say, I undid what she did to him. And don't doubt for one second that she's responsible for Jack's death.

She programmed him to kill and let him go like a wind-up toy. Have some empathy for the guy. No one feels worse than he does right now."

For the first time, Luke seemed to get that maybe Karlo wasn't an evil murderer after all.

"Am I safe, then, staying down here with her?" he asked.

I glanced across at Riley's cell. "I think so. But we need to get this trial happening as soon as possible. The longer she's here, the more danger there is to us all."

Chapter 30

$\mathcal{B}$ack up top, I could sense the wolves' unease—not just that their alpha had been hijacked, but that the creature who'd done it was even harder to kill than they were. A bullet to the brain would kill most things, as long as they were alive to start with. Sometimes even when they weren't.

I still wasn't convinced that Riley could outlive that wound in her skull, although I remembered Brandt's comment that immortality from dark magic usually resulted in madness. Could she really have made herself immortal? Was that possible?

I reached the top of the stairs and grew aware of how cold it'd got. Shivering, I went in search of my jacket. I went into Dan's room where I'd left it and slipped it on. The darkness was comforting and it was warm. I realised I was on the verge of exhaustion and sat on his bed, tempted to crawl under the covers and sleep.

While I was summoning the energy to get up and go to my own room, the door swished against the carpet as Dan pushed it open.

"Liss?"

"Oh, hi," I said. "Sorry. I was about to leave—"

"No," he said. "No, don't leave."

He stood awkwardly in the doorway. I didn't know what to say. We both knew things had changed now in a way that couldn't be undone. That single kiss in his bedroom only hours before had broken the illusion there was nothing between us. But I was so not ready to explore what that might mean. Not right now. All my anxiety around what he wanted from me was still there. Sure, I could see into him and see he really cared for me, but... he was still Dan. Which meant he could stop caring for me tomorrow and start caring about someone else just as much.

"How's Kendrick?" I asked, leaving the elephant in the room to chew on the curtains, or whatever neglected indoor elephants did.

"I think he's a bit shaken up," said Dan. He leaned in the doorway and put his hands in his jeans pockets. "Understandably."

"Does he understand the risks in trying to make Riley stand trial?"

"More than anyone. But he's also very, very angry."

That much I understood.

"So. You're a Väktare now," he said. "Not quite what I expected."

I pulled the hair away from my face and tied it back. My hands shook as I swept the elastic band around my hair one too many times, drawing it too tight. I loosened it again.

"You all right there?" Dan asked, amused.

With the lights off, I could see wet flax brushing against the windows in the wind, and beyond that, a cloudless sky full of glittering stars. What else was out there? I wondered. Dawn couldn't be too far away.

"Have you heard anything from Abigail?" I asked.

"Nothing."

"Doesn't mean anything," I said, half to myself. "We should call Tristan. Tell him we have Riley. Call their bluff." My vision was fading. I needed to sleep soon.

"Can... we talk about something else?" he said. He pushed off the door frame and held a hand out to me. I took it and he pulled me to my feet.

He started to lean in for a kiss but I pulled back, my heart pounding. There was something in his touch. Something hungry. It passed through him into me, and I was in no state to figure out what it meant.

"I need to go see what Erin's doing," I said.

I walked around him and he followed me into the hallway. "I don't get it. I thought you wanted this."

"I'll talk to you in the morning."

I headed down to the kitchen to get a glass of water and found Erin sitting at the kitchen table with Ellen and Cole. For a change, Cole wasn't drinking tea. I guessed no one wanted to caffeinate at this time of the morning; if anything, we needed sleep.

I filled a glass and sat beside Erin, dropping my head onto my arms, too tired to drink it.

"I shot her in the head," Ellen was saying. It sounded as though she'd already said it a few times. "I mean, I shot her in the *head*."

"You got her," I said, my voice muffled by my sleeve. I looked up. "She's wounded. But she can draw on her power to heal herself. Well—I think she's healing. It's hard to tell if she's healing or just holding herself together. I don't even know if she's still alive."

Cole fixed his sharp gaze on me. "What is she, Liss? And what can you see? What's this power of yours all about?"

All three sat expectantly, waiting for me to put into words something that I really couldn't put into words.

I blew out an exhausted breath. How to make them understand.

"It's like all your senses are confused with each other. Like I can taste colours and see emotions. I don't even know exactly what I'm seeing. There's a lot to take in. Too much."

"Can you find vampires?" said Cole.

"I can see where they draw their power from," I said. "Brandt draws on deep power. It looks like he's pulling lightning up out of the ground."

Erin raised an eyebrow. "That sounds cool."

"It is," I said.

"So—you can find him now?" Cole asked.

"He disappeared," I said. "So, no."

Ellen folded her hands on the table. "I guess with something like this, there's going to be a learning curve."

Cole tapped the tabletop with his fingers. "Well, perhaps you'll be able to see more tomorrow."

"I can tell you one thing," I said. "If we let Riley get back to full strength, she's capable of taking us all down. I don't think it's safe to keep her here. We should at least keep the other wolves away from her—including Karlo."

"We should just end her," said Cole. "Be best for everyone."

"I don't think Kendrick will allow that," said Ellen.

Cole snorted. "Why not? She nearly killed him tonight."

"She's also the last of her species."

"She's not a wolf, though, is she, Ellen?" said Cole. "What duty do we have to her?"

Ellen shrugged. "It's Kendrick's call while she's in his territory."

"Assuming Kendrick's in full possession of his own mind."

Ellen looked sideways and widened her eyes briefly as if to say 'here's hoping'.

"And what about Brandt?" I said. "Does he just get to walk away?"

Ellen and Cole exchanged a glance.

"What?" I said.

Cole made a face. "Maybe we should just leave him be. If he wasn't responsible for Jack's death, then we have no reason to go after him."

"What about the other people he's killed?" I said.

"What about Corey?" Erin added.

We both looked at Cole.

He spread his hands. "It's not worth it, Liss. After all this dies down, we need to concentrate on keeping the peace."

I stared at him, a lump forming in my throat.

Erin spoke up. "If the wolves are afraid to protect people—who will?"

Cole looked at Erin in confusion. "Protect them? What, you mean like they're protected from car crashes and heart disease and killing each other? It's not our responsibility to protect them, Erin. It never has been."

"Then what's the point of this power?" I said.

He sat back in his chair. "I don't know, Liss. What's the point of being a werewolf, or a human, for that matter? We are what we are. No fairy godmother tapped you with a wand at birth and decreed you had to save the world."

I was suddenly very tired. I drank as much water as I could, then tipped the rest into the sink.

"I'm going to bed."

As I opened the door to my room, Dan stepped out of the dark. "Liss. Can we talk?"

"Can we talk tomorrow? I'm about to crash."

He hovered in the hall and I could sense he had something on his mind. But I had nothing left to give.

"I'm sorry, I need to sleep."

I went into my room and shut the door. Within minutes of my head hitting the pillow, I was asleep.

I woke to the warmth of late afternoon. Orange light flooded through the curtains, and a lone cicada was doing its best to convince itself it was summer. While it would be soon, I had the feeling it would be a lonely bug for a while yet.

For a moment I imagined myself back at home, and wrapped the image around me. In that dream-blown vision, I walked down the stairs to where music was playing quietly in the lounge, the French doors open to let in the scent of fresh cut grass. I could hear the sound of a lawnmower in the distance. Jack and Andy had their heads bent over their tablets, Jack's fingers twined with Andy's as he alternately sipped his coffee and scrolled through his news feed.

I let go of the vision and waited until the concrete ache in my chest died away and I could breathe again.

I got up and pulled open a gap in the curtains. So far, the world hadn't ended. Dan was sitting alone on the steps smoking a cigarette, while Gracie and Erin sat on the grass, chatting. I wondered what they were talking about. I'd never seen Gracie having a casual conversation before. She'd certainly never had one with me.

Cole stood leaning on the porch railing, lost in thought, while a group of wolves stood chatting in a tight circle.

Everyone seemed to be enjoying the daylight while they could.

I sat back on the bed in the room's orange twilight

and felt the emptiness of loss tug at me. It was hard to care about what would come next. Hard to find the energy for hate when grief took so much of what I had.

We'd need to wait for Abigail and the others to get back before we put Riley on trial. After that, I was hoping she'd be executed and it would all be over. I was sure Abigail would make the right decision, even if Kendrick refused to.

And then what? Just ignore this new power inside me and live a normal life—pretend none of the last ten years had happened?

I wasn't going back to university. I had only grimy memories of my classes. I was pretty sure I would fail if I tried to go back.

Maybe I could get Thomas to take me back at Thomas! Cars.

That was a cheerful thought.

Something was happening outside. I jumped off the bed and went to the curtains. Dan and his brothers were arguing. There was a lot of agitated gesturing going on.

When I got outside, the wolves fell silent. Erin was staying at a respectful distance, so I figured it was wolf business.

"What's going on?" I said.

Dan looked down at the ground, gathering himself while the others waited for him to speak.

"Abigail just called. They're all okay, but they're at the Copelands' property. They found Tristan's father in the woods. He's alive, but it looks as though

Riley's done something to his mind."

"And?" I could see there was more.

"And," said Dan, "They found the rest of the Midlands pack. Abigail said their bodies were stacked in a pile in the woods. They're doing a clean-up before someone finds them and calls the cops."

"They're all dead?" I was in shock.

"Everyone except Tristan. They couldn't find him."

"Jesus."

"Yeah," he said. "So, assuming Riley and Tristan killed everyone in their pack, we"—he gestured to his brothers—"think a trial's a waste of time. We need to kill her before she does the same thing to us."

I looked up as Kendrick appeared on the porch. "Everyone inside."

Dan gave me a dark look. "You know it's true."

"Let's hope Kendrick agrees."

We crowded into the lounge where Isabella and Tane were waiting.

"By now you've heard what's happened in the Midlands," said Kendrick. "It's critical that we don't panic. The Alpha Circle will meet urgently to put Riley on trial once Abigail gets back."

"Trial?" said Cole. "We're still going with that?"

Ellen gave him a sharp look and he shrugged at her.

"At this time we have no proof that Tristan and Riley are responsible for the murder of the Midlands pack, but while it's not a leap to assume they are, there's also the vampire's role in all this to consider.

Things may not be as they seem. I don't want to play into his hands."

"Let's just execute her!" said Ben. "What are we waiting for? She admitted she killed Jack… you've seen how powerful she is. Why even try her?"

Kendrick gave him a steady gaze. "It's critical that we follow our own laws around trial and execution. That's how we've had peace for so long."

I could see that neither Tane nor Isabella agreed with him, but they weren't going to undermine him in front of his pack.

"Why do we care?" asked Luke. "She's not even one of us."

"What if she makes us kill each other before we can hold the trial?" said Ben. He turned to me. "She could do that, right?"

"Maybe," I said. "I think she's too weak right now, but I don't know if that'll last. I vote we finish her now."

I could see Kendrick was starting to get annoyed. "This is not up for vote. It's not open for discussion. This is what's happening. Abigail's bringing Tristan's father, Nicholas, back with her. We'll question him and he'll provide evidence to the Alpha Circle. Until then, we just need to stay calm. I'll continue to evaluate the risk Riley poses to ensure she does no further harm."

I looked around the room and saw simmering anger on nearly every face.

"Cole, I'd like you to question Riley," said Kendrick. "Find out what Tristan's involvement in this was and report back to me. Right, if there are no more questions, Cole, we'll let you do your job, and reconvene once the others get back and have time to debrief."

The wolves dispersed, their anger thick in the air.

As Cole started towards the stairs, I caught his attention. "You shouldn't be alone with her—she can roll your mind. If I'm down there, I can stop her reaching out with her power."

He considered me, then nodded.

"One thing, though—either I need a wolf to channel my power through so that I can protect you from a distance, or I'll need to keep physical contact with you as long as you're down there."

He scowled. "That's not going to work. Get Hair. At least I know he won't cause trouble."

I gestured to Dan. Without question, he followed us downstairs.

Riley was sitting in her cell when Luke unlocked the door. She had her eyes closed, her head drooping towards her chest. She looked up as she heard the door open, and even that seemed to be an effort.

Dan and I leaned against the cell's bars. He took my hand without speaking and squeezed it. He looked at me curiously, but I kept my eyes fixed in front of me until he looked away. I felt my face glow red; even though both our palms were sweaty, being close like this was more distracting than I'd anticipated.

Cole gave us both a warning look as he pulled his interrogation stool into the cell.

He set the stool in front of Riley and sat. "So you're the one who's been causing all the bother," he said.

Riley smiled. "I'm the one who's defending her rights to body autonomy, yes."

Cole clicked his tongue. "It's an interesting turn of phrase, that. Defending. You see, my understanding of that word is that you need to be attacked before you can defend."

Riley's smile twisted into a sneer. "It's funny, where the ruling power sees only the enforcement of a law, others may see an *attack* on their rights."

"I see." He shifted on his stool. "Do you know why I'm here?"

She nodded. "I assume you want me to implicate my lover before you try me in your kangaroo court."

"No kangaroos here, love," he said, "Wrong country for that."

She rolled her eyes. "You have no right to try me. No right at all. You're not even my *species*. Who's going to speak for me in this farcical trial?"

Cole spread his hands. "Me. That's what I'm here for. To defend you. If you want my help, I'll stand as your advocate. If you don't, I'll stand to one side and let the jury make up their own minds. But the wolves of this country don't operate by the 'slaughter everyone who opposes them' method you and your brother-slash-lover seem to employ. Now, if you don't want the good folks upstairs to give you a fair trial, that's up to you. You just let me know. I might still have some questions for you, but we might change the format."

This was more the Cole I'd been expecting when he'd questioned Karlo. He sat leaning forward with his hands resting on his thighs, his eyes locked with Riley's. The threat that boiled off him made my skin crawl.

Riley weighed her options. She glanced at me and Dan, then back at Cole.

"I believe my position is defensible."

Cole smiled. "I'm sure you do. So, would you like to start by telling me how you and Tristan slaughtered his entire family?"

Riley shook her head. "We killed no one."

"Why am I not convinced?"

Riley swayed in place and put a hand against the wall to steady herself.

"What's up?" Cole asked, suspicion in his voice.

"Ask your Väktare," she said bitterly.

Cole turned to me.

"I don't know," I said. "She's not drawing power. Maybe being underground?"

Cole turned back to Riley. "Is she right?"

Riley nodded. "I can't heal while I'm underground. If you truly do want to give me a fair trial, I need to be allowed aboveground to heal. Otherwise, you won't have to execute me." She closed her eyes.

"Riley?" said Cole.

She swayed in place.

"Riley!"

She winced and opened her eyes.

"What you need to understand is that it would be very, very convenient for us all if you were to die. No one's coming to help you. No one cares if you live or die except for Tristan, who seems to have made himself scarce. Now, I'm prepared to advocate for you if you're honest with me. But I'm not going to take you up top and give you the chance to create any more chaos."

Through heavily-lidded eyes, Riley nodded towards me. "She can stop me from attacking the wolves. All I ask is to be allowed to draw enough energy to heal. To *survive* long enough for you to give me a fair trial."

Cole gave her a cold smile. "Why would I take that risk?"

Riley reached forward and put her hand on Cole's knee. "Here's your incentive."

While no energy flowed out of her, Cole's expression changed from one of alarm to puzzlement. Riley took back her hand.

Cole narrowed his eyes. "What was that?"

"A sample of how much bigger this is than you can imagine."

"Assuming what you just showed me is true," Cole said.

Riley smiled grimly. "If I stay here much longer, I'll die. Take me outside where I can take strength from the forest and we both get what we want. You'll have your answers, and I'll gain more time to prove I only acted in self-defence."

Cole got up. He looked down at Riley, then back

across at myself and Dan.

"Can you contain her power?" he asked.

"I think so," I said.

"Think so or *know* so?"

"With enough wolves to channel through, I know so," I said.

He nodded. "All right, Riley, you get your wish."

He went to the door and Luke opened it to let us out. Before Luke could say anything, Cole shook his head.

"Luke, you've done a fine job, mate, but everything's going to be okay. Okay?"

Luke didn't look convinced, but he wasn't about to argue with Cole.

"Now go check with Kendrick if he's happy for us to do this."

Luke came back a minute later. "He says it's your call."

As Cole led Riley up the stairs, Karlo called out to us from his cell. "Watch her, Liss. All she does is lie."

Which was exactly what I was afraid of.

As we walked Riley through the wolves upstairs, the push from their anger made the hair on my arms stand on end. Cole got her outside as quickly as possible, and I felt all eyes glued to our backs.

The back garden was surrounded by beech forest and cabbage trees, their clumps of spiky leaves sharp against the blue sky.

Riley spread her fingers and closed her eyes. With my second sight, I could see green tendrils reaching from the trees to the tips of her fingers. But her own life energy barely registered as a dim glow.

As she drew on the forest, I used Dan's energy boost to cast a golden net over the wolves nearest her, in case she decided to attack—but I didn't expect big things from her.

After ten minutes of soaking up virtual chlorophyll, I was sure she had enough to keep going—but not enough to be a threat. I nodded at Cole and he grabbed Riley's arm and escorted her back into the house.

Back downstairs, Riley sank onto the bench in her cell, while Cole took up his position on the wooden stool. Glenn came down after us and handed Cole a couple of bottles of spring water. He took them and set one aside, then opened the other, drinking half of it while Riley watched. He paused and wiped his mouth with the back of his hand.

He put the cap back on the bottle. "How are you feeling now?" he asked Riley. His voice made it clear that he didn't particularly care about the answer.

Riley very deliberately looked at neither the water bottle in his hand or the bottle sitting by his stool.

"I'll survive."

"That's the spirit," said Cole. "You ready to answer some questions?"

She laughed. "Ask away. It'll be interesting to see if you're good for your word, and if you're willing to hear what I have to say."

"Oh," said Cole with a grin. "I'm all ears, love."

As much as Cole could be a prick, and as much as

he came across as a sexist jerk at times, I was getting the sense for the first time that it was intentional, rather than something truly built into his DNA. The way he was talking to Riley now was the way he used to talk to me. It wound me up, the way Cole's nicknames for the Stoke brothers wound *them* up.

Given that Cole was very aware of the effect of every word he spoke in an interrogation, I found it hard to believe he'd been oblivious to the effects of his previous teasing. Which meant he deliberately didn't make friends with other wolves. I guess it made sense, if you were expected to be their enforcer.

Cole used the bottle of water in his hand to gesture at Riley. "So tell me about Brandt. How'd he come into your life? When did he rock his sorry arse up on your doorstep for the first time, or did you go looking for him?"

Riley kept her gaze fixed in the middle distance, refusing to acknowledge the bottle of water in his hand. But she had to be thirsty. I knew I was. In fact, I was starting to obsess about this ending so I could go upstairs and get a drink.

"Brandt and I have had only the briefest acquaintance. He asked for my help. I refused."

Cole nodded. "Okay. That's one story." He uncapped the bottle and took a sip.

"It's the truth," said Riley.

Cole took another swallow of water. "Fair enough. Remember, though, love, I'm on your side—if Brandt orchestrated all of this, there's less chance the pack will throw a death sentence at you for Jack's

369

murder."

Dan and I shared a quick glance. Neither of us believed that.

"Brandt's motivations are his own. I have no interest in them," said Riley. "He thought he could use Tristan and me to achieve his own ends. He soon learned otherwise." The way she said it, with such contempt, made me think she was telling the truth.

"So who exterminated the Midlands pack?" said Cole, gesturing with the nearly-empty water bottle. "Brandt?"

"Don't meddle in things you don't understand."

Cole laughed. "Oh, that is rich. You and your brother usurp power from your father and then the rest of the pack's corpses end up stacked in a puppy pile—but you don't think we should interfere? Seems to me you're the biggest living threat to the wolves right now. I take that very seriously."

Riley shrugged.

Cole leaned forward on his stool and rolled the empty water bottle between his palms. "You realise the 'fuck off, it's none of your business' defence might not wash with some of our esteemed leaders?"

Riley finally made eye contact with him. "This is not something I'm prepared to discuss."

"Well, that is a pity," said Cole. "Because right now, you look guilty as hell to me."

He tossed the empty water bottle into a corner of the cell and picked up the second bottle. He started to twist off the cap, then paused and offered it to her.

She looked at him with narrowed eyes.

"What?" he asked, as if genuinely surprised at her response. He shook the bottle at her.

She reached for it as if she expected him to snatch it back out of reach, but he let her take it.

"Sorry, should have offered before," he said.

I could see that the gesture had unbalanced Riley. Now she wasn't sure what his angle was. She'd been expecting him to use water as leverage — yet here he was giving it to her freely.

She finished twisting off the top and took a sip, trying not to appear too desperate.

"That thing you did," Cole said as she drank. "When you put your hand on me — what's that all about?"

Riley paused for breath, half the water gone.

"Like your Väktare, I can share thoughts and memories."

"Yeah?" said Cole. "That sounds dangerous. How would I know what I see's the truth?"

"Your Väktare should be able to tell."

News to me.

Cole glanced across at me. "You a lie detector now?"

"Yeah, and I also find bugs and hidden cameras," I said. "Honestly, Cole, I don't know what she's talking about."

"Come here," said Riley. She patted the bench beside her.

Cole gave me an almost imperceptible nod and, against my better judgement, I left Dan and sat beside her. She beckoned to Cole and he slid his stool

371

forward. She placed one hand on my knee, another on his.

I closed my eyes so that I could use my sight. Through the link, I could feel Cole's curiosity and absolute confidence in himself, and Riley's intention to be honest. I couldn't help second-guessing; was I projecting those feelings on to each of them, based on what I thought they felt, or was I really feeling what was inside them?

"Concentrate, Alessandra," said Riley. "The truth is in the shape of the memory. See what I see."

I felt energy course through her fingers into me and jumped to my feet to get away from her. Cole looked at me, waiting for an explanation.

"What did she show you?" I asked him. "Sorry if I'm paranoid, but before she shares with me, I want to know what you saw."

Cole nodded. "Showed me a pretty picture of Tristan and Karlo having a little chat behind Karlo's bar."

"She's lying," hissed Dan. "Karlo warned you. Why would you believe her?"

"Oi, Hair, when I want your opinion, I'll let you know, yeah?" said Cole.

He looked back at me. "Can you do it or not, Liss? Can you tell if she's lying?"

I pushed a few strands of hair out of my face, then undid the hair band and pulled it back again, tying it tightly enough to make my scalp hurt. Could I do it? Karlo's life was dependant on me somehow knowing if a skilled manipulator was telling the truth.

"Liss, you've known Karlo as long as you've known me!" said Dan. "How can it be true?"

I looked from Dan to Cole's steady gaze, to Riley, whose husky-blue eyes gave nothing away.

Mentally, I made a decision. It didn't matter what I did, this was going to land in my lap. I sat back down and Riley placed her hand on my knee again.

Again, that power started to flow. This time, I let it.

Darkness. I could taste cold air, smell wood smoke. My body felt alien—nothing was quite where I expected it to be. An image resolved into being.

I was in the car park that backed onto Karlo's bar. Under a new moon, the car park shone as if it'd been raining, rainbows shining in oil-slicked puddles. The blue lids of the plastic recycling bins glittered with water droplets.

I was standing in shadow—*whoever I was*, was standing in shadow—watching Tristan and Karlo as they spoke together on the back steps of the bar. Karlo was dressed for work in dark jeans and a soft white shirt that contrasted with his olive complexion, while Tristan was dressed in a grey pinstripe suit and vest. He looked as if he'd just come from a business meeting. I didn't know what the Copelands did for work, but it occurred to me that it'd be useful to know. Especially if they were doing business so far from home.

Any time a wolf entered another's territory, it was customary for them to request traverse permission, or TP. If they were doing more than passing through, they were expected to speak with the pack alphas in person and ask permission to be in their territory for the duration of their stay. I could have been wrong, but I was pretty sure Abigail and Kendrick hadn't granted Tristan permission to be up here.

We were too far away to catch their conversation, but their body language was clear. Tristan wanted Karlo to do something and Karlo didn't want to do it. Karlo folded his arms, his voice rising enough for snatches of conversation to be heard.

"She'd make a better leader," said Tristan.

"She's not one of us. None of us will follow her."

"Not even if she's stronger than you?"

"I doubt that's likely."

"I think you're wasting an opportunity. By all accounts, her power when she turns could be spectacular."

Karlo shook his head and his voice was lost in a garbage truck braking somewhere nearby. " —took a risk just taking her in—"

Riley broke the contact.

My eyes were burning. I got up and briefly thought about walking out, then realised I was still needed. Instead, I went over to where Dan stood. He took one look at my face and the fear inside him leapt up a notch.

"What is it?" he asked urgently.

I shook my head. I wanted to believe Karlo was talking about Riley. But if Karlo knew Riley was a forest dog, that meant he'd known about her and Tristan's plan and had said nothing to anyone. If he was talking about me... well.

"I don't know," I said honestly. "Maybe Karlo knew about Riley's power way before this happened. It looks like Tristan tried to recruit him. He said no, but he still knew... and didn't say anything."

"No, no, if he knew this was coming, he would have told us," said Dan.

"If he didn't know about Riley, then he doesn't think much of me," I said. The truth was, that's what it felt like. It was more believable than Karlo not warning us.

"Ask your questions, Cole," I said wearily. "I'll make sure she doesn't step out of line."

I sank down to the floor and sat against the bars with my knees drawn up, my arms resting on my knees. Dan sat beside me and put his hand over mine to keep the contact.

I'd had my moments over the years of feeling excluded, left out of the full-moon parties, the wild hunts, the generally being tall and good-looking, and that sense of community that the wolves shared. I was like the geeky kid trying to be one of the cool kids—they'd let me do their homework, but they'd never let me be one of them.

Through the shared connection, Dan sensed what I was feeling. "Show me what you saw," he whispered to me.

Cole looked back over his shoulder. "Stoke, I won't tell you twice—Liss needs to concentrate, so shut it."

Ah, the Cole we all knew and loathed.

Dan clenched his teeth together and I knew he was itching to hit someone.

Cole started to ask Riley questions again, asking her to elaborate on the scene she'd shown us. Had she been there? No, she'd taken that scene from the mind of one of Tristan's bodyguards. Why was Tristan in the Westlands? It turned out the Copelands were in shipping, and he was up here talking to a contractor about signing a contract for all their international sea-freight. I tuned out.

I couldn't believe Karlo had known about Riley and not warned the pack. But how could he have said all that about me? I thought of him as a brother from another father, and until that moment I'd have told you he was a great guy. He was a close friend of Jack and Andy's, had grown up with Andy and had been the best man at his wedding to Jack.

Was he really a traitor?

Dan squeezed my hand and I looked up. Riley had her hand on Cole's knee again, her eyes boring into his. He looked paralysed. I thrust my hand out in front of me, concentrating a stream of energy at Cole that crackled over his skin in a net, blocking Riley's assault. Cole's head whipped around and he stared at me angrily.

"Did I ask for your help?" he snapped.

I was speechless.

"I'm trying to find the truth, here. Why don't you and lover boy head upstairs?"

"But she can—"

His eyes lit with fury. "Upstairs, Liss. And tell the

ACs I'll meet them in the boardroom."

"You can't—" started Dan, but Cole got to his feet. "Upstairs!" he thundered.

Dan and I upstairsed. We found Kendrick in the boardroom, speaking quietly with Tane and Isabella.

Dan knocked quietly on the door and pushed it open. "Just so you know, Cole sent us up here so he could commune with Riley. He wants to speak to you when he's done."

"Commune?" I heard Kendrick say as Dan closed the door, but Dan had clearly had enough.

He shut his eyes for a moment and then said, "Hey—have you ever been up on the roof?"

I shook my head, thrown by the randomness of his question. "There's a roof?"

"Come on. I want to go where they can't find us."

We walked down to one of the bedrooms and he shut the door behind us.

"Forgot about it until just now when I was thinking some privacy would be nice. Ben showed me this secret window when we were kids. I used to use it when I wanted to get away from Tai. Apparently *he* used to use it when I was little." He grinned. "Check this out."

He went into the wardrobe, sending coat hangers screeching along the rail out of the way. I crowded in after him. There was a window at the end of the closet, just big enough for a person to fit through.

He opened it as far as it would go and boosted me through, squeezing himself through after me.

I got to my feet and found myself standing on a

section of roof that was walled off by the steep slopes of roof that ran down in either direction to form vaulted ceilings over the two halves of the house. Over a low decorative parapet, we had a clear view of the forest, but we couldn't be seen from any other bedroom windows.

It had to have been designed this way on purpose. The flat section was tiled, sturdy enough to walk on safely.

We sat down and gazed out over the forest that surrounded the reserve.

I glanced across at him, wondering why we were here. Just escaping the chaos below, or something else?

Dan leaned back on his hands and took in a deep breath. "So. Can we talk now?"

Oh. That was why.

"Sure," I said, keeping my tone light. "What did you want to talk about?"

He looked sideways at me. "Last night, when you showed me what you could see—when we were connected—I really felt something. Something I haven't felt before."

"Mmhmm," I said, studying an ant that was making its way along a pale path of grout between two tiles.

"And then you went all cold on me."

I sighed. "I don't know what you want from me."

He took my hand and squeezed it. "I've *never* known what you wanted from me."

I looked up at him. "That's rich."

"No, Liss, that's *honest.*"

I pulled my hand away from his. He'd had years to grow something between us, and all he'd ever done was tease me.

"Come on, Liss, admit it. You clearly don't know what you want—from me at least. So how can you be angry at me for not giving it to you?"

I looked out at the hills beyond the forest. "This is possibly the worst time ever to be talking about this. Have you not noticed there's kind of a lot going on?"

He dropped his head to his chest. "Yeah. But we're still human."

"You're not." The words came out before I had time to filter them.

He raised an eyebrow.

As close as we'd gotten in the last twenty four hours, I could feel what he wanted, and there wasn't a lot of confusion there. He wanted comfort—a haven. He wanted what our current situation was denying him—his favourite coping mechanism.

He pulled off his shirt and squinted up at the sky. "At least we can get some sun while we wait for Riley to murder us all."

I rolled my eyes and looked away.

"Oh, come on Liss.

I looked back at him, and there it was. That flirty smile, the raised eyebrow, his head held at just the right angle for the sun to catch his eyes.

"This is a great place for naked sunbathing," he joked. He reached out and twined his fingers with mine.

I tried to ignore the electricity in his touch, but that connection had been opened between us too many times. I could feel everything he was feeling.

"How often did you come here?" I asked, trying to think of something else.

"Well, you know Tai."

Tai was a few years older than me, so while he was the baby of the Stoke family he was still an older brother to me.

"I wouldn't run away from him," I joked.

Dan flashed me a glance. "You know he likes boys, right?"

I did, but pretended to sigh anyway. "All the prettiest ones do."

"Hey!" He leaned in and kissed me. The kiss was exploratory at first, deepening as I kissed him back.

He pushed my t-shirt up and I shuddered at his touch, breathing into his hair as he pushed me gently back against the tiles.

He paused, his face inches from mine. "Tell me if I'm wrong, but I think this is what you want."

Just like some shitty, bad romance novel heroine, I nodded, breathless.

"Thank God." His lips met mine again.

So much for staying away from the Stoke gene pool.

Chapter 31

Dan heard the cars pull up; I was otherwise distracted. He stopped what he was doing and looked up. "They're here."

I murmured in protest and was about to make a poltergeist joke, but I could see he'd heard something that upset him.

"They need you," he said, hurriedly pulling his shirt back on.

I tidied myself and followed him back through the window. As I hopped down into the wardrobe, I wondered if any of the others from his extensive list of girlfriends had been out on that ledge. Of the alphabet, would I count as 'A' or as 'L'?

Dan sped down the stairs and reached the door as Abigail led a man I didn't recognise up the porch steps.

It had to be Tristan's father, Nicholas, the deposed Westlands' pack alpha. He looked as though he'd been stranded on a desert island. His beard was long and matted, his hair wild around his shoulders and clumped with dirt, his eyes wide and staring. I'd

never seen a grown man look so terrified of just...
everything.

We got out of the way as Abigail guided him past
us. She took him down the hall to an end bedroom.
As she passed us, Anton Gregory, who ran the Deep
South pack, gestured me over.

"I hear you came into your full power—
congratulations."

"Thanks," I said, blushing. I never felt comfortable
around him. For every one part of parental
indulgence he gave off as an alpha, he gave off four
parts macho swagger.

He was in his sixties, but could have passed for
under forty. Younger if he'd looked after himself. As
it was, his hair was a brushed-back tangle that
framed a bushy, rust-flecked beard. His faded jeans
were too tight, and everything about him stank of
leadership by violence.

"Abigail's going to need your talents," he said, his
South Island accent strong. "Nicholas's brain's a
mess—someone's been in there and stirred it up like
a concrete mixer." He gazed at me thoughtfully. "I
hear you can read minds now?"

"Not really," I said. "I mean, if he doesn't want to
share with me, I can't just read his mind."

My skin crawled as he sized me up, his green eyes
boring into me.

"Go help Abigail," he said.

"She hasn't—"

"Now." He gestured down the hall.

My face burning, I walked down the hall to where

I could hear Abigail speaking to Nicholas Copeland in a low voice.

I knocked on the door and pushed it open.

"Come in and close the door, Liss," Abigail said. Her voice was low and calm, like the voice you'd use to soothe a frightened animal. I walked into the darkened room and hovered there, unsure what to do next.

Nicholas sat on the bed, his eyes shifting between me and the curtained window.

"Nicholas," said Abigail, trying to get him to focus on her. "Liss is here to help you."

She waved me over and I came and stood in front of them.

"We can't get through to him—he doesn't recognise anyone. I hear you can share thoughts, mind to mind—I was hoping you might be able to get through to him."

"I can try," I said.

Nicholas watched me warily as I crouched in front of him.

"Hey, Nicholas, I'm Liss."

His eyes widened as I reached for his hand, but the moment I made contact, he seemed to calm.

"I'm just going to take a look at your mind," I said. "I promise I'm not going to hurt you."

He let out a small breath and his fingers relaxed.

I closed my eyes and looked at him with my second sight. Anton's analogy of his brain being stirred up wasn't far off—Nicholas had the same scarring I'd seen in Karlo, only in several places, with scorched trails running between them. The knots looked dense, like tumours of scar tissue.

Well, I could only try my best.

I sent a flow of golden energy into him, concentrating on the lesions. His fingers twitched as I channelled the energy in a steady stream, breaking down the angry red tissue and clearing the channels the scarring had blocked.

As the knots began to heal, he gripped my hand with both of his. I opened my eyes and saw the animal wariness in his eyes had gone.

"Thank you," he whispered.

"Are you okay?" I asked.

He nodded, tears running down his face into his beard.

He let go of my hand and I straightened up.

Abigail looked at me in wonder. "What did you do?"

"I undid the damage Riley did to his mind. I did the same for Karlo. Her control, it leaves scars."

"Locked in my mind," said Nicholas, half to himself. "Locked behind the wolf." He put a hand to his face and felt the beard, then looked down at his filthy clothes.

"We'll give you some time to yourself," said Abigail. "I'll have one of the boys bring you a towel and some fresh clothes."

"And a razor. Please," he said.

Abigail shut the bedroom door behind us as we left.

"Thank you, Liss. I wish I'd been here to see your

384

transition. It seems we have a lot to talk about. But right now, I need to speak with Kendrick. I'll come and find you later." She gave me an encouraging smile as she headed up the stairs.

The lounge felt like a war encampment between battles, everyone tense, resting while they could, staying close together. With our number one enemy locked in the basement, everyone was on edge.

And, I realised, the full moon was coming. Even in daylight, I could feel its pull.

Dan nudged me with his elbow as he walked past.

"We're going to play poker to pass the time."

"Pass the time before the executions start?" I asked dryly.

"Execu*tion*. You got a better idea?"

I did, but since the only place we were likely to have any privacy was the roof, and since it looked as though it was about to rain, cards it was.

I sat down next to Erin, consciously avoiding sitting too close to Dan. Whatever might be going on between us, I didn't want anyone else to start asking questions before I knew what it meant.

"Where have you been?" asked Erin.

"Doing stuff," I said, as Ben shuffled the cards and started dealing.

"I thought you knew better!" she hissed. I glanced across the circle at Dan, who was pretending he couldn't hear our conversation over the general noise.

"Some stuff happened," I mumbled. "Now's not a good time to talk about it."

She glared at me. I picked up my cards and fanned them, deliberately not meeting her gaze.

Cards and drinking were usually the wolves' prelude to the monthly full moon celebration, so it was unusual for me to be included. But thanks to Jack's coaching over the years, I not only knew how to play poker, but how to win.

After the fourth hand, the wolves were looking less than impressed as I raked in the chips yet again.

"Okay, does anyone else here feel like there's a shark in the swimming pool?" Glenn asked. The others chuckled.

"Feel free to get out of the pool," I said with a grin.

Dan laughed quietly to himself, even though I'd taken as many chips from him as I had from the others.

Two more hands later, I was starting to wonder if I should give them a break. Glenn had two chips left and my stack looked like the pre-2001 New York skyline.

"Anyone need a loan?" I asked, to a bunch of comic growls.

Suddenly Dan went still, listening. The others soon followed. I couldn't hear anything—no, wait—raised voices from upstairs.

I couldn't make out words, but apparently the wolves could. They glanced at each other.

"Someone fill me in?" I said.

"Cole doesn't want to tell the ACs what Riley showed him," said Glenn.

I imagined that was going down like a bucket of

cold sick. I got up and headed up the stairs, knowing what was coming next. As I knocked on the boardroom door, Kendrick opened it.

"We were just about to call you," he said.

"I figured."

He gestured me in and I sat in the one free chair in the room. I swivelled nervously in my chair as Kendrick joined Abigail at the other end of the table.

Cole's expression was grim. "Liss, for the love of God, I need you to trust me right now and *say nothing.*"

His tone was fierce, but under it was a note of fear. I closed my eyes and looked at him with that other sight. I had no idea what honesty looked like, but I could search him for signs of Riley's influence. As far as I could see, there was no scarring, no blue tint to his mind that might indicate he was under her spell.

I opened my eyes again. Cole silently pleaded with me.

"I hate to say it, but if Cole doesn't want to tell you, maybe there's a good reason."

Abigail's voice was frosty. "That's not how a hierarchy works, Liss."

Cole appealed to Ellen. "Ellen. You know I wouldn't withhold information for no reason."

"Why don't you want to tell us?" she asked. "At least tell us that."

Cole opened his mouth, trying to find words he could use in front of the Alpha Circle. "I can't. Not right now. All I can say is that anything I say now puts us all in danger."

"We're already in danger," said Kendrick calmly.

"How long have you known me, Kendrick?" Cole brought his hands down on the table. "My first priority is my kind, always has been, always will be. If I'm not telling you something, there's a good reason."

"Liss," said Ellen.

"She's not controlling him," I said, "and I can't see any evidence she's been in his mind."

The ACs began to speak among themselves. How could they hold Riley to trial without all the information Cole had? How could they fight an unknown enemy? And what right did Cole have to think he knew better than the Alpha Circle?

Ellen spoke up. "Cole, will you tell any of us — anyone who can vouch for you — so that at least one of us knows that whatever you're holding back isn't just a way to protect yourself?"

Cole stared at her. "You think I'm in on it too now?"

"I'm saying proof that you're not would help," she said.

Cole stared around the table, his gaze finally settling on me.

"Yeah, all right. I'll tell Liss. In fact, I'll *show* Liss. Will that satisfy everyone?"

The other alphas clearly weren't happy, but Abigail put up a hand. "I trust Liss. Liss, if you wouldn't mind."

I got up and went around the table to where Cole was sitting and put my hand on his shoulder. I closed my eyes.

I could feel his gaze on my face as I looked inside him.

'Can you see my mind?' he asked through that link. *'Show me.'*

At first, all I could see was darkness. Then out of that darkness, a face loomed. Anton Gregory. His face swam out of sight again and the focus changed. I found myself lying on the ground on my stomach. All around me were the corpses of wolves, some in four-and-fur, some in cocktail frocks and suit jackets. Blood was soaked into the ground in front of my face and my quivering fingers were stained with it. I was hurt. Badly hurt. Two feet away, a string of entrails tugged out of a wolf's stomach steamed in the cold air. The night smelled like a butcher's shop, ripe as a sweaty copper coin.

At the edge of the slaughter stood two dark-coated wolves, their fur matted with blood, and Anton Gregory. He was dressed in biker leathers, and as he turned away from me, I saw the Southland Wolves patch on the back of his jacket.

I closed my eyes and rested my head against the damp, stinking soil, pretending to be dead. A moment later, someone seized my hair, pulling my head back. I opened my eyes and stared into Anton's cool green gaze. There was a sharp pain against my throat, then blood spurted on to the ground in front of me. I choked on the blood, couldn't breathe, couldn't—

Everything went dark.

I opened my eyes, panting hard in shock. I put a hand to my throat, running my fingers over the perfect skin that a moment ago had been ragged and torn. Cole stared at me, willing me to be on his side.

I glanced at Anton, who was amusing himself doodling on a notepad. He looked bored.

Cole pulled my hand down. Through his touch, he sent me a warning. *'Don't give it away, Liss. Not until we know if this is true.'*

He let go of my wrist and folded his hands on the table in front of him, handing the decision to me.

Abigail looked at me questioningly.

"What Riley showed him is garbled," I said. "It's useless. You have to trust Cole when he says he needs to know more before he can brief you."

There was a knock at the door. Nicholas pushed the door open and Abigail motioned him in.

He cast his eyes around the room, and I noticed his gaze flicker over Anton and slide away. Anton watched him with a predator's stillness.

"Uh, Abigail, Kendrick—I need to speak with you alone."

Only I noticed Anton's brief flicker of surprise. So, when he'd sent me to 'help' with Nicholas, he hadn't expected me to be able to do anything.

"Please excuse us," said Abigail. She and Kendrick rose from the table.

Cole stood with them. After a moment, Abigail nodded to him.

"You too, Liss," she said to me.

With werewolf hearing being what it was, the only

way to get privacy was to leave the house.

We walked out together into the dreary late afternoon. Somewhere not too distant, thunder rumbled. The clouds that hung over us were heavy with rain, filtering the light to a jaundiced yellow.

"Firstly, please tell me what's happened to my family," said Nicholas.

Abigail gave him a sad look. "We found Amanda with the rest of the pack—they were murdered. Tristan wasn't among them."

Nicholas shook his head, his face crumpled in disbelief. "No."

"I'm sorry, Nicholas, I really am. But it looks as though Riley was involved."

"Involved?" he said. "Is she all right?"

"She's in our custody," said Abigail. "You should know, she attacked us and she's being held for trial. She's admitted to murdering Jack Koestler."

"Attacked?" He was incredulous. "Murdered Jack? Why would she do that?"

"She believed the Alpha Circle was infringing on her right to continue her species."

Nicholas frowned, clearly struggling to process what she was saying.

"But she's human. I don't understand."

"She's a forest dog," said Abigail. "You didn't know?"

"What? No!" Nicholas ran a hand through his hair.

"So she never asked you about getting permission to have a child with Tristan?"

391

Nicholas's eyes squinted in confusion. "With Tristan? No. I mean, obviously she and Tristan know the moratorium is in place—the whole pack knows. We told the kids we'd help them out if there was an accident, but no, my adopted daughter never asked for permission to have a child with my son."

He put his hands to his mouth. "Oh God, Amanda."

I understood. It was so easy to hear the words and instantly forget they were real.

"If I can intervene," said Cole, "we have a fairly delicate situation here, Nicholas. What do you remember?"

Nicholas took a shuddering breath and shook his head. "Nothing."

"You remember," I said quietly. "I undid the damage. But I understand why you don't want to look."

He gave me a tortured look.

"You can show me," I said. "If you don't want to say it out loud."

I could see his answer in his eyes, see that he'd rather die than relive whatever was in his head.

"Let me show everyone," I said. "And you'll never have to talk about this again."

Nicholas bowed his head. His body shook with sobs and Abigail put an arm around him. She gave Kendrick a helpless look.

Kendrick put a hand on the other man's shoulder. "Nicholas, whatever happened, lives are still at risk if we don't act now. Riley is a very dangerous person to have in captivity."

I took Nicholas's hand and Cole rested a hand on my shoulder.

"Show me," I said to Nicholas. I closed my eyes.

At first there was darkness—then the sound of people chatting, and the clink of bottles on the rims of glasses faded in. I could smell smoke, feel heat, as if I was standing next to a brazier.

'*Let me see*,' I thought to Nicholas.

A moving image flickered into focus.

I found myself in the kind of garden you usually have to pay entry to see. What passed for the Copeland estate's back yard. Wow, these guys were loaded.

I felt a tremble of indignation from Nicholas and tried to suspend my sense of self and sink into the memory. I could judge him later when I wasn't connected to the most painful experience of his life.

This was the garden that lay at the rear of the house. The ground sloped down towards a stand of oak trees that bordered a neighbouring park and had been carved into tiers, each tier supported by a bluestone retaining wall, with stone steps running down the centre. Cocktail leaners under freestanding patio heaters dotted the manicured grass. We were having a party. It was someone's birthday—

'*Riley's*.'

Riley's birthday. The heat came from the outdoor fireplace in front of me. Amanda, Nicholas's wife, stood in front of me. She was draped in an elegant ivory cocktail frock, her short blonde hair swept

393

across her forehead in a slick wave. Nicholas was filled with love and pride as he took his wife into his arms and kissed her gently.

I felt a shock at the realisation his wife had been human. Tristan wasn't even a full-blooded wolf.

The doorbell rang and Amanda's fingers trailed from his as he headed back into the house to answer the door.

As Nicholas, I felt a shock of distaste at finding Anton Gregory and two men he didn't recognise—

'Caleb and Joey,' I thought.

—on his doorstep.

"Heard there was a party," said Anton. He stank of leather and sweat. But Nicholas knew who he was, and a visiting alpha expected to be greeted with respect when they announced themselves. Then again, calling ahead was kind of a given, too.

Nicholas wanted Anton off his doorstep. His kind had no place in his home.

"Thank you for the courtesy call, Anton, but we're having a party tonight. I'm happy to skip the formalities."

Anton smiled. "Don't mind if we pop in for a bit, do you?" He looked past Nicholas. "It's been quite a long drive. Besides, I've never seen the old Copeland family home before."

As Nicholas, I didn't want this man in my territory at all, and I wanted him in my house even less.

"I didn't know you were coming, but you're welcome to pass through."

Nicholas stood a little taller, letting Anton know

his rudeness was reason enough not to let him in.

They stood eye to eye for a long moment.

Anton scratched behind his ear with one finger. 'I'd really like to come in."

Caleb and Joey stood either side of him like bodyguards. Waiting.

Nicholas knew he could ask him to leave—but he was pretty sure it would spark a confrontation if he did. It was his daughter's birthday. He wasn't in the mood to be challenged to a fight by some sweaty thug from the South.

Letting him in seemed like the lesser of two evils.

A man approached with a tray of champagne-filled glasses.

"Don't mind if I do," said Anton. He took one in each hand and walked past Nicholas into the lounge. His bodyguards followed.

Riley rushed into the lounge, her face flushed. She was wearing a pale blue dress, the same colour as her eyes.

"Dad, come on, we're about to cut the cake." She grabbed his hand, then stopped as she noticed Anton. He inclined his head and gave her a smile that made me bristle on her behalf.

"Sweetie, this is Anton Gregory. He's the alpha for the Deep South pack. He's come by for…" Nicholas trailed off. He didn't know why Anton was there.

Anton extended his hand for Riley to shake. "Just passing through," he said.

"Hi." She glanced back at her father.

'She's not this innocent,' I thought to Nicholas.

He pushed back at the thought with anger.

Mentally, I shrugged. *'Show me what happened next.'*

"I'll be out in a minute," he said to Riley. "Ask your mother not to light the candles just yet."

She left, casting a backward glance at Anton.

Nicholas felt a flicker of irritation as Anton threw himself down on the couch and put his feet up on an exquisitely carved coffee table, while Joey hijacked a tray of canapés and sat in a chair, wolfing them down. Caleb disappeared to find a bathroom.

Nicholas knew he should run them out of the house, and on another night he'd have sent Anton packing with a scar or two to remember him by. But there was no way he was going to get these three to leave without ruining the night.

Anton made a gesture with his head, *don't let me keep you*, and Nicholas left them to their own devices and went back outside.

A crowd had gathered around the tiled outdoor entertaining area to watch the cake being cut.

The cake itself was a feat of culinary construction, decorated all over with piped icing roses, graduated from deep red at the bottom to pale pink at the top. Looking at it, I wasn't sure how they were going to cut it.

Tristan watched from the edge of the crowd, sipping champagne.

Amanda lit the candles and came to stand beside her husband. He put his arm around her.

"Who was at the door?" she asked.

He shook my head. "Don't go in the lounge. Anton Gregory's decided to pay us a visit."

Her eyes widened and there was a sound behind me, like the sputtering jolt of water from a hose when it was first turned on. People started screaming. Nicholas looked back to see a dark grey wolf with its jaws buried in the throat of one of his own.

"Go," he said over his shoulder to Amanda. "You're human, go!" He pushed her away from him and put his hands up to his shirt to tear it open so that he could change, but froze in place, his fists wrapped in the fabric. He was paralysed, every muscle locked in place. He watched helplessly as the dark grey wolf lapped up the blood of—

His name was Kyle.'

—his kin, its yellow eyes filled with satisfaction.

Anton, flanked by another huge wolf, walked past him down the stone steps. I wanted to see, wanted to follow him, but Nicholas was held in place watching this wolf eat his friend. Its eyes stayed fixed to his as it tugged away a flap of flesh and swallowed it.

The sounds behind me were straight from a horror movie. A voice began pleading. Amanda.

Nicholas couldn't turn his head. "Don't you hurt her!"

Anton came into view, dragging Amanda by her hair. He pushed her to her knees in front of Nicholas and pulled her head back. Her eyes pleaded with him to help her, but he was frozen, as helpless as she was.

Anton pulled a knife from his pocket and flicked it open. With casual deliberation, he drew the knife across Amanda's throat, parting the skin to reveal flesh like the inside of a tamarillo.

Her hands fluttered at her throat and her scream choked off into a liquid gurgle. Anton let go of her hair and she fell forward, the last of the light leaving her eyes as Nicholas watched, unable to do anything to help her.

Anton reached down and wiped his blade on her dress.

The memory ended and, back in my own skin, I opened my eyes to the bruised afternoon light. I lurched away from Nicholas, certain I was going to throw up. But the moment passed and I turned back to the others, the taste of bile in my mouth.

"You don't remember anything else?" Cole asked Nicholas. He looked as ill as I felt.

He shook his head. "Nothing."

Agitated, Cole rubbed the back of his neck and turned away from the circle. He turned back a moment later with a look of frustration.

"I don't get it, Nicholas. Why would they spare you? You were the one standing in their way."

Nicholas lifted his head. His eyes were red-rimmed.

"What happened?" I asked him. "How did you get away?"

He bowed his head. "Anton went on to kill the others while he made me watch. At one point, whatever force was controlling me failed and I ran. I just ran."

I was torn between disgust that he'd run, and

empathy for a man who'd seen his entire family slaughtered.

"Did you know *anything* about Riley's power or origins before that night?" Abigail asked him.

He shook his head. "I only have your word that she has any 'powers'."

"So you thought she was human?" Abigail asked.

Nicholas shrugged. "Her birth parents were aligned with Amanda's side of the family. There was never any talk of her being anything other than human."

"We have enough to put Anton to death," said Kendrick to Abigail. "And Riley's already admitted she was responsible for Jack's death."

Nicholas looked from Kendrick to Abigail, fear on his face. "Please, tell me, how could she have killed Jack? I don't understand."

Abigail shook her head. "I'll fill you in later. Right now, we need to get Anton behind bars."

"Why would he do this?" I asked. "Does he really think the rest of the wolves won't fight back?"

"Most likely he intends to lay claim to the Midlands territory," said Kendrick. "It's not the first time that dispute's come to the fore." He nodded towards Abigail. "You know he thinks he got the thin end of the wedge when the boundaries were drawn."

"Technically, it's the wide end of the canoe, and he has more land than any other pack alpha," said Abigail.

"The Deep South's had problems with drought three years running," said Cole. "People have been migrating north—reduced population means reduced wealth in an already sparsely populated area. Perhaps it's not so much about more territory as it is better territory."

Abigail nodded. "It does seem likely."

"Ellen's been watching him," said Cole. "We did a recon down there last year after her sources told her there were rumblings of insurrection—threats to Anton's leadership. We helped set a couple of malcontents straight, just to keep the peace. Looks like it might have been a mistake."

A thought was burning in the back of my mind. There was no way this was all a coincidence. Somehow, Brandt was behind all of this. I knew it.

"Nicholas, your wife—Amanda—was human?" I asked.

His face crumpled and he wiped fresh tears from his eyes. "Yes," he said.

"So, Tristan is half human?"

He nodded. Abigail and Kendrick looked at me, wondering where I was going with this.

It was Cole who figured it out first. "Brandt—you think he got to Tristan?"

I nodded. "I just have a feeling there's a piece of this puzzle missing. If he's half human, there's a chance Brandt could roll his mind. I need to look at his brain."

They all stared at me.

"Hashtag 'Just a Väktare thing'."

Chapter 32

From what little I knew of him, it was entirely possible Brandt had messed with Tristan's mind, setting him up to take his father's place so that Brandt could start his little war. There was no way he could have done that with Nicholas. Nicholas was too mature—he'd led long enough to know when he was being manipulated. But his son... well. His son was Tristan.

I wondered who'd brought up the idea of having a kid in the first place—Tristan or Riley? And who'd fed her outrage?

"We don't have enough space at the reserve for all our enemies," Abigail said quietly.

"Liss, do you really think you'll be able to tell if a vampire's been in someone's mind?" asked Cole.

"I don't know," I said. "But I can take a look at Erin. Brandt's been in both our minds, back when we were stuck in the forest—if he leaves behind markers the way Riley does, I should be able to find something.

"What are you thinking, Cole?" asked Abigail.

"That Liss is right. That Brandt got to Tristan and manipulated him into inviting Anton to help him depose his father. If that's true, Tristan could be a ticking time-bomb, and we don't know how much influence Brandt might have had over Riley."

"Do you think Riley might be under his control?" Abigail asked me.

I shrugged. "I have no idea. One thing we know for certain, Anton wasn't when he..." I trailed off as Nicholas turned away from us, a hand pressed to his head.

"I'll go find Erin," I said. I was suddenly very afraid of what Brandt might have left in our minds. Both our minds.

I started back towards the house as the sun sank beyond the wooded hills, blinding me with the last few golden spears of light. I had a sick feeling that with the night, something terrible was going to fall on us. This wasn't over.

I knocked on Erin's bedroom door.

"Yep?"

I pushed open the door to find her reading a book. She was wearing a t-shirt emblazoned with a band logo that I was nearly certain said 'Forsaken Age'. It was hard to tell. The font was very... spiky.

She looked down at the t-shirt. "Glenn lent it to me – my stuff is in the wash."

I came in and sat on the bed. "How you doing?"

She gave me a suspicious look. "I thought you were busy with wolf and Dan stuff. What's up?"

"I need to check your brain."

I told her about the conversation I'd just had outside, about what Brandt might have left in our heads.

She put down the book. "So you want to take a look inside?"

I nodded.

"Okay. Go ahead."

I closed my eyes and looked at her with my second sight. Layer by layer, I stripped back the light of her life force until I could see the structure of her thoughts. Unlike with Karlo and James, there were no telltale scars in Erin's brain. At least, as far as I could tell. I tried to imagine what having someone's will forced on a person might do to them. Riley had inflicted blunt force trauma on her victims to keep parts of their minds from themselves. But for all I knew, the effect Brandt had on his subjects was temporary. It might not leave a trace.

"Maybe I can help," said Erin.

I opened my eyes.

"I managed to complete a year and a half of psychology before Brandt, you know, destroyed our lives. Now, this is going to surprise you, but we learned a *little* bit about what the different regions of your brain do. When you're hypnotised, there's a part of your brain called the precuneus—about here." She put a hand on the top of her head towards the back. "It's just in front of your occipital lobe, and it lights up when people are hypnotised. It's most active when you're resting, so while you're awake and doing things, it's supposed to be suppressed. It

403

does lots of work around memory and consciousness. There's where I'd look."

"Okay, so if your precu… whatever… is lit up, that might be bad?"

"Precuneus. Well, it's one place to look."

"Okay. Well, be really brain-active, and I'll look."

I closed my eyes, while Erin presumably solved maths problems or played a mental game of chess in her head. Knowing where to look helped—as did knowing that I was looking for activity, rather than scarring.

I closed my eyes again, and this time I peeled back fewer layers of light. There was *something* there. A faint glow… maybe. My grasp of cosmic Photoshop was still fairly weak.

I opened my eyes. "I don't know," I admitted. "There might be something suppressed, but it's really hard to tell."

She gave me a brave smile. "Please promise me, if I try to hurt someone, you'll stop me?"

I nodded. "As long as you promise not to murder me first."

She laughed.

"You're laughing right now, but I really want you not to murder me."

She laughed harder.

I left her to get some more sleep and met Ellen and Cole in the hall.

"What did you find?" Cole asked.

"Nothing definitive," I said. "No scarring—but

Erin thinks I should be looking for enhanced activity in the pre-cumin... in a bit of the brain about here." I showed him with my hand.

"You can see that?" Ellen asked.

I gave her a nod that said, *kinda, not really.*

"Abigail and Kendrick want more information before they take any action, so we're going to look for Tristan," she said. "I'd like you to come with us."

I was confused. "Why me?"

Ellen gave me a grim smile. "We want Tristan alive, but we don't know what kind of mind control he's been exposed to. You'll be there to make sure nothing... unusual... happens."

"Unusual," I said weakly. More unusual than what?

All I could think of was Caleb's vague smile and the casual way he'd snapped my finger on command.

Cole seemed to read my mind. "Don't worry, I'm happy to use any force necessary on those two idiots while we're extracting Tristan."

I gave him a half-hearted smile.

Ellen drove, which was, as always, a near-death experience. We arrived at the Copelands' estate just on three hours later.

With her car's engine, there was no point in trying to park far enough away that they wouldn't hear us coming. Either Tristan would be there or he wouldn't. Cole seemed to think he'd be there.

"He's not creative enough to hide," he said, when I suggested if I were Tristan, I'd be anywhere but at the house.

I knew it wouldn't be as simple as just picking the guy up at gunpoint. He and Riley were confident they'd get away with murdering their entire family. There had to be a reason why. Anton was confident enough to swagger around the reserve as if he'd done nothing wrong. All of them seemed very certain no one could touch them, although I hoped Riley had re-evaluated her position on that since last night.

We pulled up outside the front door to find Tristan standing in the lit entranceway.

As we got out of the car, something in my pocket vibrated. Something I'd forgotten about. The phone Brandt had given me. I pulled it out as we walked, and read the message. I stopped walking.

Cole and Ellen, walking ahead of me, realised I'd fallen behind and stopped.

Cole turned back to me. "What is it?"

"This is not your best idea," I read aloud.

Tristan stayed where he was, sipping his whiskey as we mounted the steps to the house. Then without a word, he stepped aside and walked off towards the lounge. Brandt came into the hall, head down over his phone. He looked up, and pushed the phone into his pocket.

"You're back."

Ellen stepped through the open door, intending to push past him, and the air warped. Brandt stood face to face with her. His steady gaze held a warning. Cole tried to move past them and Brandt put a hand against his chest and shoved him back.

"Did you want something?" Brandt asked.

I pulled EMN

"Liss, don't" said Cole.

I ignored his warning and stalked up to Brandt, who stepped back and watched me cautiously, as if he hadn't just stopped two werewolves in their tracks.

"We've come to get Tristan. For today, you're off the menu, and if you want to keep it that way, I'd find a corner and play Tetris on that antiquated piece of technology you've got in your pocket."

Brandt chuckled. "Ah, Liss, you never disappoint. But I'm afraid you can't have Tristan. You see, I'm using him."

"Does he need an adult?" I asked.

"I *am* an adult." He set his head on one side. "Besides, I gave you Riley."

I narrowed my eyes. "Did you just? Wound her up and let her go, is that it? She was more powerful than you, so you sent her to fight a battle she couldn't hope to win to get her out of the way?"

"No one could manipulate that woman's mind," he said, his tone slick as oil.

"Maybe not with mystical shit, but what about good old-fashioned lying?"

He shrugged. "I can't be held responsible for the wolves' squabbles or the draconian rules that make it so difficult for one woman to stave off her species' extinction."

"You're a real piece of work, Brandt."

I did not mean 'work'.

I glanced sideways at Cole and Ellen. They were

watching me silently.

"Have you done something to them?" I asked.

He made a face and shook his head. "No. I think they're just hoping I won't break your neck before they can do anything about it."

Cole's head twitched as if to say, *pretty much.*

"Touch me and see what happens."

It was a bluff, but I was hoping if he made physical contact, my so-far-rather-disappointing vampire-pinpointing-GPS powers would flare to life and become something more useful.

He held my eyes a moment longer then turned away. "You may as well come in. You've come a long way. Have a drink before you go."

We followed him down to the lounge where Tristan sat beside the fire, gazing into the flames.

There was no sign of Caleb or Joey. Seeing Caleb would have made me feel nervous, but *not* seeing him made me paranoid.

Brandt indicated we should sit as he poured himself a drink. We ignored him.

"Liss, are you old enough to drink yet?" he asked.

"Have been for two years," I said. "They let us start drinking at the same time they let us start voting."

"That explains a lot." He poured himself a drink from a decanter and then held it out to us.

I shook my head. "We're only here for Tristan."

He put the decanter down and took a sip of whiskey.

I closed my eyes and started peeling back the

layers of light that made up Tristan's life energy, looking for scarring.

The man had watched his family get slaughtered on the back lawn—no one short of a psychopath would be okay with that. But I couldn't find anything. No dark knots, no inflamed neural pathways. I opened my eyes.

"Riley didn't do anything to Tristan," I said to Ellen and Cole. "But that doesn't mean Brandt hasn't."

Cole gave Tristan a look of disgust. "How could you watch your own mother be murdered and do nothing?"

Tristan sipped his whiskey and said nothing.

I closed my eyes and checked again. Was there the flare in his brain that Erin had said to look for? If there was, it was too merged with the rest of his energy for me to separate it. Dark spots were easy to find. Extra light… was a little harder to see.

"We're going to take him with us, Brandt," said Ellen. "We'll fight you if we need to, or you can go now. Leave the wolves alone and we won't pursue you."

He laughed. "Such a generous offer! Here's my counter. The two of you leave Liss with me, and I don't murder you."

Ellen shook her head. "If you force us into violence, you won't survive."

Brandt scratched behind his ear. "Oh, I don't know." He held his hand out and extended his ring finger. "Do you know what this is?"

The gold band I'd seen him wearing in the club that night, so long ago. The orange stone flared in the firelight.

"Yeah, it's something you probably shouldn't be wearing," said Cole.

"Have I harmed a single wolf?" Brandt asked.

"What's your point?" Ellen asked.

"My point is—and the fact you're not shooting me in the head is evidence that you know it to be true—that you acknowledge this pact is a two-way street. I pledge not to kill you, therefore you can't kill me. That's the rule."

Ellen snorted. "Do you see anyone here who cares if you live or die?"

Tristan put a hand up. "I do."

Ellen's eyes narrowed as she shot him an angry look. She turned back to Brandt. "What do you want?"

He spread his hands. "What I've always wanted; to be left alone. Now that your fancy new Väktare has come into her power—and, let's face it, is only in the infancy of learning just how powerful she is—I want assurance that I'll be left *alone*."

"You're the one who found me!" I reminded him.

"Call that a pre-emptive strike," he said. "After all, if none of this had happened, would you not have hunted me down and exterminated me at your leisure, using the power you have now?"

I ground my teeth. He had a point.

"Who gave you that ring?" Ellen asked.

Brandt stayed silent, mocking us with his eyes.

410

"It didn't come from Tristan," I said. "You were wearing that ring in the club when I first met you—so who, then? Anton?"

Brandt's smile widened, the points of his fangs making tiny indentations in his lower lip as he did. I was pretty sure he did it to bait me, to remind me of that night on the waterfront.

"I've had it for some time. Who gave it to me is unimportant. What's important is that I haven't harmed yours. Isn't that right, Ellen?"

Ellen growled. "There's plenty I can do to you that won't kill you. And once we prove your involvement in these murders, that ring won't save your bloodless hide."

"Your choice, Ellen Kauri. But it would look very bad if you, as an alpha and an enforcer for the Alpha Circle, were to break one of the wolves' oldest covenants just because you lost your temper."

I half expected Ellen to shoot him, but instead she stood there, her eyes filled with rage. I guess no one likes having their self-control questioned.

Ellen may not have wanted to lose her cool, but no one expected great things from me in that department. I stepped up to Brandt and knocked the drink out of his hand. It went flying and shattered against the hearth.

"We're taking Tristan. Get out of our way, or I'll take you down myself!" Corny, but it had the desired effect. I didn't see Brandt so much as raise his arm, but his blow sent me flying across the room. I sat against the wall and closed my eyes, pretending I

411

was in pain. Okay, I *was* in pain, but that wasn't the point.

In my second sight, where he'd been invisible before, Brandt glowed. Maybe it was because I'd made him angry, or maybe it was because he'd touched me, but right now he was crackling with energy, the brightest life source in the room.

As humans smell something foul while a dog smells a story, so the general nausea I used to feel around vamps had morphed into something more complex. I could sense his thoughts... not read them, just feel them, feel what lay behind that smirk. He was afraid. Taking a calculated risk, bluffing like a pro, but he was *not* sure of himself at all. He was relying on that tiny orange rock to stop us killing him. And if we thought for one second—if we could prove he was behind any of the attacks on the wolves—that thin orange safety barrier would shatter.

This power of mine, the Väktare's power, was so much stronger with vampires—I could see that now. With the wolves behind me, I could destroy them all.

I opened my eyes to find Cole holding out a hand to help me up.

"Taking a nap?" he asked. But he knew what I'd been doing. I could see it in his eyes.

I let him pull me up. Ellen had her gun trained on Brandt, while he watched her with a knot in his jaw. As I walked back towards them, I tripped over the edge of the rug and fell into Brandt. I felt him freeze under my touch and knew if he'd had any inkling I was deliberately trying to touch him, he'd have got out of the way. Instead, he instinctively caught me. And I caught him.

His expression froze as I ran golden energy into him. With my hands on him, he was paralysed.

I knew the smile I gave him was probably unsettling. After all, one way or another, I held him responsible for what'd happened to Jack.

I closed my eyes and injected power into his mind. In my mind's eyes, I watched gold electricity spread through his system until his brain glowed white hot.

Cole put a hand on my shoulder and I felt him join my mind in Brandt's.

Brandt was terrified by the invasion. I savoured his fear, finally able to give him a taste of how it felt to be helpless.

'Show me what I want to see,' I commanded. He was powerless to argue.

I stepped into his skin, forcing my way into his private space. Where I'd shared memories with others before, I'd only seen the images they wanted me to see, but here... here I was in control.

'Show me your first memory of Riley.'

I could feel his nervousness escalating as I massaged his mind back in time.

Brains don't store static images or detailed recordings of things unless you're really paying attention. Memories are a broken stream of experiential video, sketched outlines of things that weren't important at the time, and vivid sensory detail of the small things that mattered at that moment. And if you don't know the point in that mess of images and half-finished animation that you're trying to find, there's a lot of scrubbing involved.

'Find it.' I made it a command he couldn't refuse.

Images flashed in front of my eyes as he strove to remember the right moment.

He showed me Riley's face on the night he took me to the Copelands' mansion.

'No good, try again!'

I could feel his panic resonating through me as I stood inside him.

More flickering images, then stillness. The first thing that hit me was the smell. It was the smell a particularly cold night has, when the cold burns your nose and you can't smell anything but the strongest scents. In this case, pine needles.

As Brandt, I was standing among pine trees. The air was cold, as I might have mentioned, but as Brandt, while I knew it was cold, I didn't feel it, but it did affect my sense of smell. That was, when I bothered to breathe. To breathe. I wasn't *breathing*.

My throat closed and my chest constricted as I stood inside his body and felt no movement of air at all.

'Are you sure you want to be in here?' he asked with savage satisfaction.

'Shut up!'

I forced myself to take steady, even breaths, even while I stood in the memory of a walking corpse. This was going to take some getting used to.

I focused on what was in front of me. Riley was standing in a clearing, her arms held out to the trees. There was a book on the ground at her feet. I could just make out scribbled symbols.

She spoke in a language that sounded like Old Wolf, and after a moment I understood the words. Brandt's mind, translating. So, he could speak Old Wolf. I wondered what else he knew about the wolves and about the forest dogs that we didn't know. What he knew about me and my kind.

"I call to my ancestors, to the line that goes back to the beginning of time. Bind my spirit with the old world, under the moon, under the sun, make me flesh and fur. Give me life from the forest, spirit from the trees. Make me whole and two, as I was meant to be."

'*Make sense,*' I ordered him. '*Show me how this started.*' I pushed power into him until I felt him shrinking from me in pain.

We went back further. Cold, again, but this time the smell wasn't pine—it was death. We were in a morgue. He pulled open a drawer, and in it was the corpse of the man Erin and I had killed; the forest dog. Brandt drew a sigil on the man's chest in blood—whose, it wasn't clear—and laid a white animal pelt over him. The man's eyes fluttered, then his body twisted in a mind-bending contortion and the pelt wrapped itself around him as his body distorted into the shape of a dog. A white dog.

So, that was where Riley had got her army from. At least we hadn't killed living creatures. I'd have felt bad about that.

'What else?'

We were back in the forest. Riley lifted her arms to the moon, her eyes on the book at her feet.

"I call on the spirits of my ancestors to walk beside me."

Forest dogs melted out of the trees. Dozens of them. Riley's expression was ecstatic. She honestly thought she'd called them from nothing.

'Back, Brandt. Where'd she get that book from?'

He pushed back against me, but his will parted like candy floss when I ran my golden energy through his mind.

Brandt stood in front of Tristan. He stroked Tristan's blond hair back and cradled the back of his head in his hand.

"Let her find this book. She can't know you left it for her to find."

Tristan nodded into Brandt's hand.

The book in question was a two-inch-thick leatherbound thing that looked as if it'd been handmade from people skin by evil priests.

No, this wasn't where it had started. There was more.

I pushed us back, back so far I could feel a natural end point—or rather, a beginning.

I was holding the huge leather-bound book. The blackened pages seemed to be made from animal hide. The writing on the pages was gold leaf, and I knew, from inhabiting Brandt's thoughts, that it was over fifteen hundred years old. The text was in symbols—

'Germanic runes.'

—and held the history of a race of guardian beings called skoghunds, whose origin was older than the book by thousands of years.

The legend told that these creatures existed before mankind made the evolutionary leap to our present-day species, in a time where there were more races like them than not.

Brandt translated the text to English as he read the symbols.

'To call the dogs to your side is to win the war but surrender the land to them, for awakened they possess the land, and only by their permission or their slumber may you walk upon it.'

'Superstitious nonsense,' he thought at me derisively.

'Is it?' I asked.

With a sudden, disorienting heave, he threw me out of his mind. I staggered and Cole steadied me as I blinked into the harsh electric light of the living room.

"Did you guys get any of that?"

They both nodded.

"Endast med deras tillåtelse eller sin slummer," I said. Whoa. After being in his head, I found I understood the language. At least, the words he understood. *"Only by their permission or their slumber.* What have you done, Brandt?"

His gaze was defiant. "Du är på farlig mark," he said.

"Yeah, well, you're on dangerous ground too," I

muttered as I got to my feet. I dusted down my jeans. "So, you woke the skoghunds. What's with all the dead guys?"

Brandt said nothing.

"Do you want me back in your head?" I asked.

He blanched, which was no mean feat for a vampire.

"When a skoghund dies, its skin is preserved. That skin can be reanimated if it's attached to a body that still has its *hamingja*."

"Why are you saying 'harbinger' without any consonants?"

Brandt briefly closed his eyes and put his teeth together. He shook his head and opened his eyes again.

"The wolves had this belief too," Ellen said. "In Norse mythology, a part of the person—their spirit, for argument's sake—stays with the body until it's destroyed." She said to Brandt, "Reanimation isn't part of that belief."

"It's part of theirs," he said. "During the period in which skoghunds were traded as slaves and for their pelts, sorcery was reaching a new era. You know of *fylgjur*?"

"Familiars?" she asked.

He nodded. "Familiars, followers. Sorcerers used the pelts of the skoghunds to bind a human soul into a being that could be easily controlled and used as a foot soldier. Or a guardian."

"Sorcerers," I said. "Like you?"

"Like me," he said, enunciating the words.

He held my gaze until Cole interrupted.

"So Riley—is she one of these *fylgjur*?"

"She is a skoghund."

"Not before she met you," I said. "How does that work?"

He gave me a look that told me he found this conversation both boring and annoying.

"Skoghunds don't receive their memetic inheritance until they first shift. In order to first shift, they need to learn to draw energy from their environment. Until Riley learned to do that, her full capability wasn't open to her."

"Memetic inheritance?" said Cole.

"Explain yourself Brandt, you're doing us a confuse."

Brandt gave a long-suffering sigh. "Must you, every time?"

I put my hand on his arm and he shuddered under my touch. "I could always just tear it out of your mind."

His eyes slid to the hand on his arm, then back to my face.

"Memetic memory, a bundle of memories and cultural knowledge, is locked inside a skoghund's brain and released at first shift. It contains memories of their origin, their journey, their trials, their practices."

"Someone's been studying," I said. "Although, I suppose a guy your age has nothing better to do than read dusty old books."

A small smile twitched the corner of his mouth.

"I'm sure you're right."

"So let me get this straight," said Cole. "You somehow found out Riley was a forest dog, you gave her a book that told her all about it, and she learned to shift. Why?"

Ellen shook her head. "Isn't it obvious?" She gave Brandt a look of disgust. "To prevent the Westlands from consolidating with the largest pack in the North Island, you got into Tristan's head —you convinced him he wasn't ever going to reach his potential while his father was alive. You fed him the information you wanted Riley to have. Then you gave her the ultimate reason to fight: to save her species from extinction. Tristan was never going to kill his own parents, and Riley wasn't going to get her hands dirty. You needed an executioner. So you brought in Anton, who was more than happy to help."

I was getting it now. "But you're afraid now, aren't you?" I said. "Riley was supposed to fight and die, or at least be weak enough that she wasn't a threat to you. But she's not. She can control any wolf, and that means Anton, too. If she chooses to come after you, you're fucked."

"Why would she come after me?" said Brandt. "I helped her to power. Besides, she can only control wolves. She wouldn't stand a chance against me."

"Not by herself. And then there's that pesky magical immortality with a side serving of insanity. You'd better hope she doesn't put you on her shit list and drag a bunch of wolves along for the ride."

He gave me a cool look.

"Cole, watch him," said Ellen. "Liss, come outside with me."

She led me out into the back garden. There was no sign of the slaughter that'd taken place there, just a neatly manicured garden stepping down to a copse of trees.

"Liss, as long as Tristan's alive, we can't take out Brandt. But we can take him back to the reserve as an accessory to the murders of Tristan's pack. Before we do that, I want to know if there's a risk in putting him near Riley."

"He can't control wolves," I said, "Only wolves that are part human."

"And then there's proving he's done anything wrong," she said.

I frowned. "What do you mean? He set up Riley! He created her *filgyurs* or whatever they're called. Her followers. He killed Corey. He killed all those other people—that little kid's mother—"

"But he hasn't actually harmed *wolves*," she said. "Our laws are very clear. We don't take issue with harming humans."

I stared at her. "So he gets away with it? What about giving Riley an army?"

"Unless he directed them, he's technically done nothing wrong."

I ground my teeth. "He manufactured this whole thing. And we can't kill him because of some stupid ring?"

She pressed her lips together in frustration. "As long as Tristan's alive, no."

She gave me a long look.

"Are you suggesting what I think you're suggesting?" I asked. "Kill Tristan?"

"Cole won't argue."

I blinked in surprise. "But what if Riley was controlling him? What if none of this was his fault?"

"We don't have any proof that she has any kind of supernatural hold on him."

"If it wasn't her, it must have been Brandt. He can't have watched his mother be murdered and felt nothing."

"It's up to you, Liss. Jack was your father. We *will* put Riley in the ground. But while Tristan's alive, even if he's tried, he's a witness to Brandt's ring."

"How do we know it's even real?" I said.

"Maybe it's not," she said. "Maybe someone can verify that—although you know as well as I do that Karlo's the best person to do that, and he's lost all credibility. And if it's real, as soon as it's witnessed by the rest of the pack…" She trailed off. I got it. This was our one chance to take out Brandt. But it meant killing Tristan, whether he was guilty or not.

"We would say he attacked us," said Ellen. "I'll make it quick."

I glanced back at the house. "And Cole won't have a problem with this?"

"It's not his decision," she said.

I looked back at her. "So when you go out to impose justice, you decide who lives and dies?"

She shook her head. "This is your call, Liss. This is the only way you'll see justice."

My call. I sank into a patio chair and rubbed my throbbing forehead.

"If we take Brandt back to the reserve, we can try him, but we can't hold him indefinitely," she said. "Either we execute him or we have to let him go. If we let him go, chances are, he'll keep playing this game. If we find Tristan not responsible for his actions, there's nothing to stop Brandt going back to manipulating him once we release him."

She was right. If we let Brandt go, he could keep toying with us and there was nothing we could do about it. Not while that ring was on his finger.

But what if Tristan was innocent? I didn't know him well enough to know if he had always been like this, or if Brandt was controlling him. We couldn't just slaughter an innocent person.

But if we didn't, we would end up letting Brandt go.

I let out a scream of frustration.

Ellen knelt in front of me. "If this is not an easy decision for you, don't make it. We'll take them both back to the reserve and let justice take its course."

"Justice," I choked out. I knew exactly how much justice Brandt was going to get.

She straightened up. "You have to live with your actions. I don't think you can live with this."

"And if he fights us here and now?" I said.

She held up her gun. "Silver bullets. Unless he's developed powers I'm not aware of, it should be enough to put him down. Let's hope he *does* fight. I'd quite like to shoot him."

I smiled grimly and stood. "Okay. The hard road it is."

Chapter 33

Back in the lounge, Tristan was still staring into the flames, sipping whiskey as if people weren't threatening to kill each other all around him. I was glad I hadn't decided to murder him—he had to be under Brandt's control. Either that or he was genuinely disturbed.

Cole had his gun trained on Brandt's chest, pointing in the general area of his heart. Assuming the bastard had one.

"Right, let's get back to the reserve," said Ellen brusquely. "Brandt, you're coming with us."

He gave a low chuckle. "I don't think so."

She lifted her gun and shot him in the shoulder. His body jerked back, and the look of surprise on his face was priceless. I lunged at him, pinning him against the wall, and ran energy into him before he could move.

Keeping one hand around his throat, I pulled him away from the wall so that Ellen could cuff his hands with her silver handcuffs. Bound with silver, Brandt went from being an all-powerful vampire to a guy who had the strength of a kitten. A kitten with a cold.

Ellen pulled the ring off his finger and slipped it into her pocket. "We'll verify this later and figure out if you get to die or not."

Cole walked over to Tristan and hauled him to his feet.

"Get off me!"

Cole pulled him roughly around and bound his hands with silver cuffs. Tristan let out a howl of pain and struggled against them while Cole pushed him towards the doorway.

I winced as I saw smoke curl up from the silver against Tristan's skin. That had to hurt.

"Move." Ellen pushed Brandt and he sneered at her.

"You'll regret this moment. And sooner than you think."

Ellen looked amused. "Mmhmm."

As I followed them out, I heard a rustle of fabric and turned back to find Joey disrobing behind me. I stared at him as he stood there, his head lowered, tattoos flowing across his chest and biceps. The look in his eyes was pure predator.

"Ellen!"

I pulled my knife.

Slowly, deliberately, he got on all fours. I backed towards the entrance to the lounge as he started to shift.

Where the hell was Ellen?

I backed into someone else. Caleb. He put his arms around me almost tenderly, then sank his teeth into my shoulder.

"Get the hell off me!" I elbowed him and broke away from him, trying to keep them both in my line of sight. I put a hand to my shoulder as blood soaked through my t-shirt. *Who bites a person? Who does that?*

I had just enough time to raise my knife as Joey leapt at me, pushing me flat. I jammed the blade into his neck, aiming for anything that might bleed him out.

He twisted on the blade, his claws digging into my arm as he pulled himself off the knife and staggered away, blood jetting from the wound.

I got to my feet and found Caleb was now a wolf. In his wolf form, he was no longer a skinny guy in a hoodie. He was a lean animal with murder in his eyes.

I ran for the front door, the two of them skidding on the wooden floors behind me.

Ellen jogged back up the front steps as I reached the foyer.

"Caleb and Joey," I said breathlessly.

She drew her gun.

I looked around. There was no sign of the two wolves.

"Let's get out of here," Cole called to us. He pointed to the Copelands' silver Audi R8. "I'll take Tristan in one of the Copelands' cars—I don't want these two in the same metal box."

The R8, eh? Yeah, it was all about safety.

Ellen gave the house a last look and said, "Don't worry, Liss, we'll get them later."

We headed back to her car, Ellen covering our retreat.

As we pulled away from the house, I saw Caleb and Joey in wolf form standing among the trees at the edge of the garden, shadows among shadows.

I sat in the back seat with Brandt so that I could keep an eye on him, while Ellen set off at escape velocity. Unfortunately for me, she and Cole decided to start racing each other.

Brandt wasn't inclined to talk, but as dawn approached, I could see that he was getting edgy.

I'd never seen a vampire turn to dust in sunlight, and wasn't even sure if that part of the legend was true—but the way he was acting, I got the feeling being bathed in sunlight would be a very bad thing from his perspective.

He glanced across at me. "You had better hope that we reach our destination soon."

"I'm pretty sure Ellen's driving as fast as she can," I said, as we overtook Cole without a hundred metres of clear road.

"I'm serious—all the silver handcuffs in the world won't be able to contain me if the sun comes up and I'm stuck in the back of this Grindhouse-school-of-driving death machine."

"I can't do anything about that—we'll get there when we get there."

"You realise if she Paul-Walkers this car, you're the one most likely to die?" he said.

"What do you want me to do?"

"Ask her to pull over."

"I'm not pulling over," said Ellen, swerving around Cole and boosting up the highway.

The sky was starting to lighten in the east, the Bombay hills outlined with a stroke of orange that faded through gold to light green.

"Liss!" Brandt's eyes were wild and staring.

"Ellen, we need to find shelter. He's a vampire. We're not going to make it home before the sun comes up."

"Can you deal with him, Liss?" she said, her eyes fixed to the road.

I didn't bother to point out that I was trapped in the back seat of a car which didn't have much room to start with, never mind being forced back against the seat by her unnecessary exhibition of speed and acceleration.

We were at least an hour and a half from home, by my calculation. But then, my calculation was based on driving at a sane speed.

"How long till we get there?" I asked Ellen, raising my voice to be heard over the noise of the engine and Brandt's ever-more frantic breathing.

"Forty-five minutes," she said. "I can't go any faster or I'll pick up a cop."

Brandt leaned forwards. "If you drive any faster, you'll pick up an air-traffic controller."

"Stay calm. We'll be home soon."

Brandt bared his teeth. "Liss!"

I shrugged. What did he expect me to do?

The sky was getting lighter. As we crested a rise,

the first rays of sunlight glittered over the ranges to the east, spears of refracted light slowly rotating over the horizon.

Brandt stared around the car in panic, mumbling insensibly.

"I can't understand you."

"Burning!" he screamed in my face.

Okay, that I could make out.

There was no smoke, nothing to see, just Brandt screaming and thrashing as he tried to get the cuffs off.

"We need to cover him with something!" I called desperately to Ellen.

"He'll be fine!" she called back, somehow managing to accelerate, despite already driving at the speed of light.

How the hell was Cole keeping up with us? The R8 was powerful, but Ellen was driving as though the road was collapsing behind her.

Brandt started hyperventilating as more orange appeared above the skyline.

The light in the car grew to a golden orange glow and Brandt started to scream.

"Calm him down!" shouted Ellen. "I can't concentrate!"

How the hell was I supposed to do that?

Brandt rammed his shoulder into the back of her seat.

"BURNING!"

Ellen cast me a furious glance. "Take his mind or something!"

Sure. Take his mind, while I was in the grips of fearing for my own life.

Holding on to the grab handle with my left hand to stop being thrown around, I grabbed Brandt's wrist with my right and closed my eyes.

He stilled instantly. At the same time, I felt the most intense pain I'd ever felt in my *life*.

Worse than having my arm torn up by a vamp, worse than being bitten by wolves; even worse than becoming a Väktare.

Without thinking about it, I threw a shield of energy around us both. The sickening sensation of being thrown around in the back of the GTR was still there, but the burning stopped. I opened my eyes to find Brandt's wild eyes fixed to my face.

"I should let you burn," I said. "After everything you've done—don't think just because we took you alive, you're going to stay that way. I look forward to staking you out in the garden under the midday sun."

He said nothing. I closed my eyes again so that I could keep up the shield, but I could feel his eyes boring into me.

We skidded up on the loose gravel at the reserve and Cole pulled up seconds later. I kept hold of Brandt as Ellen jumped out of the GTR.

As the engine died, Brandt and I sat in the back seat in the ringing silence. I realised I had my hand on an enemy I'd been afraid of for months. Someone who'd instilled fear in me then killed one of the most important people in my life. Someone I hated. Someone I owed a whole world of hurt.

Cool morning air seeped into the back seat from the open driver's door.

"Can you speak?" I asked Brandt.

"Yes," he said quietly.

"Do you understand your position?" I asked.

A muscle in his jaw twitched.

"What, no witty rejoinder?" I asked.

"That's a big word for you," he said, with a touch of his old condescending self.

"That's better," I said. "See, unlike you, I would feel bad beating up on someone I thought was afraid of me."

He gave a single, soundless laugh. "Afraid of you."

"Afraid of me. Isn't that why you did all this in the first place? You came after me before I had the power to hurt you."

He considered me. "Did you ever wonder why I didn't just kill you?"

"Because the wolves would have come after you. United. Exactly what you were trying to avoid."

"What if I told you that's not the reason?" he said. "Or, at least, not the only reason."

"Then you'd sound like clickbait."

I was aware of Ellen and Cole speaking together in the car park, of them pulling Tristan out of the Audi and escorting him inside—all of it muted in the background.

"So." I shrugged. "Why didn't you kill me?"

We were parked in the lee of the house, and while the sky was growing brighter, direct sunlight wouldn't hit this side of the house for hours.

He considered his words carefully, his mouth moving as if he was trying different ways of saying what came next.

"We have a common enemy. There will come a time when we need to work together—"

He stopped speaking as Anton came to greet us. He slapped his hand on the roof of the car as he bent down to see into the back seat.

"This must be the vampire," he said.

"Don't let go," Brandt said to me desperately.

"Don't be a pussy." Anton pulled the driver's seat forward, grabbed the collar of Brandt's jacket, and hauled him out of the car. The second we broke contact, Brandt's face contorted with pain. I climbed out after him as Anton started leading him towards the house. Halfway across the yard, Brandt fell to his knees, screaming in pain. He covered his head with his hands, trying to pull his jacket over his head.

Anton kneed him in the back. "Get up!"

I scrambled out of the car and ran across to Brandt. "Anton! Let me!"

I grabbed Brandt's arm and cast a net over him as I pulled him to his feet.

"You owe me, asshole," I said quietly.

Panting with pain, Brandt let us escort him into the house.

Once we got inside, I left Anton to lead him down the cellar steps while I wondered where the hell everyone was.

Cole came into the hall and pulled me down towards the kitchen. He looked around, checking to see if anyone was listening.

"Why isn't Anton locked up?" I hissed.

"We've got a situation," he said. "I think Riley and Anton have done something to the others."

"What?"

"I can smell everyone, but I'm not sure where they are. Ellen's doing a sweep."

"Can you smell death?" I asked, my voice rising.

"No, no death. Stay here and don't get caught. If Riley's running on full juice, you're the only one who can get us out of this."

He pulled his gun and went back into the hall. I got a cold feeling in my gut. A feeling that something bad had happened.

Then I remembered that, of all of us, I had a way of finding them.

I closed my eyes and looked with my second sight. There was a concentrated mass of life signs in the basement. I was betting that was where everyone was. If Anton had managed to cage everyone, that probably meant Riley was back at full power. We should have killed her while we had the chance.

I watched Cole's solitary life sign head down the hall and ran after him to warn him. I found him at the top of the stairs to the basement.

"Don't go down there, Riley has everyone trapped!"

It was too late. She had him. He turned towards

me at the sound of my voice and raised his gun to point at me with shaking hands.

I turned and ran, diverting up the stairs to the second level, knowing I had to hide. There was only one place they wouldn't look for me.

Voices floated up from below. Anton's and Cole's. Anton forcing Cole to tell him where I was.

I got to the second floor and hurried down the hall desperately trying to remember which room had access to the hidden balcony on the roof.

Was it the third bedroom on the right or on the left?

Footsteps clumped on the stairs, slow and deliberate. Anton knew there was nowhere I could go.

I ran into a bedroom and pulled open the closet door. Not the right one. I glanced around desperately. He was at the point where the stairs curved back on themselves. I pulled open the window and rubbed myself against the windowsill. Might work. Probably wouldn't, but it was worth a shot.

I ran back out of the bedroom and went into the next room. I pulled open the wardrobe. Yes! I shut the bedroom door behind me.

Footsteps on the stairs. Slow. Heavy.

I looked around. One of the wolves was obviously using the room—probably Tai, looking at the clothes strewn around. I grabbed a bottle of cologne from the open suitcase on the bed and sprayed it around the room, then threw it on the bed and opened the window.

Footsteps in the hall. A bedroom door opened, and those same deliberate footsteps travelled across the floor of the room next door.

I rubbed myself on the windowsill again, then ran back to the wardrobe, sliding the door shut behind me. As I struggled out the narrow window and pulled myself onto the roof, the bedroom door opened. I draped my jacket over the window, hoping if he opened the wardrobe door, he wouldn't notice the rectangle of light at the end.

I knelt there, holding my breath, as the wardrobe door slid open. I closed my eyes and looked with my second sight. Anton paused at the wardrobe door for a moment, then moved to the window.

The way the roof was structured, he couldn't see me from there—but he could smell me. Well—he could smell Hugo Boss.

A thunderous sneeze echoed out into the dawn. Roosting pigeons took flight. I took a breath and held it again.

Anton mumbled something I couldn't hear and moved away from the window. He spent some time in the room, maybe checking under the bed, but before long he moved on to the next room.

I took in air, fighting back stars from oxygen deprivation, and sat with my back against the window.

Another window slid up.

"You're not a runner!" Anton shouted, loudly enough that I was pretty sure he wasn't aware I was there. "I know you're out there. Come back and we'll talk!"

A pigeon on the ridge of the roof cooed.

He moved away from the window and I followed him with my second sight until he was downstairs.

What the hell was I going to do? With Riley holding the wolves captive and Anton, the guy who'd slaughtered the entire Midlands pack, roaming the reserve, I wasn't left with many options. I was going to have to take him out.

I thought of soil slicked with blood, of the corpses of wolves spread across the Copelands' manicured lawn.

Riley couldn't control me. Brandt couldn't control me. I was the only one who could stop him. Yep, I was the only one who could take on Anton. No problem. I'd just sneak up on him and stick my knife in his back. How hard could it be?

Think, Liss!

Maybe I could trick him into going outside, lock the door, and release everyone.

Yeah, that'll work.

A car rattled over the cattle grate at the bottom of the drive and I sat up. Reinforcements?

I crawled to the edge of the roof. A blue SUV crunched its way up the gravel drive towards the house. It didn't belong to anyone I knew. I stayed flat and listened. Doors slammed and voices I recognised rose as Anton greeted them. Caleb and Joey. Goddamnit. I should have killed Anton while he was alone. Now there were three of them. And Brandt. At least I knew he wasn't going to come after me during daylight.

"Spread out and find her," Anton ordered.

Joey walked along the narrow strip of grass that lay between the back of the house and the tree line. He couldn't see me unless he went further into the trees and looked back at the house, and even then, if I lay flat, the rise and fall of the roof should hide me. But I could hear him just fine.

"Alessandra!" he bellowed in his best cockney English. "Everyone you know and love is currently locked behind iron doors under this house. How would you feel if they all burned to death?"

That was one damned unfunny joke.

"Alessandra! I know you wouldn't run and leave 'em all to die, now would you? Anton's very impatient to have a dialogue with you. The kettle's on—why don't you come join us?" He gave the word 'kettle' two silent Ts. I could imagine him and Cole having a conversation. They'd only need half the alphabet.

"Alessandra! We don't have all day!"

He pulled out a Zippo lighter and flicked open the lid with a metallic *shink*. Clicked it shut. Flicked it open again. He lifted his nose to the air and I ducked away from the edge of the roof.

"Fuck it." He walked back towards the front of the house. "You asked for it!" he called to the forest.

If the threat was real—if Anton truly would burn the house to the ground with everyone in it—

If?

If he'd do that, then my priority had to be getting everyone out of the basement. Take away his leverage. If I could get them out in the open, I could channel through one to protect the others and hopefully between us we could put Riley down before Anton killed us all.

Using my second sight, I looked for Anton. He was in the lounge. Caleb was out the front, no doubt searching for me with slitted, bloodshot eyes.

I dropped back into the wardrobe and went into the hall. The door to the basement was directly beside the entrance to the stairwell, so all I needed to do was get downstairs without being noticed.

I crept down the stairs. Those damn, creaky old stairs that'd suffered years of abuse under the thundering footsteps of five werewolf brothers.

Four steps from the bottom, I closed my eyes to check where everyone was. Caleb was heading for the house.

There was no way I could get around that corner without being seen through the open front door. I swung myself over the banister into the passage to the kitchen and ducked down as Caleb came into the hall and headed up the stairs. If he looked down, he'd see me.

I slipped into the kitchen and crouched below the breakfast bar so that I couldn't be seen from the lounge.

Halfway up the stairs, there was a creak as Caleb stopped. He took a couple of steps back down and scented the air.

I stopped breathing and willed him to go away. He took another step down. I edged back further, trying to stay out of his sight line. I was running out of kitchen.

Caleb called out, "She's here somewhere. Someone should check out the back."

I went back into the hall just as Anton's heavy footsteps moved towards the entrance to the lounge. There was no time to get to the basement door. I opened the back door and stepped through, just as the tip of Anton's boot came into the hall. I closed the door and turned to find myself face to face with Joey.

"What 'ave we 'ere!" he drawled. If Brandt had been raised on the right side of the tracks, Joey had been raised in ditch. Maybe a Shoreditch. This was the accent Cole would use to talk to tradies when they came to fix the things in his house that he couldn't fix himself.

"You're looking well for a guy who recently took a knife to the throat."

He backhanded me across the face.

Yeah, that was probably fair.

I punched but he blocked, and there was nowhere to go in the alcove except through him—and he was a guy who could punch his way through my face *and* the door without trying.

I reached for EMN and he pinned my arms against the door with wolf-strength. His breath was hot against my face and smelled faintly of beer.

"I thought you learned from the last time we tangled that I don't appreciate obscenity from the fairer sex."

"Go tell Ellen," I said to him, struggling to loosen his hold on me. His grip was leaving dents in my bones and he wasn't even trying to hurt me.

"I've had a chat with Ellen," he said. "She and I didn't see eye to eye."

"Being as how neither of yours are black, was she asleep at the time?"

"Ha, ha, ha," he said. He pulled me away from the door.

"Didn't you say Anton wanted to talk?" I asked.

"Soon," he said. He pulled me towards him, grabbed my hands behind my back, and moved around me so that I was facing the forest with him behind me.

"Walk," he said into my ear.

I tried to kick backwards, but he moved his body out of range and growled. His fingers dug into my arms.

"Walk," he said. His breath was hot against my neck.

There was one move I knew that didn't rely on strength that was worth a shot. I turned my wrists inwards to break his grip, but instead he increased his pressure on my arms until I was sure my bones would break.

"Do you speak English? I said, 'walk'. So do that."

He kept hold of my arms and shoved me forwards, propelling me towards the trees.

There was the rattle of a metal knob as the back door opened behind us.

"Joey! Stop wasting time!"

I recognised the voice as Anton's and glanced over my shoulder to see him standing on the top step.

Joey looked down at me with a smile that made me queasy. He extended my right arm out from my side, setting fire to the bite wound in my shoulder, and ran his hand down its length until he got to my fingers. He squeezed the broken finger and I hissed with pain.

"I *will* get my chance to be alone with you."

"Better you than Caleb."

He shook his head. "Caleb just takes orders. I have imagination."

"Imagination, antisocial personality disorder..." I gave him the internationally recognised facial expression of *same, same, but not really.*

He chuckled. Of course the psycho *would* be the one person who found me funny.

Anton, Tristan, and Caleb were waiting in the lounge. Brandt sat in an armchair, his head propped on his fingers. His sullen expression told me he wasn't happy being trapped in the house by the sun. Both he and Tristan had marks around their wrists where Ellen's cuffs had eaten into their flesh. Silver wounds on vamps and wolves took a while to heal, and often scarred. Contact with the metal weakened them. It sapped their strength and burnt into them as if it was super-heated if it sat against their skin too long.

One thing you could be sure of with supernatural

creatures—they'd never steal your silverware.

"Right, let's get on the road," said Anton.

Oh, no, that was not a good idea. As a child, Jack and Andy had always made it clear, if someone wants to do something bad to you, make them do it where your body will be found. Not their exact words, but I'd got their point.

"Isn't this lovely," I said. "Tristan, do you remember Anton slaughtering your family?"

Joey threw me into an armchair with a look of amusement while Tristan stared into the middle distance and ignored me.

"He can't hear you," said Brandt.

"Why not?"

He tapped the side of his head.

"So what, you control Tristan for Anton, while Riley controls the rest of the wolves... for Anton? And everyone here does what Anton wants?"

There was a flicker of annoyance in Brandt's eyes. "We have an arrangement."

"Keeping you in the lifestyle you're accustomed to, is he?"

Brandt gave me a look that said he'd remember that.

Anton grinned broadly and stroked a hand over his orange beard. "You see, Liss, everyone was ready for a change."

"Yeah, most people just vote Labour for a term. They don't kill their entire family." I thought about it for a moment. "Well, there was that one guy, but they never proved it beyond a reasonable doubt—"

443

Anton went on as if I hadn't spoken.

"The Alpha Circle worked for a bit, and Abigail and Kendrick didn't do too badly. But it's time for new leadership. Less... restrictive rules."

"Oh, I can already see it's going to be free love and chocolate cake for everyone," I said. "Is there going to be anyone left to enjoy your reign as the ginger king of Aotearoa?"

He considered me. "A ginger king needs a ginger queen, Liss."

I clucked my tongue. "Shame I'm not a ginga."

"Not you, m'dear!" he said with the kind of gut-born belly laugh you'd expect from a six-foot-tall Viking. "But Riley, she's got enough power to rule, don't you think?"

It was my turn to give him the evil eye. "How does Tristan feel about this?"

He chuckled. "In name only, of course. Tristan keeps his missus. I'm not a complete bastard."

Well, that was an outright lie.

"So what do you want me for?"

Anton crouched in front of me with an air of fatherly affection. "I'd rather not kill your family, Liss, God knows you've been through enough. But I can't have them interfering. And I can't have you interfering. So it's best that we work together."

"That's your offer?" I said. "Come help me terrorise the rest of the country or I'll kill your family?"

He patted my knee. "No one's getting terrorised, Liss."

444

"You don't think threatening to kill someone's family counts as terrorism?"

"Sometimes you have to take a stand." He straightened up. "You see, Liss, since the dawn of our species, wolves have fought wolves for supreme control over territory. Abigail and Kendrick put a stop to that. You could say they halted the natural order of things. Wolves work cooperatively in a pack, in a family. But they don't cede territory to each other. Strong packs expand."

"I don't know what bulletin board you signed up to, but you misheard if you think I have skills that are useful to you."

"He needs you to protect him from Riley," said Brandt.

Anton cast him a glance. Brandt shrugged.

Anton scratched the corner of his mouth. "Yeah, the vampire's right. Keeping Tristan around only offers so much protection. I need someone who can keep Riley's power in check. So you'll come with us. It'll be good, don't worry, I'll put you up in your own room, and get you a PlayStation 2 or a Sega Mega Box, or whatever you kids play these days—and you'll work alongside us to make sure everything runs smoothly."

"You're not a bad egg, really, are you?" I said. "Apart from the murder, the slavery, and the bad smell."

Anton gave a snort of laughter. "You'll adjust. Now hop up, it's time to go. Chop chop, everyone." He rubbed his hands together.

"I might stay here," said Brandt. "If it's all the same."

Anton folded his arms. "You having second thoughts, vampire?"

Brandt gestured to the sunny outdoors. "I often have second thoughts when someone asks me to walk into a crematorium."

Anton snorted. "You'll survive. We'll chuck a blanket over you."

"I'd rather not. We'll catch up in the weeks to come, I'm sure."

Anton rubbed a hand over his beard. "You look worried, vampire. You don't trust me to hold up my end of the bargain?"

Brandt gave a light shrug. "You have what you need. I'll throw the keys to the wolves after dark and make sure they don't starve to death."

Anton nodded slowly. "Tell you what, we'll all go after dark. How's that?"

Brandt said nothing.

Anton slapped Tristan's chest with the back of his hand. "Why don't you go get some sleep? You look pale."

Tristan gave him a vacant look and headed down the hall towards the bedrooms.

"I'm going to have a kip m'self. We've got a long drive head of us. Joey, can I trust you to keep an eye on Liss?"

Joey smiled.

"Caleb, keep half an eye on them downstairs. Brandt, I trust you'll make sure everyone stays in

446

line?"

Brandt inclined his head.

Anton disappeared towards the bedrooms.

"You need help, bro?" Caleb asked Joey.

Joey shook his head. "I'll entertain Liss in the boardroom. Stay here, and make sure the vampire doesn't try to leave."

Caleb gave me a lazy, empty smile. "Have fun." Joey pushed me towards the stairs. At least he'd said the boardroom. That was infinitely better than the bedroom.

Chapter 34

Joey pushed open the boardroom door and shoved me through. Once we were inside, he locked the deadbolt on the door behind us and pocketed the key.

I put the huge oval table between us and did my best to stay calm. Yes, it was true, I still had my knife. But Joey was a werewolf. Strength for strength, wolves and newborn vamps were probably equal, but Joey would be ten times faster, since he wasn't adjusting to being newly dead.

I figured I might manage to stab him a few times if I was lucky, but that'd just annoy him. My best bet was to try and use my words.

He put his hands in his pockets and considered me.

"Relax, Liss, I'm going to do you a favour."

"Yeah?" I said. "That sounds likely."

He stepped up to the table and leaned forward on his hands. Veins twined around his forearms and bulged under the tattoos that circled his biceps.

"We have a score to settle."

"Oh?" I asked, folding my arms.

He put a hand to the collar of his t-shirt and pulled it down. A livid scar two inches long ran across his breastbone.

"Like for like," he said. "Cancels out the debt. Then you don't have to worry about what I'm going to do to you anymore."

"Honestly, I'll be fine. I'm used to living with uncertainty."

He grinned. "It's not as though you have a choice."

I twisted off the sphalerite ring and held it up. The stone glittered with trapped firelight. I set it on the table.

"You can't just take it off, Liss."

With acrobatic grace, he leapt onto the table and stalked towards me. I bumped into the wall as he walked off the end and leaned back against the table. His gaze locked to mine, he reached down and picked up the ring.

He held it out to me. "You can't back out of the vows that easily."

"At this rate, there won't be any witnesses left to care what I do to you."

"Put it on, Liss."

"Why?" I asked. "So that you can assert your dominance? I don't know what's wrong with you, Joey, but you and Caleb have some serious issues."

Joey lunged forward and grabbed my right hand. He pushed the ring back on to my finger.

"That's better." He studied my face. "You're afraid

449

of me. I like that."

"Careful, Joey, you're starting to sound a bit rapey."

He looked highly amused. "Just a guy who knows what he likes."

"Frightened women who have a fifth of your physical strength?" I asked.

He nodded. "With some fight."

I tried to move around him, but he caught my arm and pushed me back against the wall.

"I owe you a scar," he said. "How would you like it?"

My pulse sped up. Timing was going to be everything if he attacked me.

"Go ahead, pull your letter opener," he said. "I'm not a complete monster."

I pulled EMN. "You really want to do this now? Doesn't seem like a fair fight when I have a broken finger."

"You did this with a broken finger." He traced a finger over his scar. "So. Where do you want yours?"

"I'll make you a deal. You leave me alone, and I won't gut you like the pig you clearly are."

Some of the amusement left his eyes. He stood up taller, his muscles flexed to bulging.

"I think I'll mark your face," he said. He ran a finger from his cheekbone to his chin. "From here to here. So you remember me when you look in the mirror."

I spun EMN in my hand. "Go for it."

Yeah, don't say shit like that to werewolves.

He morphed claws and lashed out at me with the speed of a snake. His claws tore into my cheek, leaving trails of fire behind. I put a hand to the wound and touched the torn flesh with quivering fingers, as blood poured down my face like water.

He put away his claws and watched me intently, willing me to retaliate. My pulse thudded in my ears, my breath painful in my chest. I didn't want to retaliate. Because I knew—*I knew*—one of us would die if I did. And it wouldn't be him.

Instead, I put EMN back in its sheath. I was shaking badly, but my voice came out strong. "Are we done?"

He frowned.

Blood ran down my neck. My cheek felt as though someone was holding an iron to it.

Seeing I wasn't going to react, he folded his arms. "You're going to try to kill me, aren't you?"

I shrugged. "No. I'm not going to *try*."

He scratched his head. "It's a shame you're so fragile. I like you."

I shook my head, unable to find words to respond to that. Blood was trickling into the collar of my t-shirt where Caleb's bite was starting to throb in harmony with this latest wolf-inflicted injury.

I put my hand up and felt the bite marks. Then stopped. Caleb's teeth in my shoulder. Joey's claws in my face.

How long did I have? Could a Väktare even be turned? As much as I loved my adopted family, did I really want to become a furry?

"What?"

"Caleb bit me," I said stupidly.

"And?"

"He bit me, Joey, and you just stuck wolf claws in my face. Think about it. What does that mean?"

It took a second for it to dawn on him. He laughed. "Got the sweats already, have you?"

Well, yes, but it was hard to know if it was psychosomatic or the first sign of lycanthropy.

"Joey, we have to undo this. I can't turn; I don't want to be one of you. I may have scarred you, but being turned into a whole other life form, that's a bit more than a scar, don't you think?"

He shrugged. "Just means next time you'll be able to fight back properly."

"You're missing something very important here. How do you think Anton's going to react when he finds out you two gave me superpowers?"

His eyes widened. He was smart enough to suspect I was trying to manipulate him, but he also knew I was right.

"Who's going to watch me, Joey, when I have wolf strength and all the power of a Väktare? Do you really think you'll be able to control me if I turn?"

'All the power of a Väktare' didn't amount to much just yet, but he didn't know that.

"You need to fix this, Joey. Before shit gets real. Take me down to the others—if there's a cure, Karlo will know."

"I'm not taking you down there."

"Suit yourself," I said. "What does Anton do to

452

stupid people?"

He narrowed his eyes. "You honestly think Karlo can help you?"

I shrugged. "I know he's my only shot. And yours."

He unlocked the boardroom door and led me downstairs.

Chapter 35

Joey stood guard at the bottom of the basement stairs while I looked around.

"Oi, Liss, over here," hissed Cole through a small window in an iron door.

"She got ya, huh?" I asked.

He frowned as I got close. "What happened to your face?"

"Yeah, I might need some of Dan's healing-circle cosmetic surgery after this."

"Speaking of healing, that she-bitch isn't remotely hampered by being underground," he said. "It was all part of Anton's plan."

"Where's everyone else?"

He pointed his finger through the bars. "The kids are in those cells. I don't know where the ACs are."

I held his gaze. We were both thinking the same thing. I didn't want to believe it, but Dan's words rang in my head.

Someone's slaughtered them all. She said their bodies were stacked in a pile in the woods.

"Two seconds," I said, and walked over to Riley's

cage.

"So how come you're still here?" I asked her.

She smiled smugly. "I am watching the wolves."

"From a cage?"

"Protection," she said. "I'm wounded, after all."

"You're a fucking *bitch*!" shouted Cole through the hole in his door.

Riley looked amused. "Besides, I have the keys." She held them up. It was true, she had the keys. To *all* the doors.

I closed my eyes and saw that she was steadily drawing dark green tendrils from above. Her head wound was mostly healed.

"Where are the ACs?" I asked.

"Joey, why is she here?" Riley asked loudly.

Joey turned back to his, his arms folded. "Anton's orders are to keep her down here with the others until we're ready to leave," he said.

A look of annoyance passed across Riley's face.

"He said to put me in the cage with you, actually," I said to her.

Joey twitched at that. But how else were we going to get her to surrender the keys?

"Really?" Riley said. "That seems unwise."

Joey put his hands up. "Hey, I'm not the alpha."

"You certainly aren't," said Riley.

He gave her the look a husky gives you when you only pretend to throw the ball.

I glanced back at him. He needed to get those keys.

He strode over to me and shoved me against the

455

metal bars.

"If she does anything weird, I'll personally beat the crap out of her for you."

With the metal bars pressed painfully into my ribcage and my face in shreds, she must have figured he meant it. I knew I was convinced.

"Fine." She handed the keys to Joey, who handed them to me as Riley looked on in indignation.

"What are you doing?"

He ignored her. "Hurry up," he said to me. "You try anything stupid and I'll break more than a finger."

I walked quickly to Cole's cage and started trying keys in the lock.

"Hey, idiot, if she opens those cages, what's going to stop her wolves from turning you into mince?"

He looked from me to her. "You. You can control them, can't you?"

"Sure, when *she's* not here. That's the point of Anton's plan, dumbass."

I was out of time. I pushed the keys through the hole in the door just as Joey reached me. He grabbed me by the shoulder and I yelped in pain as he pulled me away from the cage.

"What'd you do?"

"I told you, I *need* their help. You need to figure out what you're more afraid of — Anton finding out you damaged his Väktare, or my pack tearing you apart. How about we make a deal? Cole throws the keys back, you unlock the door, shove me in there with them, I talk to them and figure this out. You have the keys, you have the control."

"Keep her outside that cage!" said Riley. "She can only stop me if she can touch them."

"Hey, Riley?" I said. "Why don't you just control Joey and make him do what you want him to? Or Cole?"

She looked uncomfortable. "I'm healing."

Controlling everyone before seemed to have set her healing back. I could see the glowing knots where Ellen had shot her.

"Mmhmm," I said.

"Oi, East End." Cole called to Joey. He jangled the keys. "If I give you these, will you play nicely?"

I could see Joey was struggling to decide what to do.

"Idiot," said Riley. She sat on her bench and folded her arms.

"Okay," Joey said finally. He spun me around and took EMN from its sheath at the back of my belt.

"Here's what's going to happen. You throw me the keys, I unlock the door, your Väktare steps inside. You try and push your way out, I shove this blade through her back and out her front. You feel me, you cockney bastard?"

"Consider yourself felt," said Cole. He handed the keys through the bars to Joey.

So I was trapped again. At least while I was down here, I knew they wouldn't set fire to the place.

Joey unlocked the door and kept the knife's sharp point pressed against my lower back until I was in. He slammed the door and locked it.

"Right. Figure it out!" he said.

He went back to the foot of the stairs to keep guard.

The cell was crowded. Karlo, Cole, Ellen and Dan were all packed into the 8 x 6ft iron box.

"This is cosy," I muttered. It was like standing in a lift.

Dan put a hand up to my face. "Jesus, who did this?"

"Joey," I said. "That's kinda why I'm here."

He frowned. "We haven't got enough to heal you."

"Not that," I said. I pulled away the collar of my t-shirt and showed him Caleb's bite mark. "You know what happens when werewolves bite and claw you?"

It dawned on Ellen first. She put the back of her hand to my forehead. "How do you feel?"

"I've felt worse," I said. "Look, the thing is, as much as I love you guys, I really don't want to be a wolf."

Dan snorted.

"What?" I said.

"Liss, you've *always* wanted to be a wolf. Yeah, I've seen you, slinking off when we have our full-moon parties. You're always in a foul mood when we go nature."

"There are a lot of reasons I could be grumpy around the full moon," I snapped back. "And you're wrong. Just because I felt excluded, doesn't mean I had a burning desire to become a mutant."

A stunned silence fell across the cage.

458

"Tell us what you really think," said Cole.

Looking at their faces, I felt ashamed, but there was no taking it back.

"Well, fuck you too," said Dan. He turned his back on me. The others moved to the sides of the cell, arms folded.

I licked my lips. "Look, I'm sorry, just... this is stressing me out. I can't be a wolf. I'm a Väktare. That's, like, two separate species. What if by becoming a wolf, I lose my powers? That'll leave every one of you vulnerable as long as Riley lives."

Ellen sighed. "You're right. It's a risk. But, Liss, what do you think we can do about it?"

I shrugged. "I don't know. It's a disease, right? Like, a blood disease? Isn't there a cure? Something ancient, passed down from generation to generation, with ingredients that just happen to be within questing distance?"

Ellen shook her head. "Not that I'm aware of."

Karlo stepped up to me and put his hands on my shoulders. I winced, and he made a face and took his hands down again.

"Liss, this might not be such a bad thing. The chances of you losing your powers are slim—why don't you want to be one of us? I've always thought of you as pack."

I stared at him. "Really? So you don't remember telling Tristan Copeland that I'd never be one of you?"

He looked confused.

"You don't remember the conversation you had

459

with Tristan behind your bar, where you told him you'd never follow me and I'd never be one of you? Or did you mean Riley? Because if you knew about her, then you have a lot of explaining to do."

Karlo's face reddened. He let his hands drop to his sides.

"I was talking about Riley."

Dan turned back to us. "What?"

"Why the hell didn't you tell anyone?" I asked.

"Tristan came to me, yes," said Karlo. "He dropped into the bar and asked if we could talk. I didn't see the harm in it. He proposed that a few of us—myself and some of the other wolves who he said would never move anywhere in the hierarchy— branch out with him. He said he was building a pack. I asked where their territory would be—he said he'd carve it out. I said how—he said Riley. I know the legend—but it didn't matter what Riley was, she wasn't a wolf. And I'm loyal to my pack." He looked past Cole at Dan. "I told him to take a walk."

"Why didn't you tell the Alpha Circle?" Ellen asked.

Karlo looked down at the floor. "The second he walked away, I forgot I'd even spoken to him. I only remembered when Liss unlocked my mind. And at that point, I didn't really want to give the Alpha Circle any more reasons to execute me."

Dan looked at him in disgust. "You could have saved us a lot of time."

Cole put out a hand to Dan. "Forget it. We have bigger problems."

Karlo turned to me. "Getting back to the point at hand—Liss, if you were bitten, you'll either turn or you won't. Most people don't—you have to have the recessive gene for lycanthropy in order for wolf saliva to activate the change. If you were going to turn, you'd know within an hour of being bitten."

I leaned back against the door with a sigh of relief.

"Are you lot finished?" Joey called through the door.

We looked at each other. This was our chance.

"All done," I said. "You can let me out now."

"That's okay," he said. His face appeared at the small window in the door. "You can stay there."

He disappeared.

"Anton wouldn't want this!" I shouted after him.

"Anton would find this hilarious," he said, his voice receding with his footsteps as he headed up the stairs.

"Anyone got any bright ideas?" I asked.

Cole held up two keys.

I grinned.

None of us knew if Riley had the wolves' exceptional hearing, but it was an unspoken understanding between us that she probably did.

I gestured towards the lock on our door and pointed at the keys. He shrugged. Well, it was a two in ten chance. As I was closest to the door, he handed me the keys. I tried one—it wasn't even the right shape for the lock. I tried the second one, stamped with what looked like a Russian brand name. It turned. Lucky for us the Stokes kept the master and a

461

copy of the key to this door on the same key ring. What were the chances?

"What are you doooing, Alessandra?" said Riley. I swung open the door and walked over to her cage.

"Finishing this."

She stood, her eyes wary. "You don't have the key."

Cole stepped up behind me and handed me the other key. I tried it in the lock. She was in luck—it didn't turn.

I handed the key back to Cole and he tried the other doors. One swung open. Ben and Luke joined us.

"How many others are trapped?" I asked Cole.

"Two more cells," he said. "The little goth girl and baby Stoke are in one—the girl with grey hair is in another cell by herself. For some reason she got five-star treatment."

Gracie, Tai, and Erin.

Ellen walked over to the work bench where Anton and Joey had left our weapons locked in a metal cabinet, and wrenched it open, tearing off the lock. She handed Cole's gun to him, and tossed my knife to me.

"You got any spare ammo?" Cole asked.

She handed him a clip. "Right, let's go."

"Wait!" I stopped her. "What are you going to do? Is this a shoot-to-kill situation?"

Cole glanced sideways at Ellen.

"Yes," she said. "We can't afford to let Anton get the upper hand again."

I pointed at Riley. "Then start with her."

Riley's eyes widened.

Ellen considered her. "Will she actually die?"

"She will if I want her to," I said.

"Wait!" said Riley, rising to her feet. "Don't I at least get a trial?"

"You don't stop in the middle of a war for a trial," I said. "Didn't Sun Tzu say, if someone tries to kill you, you should try to kill them right back?

"No," said Cole. "He didn't."

Well, something like that."

"Killing a prisoner of war is a war crime," said Riley.

"Have you noticed," I said to the others, "that the bad guys seem to be able to do whatever they want to us, but our rules are stopping us from stopping them doing it?"

Ellen's eyes darkened. "That's what makes us civilised."

"We won't be very civilised if we're dead."

"I'm with Liss on this one," said Cole. "We can't afford to let Riley live. She's too powerful."

"We have to stop her, but we can't just murder her in cold blood," said Karlo. "Can't you stop her using her powers, Liss?"

"I can't babysit twenty-four hours a day. You, of all people, must realise how dangerous she is," I said. "Or do you not remember what she made you do?"

Karlo looked stricken. I knew I was being cruel, but I also knew underestimating Riley would get us all killed.

"So we vote," said Ben. "Put an end to her now and deescalate this situation, or risk her banding with Brandt again to overpower us."

Ellen looked around the small group. "Who votes we execute Riley?"

Ben, Luke, Cole and I raised our hands. Karlo, Ellen and Dan didn't.

"Dan? Really?" I said.

"She's entitled to a trial," he said.

"You're not listening! She will make you turn on each other and rip each other apart the first chance she gets."

"Hey!" Erin called between the bars of her cell. "What about us?"

"They should have a say," said Karlo. "This affects all of us. If word gets out that we killed an unarmed prisoner to the wider wolf community, we could all be executed."

"She's not unarmed!" I said, exasperated. "Erin!" I called out. "How do you feel about ending Riley before she does any more damage?"

"She killed Jack. Don't give her the chance to kill anyone else."

"Don't do it, Liss," said Tai. He took Erin's place at the small panel in the door. "You kill her and this goes on your soul."

I didn't believe in souls, but this was no time to be having a theological argument.

That took the count to five against four.

"And Gracie?" I asked. Gracie's cell didn't have a window in it.

I banged on the metal door. "Gracie, can you hear us?"

I thought I could hear a voice, but it was muffled. "Dan? What's she saying?"

He gave me a sullen look. "I don't know."

"Then it's settled. We put a stop to this now."

Through all this, Riley had been watching us with horror. I was torn between a perverse sense of joy at her fear, and real anger when I thought of the trail of blood she'd left behind her. We still didn't know where the rest of the alphas were.

Dan shook his head with disgust. "Look at her, Liss. She's harmless right now. You really want to kill her? Locked in a cell?"

"I want this to end," I said. "You don't want to watch, don't watch."

Ellen put a hand on my arm. "Liss. If you kill her now, there will be consequences."

I shrugged. "What am I supposed to do? Let her kill someone else I love? Who's going to judge us? Who's going to be *left* to judge us?"

I put my hand out to Cole. After a moment, he checked the safety on his pistol and handed it to me.

"Have you used a gun before?" he asked.

"Surely if a three-year-old can kill with one, I can."

I stepped back from the cage and sighted on Riley. The gun was heavier than I'd expected it to be. My arms trembled as I held the gun out straight with both hands.

Riley's arms hung limply at her sides, her pale eyes filled with disappointment. *At what?* I

465

wondered. *Herself? Her life ending this way?*

I closed my eyes and saw the curling tendrils of power that flowed into and around her, the denser concentrations where Ellen had previously shot her now completely healed. To kill her, all I had to do was cut her off from her power and shoot her in the head. To do that, I needed to touch her, or channel through a wolf. I had no intention of touching her while I blew her brains out.

"I need someone." I glanced back at the others. "I need a conduit to stop her healing."

Cole stepped forward and I rested my left hand on his shoulder. My right hand was pulled down by the weight of the gun. But from two feet away, there wasn't much chance I'd miss.

I closed my eyes and threw a net of power over Riley. The tendrils of power she was calling into her curled and dissipated like smoke.

I opened my eyes again, holding that power over her.

"Any last words?"

There was a hiss of annoyance from behind me and a scrape of shoes on concrete as Dan turned away.

"She won't be harmless forever, Dan," I said, without turning around. "And when she's back at full power, she'll happily murder you."

"Shoot before your arm gets fatigued," said Cole quietly. "Make sure you keep your eyes open."

I locked my gaze to Riley's and squeezed the trigger.

466

Nothing happened.

"The safety," said Cole.

Shaking, I checked the gun. Cole pointed to the tiny lever that held the slide in place. I flicked it down, then pointed the gun back at Riley. I'd dropped the net.

Shaking from the flood of adrenaline, I cast the net back around her and got a better grip on the gun.

Breathing hard, Riley walked up to the bars and pressed her head against them, so that the gun was inches from her face. Her eyes dared me to do it.

"You're not a killer, Liss!" said Dan. "Please don't do this."

"For Jack," I said. I steeled myself. There was going to be a mess.

Riley gripped the bars with her hands. Her blue eyes were as pale and clear as ice. "You're wasting time," she said in whisper. "And that's what costs heroes their victory."

My teeth slid against each other as my jaw clenched. The gun was slippery in my hand. I could feel all the wolves behind me, feel their bubbles of power as a heavy weight at my back.

"It's okay, Liss," said Cole.

I jolted as Riley reached through the bars and grabbed my wrist. But rather than trying to take the gun, she pushed an image into my mind.

She showed me what she saw; my eyes squeezed shut, my face pale and glassed with sweat. I so very clearly didn't want to shoot her.

She spun the image around and showed her own

face.

"Do you want this?" she whispered.

She showed the bullet leaving the gun, collapsing into her forehead like a pen through tissue paper. The back of her head split open and there was a splat like the sound spaghetti and meatballs makes when it hits the floor. All that red. All those pieces.

My stomach heaved and I staggered away from her and leaned against the wall, fighting back the urge to vomit.

No one spoke as I rested my head against the cold stone.

Cole took the gun gently from my hand. He put a hand on my shoulder.

"Without your vote, we're tied." There was no judgement in his voice. I guessed he'd seen the vision too.

"She can kill you all," I said weakly. I turned back to the others. "This won't end as long as she's alive."

"You could try talking to me," said Riley. "Maybe I'm not the monster you imagine me to be."

I walked back to her cage and stood in front of her. "You helped Anton kill the entire Midlands pack. You killed Jack. You won't tell us what you've done to the ACs. If you're not a monster, what are you?"

"Someone fighting for their rights," she said. "And maybe someone who was manipulated into believing they were doing the wrong thing for the right reasons. Just like you."

"Where are they, Riley? Where is everybody?"

She was silent for a moment. "I believe they're dead. But it wasn't my—"

Cole shot her. Six times.

Chapter 36

$\int$hot after shot jerked into Riley's chest. I put my hands to my ears as a high ringing started. The last four shots I felt, rather than heard.

Standing in that small room with the scent of gunpowder and fresh death, I decided it was time to get out of the basement.

I headed for the stairs and Ellen tapped my arm and motioned me behind her. She went up the stairs, gun drawn.

There was no sign of Anton. How could he not have heard six gunshots? Maybe he'd wisely decided to run while he had the chance.

The wolves fanned out to search and I went out onto the lawn to breathe air and get my hearing back.

I sank down heavily on the grass with my legs crossed and put my head in my hands.

Cole hadn't shot her in the head, but that hadn't made it much cleaner. The first three shots had hit her while she was upright and the last three had jerked her body as she lay on her back, her eyelids fluttering with each explosion. I'd felt the last of her power drain away like water into sand.

She was dead, I was sure of it. She was dead.

I couldn't get the image out of my mind. So many creatures I'd killed without remorse, but lately, the things I'd killed had been far too human for my liking.

It was good to be outside. My hearing was still screwed, but the scent of the earth and the warmth of the late afternoon sun were enough to calm the shaking in my hands, the nausea in my stomach.

It was what I'd intended to do anyway. I'd been about to shoot her. To take her life. And she was responsible for the slaughter of dozens of innocent people.

Maybe.

I guessed we'd never know what she'd been about to say.

I put a hand to my head. Cole had done the right thing. Riley had taken away Jack. She'd brought Anton to our territory, where he'd do to the Westlands what he'd done to the Deep South.

Gradually, my hearing came back and I realised shouts were coming from the house. I jumped up and ran inside as Dan came running down the stairs. "What was that?"

"I don't know."

There was a cry of pain from the bedrooms on the first level, then the sound of breaking glass from the kitchen. A moment later, Anton sprinted across the yard and into the dense bush beyond.

Dan took chase.

A waft of smoke floated out of the lounge. No. No, he wouldn't.

Of course he would.

I ran down the hall and skidded into the kitchen, looking for the fire extinguisher that was always on the wall. Across the breakfast bar, I could see flames climbing the lounge curtains.

The fire extinguisher wasn't there—but the ranch slider in the lounge was smashed. I was guessing that's where the fire extinguisher went. There wasn't time to look for it.

I ran back down the hall to where I'd heard sounds. Gracie, Erin and Tai were trapped downstairs. I needed the keys to free them—I needed Joey.

I reached an open bedroom door and found Ellen and Cole wrestling with Brandt. Ellen fired two bullets into him, but it didn't slow him down. He broke free and faced off against them, snarling.

"Forget him, the house is on fire!" I shouted. "Get out! And find Joey—he has the keys to the cells!"

I didn't wait to make sure they got out—it was up to them now.

I ran back up the hall, my mind buzzing with panic. I had to get them out. I *had* to get them out.

"Joey!" I screamed, up the staircase, out the open front door. "Where the hell are you?"

I closed my eyes, and without thinking about it, that second world swam into view. There was a glow of energy above me. If it wasn't Joey, I'd cut pieces off them until they told me where he was.

I jogged up the stairs, searching frantically for the life sign. Not in the bedrooms, not in the boardroom.

The bastard was on the roof.

I found the room that smelled of cologne and pushed open the door to the wardrobe. The tiny window was open. I boosted myself through.

As I dragged myself onto the concrete tiles, I looked up to find Joey's boots inches from my face. He hauled me to my feet and punched me.

Things went black for a couple of seconds, and there was pain. Lots and lots of pain.

As daylight came back, I felt blood running from my nose and wiped it away. My face was having a rough day.

Still, he'd been gentle. I was still alive, even if I was weaving on my feet, ready to pass out. I was glad Anton didn't want me dead. The second he did, Joey was going to stop being so agreeable.

I put my hand up. "Stop, Joey, I'm here because the house is on fire."

He shrugged. I guessed he could just jump off the roof. Nice for some.

"Please, Joey, there are people trapped in the basement. Give me the keys—don't let them burn to death."

He put his hands in his pockets and grinned. "Came up here following an unusual scent. Found *your* scent all over this place. And the Stoke boy's."

"That's great, you giant pervert, but the house is on *fire*. People are going to die."

He pulled the keys from his pocket. "You want

these?"

I held out my hand. "Please."

He held up the key ring and started to wind one of the keys off the ring.

"Joey, please. Don't be a dick."

He shook his head and tutted at me. "Resorting to begging already. I thought you were supposed to be fierce. I thought you were supposed to be scary."

He held up the single key. "You want this? What'll you do for it?"

I sighed. "I asked nicely."

Before I could stop him, he turned, pulled back his arm and threw the key into the trees below.

I ran to the edge of the roof, but there was no way of telling where the key had landed. I turned back to him, furious, as he started to wind another key off the key ring.

"Like I said... what are you going to do for it?"

There were copies of all the keys on that key ring, right? I'd counted ten keys before, and there were only four cells — as long as he didn't drop any more, we'd be okay.

"What do you want?"

Holding the separated key up, he advanced on me and put an arm around me, pulling me close to him. "Whatever you gave Stoke would be just fine."

Dear God. Yeah, I wasn't going to do that. My hand was already behind my back, reaching for my knife. I lifted my face to his. As he leaned in for a kiss, I slid EMN between his ribs and pushed it all the way into him.

He looked at me in shock as he fell back. "Did you just fucking stick me again?"

He dropped the keys and staggered away from me, the knife slipping free with a wet sound as he did. He pressed a hand to his wound and looked down at it in horror as blood flooded between his fingers. "You *bitch*."

I walked after him and kicked him back against a sloping piece of roof with my boot. "Right back at ya."

His eyes were wide with fear and his breathing had become ragged. The silver must have hit something vital.

I collected up the bunch of keys and walked back to him.

"This is for every wolf you killed in the Midlands."

I slid EMN back into his stomach and turned the blade.

He made a sound that was part groan of pain, part surprise. I had to make sure he didn't heal, because if he healed, he was going to murder me.

He made a choking sound as I pulled the knife out, and fell to his knees, blood pulsing from his wounds.

Before I could slit his throat, he collapsed on himself like a wet sack, and in seconds stopped moving. Too many silver-burnt wounds for him to heal.

I dropped back through the window and found smoke was already drifting up the stairs. I headed down to the basement, taking the stairs two at a time.

My hands were shaking as I started trying keys on Erin and Tai's cell door. I was guessing we had less than a minute before the fire destroyed our way out.

The keys slid through my sweaty fingers as I threaded the key Joey had removed back on to the key ring and forced myself to try each one twice to make sure it wasn't my fumbling that was stopping them from turning.

Finally, the lock moved.

I hugged Erin. "The house is on fire. Go, I'll get Gracie out."

I went straight to Gracie's cell and started trying keys.

"We're not leaving you here," said Tai.

"Go, get out, there's no point in us all burning to death!" Above us, there was an ominous creak.

Tai looked up nervously. "If the roof goes, it'll block our only way out of the basement."

I swore under my breath and kept trying keys.

Erin ran to the top of the stairs and opened the door. She coughed and slammed it shut again. I could feel their eyes on me as I tried yet another key.

This was the last one on the key ring, I was sure of it. I'd separated them out so I didn't get confused. There were two of every other key. There couldn't be just one for this door. Joey couldn't have thrown away the *only* key to this door.

Oh shit. The second key he'd taken off. I hadn't seen it, hadn't picked it up. It was probably lost in the huge pool of blood that'd come out of him.

"Gracie! I'm trying to get you out, but I can't find the right key! I'm trying, okay?"

A muffled sound came from behind the thick iron door.

"She said 'Go, she'll be okay'," said Tai. I knew he was lying.

"Can she survive this?" I asked desperately as I tried another key with slippery fingers.

Tai looked away. "Maybe."

"Maybe's not good enough!"

He put a hand on my arm and took the keys out of my hand. "Liss, come on — Gracie might survive, but you definitely won't — we're running out of time!"

The fire would make getting the key from the roof impossible; the key he'd thrown into the trees was our only hope.

"The key we need — I think Joey threw it into the bush out the back. Can you go look for it? With your nose..."

"Out the back?" said Tai. "Liss, the air's full of chemical smoke — there's not a chance in hell I'll be able to smell anything and there's no time!"

"Please, Liss," said Erin.

I snatched the keys back from Tai and started again. "Go. At least try and find it."

Tai started towards the stairs and looked back, desperation in his eyes. "I'll look — but come with me. If I find it, I promise I'll come back down and get her out."

I didn't believe he'd go back into the burning house. I didn't believe he'd let me go back in either. I had to stay there. It was the only way.

"Liss, the hall's blocked with smoke," said Erin. "We have to go!"

"Go find the key," I said, trying the lock again. I was halfway through the keys I had.

Another crash from above made us all jump. The keys slipped out of my fingers and I swore.

"Liss, Gracie will understand," said Tai. "We're not leaving you here — we have to get out now, before the whole house collapses on top of us."

As if to accent his point, the roof creaked and cracked open. A beam pierced the ceiling, raining down a shower of sparks. Four more keys to go.

I tried them — tried them all. None turned. The fire raging above had to be close to consuming the house.

I threw the bundle of keys at the wall and let out a scream of frustration.

Tai turned me to face him. "We go, now."

I nodded. I followed him up the steps to where Erin was standing.

"We have to crawl," she said. "It's mostly smoke, no fire in the hall yet. Go straight ahead, we should be able to get out."

She got to her hands and knees and started into the smoke. Tai did the same and I waited behind them for them to move forward. Once Tai was clear of the doorway, I stood and slammed the door behind them. I pulled across the bolt on the inside of the door. "Get the key!!"

I ignored their shouts and pounding on the door and went back to where Gracie was trapped.

I picked up the keys from the floor and tried each of them in the door again. Nothing moved the lock. I screamed in frustration and pulled at the iron handle. It didn't so much as rattle.

"I'm trying!" I shouted to Gracie. "You have to believe me!"

I started going through the drawers on the work bench, then checked the cell where Cole and the others had been trapped, in case he'd dropped a key when he'd taken the others off the ring.

Nothing. I had to be realistic. Joey's last act of assholery had made sure he didn't go down alone.

I banged on the locked cell door. "I don't know what to do. I don't know what to do!"

I laid my head against the cold metal.

There was a muffled sound from behind the door. I couldn't make out words, but the tone was urgent.

"I can't get you out," I said. I started trying the keys again.

Another crash from above sent sparks and pieces of plaster cascading down. The lights flickered and died.

From inside her cell, Gracie banged on the iron door, the boom resonating through the dark.

With an explosion of wood and metal, the door at the top of the stairs burst open.

Tai bounded down the stairs.

"Did you find it?" I asked.

"No! Come on!"

He grabbed my arm and manhandled me up the stairs, pushing me into the hall in front of him.

Coughing, my eyes streaming, we ran together through the smoke. He shoved me out into the night as the roof over the hallway collapsed behind us.

"Move back!" he said, dragging me further from the flames.

I got halfway across the lawn before the ceiling over the kitchen collapsed, taking the upper story with it. Moments after it gave way, the rest of the house buckled in on itself, spilling flaming debris across the lawn.

Tai pushed me to the ground, shielding me from the worst of it with his body.

Somewhere distant, sirens sounded.

Dan came crashing out of the bush as a scream rose from the burning remains of the house. His eyes met mine with a question. "Who?"

"Gracie."

His face crumpled into grief. Tears spilled down his face and he turned away, his head bowed.

The screams stopped abruptly and a new smell joined the air.

I'd had enough. I pulled away from Tai and walked down the drive, shielding my face from the heat with my arm.

I heard Erin yell after me and Dan's voice, lower, urging her to let me go.

No one followed me.

Chapter 37

J limped along the road under a flawless night sky, the only sound the crunch of my boots on the gravel at the side of the road and the wail of sirens getting closer.

There wasn't much of me left. Pain had taken every inch of my body. I was exhausted with grief, with anger, with the pointlessness of it all.

Anton's hunger for better territory, Tristan's hunger for love and respect. Riley's thirst for revenge and autonomy, and Brandt's hunger to create chaos—all of it meaningless, all the suffering they'd caused, the lives that'd been lost. All of it for nothing. No one had won. None of them had got what they wanted. *Yipee-kai-yay, motherfuckers. I hope you're happy with yourselves.*

I wanted to scream, but I didn't have the energy. It was just me and the empty countryside that'd existed billions of years before this night and would exist long after every one of us was just another layer of sediment.

I stopped and sank down at the side of the road,

then lay back on the asphalt and stared up at the moon.

I could stay here. The ground was hard under me, but the pain was going away. I was going away.

There was nothing I could do.

No.

There was something I could do.

Riley was dead. Joey was dead. But Brandt and Anton were still alive, which meant it wasn't over yet.

I sat up and rested my arms on my bent knees.

Anton was the one who'd set the fire and killed Gracie. When I caught him, he'd die a slow and savage death.

As for Brandt, death was too good for him. For Brandt, I wanted something else. It would take time and planning. He wouldn't let himself be caught easily. But as long as I was alive, he would be in my sights.

A heavy engine accelerated down the highway as a fire engine rushed past, its lights spinning dizzily across the trees, its siren silenced. No traffic, no need for sirens. Like ambulances when the victim was already gone.

Another engine rushed past. Behind it, car headlights washed the road. The car slowed and pulled over. Andy.

He helped me up and pulled me into a hug, then held me at arm's length to look at my face. "What happened to you? Glenn rang and said the reserve's on fire."

"I want to go," I said.

He nodded and helped me to the car. Inside, he turned on the overhead lights.

"Those injuries look bad. Really bad. You need stitches." He looked around, agitated. I knew what he was thinking. If we went to a hospital, questions would be asked that would be difficult to answer.

"You can patch me," I said. "It's okay."

"You'll scar," he said wretchedly.

I shook my head. "I don't care. Just take me home."

I closed my eyes and laid my head back against the seat. Then I remembered. We couldn't go home. Home was filled with Jack's blood.

"We'll go to the summer house," he said gently. Then, "It's going to be okay, Liss."

I didn't bother to argue. I was just glad he was still alive.

Chapter 38

The fire was still burning on low when we reached the house, and the warmth wrapped around me like a hug. Rattan lamps threw golden nets of light and shadow across the walls, as I dropped down on the white leather couch in front of the fire. I stared into the flames while Andy went to the bedroom to call Glenn and tell him where I was.

He came back and looked from the white leather to my soot-stained clothes, then back at the leather. With a sigh, he sat beside me and put his arm around me. His cologne, which Jack had dubbed 'Gucci Pour De Loup', surrounded me in a cloud, a counterpoint to the bitter stink of smoke that clung to my clothes.

"Do you want to talk about it?"

I watched flames wash up the glass firebox door. "Not really."

I kicked off my blackened trainers.

"Dan asked if he could come by—"

"Not tonight."

He squeezed my shoulders and I felt a tremor run through him. Glenn must have told him what'd happened. What we'd lost.

"I need to stitch up those cuts in your face," he said gently.

"Does it have to be tonight?" I wilted at the thought of more pain.

"I'll be as quick as I can," he said. "But the sooner the better."

I sighed. I could do this. "Okay."

I didn't tell him about the bite to my shoulder. That could wait.

He got up and came back with his surgical kit. Andy wasn't a doctor, but a lot of the wolves had basic medical training. Most of the time they could heal themselves by shifting. On the odd occasional that wasn't practical, they needed to be able to treat each other without going to a hospital. Some packs had vets or doctors, but not everyone was cut out to be a doctor. Our pack didn't have anyone medically qualified, but we did have an abundance of first-aid trained system administrators.

He gave me a sedative and had me lie down on the couch. Once the sedative kicked in, he injected a local anaesthetic into the wounds, then syringed water through them to clean them. By the time he started threading the needle into my skin to close the lacerations, the pain and the pulling of the needle through my skin was easy to shut away.

I didn't dream and woke at dawn. Someone was knocking on the door. I winced as I swam up to consciousness. My face ached. My shoulder ached. Everything ached.

Grey light filtered between the lounge curtains. It was either very early morning, or it was seriously overcast.

The knocking came again and I rolled off the couch. I wiped the sleep from my eyes and swore as I brushed my palm over the nylon zigzags in my cheek. Moving my mouth hurt. I could see this was going to be fun until it healed.

I opened the door to find Dan on the doorstep. I was right, it was early morning. He had a very precise sense of 'tomorrow'.

His eyes filled with dismay as he looked at Andy's handiwork, but he was smart enough not to comment.

I went back to the couch and winced at the mess I'd made. The white leather was smeared with blood, soot, and grime. It looked like a crime scene. Ah well. I'd clean it later. I sat back in my filth as Dan shut the door and followed me into the lounge.

"Did they catch Anton?" I asked.

"No word from Ellen yet."

"Brandt?"

"Not yet," he said. His tone told me they didn't expect to catch Brandt and probably weren't trying.

"So why are you here?" I asked.

"I wanted to see you. Andy said you were in a bad state."

"Wait, did he ask you to come here?" I said.

"He went to help with the others. He didn't want you to be here on your own. In case..."

"In case the big bad wolf came after me?" I asked.

486

"In case you went after him by yourself, actually," he said with a tinge of annoyance. "Anyway, *I* wanted to see you. Plus, everyone else has headed to the motel down the road and I wanted some privacy." He looked down at his filthy clothes. "Can I use the shower?"

I waved a yes and leaned back into the couch and closed my eyes. A moment later, I heard the shower start up.

Ten minutes later, he reappeared with a white spa towel wrapped around his waist and his hair in damp spikes. "Ah—do you think Andy would mind me borrowing some clothes?"

"Pretty sure he'd be fine with that," I said. "Bedroom's that way."

While he was getting dressed, I grabbed some clothes from my room and headed for the bathroom.

The bathroom was my favourite part of the summer house. The shower had a rainwater showerhead—a wide, flat head that simulated rainfall—and the bathroom was tiled with honey-coloured marble. The base of the shower was lined with flat river stones, and ferns in pots surrounded the glass walls. It was like being in a steamy rainforest. I anticipated using whatever was left of the hot water.

I stripped carefully, peeling my t-shirt away the wound in my shoulder. I checked Caleb's bite in the mirror. Two dark circles, crusted with blood. He'd bitten hard enough that each of his teeth had left a separate indentation. Only unlike a human bite, his canines had punctured right into the muscle.

I washed the last of the dirt from my face with a facecloth, since running water over stitches wasn't recommended, and rested the facecloth over the bite in my shoulder so that water wouldn't hit it directly.

Dan knocked on the bathroom door as I stepped under the stream.

"Did I leave my phone in there?" he called through the door.

"Don't know," I said. I closed my eyes as hot water hit my back.

"Ah, there it is." His voice came from inside the room. I slicked my wet hair back and opened my eyes. He was standing in front of the glass shower door—and he apparently hadn't found any clothes that fit.

"Can I come in?"

I nodded mutely.

He opened the glass shower door and stepped inside. The warm rain from the shower ceiling fell on to his already-damp hair, plastering it flat. He put his arms around me and our mouths met, both of us hungry to forget.

"This couch isn't coming clean," Dan called from the lounge, as I finished dressing.

"Try some Jif!" I shouted back as I dried my hair.

"Oh, that works," he called a short time later.

I nodded to myself and muttered, "Yes, it does." I'd spent years marking Jack and Andy's leather furniture. I don't think I would have lasted as their foster kid if they hadn't figured out how to get it clean.

I came back to the lounge, now brindled with early morning light.

Dan put his hands on my waist and kissed my forehead. "You look a little more civilised now," he said.

"That's my superpower," I said, resting my head on his chest. "The ability to pass as civilised."

He put his arms around me and laughed. "Good thing I know better."

"And yet you mock me."

His heartbeat thudded in my ear, solid and reassuring.

I looked up to find him smiling down at me. "It's not as if you can hurt me."

I frowned.

"What?" he said. "I mean, feel free to try." He was grinning. I wasn't.

I pulled out of his arms. "Breakfast?"

"I'll make it," he said. "Your French toast always looks like it's been napalmed..."

He broke off as he realised what he was saying, and with a rush, it all came back. Here we were, playing house in a stolen hour, while one of our friends lay burnt to death underground and her killer ran free.

A wave of dizziness washed over me. I leaned against the bench, shivering as I remembered Gracie's scream, that smell in the air.

"Liss?" Dan put his hand on my back. "Don't. Not

now. When it's over, we will grieve, I promise you. But not now. Now, we eat, we make sure we're rested, and we get back out there and finish this."

"How can you?" I asked. "How are you still standing? I know you loved her. You guys have been inseparable since the day you met. She died screaming because I couldn't get her out. But you're still talking to me. You're still standing there as though nothing's happened."

Dan blinked and wet his lips as emotions chased across his face.

"One day I'll ask you what happened, but not today. I've got to keep going because otherwise I'll lose it and be no use to anyone. We don't know where Mum and Dad are. They might still be alive. If they are, we have to find them."

He put his hands on my hips.

"After this is over, I might need to get away — maybe go nature for a while. But right now, being weak is not an option."

He let go of me and started searching through the pots for a frying pan.

"You can't kill Anton or Brandt if you find them," I said.

Dan paused with his back to me. He put the pan on the gas hob with deliberate care.

"Why not?"

"If we catch them, they're mine."

He shook his head. "That's not a good idea."

"Oh yes, it is. In the car, when we found out about Jack, you promised me Brandt would suffer.

Creatively. Death is not suffering. Death is mercy. You promised me."

He reached across me to fetch plates from the cupboard.

"That was Brandt."

"The same goes for Anton. Don't you want revenge, after what he did to Gracie?"

"Keeping him alive so you can torture him would be ten times harder than killing him outright. Where would we put him, Liss? We don't even have a home anymore. Let's just get it done."

I put my arms around him and rested my forehead against his back.

"I need this," I whispered.

He put his hand over mine and patted it.

"Can you grab me some eggs?"

I got him the eggs, but the conversation was far from over.

We ate and rested until mid-morning, when Andy came back, flushed and upset.

"Are you okay?" I asked.

He shook his head. "I can't process it." He put his hands to his head, pushing his fingers into his blond hair.

"Any lead on the ACs?" asked Dan.

Andy shook his head. "Nothing. We combed the forest all night, but Anton's trail went cold at the main road—he either had a car waiting, or he hitched a ride."

"Abigail and Kendrick—they have to have left a

trail," I said.

"There was nothing," said Andy. "It's as if they all got in cabs and drove away."

Wherever they'd gone, our detour to pick up Tristan had given him over eight hours to transport them somewhere, murder them, and get back to the house to greet us. They could be anywhere.

"What about Tristan?"

"As far as we can tell, he followed Anton. His trail went further up the road, but like Anton's, it disappeared. Ooh, before I forget." He fished around in his pocket and brought out my phone. "Tai said it should be safe for you to use this now."

I powered it up. Tai, bless him, had charged it.

I took the iPhone out of my pocket. It was long-dead. I left it on the coffee table—I'd destroy it later. Maybe with fire.

"Tai put Ellen's number in there—he knew you'd want to stay in contact. Cole's, too."

"See, Dan, Tai knows what a lady wants."

Dan snorted.

"Anyway, I came back to see you two, and to tell you that the others are meeting at the house at noon to remove Gracie's body. I thought you'd want to be there."

Sure. Why not.

As we pulled up at the reserve, the chemical stink of the ruins sat heavy in the air. Not the comforting scent of wood smoke you got on a cold night, but the smell of melted plastic and treated wood.

492

The upper two levels of the house had collapsed completely, leaving only the skeletal remains of one wall standing. The rest was a pile of beams burnt to charcoal, twisted metal and brick.

I exhaled through my nose to clear out the stink, but as I got out of the car the wind changed direction, bringing the summer smell of cut grass and sunshine from the fields that lay opposite the reserve.

I took a deep breath in, savouring the scent while I could.

The wolves hugged me in turn, with Tai waiting till last to lift me off my feet. He buried his nose in my hair and sniffed. "You smell so clean. I hate the shampoo at the motel. I know I'm going to get split ends."

He inhaled again deeply then stopped, confused. His eyes flickered sideways to Dan. He raised an eyebrow but I ignored him.

"Okay," said Glenn. "The first thing we need to do is clear out the rubble. Be careful when you're working over the cellar. The iron may have thinned in the fire. And of course, the stairwell will have collapsed, and there'll be a hole somewhere in the middle."

He handed out leather gloves to each of his brothers and pulled on his own. There were no gloves for me.

"Glenn, I can help," I said.

He shook his head. "You're in no state to be doing heavy lifting. We've got this. Besides, I want you to do something else for me. Can you keep an eye on

493

the forest while we're working? I don't believe for a second that Anton's done with us."

"You honestly think he'd risk coming back?"

"He doesn't operate alone. If he comes back with his pack, I don't want to be caught off guard."

It seemed to me that he was just trying to make me feel useful, which just made me feel all too weak and human. Any injuries they'd sustained in the fighting the day before had already healed. My shoulder—and my face—would take weeks. My little finger, still bound, ached. The only thing that was keeping me on my feet was anger. Maybe Anton would come back. Maybe I wanted him to.

I sat on the grass and felt the solid earth under my hands. I closed my eyes and looked into my second sight. The small stars of birds drifted overhead like satellites in a night sky, while all around me were the tiny life energies of insects, and that dark green warmth of the forest.

I looked back towards the house, where the wolves blazed brilliant white.

I jumped to my feet, gasping for breath.

"She's still alive. She's still alive!"

The wolves stared at me.

"Gracie?" asked Dan.

"Yes! She's still alive down there!"

I closed my eyes again to check. Her sign was fainter than the others, but it had to be her, glowing under the earth.

"Down there." I pointed.

Dan clambered over the debris and started

clearing the rubble from the area above Gracie's life star. Glenn joined him, and soon they were all flinging cracked roof tiles and pieces of charred wood on to the grass.

"Here!" called Dan.

He'd uncovered a section of iron—the ceiling of her cell.

"Gracie! Can you hear me?"

There was no reply.

"Get the rest of this rubbish out of here," said Glenn. "I've got a reciprocating saw and a genny in the truck I can use to power it."

He jogged back down the driveway and drove his truck up to the house. The others stood by nervously as he uncoiled an extension lead and started cutting into the iron sheeting.

The screech of the blade chewing through metal made us all wince. When Glenn had made a hole big enough for a person to get through, Dan got onto his hands and knees and put his head inside.

"Gracie?"

There was no reply.

"Can you see anything?" I asked.

He pulled his head back out. "Nothing. It's too dark. Although, there's a faint glow from... something."

A chill ran down my spine.

I looked with my second sight. All I could see was Gracie's white light, burning low—but still bright enough to eclipse any other life sign around her.

"Be careful, Dan."

"You really think Riley survived being shot six times?"

"I don't know; how did she survive being shot three times?"

Karlo brushed charcoal down his jeans and stood beside us. "In the books I read, the legend implied if the skoghund thought it was about to be injured, it could collect energy into itself to create a buffer from the attack."

"She died," I said. "Her light went out."

Glenn brought over a large Dolphin torch and some rope.

Dan lowered himself into the hole and took the torch.

He let out a sob of air. "Oh, Gracie." He tossed the flashlight back to Glenn, who lit the hole as best he could. Dan came back to the opening with Gracie in his arms.

She was in wolf form, her coat a mass of blackened skin broken by patches of raw red and fur. Her eyes were closed, and she was breathing in uneven shudders as if breathing hurt. Ben pushed his way to the side of the hole.

"I'll take her."

Dan spoke gently, "I'm sorry, Gracie, I'm going to have to pass you up to Ben. Are you ready?"

She gave a faint whine and Dan lifted her as high as he could. She let out a yelp that devolved into a shivering keening as Ben got hold of her under her front legs and lifted her out. He cradled her in his arms and picked his way out of the debris to the lawn.

Glenn gave Dan a hand up out of the hole.

"Was she down there?" I asked.

"Riley? Not that I saw."

"The glow?"

"I must have imagined it."

I followed him out of the ruins to where Ben had laid Gracie on the grass.

Although she'd already begun to heal, most of her fur was gone and her blackened skin was marked with raw wounds which were only lightly scabbed.

Her eyes were squeezed shut with pain, her lip curled in a snarl.

"She needs a doctor," I said. "Now."

Glenn shook his head. "Honestly, Liss. We could take her to a vet, but there's no way they'll mistake her for a dog."

"We can heal her," said Dan. He looked around at his brothers. "Can't we?"

Glenn bit his lip. "If there aren't enough of us..." He trailed off.

"Surely it can't hurt to try?"

Glenn shook his head. "No. We might end up hurting more than helping."

Dan's eyes burned with desperation. "We have to help her!"

Gracie's legs twitched and she let out a shivering cry of pain.

"Six, Glenn. Six is the minimum, right?" asked Dan.

"Six *wolves*," said Glenn.

497

"Can someone *please* tell me what happens if you don't have enough wolves?" I said loudly.

Glenn gave Dan a look, urging him to explain.

"If we start the heal and there isn't enough of the right kind of energy, there's a good chance she'll part-heal—or the heal will undo itself. Either way means agony for her."

"Or a moment's relief," I said. "Will she die?"

Glenn looked solemn. "Some have," he said. "The shock of the pain being momentarily removed and then restored can stop a heart—especially if the person being healed is very weak, as she is now."

Dan sank to the ground beside Gracie and stroked the down on the top of her head. She kept her eyes squeezed shut.

Dan looked up at his brothers. "We have to try."

"She'll heal in time. It'll hurt, but there's less risk," said Glenn gently.

"Guys, I don't think she's going to heal," I said.

Gracie's breathing had begun to rasp in her chest.

"She's in too much pain," said Dan. "Even for us, injuries like this—they're too much! Come on, we're her only hope!"

The wolves exchanged glances.

"What?" I asked.

"We need your power, Liss, but if we take too much, we might kill you."

Oh. Was that all?

"I can do it," I said.

Glenn shook his head.

"Let her!" said Dan. "Come on, we're wasting

time!"

Gracie's breathing hitched. Dan ran a shaky hand above her flank, afraid to touch her wounds.

"You understand the risk?" said Glenn.

"Yeah, let's just do this," I said. Before I chickened out.

"Gather in," said Glenn. The wolves knelt around Gracie. Glenn put one hand on my shoulder, Karlo a hand on the opposite shoulder.

"Liss, place your hands on Dan. Dan, you know the drill," said Glenn.

Dan bent his head. I felt a soft tug as energy started to flow through the wolves. The tug grew stronger as the energy gathered speed, magnifying as it ran from wolf to wolf, through me into Dan.

The end of the chain, Dan collected what we gave him, condensing it inside himself until he blazed white in my second sight.

There was a tug at my insides as Dan released it all into Gracie. He glanced at me desperately. "It's not enough!"

The pull increased as he tried to draw more. But there was no more.

My organs felt as though they were being pulled through the front of my body. The connection between us all spat and crackled as Dan drew faster than any of us could give him our energy.

"Dan, stop!" shouted Glenn. I could sense the wolves' fear and their struggle to stay in their human skins as Dan dragged at their life essence.

But he didn't stop.

Under his hands, Gracie's body started to change. Her blackened skin grew pale and smooth, the scabbed blood and burnt hair flaking away as fur began to sprout.

"Please," Dan said, almost a sob. "Come back, Gracie."

His muscles tensed under my touch as he doubled his efforts, but one by one, the well inside each of the wolves slowed and petered out, until there was only me. The wolves fell outwards from us like petals from a dying flower, convulsing as they changed into wolves that lay as still as death.

Sensing we were tapped, he tore the last of what he needed from me.

My fingers tingled as if even my blood was draining into him through my fingertips.

I couldn't speak anymore to ask him to stop. My body got cold, colder, until I was numb.

I sent Dan a desperate thought.

'You're killing me.'

With a jerk of realisation, he shut off the flow.

I fell back as the world spun in lazy circles around me, the sunny afternoon dulled to half a shade of darkness.

As the world faded to black, I heard a whimper from somewhere nearby and Dan whispering over and over, *"I'm sorry, Gracie, I'm so sorry."*

His voice faded and I sank into the cold.

ABOUT THE AUTHOR

Read more in the second book in the Väktare series,
The Hungry.

For updates on the next release, head over to
www.kaialeigh.com

www.ingramcontent.com/pod-product-compliance
Lightning Source LLC
Chambersburg PA
CBHW021117260626
47169CB00005B/1320